JASON MINICK

THE THREAT

RUNS

DEEP

DILUVIAN

Published by Jason Minick

ISBN: 978-1-9996620-4-2

Cover design, illustration & interior formatting:
Mark Thomas / Coverness.com

This book is dedicated to anyone whose carpet I have spilled a drink on,
especially if it was red wine.

Sorry, but I honestly cannot help it.

PROLOGUE

Eight Years after Arcam:
Friday 18th June – Gakona, Alaska

Professor Romano had been meticulous, even by his standards. However, the extra checks were justified, given the stakes.

One final tap on the keyboard interrupted the eerie hum of electronic devices in the deserted control room. He undertook a final review of the indication system. The display before him confirmed that all was functioning normally, including the Faraday cage electromagnetic defence system.

The deception was complete.

The professor rubbed a tanned, wrinkled hand over his white beard as he took one final look around the laboratory, now confident that everything was in place. He brushed aside his own silly melancholy as he considered that he might be seeing the establishment that had become his second home for the final time. It was for a greater good, he hoped, as he dabbed a handkerchief against his sweaty forehead.

The corridors of the facility were deserted, with most employees having departed for the weekend, all except those who were most ardently married to their work. Like he had been for his entire career.

Swing doors swayed behind him as he stepped into a grand concourse and looked across at the tall security guard. The large woman's eyes that shone in his direction were accompanied by a wide smile. Romano returned his own, typically affable smile as he hobbled on worn knees in front of the reception desk.

'Ciao, Veronica.'

The guard winked at him.

'Goodbye, Professor. I hope you have a lovely holiday! See you in a couple of weeks.'

'Thank you, Veronica. Yes, I will see you soon,' he lied, tipping his flat cap as he passed a couple of security guards and exited the high security facility.

Outside, he inhaled deeply then spluttered instantly as he felt the freezing air fill his lungs. He stopped amid the near-deserted car park and fumbled with a pill before casting it back down his throat. The palpitations in his frail heart had been growing for the past few months and, as the day had grown ever nearer, his anxiety over the mission had threatened to render him totally paralysed, particularly in the last few days.

Even now, with his job irreversibly complete, the foreboding feeling would not subside.

CHAPTER 1

Friday 25th June
Belmarsh Prison, South-East London, England

Prisoner AB6794AA stood completely still and stared fixedly out at the free world he longed to be a part of again. He felt the teeming rain soften his soul, evoking memories of what seemed like a distant past. The guards on either side of him maintained their firm grips around his biceps, which were forced into their elongated state by the cuffs that bound his wrists together behind his back. The screws were oblivious to the teardrop that escaped from a corner of one eye as the prisoner remembered his former, simple life in charge of his beloved and ancient little harbour.

Several yards away, sodden mud sprayed from beneath the wheels of the white, cuboid van as it performed a U-turn in front of them. Inside the vehicle, the driver and passenger both offered the faintest of acknowledgements to the two prison guards, while ignoring the convicted man that stood, soaking wet, between them.

For a moment, the guard on the prisoner's right betrayed a glimpse of self-doubt. Although it had been brief, the prisoner had noted and enjoyed the unmistakable sign of nerves. He did not need to twist his tattooed neck round to know that the prison official was doing his absolute best to cover up his silent, albeit involuntary, acknowledgement of the prisoner's strength. The detainee had stood firmly rooted to the spot, despite the increasing force applied by the two guards, who had tried to coax him towards the van. It was silently clear, when they eventually began moving, that it had been of the prisoner's own free will.

The newly arrived escorts had not failed to notice the tense encounter and, consequently, they too revealed the slightest hint of nerves as their new passenger was guided into the back of the vehicle. The last thing they needed was a troublesome prisoner, so it was a relief to see the athletic man finally comply.

With his back to the officials, the prisoner allowed himself a wry smile as he ducked into the cramped, mobile cell. As he sat his lean, powerful frame on to the hard bench, he remembered how, only a few years earlier, he would have found it exceedingly difficult to fit into such a tiny space. But he was a changed man now, both physically and psychologically.

The doors to the van slammed closed and the prisoner heard the guards exchange light-hearted banter outside, evidently having regained their confidence. A moment later he heard the doors at the front of the van crashing shut and his head flew backwards as the vehicle lurched forward, unnecessarily abruptly, he noted.

Have your fun while it lasts, the prisoner thought as he composed himself.

He began to mentally prepare for the imminent long journey in the sweatbox. He put his hands out in front of him to counter the effects of the uneven road surface on his body, which vibrated inside the rumbling metal enclosure as they departed the formidable prison walls.

Jacob Miller was finally on the move.

*

Meanwhile, two armed men watched a helicopter appear from over a nearby mountain peak and thunder towards them. The soldiers remained motionless apart from blinking, as the pilot lowered the machine on to the dusty terrain which swirled beneath the turbulence created by the spinning rotors.

A lone figure appeared from the side door of the aircraft and, after hopping out, proceeded towards them with an assured gait, despite the wild terrain. They all exchanged friendly smiles and took one last look at the sky as the aircraft returned in the direction from which it had just arrived.

The two soldiers flanked their superior, as the three of them proceeded towards the entrance to their secret community.

CHAPTER 2

The prisoner, Jacob Miller, sealed the top of the urination bag and bent down to pass it through the small hole at the bottom of the cell door. The van took a sudden turn to the left, causing the right side of his skull to smash against the metal shell. He imagined his two escorts in the front exchanging satisfied smiles when they heard the loud bang.

He thought he heard a snigger.

Let's see if you're both brave enough to laugh at me a little later, you pair of glorified fucking bus drivers ...

Miller adjusted his position as far as possible within the constraints of his confinement. He began to adopt the same meditative state that he had been in for the first three hours of the journey, prior to his 'toilet break'.

Planning had begun for this day long before the moment when he was formally advised that his status was being downgraded from 'Category A'. The downgrade was, ostensibly, his reward for being 'so well behaved' during his time inside the formidable walls of HMP Belmarsh. That he was being transferred to the more relaxed environment of a 'Category C' facility in the midst of Dartmoor was beyond his wildest dreams. Not that he was ever planning to see inside Dartmoor – this 'model prisoner' had other plans.

Considering the high-security risk which the sentencing judge said he had posed, he knew that a major justifying factor in the decision to authorise such a significant downgrade was the undeniable issue of overcrowding, rather than any great amount of trust on the part of the prison officials. That, along with the fact that he had influential friends. That he was not being afforded a toilet break, even on a five-hour journey, appeared to confirm that he was not entirely viewed as being without risk.

Miller closed his eyes and slowly regulated his breathing, preparing himself for what lay ahead.

CHAPTER 3

Wednesday 23rd June (Two days earlier)

Jack Robson shook his head and let out a sigh of resignation.

It was not that he had no interest in the party planning. He simply did not have any worthwhile suggestions to offer for a girl's fourteenth birthday. And the girls seemed to have it all in hand. At lease it seemed to be helping to take the edge off Sarah's nerves. Her big day was now just over forty-eight hours away and her fiancé was going to be out of town until the night before the wedding.

He carried the tray of tea into the living room, feeling useful at last.

'Okay, Dad. It's going to be a disco!'

Robson maintained an even expression while he lowered the tray on to the table.

'Oh great, that's what I was hoping you'd say.'

Jasmine giggled, always a sucker for her father's dry wit. She threw her arms around his neck as he rose from depositing the drinks.

'We know. That's what swung the decision, Jack.'

Sarah grinned, still looking at the laptop in front of her, which displayed the details for a local DJ.

'Sarah and Mark will be back from their honeymoon, so they'll be able to come along too. So, you'll have a friend to talk to,' said Jasmine.

'That's if my husband-to-be manages to get back in time for the wedding,' Sarah added.

Suddenly her cheeks began to flush, her mind swimming with outstanding tasks as she identified everything that could go wrong between then and Saturday. Robson, sensing her anxiety, attempted to reassure her.

'I think Mark is well aware of his commitments, Sarah. He said that he'll be back by five o'clock on Friday, and he will.'

'How can you be so sure?'

Sarah's eyebrows rose suspiciously.

'Because he's coming over to mine for a curry.'

'What? So, you get to see him and share a nice takeaway, but I have to wait until Saturday?!'

'I believe that's tradition, isn't it? And Jasmine has your last evening of freedom all planned, isn't that right, Jazzy?'

'We've got two movies and loads of popcorn!' the young girl enthused. 'And Granny's coming!'

'And anyway,' added Robson, 'we're not having a takeaway – I'm cooking my speciality, beef Madras.'

Sarah winked mischievously at the young girl.

'Oh, I see. In that case, I'm happy with the popcorn, Jazzy.'

CHAPTER 4

Friday 25th June

'Nice sleep, Geoff?'

The prison guard kept both hands on the steering wheel of the van and smiled mischievously. His colleague responded with a single grunt, indicating that he was not entirely appreciative of his workmate's sarcasm.

'Hardly. I only had my eyes shut for five minutes.'

'Oh yeah. Well, we've just broken the land-speed record then, I reckon.'

'What?'

'Considering where we were when you dropped off, we've just managed to travel between Exeter and Dartmoor in five minutes, according to your timekeeping!'

'Oh, piss off, Smithy! When I drive, you're usually out like a fuckin' light within five minutes!'

Smithy's wicked laugh was irresistible, and Geoff's grumpy visage soon broke into a broad grin at his colleague's typically impish performance.

'We're on the home straight now, Geoff. Last few miles across this bloody desolate moor, then we can have a nice brew.'

'A nice brew sounds good, pal. But I need to make some room for it first. I'm bloody dying for a piss!'

'Should've used one of our passenger's bags.'

A sign indicated that Princetown was five miles away. In the distance beyond, a man in the next lay-by paid detached attention to the passing prisoner transport vehicle, as he stood outside his own parked car. He took another drag on his cigarette before returning his attention to the wild yellow and green landscape provided by the surrounding gorse and heath.

While the guards gazed out of the front windscreen at the remote wilderness, the prisoner in the rear began to compose himself. His mental timekeeping told him that they must be close. And he hadn't missed the unmistakable rumbling of a cattle grid beneath the van's wheels a few minutes ago, which could only mean one thing: they had entered the moor. The rendezvous would be imminent.

The bleak and deserted terrain never ceased to capture Geoff's imagination. He remembered bringing his family to the area for a picnic during a holiday some fifteen years ago. That seemed like a distant memory now – his offspring were no longer children and had flown the nest – but he still remembered vividly how the two boys had taken such pleasure from the open space. With only a few sticks for props, they had raced over the bumps, pretending to be aboard scrambling bikes.

The sudden, loud bang summoned Geoff from his daydream and his eyes darted between the yellow-flowering bushes and the driver. His colleague seemed equally stunned by the sound as he struggled to get the vehicle under control, his arms now rigidly outstretched as his hands grasped the steering wheel.

Finally, they skidded to an abrupt stop as the left wheels lodged themselves into a ditch at the side of the empty road.

'What the hell was that?'

Geoff was momentarily frozen in the passenger seat and noticed the shock in his own voice. A few, silent seconds later, as he looked across at Smithy, it became clear why his friend had not responded.

Smithy's eyes were fixed wide open, his chin resting on his chest, while blood oozed down his nose from a small hole in his forehead.

The stunned guard stumbled from the vehicle and stood in confused silence.

Apart from the car parked in the layby they had just passed, no other vehicles occupied the moor as far as his eyes could see. His vision suddenly picked up the Stinger device that had been laid across the road fifty yards back. As his mind struggled to compute the possibilities, he heard movement inside the back of the van, whose burst tyres sat in a ditch on one side, causing the vehicle to sit at an angle. The sound from inside the van caused him to snap out of his panic-induced paralysis and he began to revert to well-practised protocol. Geoff grabbed the phone from inside his pocket and began hastily pressing the keys.

Before he could finish dialling, a voice from behind stopped him from making the call.

The bewildered guard obeyed the calm voice and dropped his phone. It bounced off the cushion of thick, wild grass, and the man who had been smoking alongside the road earlier appeared in his vision, now holding a pistol instead of a cigarette.

'Give me the keys to the hatch … very, very slowly.'

The guard did not have to think about his response.

'I can't. There's a code, I only know part of it, the other half was known only by my colleague.'

The guard shuddered as he thought of his friend. They had worked together for five years now and he couldn't imagine what this would do to his wife, Jean, not to mention their two sons. To learn that their husband and father had been murdered while at work …

'Don't fuck about with me, old man. You know very well what I mean – I want the keys to the escape hatch at the top. You can either give them to me, or I'll find them once I've shot you. But any more stalling for time and you'll meet the same fate as your partner.'

Geoff knew he would only need to buy another few minutes. They were close to the prison and at least two minutes had already elapsed since he had operated the emergency signal, which would by now have been escalated. He would fetch the keys – slowly, as instructed. The nearest armed police unit would have plenty of time to get to the scene before the gunman would be able to get the convict out of the roof.

CHAPTER 5

DCI Jack Robson smiled at the song being played by the radio DJ as he continued to chop the curry ingredients in preparation for the impending 'last night of freedom' celebrations.

He looked up from the chopping board and allowed himself another sip of cool beer from the bottle in front of him as he peered beyond the trees outside. The channel looked murky beneath the grey sky, both heaven and earth seeming to reflect melancholy back at one another. He still loved the view and hadn't for one second regretted their decision to relocate to the area from their former home in London. The move had been beneficial to him, Sarah, and, most importantly, Jasmine, even if many of the landmarks in and around North Somerset still often caused him to shiver, unfailingly evoking memories of the Arcam case eight years ago.

Regularly he wondered what Isabelle would have thought. She was certainly always very appreciative of natural beauty; but he had a hunch that the stubbornly slower pace of life in the south-west would perhaps have bored her slightly.

The fact that their relocation had in no small part been influenced by an ulterior motive of living closer to his new female companion was ironic, given that she had now flown the area to take up an exciting new career opportunity based in the capital. They had almost literally swapped locations.

Often during the last few years since their parting, he had lamented the lost opportunity, but he told himself that fate had played its hand. Alas, that didn't entirely suppress the craving he felt in his soul. And he knew he wasn't the only one that missed Emma Wilson. Jasmine had grown close to Emma and she had not only been upset but, for a while, also angry at her father's apparent acquiescent attitude, in allowing such an obviously well-matched partner to depart their lives.

At least they still had Sarah ... just about. But she was about to embark on a new life of her own.

CHAPTER 6

The assassin tucked the keys into his pocket before placing a ladder against the rear of the abandoned prison van and scrambling hastily on to the roof. He led with his left foot as he leapt off the top rung. His right foot, which had provided the propulsion for the jump, remained firmly rooted to the ladder step. His scream wasn't a reaction to slamming face-first on to the tin shell, but instead, was due to the pain from his ligaments as his ankle joint opened.

He raised himself up on to his elbows and, from his new elevated vantage point, he watched the bright blue flashing lights emanating from two cars that sped across the moor towards them about three quarters of a mile away. He winced as he pulled at his right foot, which refused to move from the ladder. The assassin did not panic. He looked down to examine the cause of his immobilisation. A shoelace had become wrapped around a bolt that had worked its way loose from the ladder. He calmly removed a dagger from inside his jacket and slashed the lace.

As he stumbled forward, ignoring both the hot pain coming from his right ankle, as well as the sound of sirens being carried across the barren moor by the wind, the metal roof clashed like a huge gong. He stopped at the hatch and deployed one of the dead guard's keys in the lock. The hatchway opened easily, and he paused for a second to gaze through the opening. A pair of dark eyes peered back. Nothing else about the prisoner was familiar in that darkness – but he recognised the eyes from their only other prior encounter.

The assassin felt surprised by the athleticism of the occupant as, declining the offer of his outstretched hand, the prisoner leapt to gain a grip on the lip of the opening, before pulling himself through and up on to the roof. The assassin eyed the newly liberated man, patiently waiting for his greeting, despite the oncoming cavalry. None was forthcoming. The assassin looked the escapee up and down – the man was not huge but looked as hard as nails.

As they both descended the ladder in silence, the escaped prisoner's veins bulged under the tattoo on his neck as he turned to survey his emancipator's handiwork. The two guards were sprawled five metres apart, each with a single bullet wound to their foreheads, correlating with the shots he had heard from inside the van. The second had followed the first by a few minutes, indicating that the assassin had ensured he had what he needed first. *Very professional.*

Finally, the prisoner extended his hand in a gesture of greeting.

'Jacob Miller.'

The other man grabbed the outstretched hand and tried his best to act nonchalant at the incredible strength in Miller's grip.

'Harry Arkwright.'

The sound of the sirens grew louder.

Miller jogged behind Arkwright towards their waiting vehicle until the man in front stumbled on his injured ankle. As he did so, his loose right shoe was jolted by his reaction, off the road and down a steep bank.

'Shit!' cursed Arkwright.

'Just leave it, there's no time …' insisted Miller, as they both watched the police vehicles scream around the corner to their rear.

They both scrambled to the car. As Miller dived inside the passenger door, Arkwright turned the key in the ignition. The sound of the engine firing into life added to the growing wail of sirens. Arkwright glanced at the flashing lights in his rear-view mirror as he pulled away, spraying wet mud behind the spinning wheels beneath them.

Seconds later, on hearing the bangs behind, Miller looked back to see that both police vehicles had been disabled by a second Stinger which had clearly been laid for that purpose. He allowed his large head to drop back an inch against the rest, and he settled into the passenger seat, enjoying the relative size of the space which allowed him to extend his short but muscular, aching legs.

''Ow far to the changeover point?' growled the ex-harbour master.

Arkwright inhaled through his nose.

'Half an hour, tops.'

'Good. The second vehicle's well-hidden I presume, lad?'

'Oh yes, there'll be no problems there, sir.'

'And the key will be there to collect, as planned?'

'Yes.'

Miller nodded but showed no sign of gratitude. Nor did his stern demeanour indicate any sense that he was impressed by the professionalism of the operation to date. *Except for the fucking shoe!* Arkwright cursed inwardly.

The assassin glanced across at the escapee. Then, returning his attention to the flooded road ahead, he raised his voice to overcome the noise of rain rattling against the car's shell.

'You must be pleased to be out since we're having such a lovely spring. Half the country was cut off by floods last weekend.'

After several seconds, Arkwright shuffled awkwardly in the driver's seat, understanding that his new travel partner was not interested in small talk.

In the passenger seat, Miller adopted a disciplined poise, his back plumb straight. He closed his wrinkled eyelids and ran through the next forty-eight hours in his head, a process that he would complete several times over before they reached their next check point.

CHAPTER 7

The soldiers remained stubbornly vigilant despite the remoteness of the location, as Naamah and the professor wandered among the enormous forest of steel masts. The virginal white powder crunched softly beneath their boots as they paced slowly between the antennae, assessing whether the severe storm had caused any damage.

They had anticipated adverse conditions and had planned accordingly. As a result, the damage to the installation was minimal, but the completion of their project would be delayed slightly. The importance of the test had been vindicated – they had to be able to demonstrate that they could sustain their existence in the most adverse environments. The professor knew that to be so, yet he silently worried, awaiting his leader's reaction to the set-back.

However, unlike Noah previously, their new leader, Naamah, generally possessed a more evenly balanced temperament, at least on the surface. It was that calm, assured nature that permeated among Naamah's devoted followers, currently occupying the facility directly beneath their snow-laden feet.

'So, what do you make of the impact, Alberto?'

Naamah had stopped in the space directly between two huge masts, whose peaks touched the precipitous white fluff above. The professor turned to face his leader, as ever appreciating the beautifully high cheekbones and huge blue eyes.

'We've probably lost about five per cent of the antennae, Naamah. I'd say we're about a week or two from being fully operational.'

Naamah enjoyed the professor's romantic, Latin inflection as he spoke, simply nodding at the response, while thinking of how, eight years previously, no one would have predicted who the successor to the inimitable Sir Geoffrey Charlesworth would be. Fate had played a significant role – if it hadn't been for certain circumstances, things would have turned out differently.

*

Over two hundred miles away, the driver of a saloon car breathed a sigh of relief that his awkward journey was coming to an end. For the first time since being given the cold shoulder earlier, he spoke to his passenger again.

'This is us,' he stated forthrightly, and turned his head to the left just enough to catch his passenger in his field of vision. It seemed that, once again, there was not going to be a response.

Another mile further along the remote country road, they drove through a pair of rusty gates and approached a large crusher. Beside the battered machine, there lay a gigantic pile of metal in the centre of a large yard. Before reaching the scrap heap, Harry steered the car to the right to pull up alongside a Portakabin. Upon arrival at their interim destination, Miller finally chose to speak, albeit briefly.

'Good.'

As they both got out of the car, a small, dishevelled man approached. He held a hammer in one hand, and a hand-rolled cigarette hung from his lips, giving the impression that both were permanent fixtures. Their host raised a blackened, grease-covered hand to briefly remove the thin cigarette from his mouth.

Harry spoke first.

'We're here on behalf of Naamah.'

The grease-laden man confirmed the phrase to himself before responding with his own pre-agreed line.

'The harbour-master's vehicles are ready.'

The scrap merchant spoke with an unashamedly agrarian accent, which was laced with a typical smoker's gruffness. As they exchanged a handshake, Harry felt the man's warm, calloused skin.

'Afternoon, gents – follow me if you will,' croaked the greasy man.

The scrap-dealer's filthy, oversized overalls hung from his dishevelled frame as he meandered towards a steel garage door. Above their heads, the roller let out a piercing screech as the door opened to reveal two vehicles inside. Miller remained at the entrance to the lock-up with the scrapyard owner. Together they watched Harry approach one of the vehicles.

Suddenly aware that he had entered alone, Harry stopped and turned. He felt an intense foreboding as the other two men began to approach silently. The hammer that hung from the small man's wrinkled paw suddenly seemed threatening. He noted Miller's muscular neck grow tense.

Neither Miller nor the scrap dealer withdrew eye-contact as they approached Harry.

Harry switched his eyes from Miller to the older man, remaining calm. He towered over them both. The scrap-dealer's dark eyes appeared suddenly menacing as they reflected the soft glow of the filament bulb directly overhead. Harry had been trained to be able to identify an imminent attack before it happened, and he watched the scrap-dealer's filthy fist flinch as he squeezed the hammer. The small man began to mumble through a small opening in his mouth while continuing to grip the roll-up between his lips.

'You're takin' t'other one, my friend.'

He used the hammer to point to a small silver hatchback parked alongside the jeep that he currently stood beside. Harry's eyes flickered towards the hammer. The scrap merchant appeared to become aware of the implied threat and instantly dropped the tool on to a wooden workbench, giving off a loud thud.

As Harry passed Miller, a muscular forearm shot out into his path. He turned ninety degrees so that they stood face to face. The scrap dealer approached from the side, before pulling something from his pocket. A bunch of keys jingled as he tossed them towards Harry.

'You'll need these.'

Harry caught the keys without turning away from the challenge apparent in Miller's peculiar expression.

'Well, I'll be off then, unless you need anything else from me?'

Miller moved his chunky forearm closer and opened a large palm. Harry tossed the bunch of keys into his left hand and reciprocated the offered, unnecessarily firm, handshake.

The rumbling of the hatchback's engine echoed inside the garage and Harry wasted no time in getting the vehicle in motion. He operated the button to his right and the window whirred down beside him.

'See you soon, Jacob.'

Miller nodded.

'Thanks for the lift … Harry.'

The window rose again as he negotiated a path around the huge crushing facility, finally muttering to himself as he approached the gate of the remote plant.

'You're most welcome.'

Ten minutes later, Miller replaced the small electronic device, along with his new identity documentation, back in the glovebox, satisfied that everything was in order. He turned his thick neck to witness the crusher squeezing the remaining life from the vehicle they had arrived in, before tipping the dirty machine operator a farewell nod.

He paused at the open gate to confirm to himself that the firearm was loaded and placed it in the door compartment to his right. The speakers let out a ringing sound as he moved to make his first contact on the vehicle's phone. He would confirm that the first phase of the operation had been successful, and he was en route. Naamah would be delighted.

At the same time, now several miles away, Harry felt beneath the steering column with one hand, while with the other he continued to guide the vehicle through the waterlogged country roads. He let out a satisfied sigh as he located the device. The correct one.

The scrap dealer had done well.

CHAPTER 8

Saturday 26th June

Robson could not be sure what had triggered the sentimental response. It might have been the sight of his precious daughter in her bridesmaid's dress, or that of his late wife's lifelong friend as she glided down the aisle. Whatever the reason, it certainly had not been easy keeping his emotions at bay.

He thought he could partly attribute the relaxation of his usual self-control to the slightly excessive consumption of alcohol the previous night. Having waited until nine o'clock for Sarah's fiancé to finally arrive, Robson had already been through a significant amount of beer. That had been before the bachelor night had even begun.

The two revellers had finally hit the sack at just after three in the morning, which, for DCI Robson, was when the faded memories of his own wedding preparations unexpectedly, but vividly, surfaced. Now, several sobering hours later, he felt sorry for Mark. The poor man had enough on his plate – preparing for the most important day of his life to date – without having to contend with a middle-aged wreck. Fortunately, Mark was a good listener. And he never judged, which was perhaps why, for the first time in a long while, Robson was prepared to label another person as a 'friend'. Sarah had chosen well.

Robson squeezed his eyelids shut, attempting to moisten his bloodshot vision, before forcing a smile for the elegant bride.

'The sun shone for you then?' he croaked.

Sarah extended a white lace covered forearm and took his hand tenderly. He appreciated her choice of perfume as she stood on tiptoes to peck him on the check.

'It wouldn't dare do, otherwise, Jack.'

Robson's open palm covered the small of her back as he held her towards him.

'No. Quite true.'

'How are you feeling?'

Reluctantly, Robson released her petite frame.

'Me? It's your day, Sarah, not mine!'

'Mark told me you had a bit of a late one.'

'Yes, you could say that.'

A young waitress stopped beside them and smiled politely while delicately balancing a silver tray, which was laden with champagne-filled flutes. She flushed slightly as Robson held her gaze and returned her smile. He took a glass in each hand.

'Thank you.'

The young woman approached the next guests, wearing the same immovable smile. Robson handed a flute to the bride, who now appeared to be wearing her patent maternal expression.

'You don't look as though you really want that,' she said, mischievously.

'I'm not used to all this partying.'

'Mark seems to think you had a bit of a head-start before he arrived back last night.'

'Perhaps. I hope he doesn't work that late on a regular basis mind you, or you two won't be seeing much of one another.'

'He won't.'

'Of course not. Have you seen Jasmine, by the way?'

'She's in deep conversation with my aunty. Isn't she looking stunning, Jack?

She reminds me so much of Isabelle, I could just cry.'

Robson nodded and looked away from Sarah's eyes, which suddenly seemed to moisten. He swallowed the lump in his throat.

'It wasn't so long ago,' the bride continued, 'that a few of us were expecting this to be you and another certain officer of the law.'

Robson knew that, however taboo he had made the subject, it was inevitable that it would be brought up again some time. Privately he reflected that a wedding was the obvious timing.

'There's only ever been one bride for me, Sarah.'

Robson did his best to present a nonchalant expression, but Sarah knew him better.

'Jack, I know you don't want to hear this, but it's such a shame. Anyone could see that you two were great together—'

'She had other plans, Sarah. A career opportunity that couldn't be refused. I couldn't let her throw that away on me.'

Sarah brushed her veil back as the breeze caught it and shook her head in frustration.

'Jack, after all these years, have you really not learnt anything about the female species? Emma wasn't making a choice between you and her career. She just wanted to know where she stood.'

Robson remained silent.

'She wanted both, Jack. You must have seen that.'

'Ancient history, Sarah. Today is about you and Mark.'

One of Sarah's female friends arrived as she let out a long, frustrated sigh and placed a hand on the bride's shoulder.

'Sorry to interrupt. Sarah, can I introduce you to someone please?'

Sarah's eyes remained trained on Robson for a moment, before she turned away and glided towards a small huddle, holding the hand of her female companion.

Robson emptied the champagne flute and felt his heart ache slightly. He knew he had been a coward, but out of genuine affection he had felt he owed it to Emma Wilson to release his grip. Detective Inspector Wilson had awoken strong feelings of affection in him which, while being wonderful, also frightened him to the core.

Friends and family had been remarkably supportive and positive about the relationship. Jasmine adored her, but Robson hadn't been prepared to take the risk, instead choosing to allow fate to dictate the outcome. At least, that is what he had been telling himself every day for the past couple of years since they had parted.

CHAPTER 9

Monday 28th June

Inside his newly acquired vehicle, Miller completed the brief phone call from the car park as he looked out of the windscreen at the dark rainclouds that smothered Porlock weir.

"I fear your concerns regarding Arkwright might have been justified, Naamah. It seems the electronic key is a decoy."

"That's a shame, Jacob," responded the voice at the other end. "Fortunately, we traced Arkwright, so that situation will be dealt with promptly, have no fear. You can focus on your own objectives."

"Thank you, Naamah, speak soon."

"Goodbye, Jacob."

The familiar saline smell was the first thing to pounce on Miller's senses, as the ex-harbour master arrived back at his old stomping ground. As he entered the Ship Inn, further memories were awoken as he inhaled the atmosphere of the tavern. Most of the tables lay empty, with the fishing folk out in the channel and it still being a little early in the year for the peak tourist season. That suited Miller just fine – he didn't want to be recognised. Although, given his changed appearance, recognition would have been unlikely. Even the landlord, who had been expecting him, performed a double take when his visitor arrived. He was astounded at how much the man had changed, even though he had been told to expect a significant difference. Their prior communication had occurred through third parties only, as they couldn't risk direct visits.

Suppressing his surprise, the landlord approached Miller on the other side of the bar and acted as though he was greeting a stranger.

'Good afternoon, sir. What can I get you?'

The landlord continued to hold the visitor's gaze, confirming to himself that it was indeed the formerly overweight, gregarious harbour master of eight years ago. He now faced a lean figure, who perhaps possessed the same impish sparkle deep behind those eyes, but now they also appeared colder. The landlord noted the impressively toned, muscular arms that emanated from the customer's t-shirt sleeves as he placed his order. The large hands, synonymous with a fisherman, were the only familiar aspect. *Apart from those eyes.*

'Afternoon landlord. I'll take a flagon of whatever you recommend, and oi'd be glad to buy you the same, if you'd care to join me in a wassail.'

The landlord noted to himself that the prearranged password had been used before responding with his own.

'Why thank you, sir. I'd be glad to join you in a glass of Natch.'

The landlord poured them each a pint of amber-coloured, slightly cloudy liquid. He presented Miller with a beer mat on which to place his drink, and the customer handed his payment across the bar.

'I thank you, sir,' said the landlord, as the two men clinked their glasses together.

The landlord retreated to the opposite end of the bar to take an order from an elderly man, who had staggered to the bar for a top-up.

Meanwhile, Jacob Miller observed the message that had been scrawled on the beer mat, as he lifted the glass of cool liquid to his dry lips.

Shangri-La. Berth 4.

By the time the landlord was taking payment from the old man, Miller had necked the cold cider and waved farewell. The landlord acknowledged his departure.

'Thank you for the drink sir, come again soon.'

Miller raised a hand and turned his head slightly, ostensibly to offer a farewell, but also to check that no one was watching him as he threw the beermat into the dormant fireplace. He knew it would be lit later that evening due to the unseasonal cold weather, but also that its ignition had already been planned, regardless of temperature.

CHAPTER 10

Two miles east of Porlock, Jasmine linked her arm through her father's as they scampered alongside the stream. The bank had become increasingly sodden in a short space of time, due not only to the ferocity of the freak downpour, but also to the soft ground already being close to saturation even before the latest rain had arrived.

Up ahead, the newlyweds skipped along, giggling in the face of the adverse conditions. When they had strolled along that very stretch in the opposite direction only an hour earlier, they had basked in the spring warmth while enjoying the still calm of the Coleridge Way – a quintessentially English springtime scene, complete with birdsong to accompany the breath-taking views of the Quantock hills and the North Somerset coastline.

'Mark!' Robson shouted to his friend for the second time, but louder this time. They were only separated by some five metres of sodden ground, but he had to overpower the noise of rain lashing down on the lush canopy of trees above. Mark Connor and his new bride looked back together to see Robson pointing towards a wooded area in the distance.

They diverted leftwards from their course in the direction of a small area of woodland. The sodden ground squelched beneath their feet, and as they stumbled into the wood, all four of them felt grateful for the cover that was provided by the dense foliage.

*

29

The hidden man inhaled slowly to control his heartbeat as he eyed the group of walkers who were making an unexpected dash in his direction. He watched as his target stumbled on a tree root, before being helped up by the other members of the group. The sight of the DCI evoked a multitude of memories in the concealed marksman. It had been a while, and while he had seen him from a distance on a handful of occasions over the years, he hadn't been this close in eight years.

He regained his focus and carefully aimed the firearm at his quarry. The group had begun to slow down, making his prey an even simpler target. The marksman cursed to himself and lowered the weapon as he realised the group were currently located between him and his intended escape route.

I'm not wasting my ammo on all of them. Not unless it is absolutely necessary.

The gunman re-evaluated his strategy. He raised himself slowly and moved stealthily to look for a new, more efficient shooting position. The noise of cracking twigs beneath his feet was conveniently drowned out by the sound of torrential rain.

*

They eyed one another with dishevelled expressions, looking like drowned rats, before noticing the shelter that finally revealed the reason for Robson's insistence on the detour. The four walkers marched towards the wooden construction which stood in a clearing fifty yards away.

The Jubilee Hut at Webbers Post had been cleverly designed. In theory, those wishing to escape a particularly bracing wind could always find a sheltered side, regardless of its direction. The current four inhabitants were more concerned about sheltering from the downpour which continued relentlessly, rather than avoiding wind. However, they took the quadrant that seemed to offer the stillest environment, sitting in a row on the wooden bench and facing away from the forest at a forty-five-degree angle.

'This weather is insane,' Sarah commented, as she attempted to dry her sodden hair with her equally waterlogged clothing.

'This is a rubbish summer,' added the young girl to her left, 'but at least it didn't rain on Saturday for your wedding!' Jasmine beamed.

Robson allowed himself to smile as he watched his daughter, admiring yet another example of his late wife's positive demeanour. Sarah winked as she responded.

'I know. Mother Nature knew better than to hit us with rain on our big day, Jazzy!'

'Still,' added Mark, 'we can only take shelter for so long. We have a lot of packing to do before Wednesday.'

'Oh, stop fretting you, what's left to pack for the honeymoon?'

'What was that?' Jasmine interrupted.

'What?' Asked Robson.

'I just saw something move in the woods over there.'

'Probably a deer,' he answered.

Sarah chuckled.

'I expect we've taken its shelter!'

CHAPTER 11

The torrential rain had no effect on Miller, in fact, it suited him. He had his hood pulled tightly around his face, concealing his identity from anyone who might have been sharp-eyed enough to notice. He drew the hood cords a little tighter and hunched his shoulders as he meandered past his former office. He knew it to be empty, having waited until he had surreptitiously observed the incumbent harbour master arrive at the inn for his afternoon break. Miller marched towards the quayside.

Despite the suddenly inclement conditions, there were no other vessels in the dock apart from the boat that he now approached. The blue hull swayed in the dock as raindrops bounced like ricocheting bullets against the white fibreglass surface of the *Shangri-La*.

Miller was pleased that a fishing vessel had been selected. The coastguard's attention might well have been drawn to anything other than a professional boat venturing into the channel in the current conditions. He noticed the smoke rising from the stack as he climbed aboard and within moments the only inhabitant surfaced to greet the cause of the increased rocking.

The pilot exchanged a brief handshake with Miller as they ducked into the cabin in single file.

'Is she free?' asked the other man.

'Sure is,' Miller replied, nodding to confirm he had released the moorings prior to embarkation.

'Could be a rough one for the time of year,' said the boat pilot, already manoeuvring the boat through the small entrance in the harbour wall. Miller sniggered ironically to himself, before responding.

'I think I'll manage. Who's waitin' for us on the island?' he enquired.

The boat pilot turned his head slightly to respond, still concentrating on negotiating a path into the murky channel.

'Carlos.'

Miller nodded in satisfaction, picturing their trusted colleague, who had been one of the officials at the Iberian base all those years ago. Clearly, he had managed to evade suspicion in the last eight years, waiting to be part of this – their crowning glory.

The buoyancy of the churning sea still felt comfortable to Miller, like second nature, as the boat picked up pace, ploughing a course towards their next destination.

Jacob Miller had returned home.

CHAPTER 12

The overwhelming aroma of earthy petrichor dominated the air as the downpour finally began to ease. The sound of water pellets resonating off the wooden roof above them had softened sufficiently for Robson to hear the phone ringing in his sodden anorak pocket. Jasmine lifted her head from her father's shoulder to allow him to retrieve the mobile, while Mark and Sarah momentarily withdrew their attention from one another, noticing Robson's seemingly puzzled expression as he answered the call.

'John?'

'Jack, how are you? It's been a while.'

Robson visualised his friend and highly decorated ex-boss and immediately wondered at the purpose of this unexpected call. It had been a while since they had spoken so they were probably due a catch up, but there was something about Commander John Gibson's tone that seemed peculiar.

'Hasn't it just … I'm good thanks, John. Wet, but okay. What about you?'

'Fine, usual challenges here, but I'm otherwise okay. Listen, I'm sorry to disturb you, Jack. I called the station and they explained you were currently on leave. I've got some information that I wanted to share with you.'

'Really … I don't think I like the sound of this, John.'

'Well, I'm sure it's nothing to worry about, but you ought to know. It's about Miller. Jacob Miller …'

Robson pictured the plump harbourmaster he had first encountered while working alongside DI Wilson and the Somerset CID, several years earlier. He had encountered many types of crook in his time, but Miller's involvement in the Arcam conspiracy had particularly bugged him. An atypical profile for a murderer if ever there was one. He had already wondered if it had been his apparent pleasant demeanour that had persuaded HMP officials to take their recent, bizarre decision to downgrade his status.

'Oh right. Yes, I heard he was being downgraded to Category C, for exemplary behaviour, wasn't it? Couldn't quite believe it. I hear Belmarsh is bursting at the seams more than ever though.'

'Hmm, yes, well, your reservations may perhaps have been justified. There's no easy way of saying this, Jack – he's escaped.'

Mark was the first to recognise the sudden anxiety on Robson's face, shortly followed by both Jasmine and Sarah.

Robson suddenly felt claustrophobic, as though the giant trees were closing in around him. He rose stiffly and left the shelter to stand in the lightly spitting rain.

*

The large man in the woods felt energised that his patience had paid off. He had chosen his new position well and would get a clean shot at his target after all. He knew he could be out of the area before anyone would be able to determine which direction the bullet had come from.

*

'Escaped?! How the hell has he escaped, John? And when?'

Robson's speech betrayed his exasperation. He tried to remain objective while his subconscious whirred through endless permutations. Commander John Gibson spoke with his usual unruffled elocution.

'It happened on Friday, Jack. He was being transferred to Dartmoor and they were intercepted on the moor, so it seems. Both prison guards were shot, but not before raising the alarm. A local armed unit arrived in time to see a vehicle speeding off the moor. They had laid a Stinger, so both police vehicles were disabled and unable to give chase.'

'Holy shit, John.'

'Listen Jack. I don't think there's anything for you to worry about. I just thought it would be courteous to let you know. I gather that Superintendent Grayson didn't want to disturb you while on leave, but I didn't want you to get a shock.'

'Shock? Jesus, John!'

'He won't get far, there's a huge manhunt underway.'

'Well, how far have they got already, John? Have they found the escape vehicle?'

'No. It seems to have disappeared.'

In his bewilderment, Robson hadn't noticed that the rain had ceased. The others had arrived alongside him, having left the wooden shelter. He still held the phone to his ear without speaking, until, suddenly, the deafening sound of gunfire revived his senses.

On the other end of the line, Gibson heard the loud bang, shortly followed by screaming – female screaming.

The phone connection remained open.

'Jack? Jack! What was that, Jack? Is everything okay?'

Commander Gibson did not get a response.

As the rest of the group hovered over the casualty, nobody noticed the covert marksman leaving his cover and swiftly departing the wood.

CHAPTER 13

Miller's veins pulsed with vigour as he watched the dark mound grow larger. The boat was drawing them ever nearer to their destination.

The ex-harbour master exchanged a brief glance with the pilot, both closely observing the signal that was being displayed by a lone person on the shore. The clouds began to part, allowing the sun to illuminate the figure on the shore. A short, tanned man, wearing shorts and a lightweight raincoat, awaited them. There was a tangible release of tension on board the fishing boat, as the pilot became satisfied that their host ashore had confirmed that they were clear to land.

The island had been reserved for their exclusive use.

None of them had doubted that the chair of the island trust would have played their part to ensure that they would not be disturbed. The new trust had moved to secure the island only two years ago once the security services had finally released it from their grasp. It had taken more than five years, but the officials were finally satisfied that all searches had been exhausted and that the extraordinary, secret nuclear arsenal had been safely decommissioned. But it wasn't yet ready to be a tourist attraction again.

In the guise of an ostensibly well-intentioned trust, the island's beauty had begun to be reinvigorated and it was, reportedly, nearly ready to receive its first truly public opening in over a decade. There would be no public occasion today though, and the only other visitors would be those aboard the vessel which was now being secured to the small landing pier at one end of the pebbly beach.

The sun reflected off the small man's shiny brown scalp as he rushed forward to greet Miller, as soon as the ex-harbourmaster hopped ashore. He had removed his raincoat to allow the newly arrived sun to warm his bony shoulders which protruded from a loose-fitting vest.

'It's been a long time, Carlos.'

Miller spoke with a large paw resting on the other man's skinny, bronzed shoulder. The slender man remained silent for a few seconds and constantly smiled as he took in the renewed form of his former friend and comrade.

'Jacob … is it really you?!'

Miller smiled at the man's rugged Latin tones. When they had parted eight years ago, they had expected to be meeting under different circumstances, having gone to take up their positions in their own respective underground habitations. The escaped convict nodded at the grinning Spaniard.

'Do we have everything in place, Carlos?'

'Of course, General Miller. Won't you follow me, gentlemen. Naamah is very keen to receive you, but we have work to do first, as you know.'

They followed Carlos towards the familiar sycamore-lined path. They were jogging as they passed the overgrown entrance to the path and continued following their nimble-footed host. Carlos hopped off the path and stepped deftly down the rocks on to another, smaller pebbly cove. Miller constantly scanned the sea and sky for anything suspicious while he and the boat pilot remained in tow. The three men marched across the beach.

*

Sarah's face was buried deep in Jasmine's young, yet mature shoulder. The young girl couldn't take her eyes off the bloodstains on her father's clothing, as she watched the paramedics expertly load the casualty into the side of the helicopter.

The air ambulance had managed to identify just enough clearing about fifty yards from them, while Jasmine had done an impressive job of keeping the bleeding under control. At the same time, she had been doing her best to calm Sarah.

Sarah had become hysterical as she tried to process what had happened. The noise of the gunshot had shocked her, and she had spent a good few moments scanning the area for its source before finally noticing her newlywed at her feet with blood oozing from a hole in his shoulder.

Robson had flown into the wood, evidently sensing the direction from which the single bullet had originated. A few minutes later, he returned alone with his phone to his ear. His own pulse rate had risen significantly, as he processed the recent information he had been given. An event which, no sooner had it been described, had already become a secondary priority due to the gunfire that had immediately followed the news. It was difficult not to make connections between the two.

He helped a distraught Sarah into the helicopter with the paramedics. As the doors were closed, he gave his daughter a brief hug, before addressing the police officers who had arrived at the scene.

*

On the southern shore of Steep Holm island, Miller and his colleagues had reached the eastern boundary of the cove and now helped Carlos remove the temporary vegetation canopy from one of the concealed machines.

Carlos and the boat pilot smiled, admiring the light aircraft, while Miller remained impassive. The ex-harbourmaster was unimpressed by any mode of transport that did not travel on the surface of the ocean, but was silently appreciative of the fact that the A5 seaplanes represented the latest in light-aircraft technology and would be an efficient means of travelling to their next rendezvous.

CHAPTER 14

Professor Romano flicked off the television. The content of the news programme was almost entirely weather-related: floods in the south-west, storms in the north – even Siberian weather fronts were invading the typical spring throughout Europe.

He moved to the window of his little cottage and watched the rainwater gushing down the narrow road. The saturated mountains emptied themselves as fast as they were being refilled by the precipitous sky, turning the road outside into a constant, fast-moving stream. But the grey sky had temporarily given way to sunlight, which now sparkled in the new river.

The randomness of nature had always fascinated Romano, and he had spent most of his long career studying it, trying to establish what influenced weather systems to behave in such an apparently erratic fashion. He felt blessed to have been involved in some of the most advanced research ever carried out on climate change and he knew he had been privileged to have been one of the very first to gain insights that few other people would be privy to for a very long time to come, if ever.

But the latest experiment troubled him. No matter how hard he tried to reframe it in his mind, an ingrained moral code forced him to consider his actions. There were often such occasions in the progress of science – experiments that led to its perpetrators having to assess the balance of ethical concerns against the potential long-term benefits to humankind. Alberto

Romano had begun to feel that the latter was now becoming outweighed by the former.

The trouble was, he knew this realisation had come too late.

CHAPTER 15

DCI Robson and his daughter paced into the A & E department to be greeted by a scene of bored inpatients scattered around the various seating areas. A flustered male nurse stood over an apparently intoxicated man, attempting to suppress his aggressive outbursts.

Robson inhaled deeply to keep his anxiety at bay while he took in the familiar, depressing scene. With his hand at her back, he gently guided Jasmine towards the desk. However, the young girl seemed to be unaffected by the scene and surprised her father by taking the initiative. Jasmine's forthrightness even appeared to distract the glacial nurse from her indifferent disposition.

The nurse looked up from behind the reception desk at the confident, young girl.

'Excuse me, nurse. Could you tell us where to find our friend please? Mark Connor.'

'Let me see.'

The nurse visibly resisted the urge to show a condescending smile, seeing the serious expression on the young lady's face.

'When was he admitted, approximately?'

Robson joined the conversation.

'Recently, he came in with the air ambulance paramedics.'

The nurse's eyes displayed instant comprehension at Robson's clarification.

'Ah yes, let me get someone to come out and see you both. Please take a seat while you wait. Someone will be with you as soon as possible.'

Robson retained eye contact just long enough to convey that he would hold her to her parting assurance. They made their way to a section of seating nearest the desk, but noting the sudden interest in them from the most highly populated area of the waiting room, they continued walking and opted for an empty section. Jasmine tugged at her father's sleeve.

'Where do you think Sarah is, Dad?'

'She'll be with Mark. Come on, let's take a seat.'

DCI Robson looked around the large room, which seemed exactly the same as eight years previously, on his first visit to Taunton hospital. The memories invaded his mind like a film reel: the personal emotions and the extraordinary implications of the related investigation – a case that had led them to a nuclear arsenal with the capacity to destroy most of humankind, in the hands of a group of fanatics who had intended to use it to its full potential.

His thoughts jumped to the present, disturbed by his daughter's frank inquisitiveness.

'Dad, who do think that bullet was meant for?'

It was not the bluntness of his thirteen-year-old daughter's query that surprised him, but its astuteness. Every day she grew to be more like her formidable, late mother, Robson thought.

'We don't know anything yet, love. My first instinct would be mistaken identity.'

'Really, Dad?'

'Who knows? We don't know anything, Jasmine, so there's no point speculating. Let's just hope that Mark is going to be okay.'

Jasmine knew full well that her father would not share his full feelings on the matter.

But the fact of the matter was, Robson had been pondering the very same question for the past couple of hours. He couldn't help thinking that if the shot had been fired a split second earlier, it would have been him lying in the hospital bed. Or worse.

Seconds earlier he had learnt that one of the senior perpetrators from the

Arcam investigation had escaped his incarceration. The theory that Jacob Miller would choose to come after DCI Robson was not a particularly long shot. The ex-harbour master had made it clear eight years ago that the man largely responsible for foiling Arcam would one day live to regret his actions.

Robson suppressed a shudder and focussed on his breathing, as an official-looking woman entered the waiting area through the security doors and made her way towards them. The solemn expression and clipboard could only mean one thing – she was the doctor, and she brought news of the patient.

CHAPTER 16

The ocean beneath the seaplane glistened in the remaining solar rays from the low sun which peered just above the horizon. The plane began to descend from its two hundred-foot cruising altitude, having successfully flown in accordance with the predetermined route plan to avoid radar detection.

Miller remained composed in the passenger seat of the plane, while on his left, the pilot continued to demonstrate his multiple talents, having switched from sea to airborne transport seamlessly. He eased back on the control stick and the aircraft juddered slightly as the sea-wing platforms connected with the ocean surface. Seawater sprayed either side of the plane as they came to a standstill on the aqueous runway.

Miller surveyed the seemingly unending expanse of ocean, pleased by the remoteness of their destination, but while the pilot checked the GPS display to confirm that they had arrived at the correct location, neither of them noticed the antenna, some fifty yards away, protruding through the vast ocean surface.

*

Fifteen metres beneath the surface of the Atlantic Ocean, the submarine captain was satisfied that the target had been identified and ordered the withdrawal of the photonics mast, before barking his next command.

'Make preparations for surfacing.'

CHAPTER 17

Seeing her newlywed connected to wires and tubes had been tough on Sarah by any measure. Robson had tried his best to comfort her, but she only seemed responsive to Jasmine.

The waiting area had emptied over the past few hours and a different person now occupied the front desk. Despite the emptiness, Robson sensed the same sombre atmosphere in the hospital as he strode behind the two females, who walked before him with their arms linked.

He considered his next move as they made their way through the empty reception area and hoped that his own involvement in the fracas had provided an increased focus for those who currently pursued the escaped convict, Jacob Miller. Shootings in North Somerset were not a regular occurrence, but the force was stretched, and it took time to reallocate resources. Curiously, at the time of the shooting, Robson's ex-superintendent – now the commander of the national counter-terrorism police unit otherwise known as SO15 – had been in the process of warning him of Miller's escape, given that the prisoner was known to have held a grudge against Robson and his colleagues. Gibson hadn't waited for the phone to ring twice before answering Robson's call from the hospital earlier, and Robson had already concluded that the incident was being afforded an appropriate profile.

Even so, he did not expect to be confronted by a gathering of police officers and CID outside the hospital entrance. Robson recognised a couple of the faces among the team and couldn't help feeling impressed by the speed at which they had been assembled, given their existing commitments. It didn't make Mark Connor's condition any less precarious, but his instinct told him that it hadn't been a chance encounter earlier on the Coleridge Way, so the appearance of an experienced team of officers pleased him. He marched purposefully from the hospital entrance to intercept them.

Robson soon noticed the distinctly peculiar atmosphere among his colleagues. From their body language, it appeared that none of them were particularly impressed by their reassignment. Robson was on familiar terms with one of the two uniformed officers and the two CID were both his subordinates, yet the typically affable relationship between them seemed to have vanished for some reason.

As he arrived at close quarters, however, Robson realised it wasn't disappointment in his colleague's faces. All he saw was sheer tension.

'Hello folks. I'm afraid you won't get a word out of him at the moment.'

Robson chose his words carefully, knowing that both Sarah and Jasmine were within hearing distance, having stopped to wait for him. To Robson's surprise, a response came from the uniformed officer with whom he wasn't familiar.

'DCI Robson, sir, it's you we'd like to have a word with.'

Robson stole a glance at his daughter and Sarah who were watching the scene with interest, still arm in arm. Jasmine began to frown, noticing the apparent unease grow across her father's face as he addressed the unknown officer.

'Sure, how can I be of assistance? Have you come up with a lead on our mystery marksman already?'

'This isn't related to the recent shooting on the Coleridge way, sir,' continued the young officer. Robson could see the man was troubled but still grew frustrated at his procrastination. Evidently, so had his colleagues and one of the CID officers took over.

'Jack, this isn't going to be easy I'm afraid. Could you tell us where you were two days ago, on Friday 25th June?' asked Detective Inspector Matthews.

Robson felt winded as he found himself unexpectedly under the spotlight. He stuttered slightly.

'I … I'm not entirely sure. Well, actually, I was at home … pretty much all day.'

'Okay. Were you alone, sir?'

'Yes. Well, at least I was until late, when my friend arrived. What's this all about, Matthews?'

Robson watched his CID colleague swallow hard before proceeding.

'We need you to come with us, sir, for questioning.'

'In connection with what, James? Look, I don't know what you guys are after, but we've had a pretty traumatic day and the last thing I'm going to do is come to the station now. It'll have to wait until morning I'm afraid.'

The two uniformed officers stepped forward so that they were abreast of Robson, while DS Burford shuffled to one side so that she was immediately in front of him. Matthews did not seem confident holding his senior officer's gaze and he was clearly finding the situation the most difficult of all of them. Burford, noting her inspector's discomfort, stepped in.

'Jack Robson, you are under arrest, on suspicion of aiding and abetting an unlawful escape from custody, and in connection with the murder of two prison officers. You do not have to say anything, but it may harm your defence if you do not mention when questioned, something which you later rely on in court. Anything you do say may be given in evidence.'

Stunned, Robson understood that he had no choice. He returned the confused looks of Jasmine and Sarah as he walked between the officers. The sound of Jasmine crying out seemed to come from another world.

'Dad!'

The uniformed officers twitched nervously as Robson stopped abruptly, before looking back towards his daughter.

'It's just a misunderstanding, Jazzy. Go home and look after Sarah. I'll call you.'

Jasmine and Sarah continued to link arms as they both remained frozen to the spot. They were still in the same position when the police car sped away with an unmarked CID car close behind. They each stole a look at the backseat passenger, but Robson did not return their stares. Instead his head remained lowered as though staring at something on the floor.

CHAPTER 18

Atlantic Ocean (Monday 28th June)

Miller eyed an area within the vast body of water some fifty yards away. A huge shadow had begun to appear, presenting itself as the source of a sound that had been steadily growing. The two men in the seaplane were temporarily spellbound by the sight of the awesome giant that bulged beneath the surface.

The fin was the first part of the metallic structure to break the ocean's skin and was immediately followed by the remaining hundred and fifty metres of grey steel. The top of the hull bobbed momentarily, then sat menacingly still.

From their position aboard the seaplane, the sound of the airlock opening at the top of the sub was faint, yet unmistakable. A lone figure promptly appeared through the open hatch and stood on the hull, surveying the scene before him. The man pulled a device from his jacket and began speaking into it. Within seconds, the grey sea monster idled towards Miller and his pilot and, moments later, stood alongside them, further emphasising the size of the vessel.

The tension that initially showed on the worn, dark-skinned face of the man on the hull, softened to pleasant recognition as he beheld the ex-harbour master, who was now standing on a float on one side of the plane.

'Jacob! Is it really you? They said you had changed my friend, but my word!'

'Abdi. Good to see you. Let's get aboard before we indulge in small talk, shall we?'

'Of course, my friend. Please.'

The tall figure extended a short platform towards the plane to allow Miller and his aircraft pilot to board the submarine. Abdi took each visitor by their right hand as they boarded and watched them each swiftly disappear through the open hatch. As the top of their heads disappeared through the opening, Abdi swiftly withdrew a firearm from a concealed holster and held it steadily in front of him, before firing four shots and replacing the firearm on his waist.

Within a couple of minutes, the seaplane began to sink. Abdi watched for a further five minutes, observing the rate of submersion increase as the light aircraft filled with water. He watched the last of the bubbles pop on the ocean surface and turned away as the top of the plane disappeared into the Atlantic.

Abdi descended the steps, briefly stopping to secure the airtight hatch above his head. The periscope antenna withdrew and the captain, who had watched the process from inside the control room, ordered two of the sailors to go and greet their guests.

Meanwhile, the ballast tanks started to flood again, and the submarine began to disappear. In less than a minute, the surface of the vast ocean was once again still and empty, leaving no trace of the recent rendezvous.

CHAPTER 19

While the surroundings were familiar, DCI Robson felt only numb detachment, both from his environment and from the face that sat across the desk from him.

Having consented to an oral swab and giving his fingerprints, Robson could tell from the look on his colleague's face that he felt his DCI hadn't made the wisest of decisions declining their invitation for legal representation.

The door to the interview room opened and another officer entered. The slightly built, bald man held Robson's gaze impassively from the moment he entered. Robson and the new entrant nodded at one another before Robson addressed his senior officer.

'Sir.'

'Hello, Jack.'

Superintendent Grayson helped himself to the remaining seat at the desk.

DI Matthews had refused the interview, stating that he was too close to DCI Robson. The superintendent had seemed unmoved, and Matthews couldn't tell whether he had agreed with his judgement or whether he was disappointed in him. Either way, Matthews didn't care. This was one interview in which he wouldn't have backed himself to act objectively. So, instead, an officer from the major crime investigation team had been enlisted – DI Bannister – who himself had seemed rather uncomfortable at first, but now, seemingly emboldened by the arrival of the superintendent, seemed to relax.

Bannister operated the recording device on the desk and began the interview.

'Interview time 17:10. Present – Detective Inspector Bannister, Detective Superintendent Grayson, and the suspect –Jack Robson. Mr Robson has declined the offer of legal representation.'

Robson watched Bannister look up from his notepad, for the first time since speaking, to give him the same authoritative, patronising look that he had delivered himself so many times.

'For the benefit of the recording, Mr Robson, could you confirm that you do not wish to have legal representation?'

Robson's look was icy.

'I confirm that is correct.'

'Okay. Could you tell us again where you were on Friday, 25 June?'

Robson peered silently into his interviewer's eyes.

'I was at home, Inspector.'

'All day?'

Robson felt himself begin to nod, and immediately felt a degree of empathy with all those he had previously encouraged to use speech rather than body gestures for the audio recording.

'Yes, all day.'

'Were you alone?'

'Until later in the evening, yes.'

'I see. Could you tell us what you were doing?'

'I don't know. Just pottering, making the most of my day off, I think. Jasmine was at Sarah's – it was the day before her wedding. I think I did a bit of housework and gardening.'

'Do you think anyone would have seen you working in the garden?'

'I doubt it. As you know, we live in the corner of a small cul-de-sac, and it was a working day.'

Although their facial expressions revealed nothing, Robson could see the scepticism in the eyes of his interviewers.

'So, you say you were alone until the evening – who did you see later?'

'Sarah's fiancé, Mark Connor. I had invited him over for a meal and he stayed the night. It was supposed to be a bit of a bachelor party, but he didn't arrive until late … oh, and that's what else I was doing – cooking a curry.'

The interviewer nodded while the superintendent continued to watch impassively.

'Okay. Can you remember exactly what time Mr Connor arrived at your house on the 25th?'

Robson's intolerance of the situation was beginning to show, as he began to surface from his initial numbness.

'I think it was around nine before he arrived.'

Superintendent Grayson spoke for the first time.

'Where had Mark Connor been, before he got to your house?'

'He was working. He's a security specialist and had been meeting a client in the midlands.'

Robson felt his patience was about to expire and he shuffled to an upright position before facing his interviewers again.

'Look, gents, I know you're doing your job, but my family has just been through a rather shocking ordeal. I've answered your questions and allowed you to take samples, so are you going to tell me what all this is about? The charges you mentioned when you arrested me sounded pretty serious, so I wouldn't mind a little clarification, if it's all the same to you.'

Inspector Bannister resumed the interview, as though Robson hadn't interrupted.

'DCI Robson – do you know anyone by the name of Jacob Miller?'

Robson felt his blood boil. He became aware that he was nodding again and forced himself to calm down.

Breathe, Jack.

'Sorry, yes. Yes, I know Miller – as you well know I do. Come on, gents, my patience really is wearing a little thin now.'

'On the 25th of June,' Bannister continued, 'Jacob Miller was being transferred from HMP Belmarsh to HMP Dartmoor. The prison van was ambushed, and Miller escaped.'

'I know.'

'You do?'

The look in Bannister's eyes intensified.

'I received a call earlier today from the commander of SO15 informing me of the very same thing.'

Superintendent Grayson leant forward to enquire further.

'Gibson?'

'Yes. He is the new SO15 command—'

'DCI Robson – I'm well aware of who Commander Gibson is. My question is, why would a high-ranking officer from the Met be communicating such news directly to you?'

'Because we are friends. Commander Gibson was my old superintendent when I was in the Met. To be quite honest, I was a little surprised I hadn't heard the news earlier from someone local. At least there's someone out there looking out for me.'

'Both prison guards were murdered during the snatch.'

'I heard.'

'DCI Robson, our database has matched your DNA with one of the traces that were found at the scene. And your fingerprints.'

Robson suddenly became aware of his heart rate increasing and forced his breathing to slow down before reacting.

'That's impossible. Where were these traces found?'

'From an item of clothing that was found at the scene of the murders.'

'Bloody hell, really? That's your evidence? Do you really believe I had something to do with this? Me, of all people?!'

Out of the corner of his eye, Bannister noted that Superintendent Grayson had leant forward in a challenging manner. He allowed his senior officer to speak.

'DCI Robson. We have reason to believe that Miller's escape could signify that he and his remaining colleagues are planning something. Until now, the security services and Special Branch haven't been able to piece together the connections.'

'Until now?'

'Could it be that you've let these people into your head, Jack? We all know about their powers of persuasion.'

Grayson's voice was as steady as his demeanour.

'Are you kidding me? You know damn well what I went through eight years ago. And if it weren't for me, those maniacs would probably have blown us all to smithereens by now!'

'Quite. Yet the evidence is a little too compelling to ignore, Jack. It's a precise DNA match that was collected from the scene, and you don't seem to have been able to offer an alibi.'

'I'm not fucking well listening to any more of this!'

The chair fell backwards as Robson stood abruptly. Bannister signalled to the uniformed officers outside before responding.

'Jack Robson – based on the available evidence, I am confident of obtaining CPS authority to charge you with being an accessory to the unlawful escape of a convicted criminal and conspiring to murder. You will be detained until further notice. Interview terminated at 17:29.'

CHAPTER 20

The coded transmission between *Teva One* and *Teva Two* lasted only a matter of seconds. Naamah simply requested confirmation that they were still on schedule. The submarine captain confirmed over the extremely low frequency system that they were on course to their first target.

'We will be descending to two thousand feet. Our next communication will be on completion of our objective.'

'Affirmative. Out.'

Miller watched the captain intently as he replaced the handset in its holder and turned to face his team in the control room before giving his next command.

'Rig for diving. Two Thousand feet. Speed, thirty knots. Silent running.'

The nuclear submarine disappeared, silently, into the depths of the ocean, becoming invisible to all surveillance technology.

CHAPTER 21

Tuesday 29th June

For the second night running, Robson lay on the hard bench and pictured Sarah at home and what she might be going through. During his earlier permitted phone call she had seemed quite together, considering the circumstances. But the parallels with his own experiences were unavoidable and he felt her pain, almost literally. Her and Mark's moment of bliss had been blown apart in a matter of seconds. But the fact that he had ended up in a prison cell brought a whole new meaning to the word irony.

It had taken him a day to restore his mind to anything close to rational processing after such a cruel twist, and he dreaded to think how Sarah was coping. She was a tough cookie beneath that pristine exterior, but the current situation would have been hard for anyone to bear. The one consolation was that she had Jasmine with her. Aged thirteen, his daughter had been through what for most was the kind of story confined to nightmares, but she had come out of the other side stronger than ever. A true image of her late mother, in almost every sense.

The noise of the police station had died down now that evening had set in. He imagined the portly duty sergeant at the front desk, working on his crossword puzzle while sipping tea. A recurring question continued to dominate his thoughts – *who is responsible for me being here?*

Despite the late hour, he initially paid no attention to the footsteps outside in the corridor. But the noise grew nearer until the patting of shoes on the hard floor stopped outside his cell door. The sound of whispering was soon followed by the clunk of a key being inserted in the lock. The noise stopped abruptly, and the door remained closed.

Robson sat up with both hands gripping the bench. He was disappointed with himself as he jolted at the sound of the viewing hatch being slammed open but he recovered sufficiently to control his reaction to the threatening sight which followed – a pair of dark eyes peering in through the portal.

The hatch slammed shut. Robson had expected some dialogue to be exchanged. *Perhaps I'm on suicide watch!* he thought. Or perhaps they had called on the wrong guest.

Robson began to lower his back on to the wooden surface again, as the lock to the door clunked and the large metal door swung into the cell. The first thing he noted was not just one visitor, but three. As they approached him, he felt a degree of unease at the cold intent displayed in each man's expression. None of his visitors wore a police uniform and, for some reason, none of this had the feel of official police business.

'Would you come with us please, Mr Robson.'

The man's voice seemed effortlessly authoritative – it was clearly a polite command rather than a request. The two companions flanking him seemed unequivocally confident of the inmate's compliance. Robson felt perspiration running down his back. Having been in solitary silence for the past few hours, he attempted to lubricate his dry throat before offering a croaky response.

'To where?'

The man in the centre was business-like in his response.

'Your questions will be answered in due course, Detective Chief Inspector. But for now, we would really appreciate it if you would accompany us, without resistance.'

Robson found his steel, as he typically did in the face of authority. Something about the condescending nature of his visitors irritated him.

'And what if I don't? Listen fellas, I know how this works. Now, if you want compliance, you need to tell me who you are and what you want, all right? Otherwise, you can go back and tell my CID colleagues that they need to afford me a little more respect.'

It only took seconds for the two silent men to have Robson's hands fastened behind his back, before they proceeded to frog-march him from the cell. The silence of the station did not necessarily surprise DCI Robson, given the hour. But the lack of any personnel on their route seemed strange. As he was marched past the unmanned front desk, he began to feel the unfolding situation had an unnervingly non-procedural quality about it.

Outside, he was shoved into a dark, unmarked saloon car parked on the pavement immediately outside the station entrance. Robson looked back at the station and watched the apparent leader of his escorts dictate instructions to the uniformed sergeant, who had returned to his position behind the front desk. Robson thought the sergeant looked intimidated, a feeling that he could easily empathise with, as each of the two burly, suited men entered the car doors on either side of him and proceeded to wrap a blindfold tightly around his head.

His ears rang as he strained to evaluate what happened in the following silent seconds. The front passenger door opened momentarily, before a slam was replaced by silence once again. The car lurched forward, and the scream of the engine indicated they were travelling at high-speed, in an unknowable direction.

Robson's mind swam, all the while feeling muscular shoulders press on him from either side.

*

By the time the car finally came to a stop, Robson judged that they must have been travelling for around an hour. As his blindfold was removed the digital clock display confirmed his estimate was accurate. No words had been spoken since they had sped away from the police station earlier which only added to his tension.

As he was coaxed from the back seat by one of his burly co-passengers, he took in his surroundings. The sun could not yet be seen, but its light had started to radiate on the horizon, illuminating the desolate countryside that surrounded him. The cool air temperature made him shiver as he studied the only apparent manmade interruption to the natural terrain, an old farmhouse under the cover of a small group of huge oak trees.

The three men swiftly led him to the house. Once inside the front door, the first words were spoken by the same man that had seemed to be in command back at the station.

'This way please, DCI Robson.'

The group walked up a bare wooden staircase in single file before turning left onto the landing at the top. The door at the far end was opened and Robson obeyed the hand gesture to enter first.

He began to sense that this would be his last moment of life as the three men peered at him from the doorway.

'Get some rest, sir. You will find an ensuite bathroom for your use. You will be brought some food shortly.'

'Where are we?'

'We will talk later once you've eaten and had a chance to freshen up.'

CHAPTER 22

In the night, the scene had seemed surreal to Mark Connor as he sank into the comfortable mattress. To his left, a nurse had been taking his pulse. She smiled and began to make small talk when she noticed the patient had conveniently opened his eyes. Twenty-four hours had elapsed since then, his first moment of consciousness in the hospital ward.

Several hours later, his visitors had been full of emotion when, on arrival, they found him awake and eating breakfast. But, as Sarah threw her arms around his neck and sobbed, there had been a different emotion displayed on Jasmine's face.

The prognosis had been good. Connor hadn't lost too much blood, but the doctor's instructions were that he would remain under observation for a couple of days at least. Now into the second night of his stay, Connor's legs still felt weak as he struggled to get up from the high bed. He breathed heavily with the effort and leant against the large windowsill next to his bed while watching the darkness loom over the hospital grounds outside.

Connor willed his mind to become more alert as he tried to reflect on the events of the past thirty-six hours. His head was becoming a little clearer compared to how he had felt a few hours earlier, having refused his last two doses of powerful medication and instead opting for simple pain-relief.

He thought about what had happened in the woods. None of it made sense.

Earlier, the girls had told him about Robson's arrest and, as he contemplated the news, something told him that he could not afford to simply lie around. Why would Robson, his friend, have been arrested? In Connor's line of work, he got to know a little bit about double-dealing and his immediate theory was that corrupt forces appeared to be at work.

There were no two ways about it – he would have to move fast. His first objective was to discharge himself. Then, he needed to get Sarah and Jasmine to safety.

CHAPTER 23

At that moment, it felt to Naamah that they had reached the highest point on earth, both physically and metaphysically. The landscape was dominated by a blanket of white and grey cloud beneath them and, as far as the human eye could see, nothing existed at a higher altitude than them. It was extraordinary to think that, only hours earlier, there had been a clear vista of the surrounding massif which had provided obvious evidence of their location. But now, looking into the mist, the ethereal sight seemed to lend a supernatural credence to their mission.

Naamah shivered in the cool June air and wandered back to the control room. The plan had gone remarkably well, and nothing had gone wrong since Miller's release.

The woman sitting at the VDU nodded to acknowledge her leader's arrival.

'Naamah, we have received a coded message from General Miller. *Teva Two* is on-programme and will provide a further update in twenty-four hours.'

'Thank you, Sylvia.'

Naamah left the control room and headed for the elevator that provided access deep inside the mountain.

*

Robson felt the usual tension as he faced his captors. Each time they paid him a visit he expected the worst, but so far they had only called to bring him food, each time without speaking a word. But now the apparent senior of the three spoke as one of the others collected the untouched microwave meal from the small desk, the only furniture in the room apart from a camp bed on which Robson sat.

'We will be moving on tomorrow.'

'To where?'

'Our boss would like to see you.'

'Who is your boss?'

'Goodnight, DCI Robson.'

CHAPTER 24

Wednesday 30th June
Porlock Weir

Sarah and Jasmine listened to the raindrops pelting against the metal exterior as they waited for Mark to return to the car.

Most holidaymakers appeared to have decided against venturing out on another day of thunderstorms. Indeed, Sarah had considered turning back more than once during their journey; as they had approached the weir, the rainfall had become a monsoon. However, both Mark and Jasmine persuaded her that, within reason, they did not allow the weather to dictate their actions.

It had only just been possible for them to navigate the gushing water at the bottom of the steep hill. Unsurprisingly, even though the tourist season was getting underway, they found the weir devoid of visitors.

Sarah understood that Mark had been keen to venture out, understandably craving some form of normality after their crazy experiences of the past few days. But given that they were due to set off on their honeymoon in a few hours' time, it seemed a little ill-timed. There was an ulterior motive though, with which she couldn't disagree –– it was their last chance to persuade Jasmine to go with them, and they were hoping that a late morning cooked breakfast might help to soften her resolve.

While Mark's apparent resilience impressed her to some extent, Sarah was sure that the hospital had discharged him a little too early, considering the circumstances. Still, it was certainly a wonderful treat to have him back so soon after that traumatic day, only forty-eight hours ago.

Inside the sparsely populated inn, the conversation was brief. Only one of the tables inside was occupied, by an elderly couple who had evidently surrendered to the elements and terminated their walking expedition. They each sat miserably sipping coffee and looking through the small windows at the relentless weather they had escaped, as rainwater dripped to the floor from their sodden raincoats which had been hung up to dry.

'Are you still serving breakfast by any chance?' Connor asked the landlord.

'Yes, we are, sir.'

'Great. There are three of us, I'll go and fetch the ladies.'

Connor turned and immediately jumped in surprise as he came face to face with a sodden giant. The huge man wore typical fishing garb and displayed an unerringly stern expression. When he spoke, his accent confirmed that he was local to the area.

'I'm sorry, friend. Didn't mean to startle you!'

Connor forced a smile.

'No problem.'

He walked swiftly past the bulky man and bent his frame to get through the door.

The fisherman watched Connor leave before completing his journey to the bar. By the time he arrived, the landlord had made a swift exit and left via the rear of the bar, evidently having instructed his young assistant to take over. The boy did his best to present a welcoming demeanour as he held the fort. Noticing that the great man on the other side of the bar appeared to be displeased at being left with the apprentice, the young man was determined to prove himself worthy.

'Full English and tea please, my boy,' the big man commanded as he pointed a thick finger towards one of the draught handles. 'I'll pay you in a sec, lad, but I've got to go and relieve myself first.'

'No problem, sir.'

The fisherman's boots squelched as he marched his bulky frame around the bar and towards the rear entrance which led to the outside lavatory.

Meanwhile, the landlord ran from his flat at the back of the inn, holding a key, and jogged through the rain to the small office annex at the rear of the pub. He shook rainwater from himself as he stepped inside, pulling the door shut behind him. Through force of habit, he ensured he was alone, before locking himself inside.

Can't be too careful.

Samuel Peterson hadn't lied when he told his young employee that he had an important call to make.

Another figure inside the small box room remained deathly still in the corner. It was a tight squeeze, but the uninvited guest had managed to get inside before Peterson and found a spot just out of sight, obscured from view by a tall storage cupboard.

Peterson sat at the small wooden desk and unlocked the only drawer before sliding it open. He lifted the phone from inside and dialled the memorised number.

'It's Sam. I think there could be a probl—'

The impact of the short scaffolding pole on the rear of the landlord's skull prevented him from saying any more. The person previously hidden from view swiftly terminated the call then leant across and placed an index and middle finger against the vein at the side of Samuel Peterson's neck. Having verified the absence of any pulse, the attacker satisfied himself that the blow had been dealt with enough force and removed his hand.

After taking what he needed, the attacker left, swiftly disposing of the murder weapon before locking the office door.

*

'Jazzy, are you sure you're happy with this? We can take a holiday whenever we feel like it, you know. Mark is his own boss, and I can write anytime, anywhere.'

Sarah and Mark Connor both wore concerned expressions as they gazed above the three empty plates on the table. Jasmine held their gazes with her usual carefree countenance. The three of them were the only customers remaining in the old inn, which was fortunate given that the hapless young barman appeared to be fending for himself for the time being.

'Yes, Sarah. As I've already told you, it's fine. I'm looking forward to staying with Grandma, and so is she.'

The pride Sarah felt at the girl's maturity would nearly have matched that of Jasmine's own mother. The young girl already had an incredibly balanced view of life. Seeming to notice the lump forming in his wife's throat, Mark took over the plea.

'We know you'll be fine, Jasmine. It's just that, after recent events, I think Sarah and I would be far happier if you accepted our offer to join us on our trip to France. It'd be fun.'

'It really is fine. For a start, I'm not coming on your honeymoon! Gran is looking forward to me going over tomorrow – she's already made up my bed!'

Her smile suddenly waned.

'But I also want to be around for when Dad comes home.'

'Okay. But you don't need to worry about your Dad, as we discussed earlier. Like he told us on the phone yesterday, it has all been a crazy misunderstanding and he'll have this sorted out before too long. But we respect your decision.'

Mark winced with the pain in his shoulder as he reached out to briefly place a hand on top of Jasmine's.

'But if you change your mind …'

'I won't. Thank you for bringing me out for breakfast today though. Those sausages were awesome!'

The stubborn lump in her throat prevented Sarah from speaking, and instead she smiled affectionately. Mark noticed the sun shining through the pub windows at that moment and grinned.

'Wow, we ought to go and catch those rare summer rays before the next downpour. Fancy a little walk before we go home?'

Sarah and Jasmine both nodded in agreement as Mark got up from the table and began to venture towards the bar. Seeing that there were no staff present, he stopped in his tracks and turned back to the table.

'Looks like we're letting ourselves out!'

He deposited a few bank notes on the table and they departed the shade of the inn, stepping out on to the wet concrete which was now bathed in the sun's rays.

Inside the inn, the young barman returned to the bar to find it empty. He couldn't blame them for leaving, there wasn't much of an atmosphere in the inn lately. Even the landlord seemed to have had enough.

The young man had been trying to track his boss down for the last twenty minutes, to no avail. For some reason, the office door was locked but he was sure he could see a lamp on. He walked to the kitchen and plucked the spare key from the hook as he addressed the chef.

'I think we're done until lunch, Ralph.'

'Okay nipper, I'll see you later.'

'Yes, mate, see you in a couple of hours.'

As the chef departed the inn, the young man wandered back to the office and inserted the key in the locked door. As he pulled the door open, the sight of the illuminated desk-lamp seemed to confirm his suspicions.

Then he stumbled as he beheld the gruesome scene inside.

CHAPTER 25

Despite the air conditioning blasting towards his face, DCI Robson felt his shirt sticking to his perspiring back.

He had been forced to wear a blindfold since departing the remote farmhouse at midday and, after what seemed like several hours of travelling, he was beginning to feel nauseous. But it seemed the journey had finally come to an end. Robson's neck muscles instinctively tensed as one of his co-passengers grabbed at the knotted material at the back of his head.

'Relax, Chief Inspector.'

Robson leant forward to allow enough room for the large hand to untie the blindfold. As his eyes peeled apart for the first time in several hours, they instantly began to sting. He noted from the car's digital clock that it was mid-afternoon.

Daylight continued to dazzle him as he was coaxed from the vehicle. Even so, he felt slightly relieved to escape the rear seat of the dark saloon, despite the uncertainty of his immediate future. He instinctively stretched his long frame before his three captors led him forwards.

His brief relief at the termination of the car journey soon changed to anxious confusion. While it was apparent that they were heading somewhere specific, their destination was unclear to Robson. The immediate locality was a somewhat non-descript street lined with Victorian style buildings on one side.

Gradually, Robson's vision became accustomed to the new setting. As his eyes adjusted, he began to make out that there were signs above some of the doors as they moved towards the buildings, but he failed to register the curb and stumbled as his toes connected with concrete. The three other men seemed to react nervously. He straightened himself and looked along the row of brick buildings. They were now close enough for Robson to make out signs above some of the doors. Imagination and reality seemed to merge and become one as he contemplated their destination. Anything seemed possible to him at that moment.

It became clear that they were headed for the only apparently unmarked entrance in the row of buildings before them. The other adjacent doors seemed to all belong to various legal firms. Up close, his eyes rested above the unremarkable dark entrance before them, while one of the men entered a code into a combination lock to the side. Robson noticed an industrial sized cast-iron pulley, which struck him as being rather out of place amid prestigious solicitors' dwellings. More curious still was the wide, gaping air vent of the sort one might expect to see at the top of a mine shaft.

As the leading man pulled the door open, the other two continued carefully surveying the street in either direction, while also keeping a close eye on their prisoner. The growing weakness in his thighs made Robson feel as though he was close to paralysis. One of the two men at his rear gently nudged him in the back.

'Come on in please, Mr Robson. Nearly there now.'

Robson's hearing was overwhelmed with pumping blood, as the four of them crossed the threshold and squeezed together inside an exceedingly small, square chamber. The thumping in Robson's chest increased further as the door to the enclosure closed to shut them inside, then began to vibrate. He suddenly reached out, hoping to locate something to hold on to prevent himself from falling. His own motion seemed to throw him off balance and he suddenly wobbled in panic, his hands unable to locate anything to grip. Somewhat nonchalantly, two of the men silently held him under each arm to steady him. Robson composed himself, feeling slightly embarrassed. The unknown is always more terrifying than the reality, Robson told himself, as he continued to feel the two strong hands that supported his weight. His paranoia told him that he sensed a degree of enjoyment from the men, despite their impassive looks.

In a flash of understanding, he realised what was happening. He tuned into the sound of the pulley squeaking overhead, which was becoming gradually more distant. They were descending.

As the metal box which was apparently their lift proceeded into the earth, Robson's mind, not for the first time in the past couple of days, was unavoidably cast back to the mind-blowing events of the Arcam investigation eight years earlier. Once again, he was on a journey underground, only this time, he was the one being escorted against his will.

Their descent seemed to take forever, leaving Robson to contemplate how deep they must have travelled.

As their journey finally came to an abrupt halt, the metal enclosure vibrated around them, resounding like a huge gong. A deep rumbling sound echoed all around them, increasing Robson's sense of disorientation. He watched the apparent leader of his chaperones slide the lift door open, only to reveal another set of doors immediately beyond which seemed to be far sturdier than those they had entered at street level. Robson studied their incredible thickness as they swung open.

Bomb-proof?

They departed the dimly lit enclosure and stepped into darkness. For a moment, he wondered what they were waiting for and found the continued silence unnerving. His pulse raced as lighting suddenly flickered on. A subtly lit passageway sprawled out before them, continuing for at least a hundred metres. Despite its length, Robson suddenly felt claustrophobic as they began to march along the tunnel.

Déjà vu.

CHAPTER 26

It had been ten minutes since they had left the lift cage and Robson's unease grew as they continued to navigate a labyrinth of underground tunnels. It was as though his own thoughts could be heard bouncing off the damp concrete walls in the eerie silence, with each hypothesis he imagined darker than its predecessor. He knew he was close to panicking and began to focus on controlling his reaction to the situation.

As he continued to consider his likely fate, they abruptly altered their course and took another passage that connected at a ninety-degree angle. His throat felt dry as he swallowed, watching the dead end before them get closer. He imagined they had reached a location that few, if any, knew of. Should his captors select this as the spot to leave him, he would likely never be found – either dead or alive.

They stopped at the end of the corridor.

The beads of sweat running down Robson's back made him shiver in discomfort, as one of his three chaperones raised a clenched hand and began to bang on the wall at the end of the passageway. The resulting hollow sound was still reverberating inside the narrow passageway when a muffled voice could be heard, issuing a clear, simple command.

'Enter!'

The man at the front of the suited group extended a forefinger and prodded at the surface before him. The wall suddenly opened to reveal a dimly lit room beyond.

'After you, Chief Inspector,' came the same monotone voice that, several hours earlier, had instructed him to leave what now seemed like the relative safety of his police cell.

Robson entered the lit room gingerly, half-expecting to receive an impact on the back of his head at any moment. He was still bracing himself for the event when he noticed a silhouette form only twenty yards away. DCI Robson felt a jolt of recognition like a wakening slap across his face as he eyed the lithe, athletic outline before him.

Can it be?

When the shape spoke again, there was no mistake.

'It's been a long time, DCI Robson. Come and have a seat.'

He shot a bewildered look behind him, just in time to catch his three chaperones exiting the room and closing the covert entrance. After numbly dropping into the nearest seat, Robson watched his host move into the light to take the adjacent chair. Finally, he overcame his temporary paralysis to speak, in a somewhat breathless gasp.

'Emma? What the hell's going on?'

*

On board *Teva Two*, the captain scratched his chin as he contemplated putting plan B into action. He had humoured General Miller and authorised a further FLAP analysis, this time from a revised position, but it had become clear that they were sealed beneath a continuous sheet of ice, with no polynyas or fractures within the radius of their scan.

Describing the operation again to Miller seemed to increase the general's frustration at their situation. Having deliberately avoided the Gulf of Alaska and the resident, heavy American presence, they had planned to silently discharge their high-tech arsenal from the remoteness of the Arctic circle. It now seemed they had no choice but to risk breaking cover.

'How can you be sure that we can break through?' Miller continued with his inquisition.

'We have identified an area where the ice is significantly thinner - only three foot deep. We should be able to punch through if we get the manoeuvre right.'

The calm disposition of the captain told Miller that they had recruited well. They were no doubt re-enacting a mere training routine as far as the former naval officer was concerned. The ex-harbour master was at last satisfied that they were pursuing a valid solution.

'How much of the ship will need to be on the surface for us to fire?'

The captain cringed at the general's use of terminology. Any submariner would never refer to his vessel as a ship, yet this was an entirely different sort of mission, one in which submariner skills formed only a fraction of the overall requirements. Yet, come the day of reckoning, he knew those would be skills he might just be thankful for.

'Just the fin, the rest of the *boat* will remain submerged.'

If Miller had noticed the gentle attempt to place emphasis on correct submarine terminology, it didn't show. Jacob Miller continued.

'And we can readily dispatch the torpedoes under those circumstances?'

'Of course. There are three missile silos in the rear of the tower. Once we've punched through, we can pretty much let loose.'

'But presumably we'll have revealed enough of ourselves to get picked up by any airborne surveillance?'

'Yes, that is correct. But we'll do our best to ensure that there won't be anything in the skies before we surface.'

Satisfied with the approach, Miller nodded with a faint, deep grunt, and returned to his seat inside the command room, allowing the captain to discharge his orders to the staff.

The captain picked up the radio and spoke to the control room.

'Bring her to seventy feet, steady. We'll be scanning the sky. Standby for further orders. Battle stations.'

'Aye, sir.'

CHAPTER 27

Robson felt dizzy, his mind swimming with permutations as he attempted to evaluate the past forty-eight hours.

Extraordinarily, he had been arrested for allegedly playing a role in unlawfully freeing a convicted criminal. Then, involuntarily, he had been escorted from his prison cell and taken on a mystery journey to arrive at the disturbingly familiar setting of an underground complex.

Now, he sat face to face with an attractive female. A woman he had known well, and who had helped to stabilise his emotional state when they met eight years ago, but who now appeared to be responsible for the current turbulence in his life.

The extraordinary had become surreal.

'How are you, Jack?'

Robson blinked, only vaguely aware of her crossing her slender legs beneath pale linen trousers.

'I'm … I don't think I know how I am,' Robson managed to rasp through a dry throat. 'How are you? More to the point – where are we, and what are we doing here?'

Emma Wilson sat and calmly observed his obvious growing frustration.

Outwardly, she appeared to be the same, balanced woman, Robson thought to himself. She also seemed to convey an air of authority, as though subtly informing him that she was in total control. She seemed both familiar and alien to Robson all at once. There was something different, something impalpable, but he saw that somewhere deep behind those intelligent, blue eyes was a mind deep in weighty contemplation.

He had seen her compassionate nature often during the relatively short time they had known one another, but he only ever remembered witnessing her current expression once – eight years previously, to be precise – when she lay in a hospital bed with a bullet lodged in her left leg, desperate to reveal her newly discovered knowledge to Robson. That had been at the beginning of a case which had left its mark on more than just the two of them.

As he waited for his ex-partner to respond, the silence was interrupted by the disconcertingly close sound of heavy rumbling. Suddenly, the noise grew to a disturbing level. Robson leapt to his feet.

Wilson sensed his alarm and immediately adopted a more sympathetic countenance, shouting to overcome the noise.

'Just another underground train, Jack. We're not far from the Victoria line down here.'

'Not far? You're telling me! It must only be another bloody metre beneath us!'

'Not beneath us, Jack. Above. But by more than just a metre, trust me.'

She smiled again.

'We're below the tube? Just how deep is this place?'

'Just over a hundred feet.'

'Emma – do you think you could tell me what's going on here, please? What are you doing here, and why am I here?'

'Of course, Jack. I'm here because I work here. You're here because I sent for you.'

CHAPTER 28

Now that she was nearing her destination, *Teva Two* had risen to a position eight-hundred feet beneath the Arctic ice sheet. It had been an impressively swift journey, the submarine powering at two thousand feet beneath the surface for most of the transpolar sea route.

Down in the sleeping quarters, a lone figure laid flat on a bunk with his eyes fixed on the ceiling that was only inches from his face. He had spent most of the journey in quiet contemplation, knowing that he had little to offer during the current phase of their mission.

According to his conversation with the captain over dinner the previous evening, he knew that they should be close to their chosen launch site by now. Then Jacob Miller would make his presence felt, ensuring that their intended target was clear, and that the escape route was fully planned and understood. There would be no mistakes.

A few metres above Miller, on the command deck, the captain continued to issue his orders to the small, skeleton crew aboard the sub.

'Proceed on this course. We will review our position again in five hours, before commencing FLAP analysis. Until then, keep her steady and let me know the moment you come up against anything unexpected.'

Having satisfied himself that the crew had understood the order, the captain finally retired from his long shift. As he left the control room, the adrenaline finally began to leave his system. His body ached for rest more with each step. He decided to bypass the mess and head straight for his quarters. He contemplated calling on General Miller but decided against it, realising they would be interacting enough the following day. They were nearly in position.

CHAPTER 29

Robson was now running on instinct. He didn't feel in control of the questions which rolled from his subconscious.

'You mean, you're responsible for taking me prisoner? For removing me from police custody?'

'I'm sorry, Jack, really I am. I hope you'll understand once I've had a chance to explain.'

'Emma, I was in enough trouble before you sent your henchmen for me. The police think I've been involved in the escape of a prisoner. Not just any fucking prisoner, but the one and only Jacob Miller!'

He expected a change in his ex-partner's expression at the name, but Wilson did not flinch. Robson continued.

'But now I've broken out of prison myself, which is almost tantamount to a guilty admission. Why have you done this?'

'We had to get you out, Jack.'

Robson blinked, unable to construct any further dialogue.

'Tell me, Jack … and please, don't take this the wrong way … but are they right? Do you know anything about Miller's escape?

'Seriously? Emma, I'm a detective chief inspector in the CID. I have a young daughter to support. I was at home at the time the escape took place.'

'Oh, we know you weren't at the scene.'

'Well, then. And of all people, why would I – me – why would I help Mill—'

Robson inhaled as Wilson's previous comment registered. 'What do you mean, you know I wasn't there?'

Wilson's mouth opened and closed without speaking. She allowed another growing crescendo of rumbling to pass. Robson watched the ceiling vibrating above them.

'We're lucky it's not rush hour. You should try having a conversation down here when the tube is in peak service.'

Robson wouldn't allow his earlier query to pass unanswered.

'You said you knew I hadn't been at the scene of the escape. How? Am I under surveillance for some reason?'

'Not you, no. Miller was.'

'Well, I'd think about sacking your surveillance team if I were you!'

Wilson's smile did not reveal any real amusement. Hearing Robson speak in his brusque way once again was like rolling back the years.

'We didn't lose him until after he escaped, Jack.'

'Sorry? Are you saying that you watched him escape and murder two prison guards?'

Wilson remained silent. The look in her eyes was all Robson needed.

'Whose fucking side are you on?!'

Robson's raised voice was amplified by the acoustics of the empty room, and they both glanced towards the sound of the opening door. Robson's previous escorts appeared in the opening. Wilson gave a subtle, brief shake of her head while half-raising her right hand, and the suited figures withdrew again.

An unthinkable theory began to form in Robson's mind. Saying it out loud seemed to make it even more outrageous.

'Are you … are you working with Miller?'

Robson remembered how, eight years ago, Sir Geoffrey Charlesworth had managed to build a cult following from an ostensibly sober and intelligent section of the community. It had later transpired that the perpetrators' reach was more than simply local, and spread right across the globe. Having managed to bring Arcam to its knees in the nick of time – with not insignificant input from the astonishing blonde woman sat before him – the intelligence community hadn't managed to track down any more of the key allies in the conspiracy since then.

Secret bunkers had been found in several parts of Europe, Asia, Africa, America and South America, all containing the grim evidence that human inhabitants had died inside the abandoned underground dwellings.

The scene in China had been particularly gruesome, from what little intelligence Robson had been privy to. But essentially, the last underground community to be discovered had literally starved to death deep underground inside the sealed complex.

What had been clear was that, while Arcam had been foiled as a mission, the ideology had not, and there was believed to be a large group of unknown disciples still at large. It therefore stood to reason that a discreet recruitment process would still have been taking place, doubtless involving more people of influence and connections, and especially those with particularly special access or clearance.

The hypothesis suddenly drove him crazy. Could it be that the senior MI5 intelligence officer before him, his ex-colleague – and ex-lover – who had fought alongside him to stop the fanatics, had now been enrolled herself? It was too much for Robson to contemplate, and he could only stare at her, waiting for her to confirm the worst.

'Jack. Do you really have no idea where we are?'

Robson looked at her squarely, feeling confused by the apparent compassion in her eyes. *Or is it radicalism?* He shook his head.

'I've no idea, Officer Wilson.'

'We are currently sitting at just over a hundred feet beneath the streets of London – Vauxhall, to be precise – inside one of the most secret facilities in the United Kingdom. The men that brought you here are my colleagues, all direct employees of the secret service.'

Robson felt one of the nerves in his back ping as he sat up straight in the chair, correcting the slightly slouched position he had allowed himself to slide into.

'So, this is official business?'

'In a way, yes.'

'In a way?'

'Such a phrase doesn't particularly apply to much of our work, and this is one such assignment where our current lines of enquiry are not known about outside of this organisation. Just like the tunnels we're currently occupying, this investigation doesn't exist.'

'But surely you could have obtained authority to remove me from the police cell without the Bond-like drama?'

'Sort of, yes. But at this present time we are not in a position to be able to trust anyone outside of our immediate organisation. We couldn't risk raising the alarm by announcing our desire to meet you.'

Robson shook his head as if attempting to shake reams of abstract data into some form of order. He had always been quite comfortable with the undercover side of the job at CID, but the cloak-and-dagger approach of his MI5 and MI6 counterparts did not in any way appeal to him.

'And what exactly do you want me for?'

Wilson blinked, a pale collarbone coming into Robson's view as she leant forward. She formed a steeple with well-manicured fingertips.

'Well, first of all, we wanted to protect you, Jack.'

'Protect me from who exactly?'

'Why do you think your DNA was found at the crime scene, Jack?'

'I have absolutely no idea. Do you think I've been framed?'

'Do you know where they found your trace?'

Jack shook his head.

'Not exactly. Something about an item of clothing, so I was informed.'

Officer Wilson withdrew a small, transparent plastic bag from the floor beside her and handed it to Robson, who began to study it immediately.

'A shoe?'

'Do you recognise it?'

Robson tossed the bag back as he answered.

'Should I?'

'Why do you think a shoe with your DNA was found at the scene of the escape, Jack?'

'Pass. Ask me one on sport.'

She was now visibly restraining herself from smiling. Robson's dry wit was just one of the things that she missed. Robson decided to correct his facetious response.

'I find this incredibly confusing, Emma. Did you not tell me earlier that your people observed the escape? You know I wasn't there. But more importantly, who was there and why were they not followed?'

Robson's gaze dropped and for the first time he became aware of the sparkling engagement ring on her finger. Wilson straightened herself in her chair, suddenly appearing self-conscious. She deftly clasped her hands together in her lap so that her fingers interlinked.

'A Stinger had been laid. Soon after the prison van appeared on the moor, it came to an abrupt halt in a ditch.'

'Who laid the device?'

'The same guy that shot the two prison guards before freeing Jacob Miller from the emergency hatch on top of the vehicle. They left together seconds before the response arrived, but the police couldn't pursue them because the Stinger got them too.'

'So why didn't you guys take up the pursuit? In fact, why the hell didn't you stop it happening?!'

Wilson's countenance became serious, taut with apparent anxiety.

'Jack. What I'm about to tell you is highly confidential.'

'Why are you telling me, Emma?

'Because you are already involved, Jack. And we need your help.'

CHAPTER 30

Sarah twisted her neck round as far as she could. She was determined not to take her eyes off Jasmine. Meanwhile, Mark placed a strong but tender hand on the back of her neck. The last few days had been a rollercoaster ride.

A Wedding. A Shooting. Hospital. And Jack arrested!

She repeatedly told herself that they were doing the right thing. Yes, they had experienced a shock, but in the cold light of day she knew it could have been a whole lot worse. Nobody had died, after all.

In addition to the solitary phone call, Robson had been able to send her a text message yesterday which had provided a timely sense of relief. They celebrated the news that it had apparently all been a misunderstanding and were grateful to learn that he would be home again later that day. He had insisted on her and Mark continuing with their honeymoon plans on the basis that his elderly mother was more than capable of looking after Jasmine. In truth, they all knew it was really the other way around.

Jasmine, too, had seemed at ease with the arrangements, even though her father was apparently still being detained at a police station. Yet for all the compelling logic of events, Sarah's instinct would not allow her to truly relax. For some reason, her anxiety refused to dissipate.

As their cab rounded the corner and they finally lost sight of the waving thirteen-year old girl, Sarah turned and rested her head on her husband's shoulder. They remained in silence for the duration of the journey to the railway station. It was in that moment of calm that Sarah began to reflect, and it suddenly dawned on her – the reason for her anxiety.

Never ignore your instincts.

She gazed at her new husband, who looked at her benevolently. Sarah took a deep breath and promised herself that she would bury her worry, for him, and enjoy their time away together. The beginning of the rest of their lives.

CHAPTER 31

DCI Robson's face betrayed his amazement as he listened to his ex-partner reveal details of the ongoing covert operation – a mission that ostensibly involved the secret services knowingly standing by and watching an ex-Category A prisoner escape during his transfer, while his comrade murdered two prison guards in the process. Robson knew only too well that the secret service had their own way of dealing with things. It was why he could never be tempted into the unscrupulous world of espionage. However, he could see Wilson's point. He didn't like it, but he was beginning to accept the reasons for adopting such a high-risk strategy, despite the lamentable consequences. And they couldn't have known that the two guards were going to be killed in cold blood – *could they?*

'Are you going to say something, Jack? Do you understand what's at stake here?'

Robson swallowed hard and rubbed his wrinkled brow. He decided to test Wilson's theory.

'Just because it was Miller, why does that automatically imply that, whatever is going on, it's anywhere near the scale of the previous misdemeanour?'

Emma blinked, and her poker face cracked. It had been brief, but the expression was unmistakable. She looked at Robson like he was crazy.

'Misdemeanour? What, like trying to initiate a nuclear holocaust?! Jack, have you listened to what I've been saying? There is intelligence to suggest that some of the elusive members of the previous Arcam network are behind Miller's escape. These people are still at large and have evidently decided that it is time for them to resurface. Miller was our best chance of getting to them.'

'Okay, understood. Has it worked?'

'Sorry?'

'Has his escape – and the deaths of two guards – led you to any of the perpetrators?'

Robson had recognised Emma Wilson's strong will from the moment they first met. She had the same unwavering determination in her eyes that his late wife, Isabelle, had possessed. Compassion and fire, in equal measure. But now, he couldn't spot any compassion – she seemed to have developed a colder, more detached demeanour.

'Jack, as you already know, we have lost the trail. It's being worked on as we speak.'

Robson continued to stare into her eyes, searching.

'We know that Miller swapped vehicles at a scrap dealer's, in a place called Winkleigh,' she continued. 'The getaway car was immediately destroyed in a crusher. Miller and his comrade went separate ways after the switch.'

'Who was the comrade?'

'We'll come to that. Miller then drove all the way to Porlock Weir before destroying his second getaway vehicle by setting it alight on a piece of disused farmland.'

'Seriously? He actually went back to his home village?'

Wilson nodded.

'We know he visited the Ship Inn, only for around ten minutes, before leaving to take a boat from the harbour.'

'I can't quite believe I'm hearing this! Did no one recognise him and sound the alarm?'

'First of all, Jacob Miller has a significantly different appearance these days, compared to when you last saw him.'

'Even so, surely if any of the former bar staff or locals were around they'd have been able to identify him?'

'He really is a totally different specimen – I think you'd be surprised. As it happens, the landlord is the very same guy we met there eight years ago – Samuel Peterson.'

Robson recalled their first encounter with the gregarious harbour master. It had been during one of their initial searches for the unfortunate Jonny Searle, eight years earlier. Miller had been a large personality with a large frame to match. It had been he who had escorted Robson and Wilson on their first ever visit to the watering hole on the harbourside, so that they could make enquiries with the locals as to Searle's whereabouts.

Miller knew everyone, and everyone knew Miller.

Robson also remembered how the ex-harbour master had held court with the landlord and a gaggle of the fishing folk as they enjoyed a lunchtime pint of cider. It just didn't make sense to Robson that someone so popular could remain incognito, for even a second, in his own village.

'I really can't get my head around that, but if you say so …'

'We had someone inside the inn. They observed Miller engaging in brief dialogue with the landlord. There were no obvious signs of recognition and Miller bought a pint of cider for both himself and the landlord, before necking his drink and leaving. As I said, he was only inside the pub for ten minutes.'

'Incredible.'

'Our undercover operative watched Miller throw something into the fireplace on his way out. When the landlord left the bar, our guy managed to retrieve a beer mat from the dormant fireplace. The beer mat had something scribbled on it, which turned out to be the name of the boat in the harbour which, shortly after, Miller departed on.'

'Did he meet someone else in the bar?'

'Just the landlord.'

'Have you interviewed the guy yet?'

Emma shook her head.

'Unfortunately, that is not possible.'

'Emma, with respect, it seems to me that this clandestine approach doesn't appear to be getting you results.'

'We sent someone to see him today. The landlord was found murdered only a couple of hours ago. I've only just discovered this prior to your arrival earlier.'

Wilson watched Robson's reaction, knowing that he was beginning to accept the gravity of the situation. She continued, confident that she had his full attention.

'A boat, by the very same name as that scribbled on the beermat, departed Porlock Weir within fifteen minutes of Miller leaving the inn. He was on board. We had air surveillance tail them on their journey, from a distance of course, until they reached their destination.'

'Which was?'

'Steep Holm island. I believe you know of it.'

CHAPTER 32

Jasmine stood and watched pensively as the taxi disappeared, carrying an emotional Sarah and her new husband away on their honeymoon – something that had seemed unlikely only twenty-four hours earlier. But the prospect of their special holiday together had obviously motivated the charming Mark to recover in record time. The young girl admired them both immensely. She wasn't immune to anxiety, but she was already a believer in 'getting on with it'. The fact that her father would be returning home soon certainly helped her optimism.

Back inside the house, she diligently checked that all doors and windows were secure, as she had promised she would, before preparing to make her way down the sleepy street to her grandmother's house. It never failed to amaze her, the excessive level of caution that all adults defaulted to when it came to material items. Handbags, cars, phones. Houses.

Nothing ever happens here anyway. Jasmine smiled wryly, mocking her own thoughts. *Or at least, it didn't used to …*

Standing at the front door, the summer breeze blew her fair hair in front of her keen blue eyes as she made one final attempt to call Sarah's beloved cat back for its lunch. It had been clear from the emphasis in Sarah's long list of instructions, that this was the most important part of the brief.

'Heno!'

The cat almost always seemed to appear out of nowhere when he heard

Jasmine calling, so his non-appearance after several minutes of calling was unusual.

'Heno! Come on boy, lunch!'

She shook a box of pet biscuits as she shouted into the quiet street, still expecting to see the animal appear from his usual route through the hedgerows opposite.

'Oh dear, is somebody cross about Mummy going away?!'

She dropped her rucksack against the open front door and returned to the small kitchen to grab a sachet of wet food.

'You'll have to use the flap then, silly cat! I'll come back to check on you later!'

As she emptied the smelly contents of the sachet in the cat's bowl, Jasmine smiled at the dull thud that emanated from the doorway behind her. She leant over as she squeezed the last remnants from the packet, unaware of the man that had tiptoed through the open door. The intruder cursed to himself as his elbow caught the doorhandle.

Hearing the knock, Jasmine braced herself for an incoming ball of fur wrapping itself round her face – Heno's own personal greeting – and giggled in anticipation. She dropped to the floor the instant the sharp blow contacted the back of her neck. As she collapsed, a strong arm prevented her from slamming on to the hard floor. Seconds later, a mobile phone began to vibrate on the kitchen side, its screen displaying the caller id – *Gran.*

The gloved figure ignored the device and deftly bundled the slim girl into a huge luggage case. A gag had been tightly fitted to her mouth, preventing her from protesting as she lay curled up in the case, shaking in semi-conscious, confused fear, as her battered senses detected the case rumbling underneath her. It bumped roughly on its groaning plastic wheels as it was dragged across the threshold of the front door.

Jasmine tried to scream but – like one of her nightmares – no sound materialised. The only sound apart from the grinding beneath her was that of a phone ringing from somewhere. Seconds later, a door slammed shut and the ringing stopped.

Her abductor was clearly strong – Jasmine felt weightless for a moment as the case was lifted into the air and dumped on to another surface.

The intensity of her panic acted as a blocker to the pain that she might have otherwise felt, as a long needle penetrated a specially modified, soft, square section in the hard case. She felt the fine point easily pierce her thigh and remain embedded for a time. The perpetrator obviously knew that she would not be able to move and administered the pre-prepared dose easily, before swiftly withdrawing the needle.

Her chest was as tight as a zipwire as she fought to breath. The gushing of blood pumping in her ears was briefly interrupted by the unmistakable sound of a car boot closing immediately above. Just before she went to sleep, the last thing Jasmine remembered was hearing an engine roar into life.

*

Half an hour later, a lanky man wearing blue overall trousers and a polo shirt peered suspiciously through the hedgerow in the front garden of the remote house. The sight of the wide-open front door did not comply with his philosophy of surprise. In fact, it was he that got the surprise, as he beheld the sudden appearance of a giant at the door, arriving from somewhere inside the house.

But Gwen Robson was nowhere in sight. Something seemed wrong. Very wrong.

Nonetheless, the newly arrived visitor remained in position. He had taken care to park his vehicle fifty yards along the lane from the cottage's front door, so that it was close to the only other two parked vehicles in the area. Finally, he strolled back towards his vehicle, trying to look as nonchalant as possible. He didn't want to arouse suspicion among any local curtain-twitchers. Not that anyone would be particularly suspicious of a gas engineer.

It seemed that the neighbourhood watch patrol must have been on a tea break anyway, since nobody appeared to have noticed the huge bruiser roaming about their elderly neighbour's dwelling.

CHAPTER 33

Robson felt a shiver traverse his spine. It wasn't as though he had blocked out the existence of the island. Indeed, he saw it just about every day when the weather in the channel was sufficiently clear. But to hear that one of the former Arcam perpetrators had, after all this time, returned there illegally was the stuff of nightmares. He spoke through an increasingly tense jawline.

'How can this be happening again? Surely it hasn't been possible for them to rebuild Arcam.'

'Of course not. At least, not on Steep Holm island.'

'So, what were they doing there?'

'Evidently they were catching a plane. Or two, to be precise.'

'Sorry?'

'Two seaplanes had been hidden on the island. We have footage of them walking across the beach on the southern shore and uncovering something. Turns out "something" was two state-of-the-art, lightweight seaplanes which they took off in.'

'Where did they fly to?'

The frustration appeared on Wilson's face again.

'We don't know, that's where we lost them. They totally evaded radar. It seems they knew what they were doing and managed to avoid detection completely.'

'Extraordinary.'

'It's a mystery from there, Jack. And it has us concerned.'

I bet it does, thought Robson. He was somewhat surprised at his ex-colleague's maverick approach, considering that, in the past, he was the one who had always been labelled impulsive. The Emma Wilson he had known only a few years previously would never have even bent the rules, let alone flout them. But now, having decided on the most ruthless strategy, she had not only failed to locate the nucleus of the organisation that was responsible for facilitating Miller's escape, but had also allowed him to escape a second time. *The stakes have been raised.*

Robson brought his mind back to the present.

'Emma, forgive me, but where on Earth do I fit in to all of this?'

'I need to share some further confidential information with you, Jack.'

'Oh? This really is my lucky day.'

Under different circumstances, Wilson knew that she would have appreciated the sarcasm, but there wasn't currently much scope for flippancy in her world.

'Jack. We know why your DNA was found at the scene of Miller's escape.'

Robson remained silent.

'The getaway driver – the person that ambushed the prison van and freed Miller – he left traces of his DNA at the scene. It seems he lost a shoe during the getaway.'

'This isn't making sense, Emma.'

Robson's frustrated tone was partly genuine, but he was also trying to disguise the rising anxiety in his dry throat. He sensed he was about to be given further shattering news.

'Jack. There was more than one trace of DNA on the shoe. One of the traces was yours. That's why it was so easy and fast for CID to pick you up. They plugged the sample into the database, and it gave them an exact match.'

Robson interrupted.

'Even so, they assumed that their own detective chief inspector had to have been the perpetrator. Is that the level of their mistrust now?!'

'Jack, we understand that CID received an anonymous tip off about you.'

'What?'

'They're scared, Jack. They probably didn't believe it themselves, but they had to ignore their hearts, if you like, their own prejudices, and almost totally go the other way. There's already been one extraordinary conspiracy in their ranks – they dare not risk another. And not only that, but we understand that there had been a tip-off.'

'Tip off – so I was being framed?'

'Perhaps. But we think it is more likely that someone wanted to cause a distraction. Or they wanted you out of the way ...'

'Jesus ...'

'I imagine it must have felt slightly surreal for your colleagues, having to arrest you. I can't imagine many of them truly believed in your involvement, but at least any niggling fears and suspicions have been allayed now.'

'How so?'

'After removing you from the station, we advised them that your DNA trace was unrelated and that we had the identity of the actual perpetrator.'

'And you've given them the identity?'

'Not yet. But your name has been cleared.'

'What are the chances of my DNA being on that particular shoe? What the hell is going on here?'

'The chances are odds-on, actually ... considering it was your shoe.'

'Don't be fucking ridiculous.'

'Jack, one of our agents was posing as the getaway driver for Miller's escape. He met Miller on the moor, as arranged, and intercepted the prison van using a Stinger.'

Robson's eyes became slits.

'*Your* agent? Seriously? The killer that I've been mistaken for is an employee of MI5?'

'Not quite. He's an MI6 agent, or Secret Intelligence Service, to use its modern identity.'

Robson wondered at Wilson's apathy. He had once known her so well, but her new role had evidently generated a notable change in her demeanour, a

97

lessening of empathy. Outwardly, she was certainly still attractive, beautiful even, and he still saw signs of her once personable nature. But, as she described the recent events as if they were just everyday occurrences, the impassiveness of her speech astounded him.

'I'm sorry, Emma, I know you people have to operate in a less than conventional manner sometimes – but are you telling me that you support the cold-blooded murder of two prison guards – two family men? I'm afraid I can't see how their deaths could ever be justified as casualties of war.'

Wilson remained businesslike.

'Jack, I agree with you. Believe me, there is no policy within the secret service that I am aware of which permits disregarding the value of human life. The killing of those guards was not authorised.'

Robson raised his eyebrows.

'So, where is your agent now?'

CHAPTER 34

Jasmine Robson remained curled up in the foetal position as her eyelids began to flicker. The sedative was beginning to wear off.

Despite her drowsiness, she somehow understood that the calming warmth running through her veins was wholly a consequence of the drug forced into her bloodstream, and nothing to do with the situation she found herself in.

In the pitch dark, she felt a hard surface immediately above her head. The numbness in her lower limbs felt suddenly uncomfortable and she decided to extend her arms and legs simultaneously in opposite directions to see if it would be possible to expand her enclosure. Somewhat alarmingly, she felt nothing restricting her. The walls of her enclosure were not there, or at least, she could not feel them. Her anxiety, as it grew, began to counteract the residual effects of the drug. She took a long, deep breath and forced herself to think.

As she waved her arms above her head, her senses continued to sharpen. As far as she was aware, her legs were stretched out fully as she moved on to her back. Underneath her, the surface felt soft and seemed to give way when she moved. It suddenly dawned on her that her eyes were still closed. She strained to open them, and the darkness disappeared.

The light was dazzling at first, and it took a few moments to confirm that she was no longer inside a container. She now inhabited a small room, furnished only with the bed she found herself laid upon. As her eyes began to focus, she made out the outline of a wooden door in one of the four walls, and she was suddenly aware of a noise which seemed to come from the other side of the portal. Her breathing became rapid again as she sat up on the bed, listening to the footsteps outside the door increase in volume. She swallowed hard as somebody began to turn the handle from the other side.

Devoid of options, she closed her eyes again and prayed to her mother.

CHAPTER 35

Robson turned as the door opened behind them, expecting to see the three men that had brought him to the clandestine meeting room. Instead, another confident looking man entered, wearing a tieless suit over a tall, slim frame.

Emma introduced the two men.

'DCI Robson, I'd like you to meet David Vincent. Mr Vincent is a senior anti-terrorism officer in the Secret Intelligence Service – MI6. The missing agent was reporting directly to him.'

Robson met the tall man's expressionless eyes as he rose to accept his outstretched, tanned hand. Robson was not short, but felt dwarfed by the man, who stood at least four inches above him, and despite his slight stature, matched Robson's strength as they gripped one another's hands.

'Pleased to meet you, Chief Inspector. You're something of a legend in the intelligence community, as I'm sure you're no doubt aware.'

Robson did not detect any obvious sarcasm, but he couldn't quite read the man's expression, so chose not to respond. Wilson intercepted the frosty exchange.

'David, DCI Robson is probably not aware of his reputation,' she offered, before glancing back at Robson. 'Jack, Mr Vincent is not mocking you, I assure you, but if I may put that discussion on hold for a moment ...'

'I'm sorry,' interrupted the MI6 agent, in clipped, public schoolboy vowels.

'Allow me to address the query you were voicing just as I entered, Chief Inspector.'

Robson felt some of the tension disappear from his shoulders and allowed them to drop, at the same time squeezing the back of his neck. He sat back in his chair, while Vincent took a spare seat and drew himself between Robson and Wilson.

'The frank answer is that we don't know where our missing agent is. He's *AWOL*, you might say. Which is, to say the least, troubling. We couldn't risk breaking cover by pursuing the agent when he and Miller departed the scene. For a start, we don't know how much, if anything, the agent has told Miller. Secondly, the local police had arrived on the scene. And finally, there was the not insignificant matter that our agent had positioned a Stinger such that it impeded the only route from our covert position. We had to assume at that time that the agent was still on our side, albeit he had lost control of the situation by killing the guards. However, he wasn't at the agreed meeting point later in the day and has been incommunicado ever since.'

'Who is your maverick agent? And what exactly is he up to?'

Curiously, it was Wilson who visibly took a deep breath, as the MI6 officer continued.

'This is classified information, DCI Robson. But I'm going to share the following intelligence with you because you have the experience and training to deal with it. And, as I'm sure Officer Wilson has been explaining, we could really do with your help.'

Robson let out a brief, mirthless chuckle.

'I don't really see how CID can assist you with this.'

Vincent ignored the remark and continued.

'The agent in question is known to us as "Arkwright". Real name, John Harry Reilly.'

Robson continued to look blankly at Vincent, who had paused momentarily, as though he had expected some spark of recognition. The MI6 officer glanced at Wilson, giving her the cue to elaborate further.

'For some time now, Arkwright has been working undercover in connection with a highly confidential operation. He had managed to successfully infiltrate the organisation we believe is connected to the former Arcam conspiracy. What is more, he had gained the trust of senior figures, so much so that he was entrusted to single-handedly manage Miller's escape.'

Robson's mind was in overdrive as he tried to digest the information.

'DCI Robson, we have done some deep digging and found something unexpected. John Reilly, for the past three years, has been living under a different alias, part-time. When he isn't engaged in MI6 business, he is known to his recent friends … and family … as Mark Connor …'

The room span for Robson as he pictured his friend – Sarah's new husband – who, as far as Robson was aware, was currently lying in a hospital bed after the incident that had signalled the beginning of the previous, insane forty-eight hours. Unsure how to react, he forced himself to maintain a professional demeanour.

'And?'

'Chief inspector, the Mark Connor we're referring to is very same man whose wedding you attended a few days ago. The husband of Sarah Connor.'

'I beg your pardon?! I'm sorry but I really am struggling to process this. Well, if it's the Mark Connor I know, you shouldn't have too much trouble finding him. He's currently being treated for a shot wound in Taunton hospital.'

'Was.' Vincent was quick to correct Robson's statement. 'He discharged himself after twenty-four hours.'

'What? And you've lost him again?'

'We only became aware of his alternative identity twenty-four hours ago. Obviously, the first thing to come to our attention was the recent shooting at Webber's Post. We went to the hospital to find he had discharged himself the previous day, apparently against the advice of the medical staff.'

'Jack,' Emma added, 'that's also what made us aware of your extraordinary arrest. When we spoke to CID and they advised us of the DNA match, it was almost immediately obvious what had occurred, given your link to Connor. So, we wanted to get you out fast. But we don't know who Connor – or Reilly – is in league with and, therefore, we couldn't risk announcing anything in advance until we had you in our protection.'

'Protection?'

'DCI Robson.' Vincent's speech had been serious throughout their brief encounter, but it suddenly became austere. 'Do you believe that Mark Connor was the intended recipient of the bullet at Webber's Post the other day, or could it be that you were the real target?'

'Why would I be a target?'

'There's much more to tell you. But for now, we were wondering if you could tell us what Sarah and Mark's honeymoon plans were?'

Robson felt light-headed as he suddenly became aware of the potential risk that existed to his immediate family.

'Shit! Sarah and Jasmine. Are they all right?'

'We believe Sarah and Mark might be en route to their honeymoon.'

'What? They've gone? Where is Jasmine? Is she with my mother?'

Wilson suddenly seemed to find eye contact difficult. For a moment, Vincent seemed to lose his phlegmatic demeanour and now he was the one that inhaled deeply.

'There is no cause for concern yet, Jack, but we are trying to establish if Jasmine is with Sarah and Mark Connor, or whether she stayed behind. It is highly likely Connor will be travelling under a different identity.'

'Fuck!' Robson stood as he spoke, suddenly panicking.

'Jack, we've just sent people to Sarah's house, to your property, and to your mother's. Our agents haven't arrived yet, but we have asked the local constabulary to attend in the meantime.'

Robson felt nauseous as his eyes flicked briefly towards Wilson. He now saw unmistakable concern in her hitherto professional expression. Robson found it difficult to remain focussed on the MI6 officer's dialogue.

'Your mother has not answered her telephone. Do you know if she had planned to go somewhere?'

Robson shook his head sombrely.

'I know nothing about any of this. But if my mother isn't at home, that itself is troubling.'

'Oh. Why?'

'Because, for the last year, she has pretty much been housebound due to health problems. She can barely walk and she doesn't drive. So if she isn't at home, something unusual has happened.'

'Okay. Perhaps there is a simple explanation, but as I said, we've already asked the local police to attend,' Wilson intervened, nodding in understanding. She turned to Vincent. 'I think we need to get DCI Robson back to Somerset.'

The chair slid away as Robson rose abruptly, signalling he did not wish to delay. Vincent stood only to acknowledge their exit, as Robson and Wilson exited the room and joined the three men waiting outside.

The group of five began to pace through the labyrinth of underground tunnels.

CHAPTER 36

Jasmine Isabelle Robson had made her decision in an instant. Even before the door had opened, she had made up her mind to attack … regardless of her opponent. True to her plan, she was on her visitor before he had time to react. An instant later, the man screamed as Jasmine's nails tore at his eyes.

'Calm down, girl! I don't want to have to hurt you!'

Jasmine felt large, strong hands grabbing at her waist. As the man began to prise her from his torso, she tightened her grip with young, athletic legs, clinging to his sweaty body like a koala to a tree trunk. As her nostrils flared with rage and fear, her sinuses were filled with an overwhelming aroma of perspiration and musky body odour as she leant in to bite at her captor's neck. The man's stubble rubbed at her soft cheeks like coarse sandpaper.

The stocky man became angry, and his arms suddenly exploded away from his chest, sending the young girl hurtling across the room towards the bed. Jasmine fumbled around on her knees as the man pounced on her. As she felt his rough fingertips at the back of her neck, she propelled her legs against the bed frame, and flew between his tree-trunk legs before darting out of the open door.

Above her own panting, she could hear the man gasping behind her – she imagined a huge chest expelling air from those lungs. She stumbled awkwardly towards the front door of the mystery property and frantically grabbed the handle. The handle moved but the door refused to budge. She could hear the man was only a few paces behind. Instinct drove her to twist the latch just above eye level. As the door began to open inwards, she felt a large hand claw at the back of her jumper as she tried to squeeze through the narrow gap, but she was unable to move forward.

While her captor wrapped his other arm around her waist, she kicked her legs forward to gain a purchase on the door frame and attempted to heave the door towards her with two hands. The door only moved a few inches, but that was sufficient to cause a painful impact to the man's left elbow. Jasmine knew he would only lose his grip for a split second and this would be her only opportunity.

She sprinted with all the power she could muster, straining every sinew and resisting the panic-driven urge to look behind her. The audible sound of hoarse panting told her all she needed to know – her pursuant was close behind.

CHAPTER 37

The remote video system had allowed *Teva Two* to be manoeuvred to within twenty yards of the location where the vast ice sheet was at its thinnest. Approximately three feet of frozen ocean stood between the submarine and its crew's objective.

The captain instructed his crew to complete the final arrangements, as they prepared the sub to deliver an upper cut to the Arctic ice layer. On hearing the command, every member of staff on board adopted a brace position. Whether seated or standing, the drill was simple – wherever you were at that moment, hold on to something and do not let go.

A sudden, huge jolt indicated that the tower had made contact with the frozen ocean surface. To Miller, it felt like being in a car-crash. In response to the captain's command, the control room operators increased the flow of compressed air into the ballast tanks. As water was dispelled from the tanks, the huge vessel could be felt to rise slowly. The sound of the cracking ice sheet was like an almighty thunderstorm, and the entire vessel shook as she began to break through.

The captain shouted into the comms link.

'Now!'

Suddenly, the boat surged upwards at an increased speed.

*

On the surface, the white, glassy sheet gave way and shards of ice splintered into the air as the huge steel bulk protruded through the otherwise virginal landscape – a grey monstrosity in stark violation of nature's purity.

Moments after penetrating the ice sheet, Miller followed the captain through the open hatch. They both stepped out to behold a pristine, infinitely white and desolate landscape. It felt like they'd arrived on another planet – an uninhabited world. Both men held a hand up to their foreheads to act as visors against the blinding whiteness.

The captain spoke into his transmitter again.

'Control, lock the coordinates and fire at will.'

'Aye, sir.'

*

Miller ignored the freezing air biting his face as he stood on the wet surface of the submarine and watched two Tomahawk missiles erupt from their chambers and follow their pre-programmed courses towards the land mass a few miles away.

He was jolted from his moment of satisfaction by the captain tugging his coat. Miller turned to face the direction indicated by the captain's outstretched index finger.

The sight sent a shiver down Miller's spine.

Two fighter jets had appeared on the eastern horizon and were undoubtedly heading in their direction at immense speed. Without another word, both men scrambled back through the submarine's hatch. As a waiting crewman hastily secured it above them, the thunderous noise from the sonic boom generated by the aircraft seemed to cause the very sky above them to shake. Miller sprinted after the captain towards the bridge. They headed straight for the comms point and the captain frantically clawed at the transmitter.

'Action stations. This is an emergency. This is an emergency. Control – initiate emergency deep dive. Immediately.'

On the surface, the frozen ocean surrounding the submarine erupted again, as one of the fighter jets peppered the icy surface with its machine gun, while the second plane disappeared in pursuit of the dispatched missiles.

Neither fighter pilot could have known that the Tomahawks were not carrying their usual payloads.

The communication engineer's eyes were fixed on his captain, anticipating a response to the message that had just echoed from the vessel's radio. Seconds later, the same message was repeated.

'This is the United States Air Force. Please identify yourselves immediately. You have ten seconds. We have authority to fire. You are currently violating United States territory.'

The captain returned his colleague's glance, then looked away in silence as one of the crewman's voices pierced the white noise inside the control room.

'Ready to commence diving, Captain.'

'Proceed.'

Moments later, *Teva Two* was hundreds of feet below the ice sheet and descending rapidly. In a few more minutes, the nuclear sub would reach two thousand feet before adopting silent running again.

Then, *Teva Two* would disappear once more.

CHAPTER 38

The mobile phone rang again on the kitchen table while Heno sat watching the device with suspicion, still on his guard after earlier witnessing one of his favourite human friends being bundled into a suitcase.

Heno's paws made a thud as he leapt from the table on to the kitchen worktop. He had finally resigned himself to the fact that he would have to hunt for his own meal that evening. As he trotted along the worktops, his thick bushy tail swept against the frame displaying a new photo of the newlyweds, Mark and Sarah Connor, taken only days earlier.

A second after knocking it from the side, the cat landed beside the resulting mess on the tiled kitchen floor. With his head in the air, Heno marched towards the cat flap and butted into it. The little doorway swished behind his fox-like tail as he disappeared into the night to find his supper.

*

Sarah forced a smile, feeling Mark's comforting hand on her shoulder. She was exhausted. There had been quite a queue at the hotel's check-in desk, despite the late hour. Indeed, they had been waiting for twenty minutes at the front desk of the Parisian hotel, but they had at last made it to the front of the queue.

She leant her head on Mark's shoulder and looked on wearily as the only receptionist dealt with a couple of Chinese tourists. Sarah was a great admirer of her husband's patience. It was just part of his classy demeanour, but she wished that, just on this occasion, he might have exercised a little forcefulness, rather than continuing to maintain an unflappable, patient smile while the receptionist dutifully answered yet another query.

The Chinese couple now wanted to know the best time to visit the Eiffel tower. Mark wrapped his arm around Sarah's shoulder and pecked her on the cheek before facing the receptionist, as the young couple in front of them finally moved away from the desk. Sarah gripped Mark's hand and gently prised herself away from his embrace.

'I think I'll try Jazzy again while you check us in, darling.'

Mark released his arm, smiling sympathetically.

'Stop worrying, honey. She's fine. She'll be busy chatting with her Granny Robson. You know what those two are like when they're together.'

'I know, I know. I'd just like to make contact, that's all. And I don't understand why Gwen isn't answering her phone either.'

Mark placed a palm on either side of her head, cradling her face.

'Like I said – they'll be busy chatting. Anyway, you carry on, there's a nice comfy sofa over there. I'll sort this out.'

*

Inside the little cottage which was nestled at the top of Church Lane in the village of Bicknoller, a landline telephone began to ring again. The caller was the same that had just tried to call Jasmine Robson. As with that previously attempted call, the telephone rang until the answerphone message kicked in, but instead of a mechanical sounding, automated voice, this recipient had taken the time to record their own monologue. The friendly sounding voice of an elderly lady duly apologised for being unable to come to the phone before the recording tone sounded.

From her enclosed position, Gwendoline Robson listened carefully to the muffled message. It was Sarah again. Each time she called, Gwen thought she could detect an ever-growing anxiety in her speech, but now, Sarah's voice seemed positively shaky, almost as though she had guessed that Gwen was in trouble.

'Gwen? Hello, Gwen, are you there? Oh, I'm so worried, mum. We've arrived at our hotel, finally. We had to check-in somewhere else! So, we're now staying

at the Hotel Royal Monceau. There was a mix up with the booking at the other place apparently. Listen, I can't get hold of Jasmine either, the little scallywag! I'm sure you're both engrossed in a movie or something, but I'd really appreciate a call back, just so I know you're both all right. I'm just a bit on edge still after what we've all been through the last few days. Okay, it looks like we're checked in at last – Mark's on his way over. Please, please call me when you get this message. Okay, love to you both, bye for now.'

Tears formed in the corner of the elderly lady's eyes. Her wrists were stinging intensely, and she strained at her bindings to try to create some slack. But there was no give. The big, aggressive man had used some sort of twine. Her thin, veiny legs were numb, having been bound beneath her for several hours. As far as she could tell, the man had finished crashing around her beloved cottage – perhaps he had finally found whatever it was he had been looking for. Or he had given up.

Suddenly, her spirits were lifted by the sound of the front door opening. Out of desperation, she tried hammering her already bruised head against the inside of the under-stair's cupboard door. She opened her dried-out mouth to scream at the pain in her skull, but no sound emanated from the tight-fitting gag.

Gwen began to cough uncontrollably.

The darkness of the cupboard gave way to utter blackness as Gwen Robson once again lost consciousness. She slumped to her side, her head coming to rest on the inside of the cupboard door, while her shoulder dropped as far as her neck would allow.

*

Inside the luxurious Parisian hotel, Sarah continued to display an outwardly happy countenance for her husband, as the ornate elevator announced their arrival on the fourth floor. Mark Connor seemed pleased with himself. Despite the slight hiccup with the booking, he had managed to arrange a splendid alternative for them.

'Come on, honey. I've got a surprise for you!'

As Connor replaced his credit card in his wallet, he checked the other small but precious cargo was still safely tucked away inside the wallet's coin pouch. The micro sim card had already proved to be a valuable asset, justifying the effort and deception that had been required to create a clone of Robson's IMEI number, so he didn't want to lose it. For a start, without the sim he wouldn't have been able to have sent the decoy text messages which had persuaded both Sarah and Jasmine that it was unnecessary to cancel the honeymoon plans.

Hand in hand, the Connors paced across the luxury pile in the hallway as they approached the honeymoon suite.

CHAPTER 39

Beads of sweat were beginning to form at Commander Campbell's temples, as he waited for an update from his F-16 fighter pilots.

Since receiving reports of alarming activity off the Arctic Alaskan coast just over three hours ago, there had been no further validation of the claim that an unidentified submarine appeared to have dispatched two missiles towards the mainland, before disappearing back beneath the ice sheet. The radar had not picked up anything until an hour ago, when an unidentified bogey was briefly detected. U.S. military were able to establish that it was travelling at more than five-hundred miles per hour in a southerly direction, before it once again dropped to an altitude that was undetectable by their main radar system.

Campbell blinked in disbelief as the unidentified object suddenly appeared again, this time courtesy of a superior, 360-degree radar system. The navigational data showed that the bogey was only two hundred miles from them. But there was something strange. It had, evidently, already passed the air force base, apparently headed for a different destination.

As his eyes followed the spot on the huge screen at the front of the command room, the audio system crackled with an incoming communication from one of the two additional F-16 jets which had been scrambled from the 18th Aggressor Squadron as a precaution.

'Come in Slammer. Kingfish has a bogey, visual, twelve o'clock, ten miles, angels two, heading zero-nine-zero. Please advise.'

Every occupant of the command room looked towards Campbell, awaiting his order, but before the commander could respond, a second message sounded from the other aircraft.

'Break-Break. Slammer, Rambo also has a bogey, visual, six o'clock, twenty miles, angels two, heading two-seven-zero. Advise.'

Panicked murmuring grew within the command room at Eielson as they absorbed the last two messages, which confirmed what their advanced radar system was presenting – two cruise missiles now closing in on a location two-hundred miles to the south of the airbase. The bogeys approached one another from opposite directions and were currently separated by only eighty miles of airspace.

The chief air traffic controller addressed the Commander.

'Sir, the missiles seem to be heading towards one another.'

The commander studied the radar and held his finger against a point on the map as he responded, approximately marking midway point between the two unidentified bogeys.

'So I see. Are they heading where I think?'

The controller nodded.

'Both bogeys are closing in on Gakona, sir.'

Commander Campbell spoke into his mouthpiece, keeping his voice steady.

'Kingfish, Rambo – engage immediately and intercept your bogeys. You may fire at will. Slammer over.'

'Roger that, Slammer, wilco. I'm goin' to Mach 2. Kingfish out.'

'Copy that, Rambo's supersonic. Out.'

The control room fell silent again as all eyes turned to watch the screen, everyone understanding that the fate of many was now in the hands of two highly trained fighter pilots.

*

Rambo banked hard, adjusting his course to remain on his target's tail. The F-16 super-jet smashed through the sound barrier as it reached its top speed of nearly one and a half thousand miles per hour. Rambo would be on top of the Tomahawk missile within a minute. Meanwhile, Kingfish pressed down with his thumb, releasing a missile the second he received confirmation that the target had been locked.

'Slammer, Kingfish has Fox 1. This one's pickled!'

The other F-16 roared with power. Inside the cockpit, Rambo smiled confidently as he locked in on his own target and prepared to destroy the cruise missile, while silently listening to his colleague's confirmation over the radio system.

'Shit!'

Rambo's grip on the joystick tensed as the expletive echoed inside the cockpit. Kingfish spoke again.

'Come in Slammer. This is Kingfish. Disregard previous communication.'

The response from the control tower was instant.

'Kingfish, please clarify. Has the bogey been destroyed?'

'Negative, Slammer. Bogey remains in flight, evidently under external control. Target evaded fire!'

Commander Campbell's cheeks now flushed heavily as he raised his tone.

'Kingfish, reengage and fire from closer range.'

'Copy, Slammer, Kingfish is reengaging.'

Rambo remained ice-cool as he inwardly digested the dialogue playing over the transmission system. From only fifty metres range, he released his missile just as the airwaves sounded again.

'Rambo, this is Slammer. Requesting status update.'

The airman took the F-16 into a sharp vertical climb as the bogey Tomahawk missile exploded with a tumultuous bang. Two hundred metres below, civilians within a fifty-mile radius looked up at the source of the sudden explosion, while the fighter banked and reduced speed.

'Come in, Slammer, this is Rambo. Bogey destroyed!' Ten silent seconds elapsed before Rambo spoke again. 'Come in Slammer, this is Rambo. Repeat – bogey destroyed, over.'

In the cockpit, the normal background crackling had disappeared. As the pilot contemplated the loss of communication, he began frantically jabbing the control panel, which had entirely extinguished before his eyes. The course of the F-16 remained steadily declining, unaffected by any of the cockpit controls. Rambo screamed into the transmitter.

'Mayday, mayday! This is Rambo – all controls inactive, I've lost all indications!'

In the lonely silence that followed, the pilot watched open-mouthed as the missile he had recently dispatched disappeared into the distance. He had missed the target, but the bogey had exploded in mid-air.

Rambo contemplated the evidence. The cruise missile, his prey, had detonated of its own free will, or at least, at someone else's command. Frantically, he turned his attention back to the panel in front of him and tried one final operation. After the fifth slam of his clenched fist on the red eject button, Rambo redirected his physical force and began to smash both fists against the clear canopy above his head, using as much force as he could muster.

CHAPTER 40

Doctor Stevenson turned the key in the ignition again. *Bloody useless thing!* She slammed a palm on the steering wheel, reluctantly acknowledging defeat. Moments later, she pulled at the lever beneath the steering console to flip the bonnet open.

Stevenson stepped out of the car as the door flung open, wrapping her cardigan around her body and bracing herself against the biting breeze that swept the open highway. It seemed strange that the normally busy trunk road should be so quiet. She checked her watch.

17:16. What happened to rush hour?

She rested the bonnet on its holder and began to investigate, finally chuckling in self-mockery as she began to pull at the battery cables. *You're a scientist, Jilly, not a car-mechanic.* She allowed the bonnet to slam shut and decided to phone for help.

As she pulled the car door open again, it seemed peculiar that not even a single vehicle had passed. She squinted as she looked along the highway and tried to make out the shapes in the distance – stationary vehicles that hadn't moved since she'd been stranded a few minutes ago. She checked her watch again.

17:16. Shit – doesn't anything work?!

The scientist pulled a phone from her tight jeans before sitting back in the driver's seat. She pulled the door shut and looked down at the device. After staring at the strange display for a few moments, she dropped her phone on the passenger seat with its frozen screen facing upwards, still showing a random combination of letters and numbers. She sat for a moment and contemplated the sudden disruption to technology. Her pulse began to quicken as she formulated a theory.

She leapt out of the car again and stood, listening. The absence of any sound seemed so alien. The normal drone of machinery had stopped and, even though she was only a quarter of a mile outside the city, not a single light could be seen cutting through the dull background. She threw a warm coat around herself and pressed the lock button on the car key. The device did not respond.

Doctor Stevenson began to walk towards the city of Gakona.

*

Graham Stevenson looked at his watch as he considered the recent events.

Jilly should be home soon, maybe she can explain what's going on.

Despite apparently having lost all power to their home, the large plasma television glowed against the living room wall. A little earlier, he had shouted out in pain when he tried to remove the searing-hot plug from the wall, before running into the kitchen to run cold water on his burns. The absence of a display on the microwave oven confirmed that they were still without electricity.

He decided to check if his wife was on her way home. Jilly wasn't known for her timekeeping. Typical scientist, he thought, as he leant to his right to grab his phone from where it lay, charging.

The sight of a dark screen was perplexing at first but his eyes widened as he realised it had begun to melt. He lifted it closer, and the charging cable offered no resistance, instead breaking into two.

Mr Stevenson looked along the portion of the cable that remained connected to the wall. At the extremity of the cable, the plug had turned into a mess of white plastic. Another power outlet he should avoid.

CHAPTER 41

G wen Robson remained coiled and unconscious beneath the stairs when her uninvited guest cautiously opened the front door and inspected the area outside before departing the ransacked property. The huge man was in a rush and had no time to waste by checking on the condition of the homeowner.

Fifty yards along the quiet lane, the tall man wearing blue overalls sat inside his parked vehicle and watched the gated entrance to the cottage in the van's rear-view mirror. Apart from the large, conspicuous looking man who was just leaving Mrs Robson's property, nobody else moved on Church Lane, which wasn't unusual for the sleepy village in the middle of a working day.

As the colossus moved away from the front garden gate, the man dressed as a gas engineer started the ignition, already having realised that he had been beaten to it. His frustration began to boil over into anger, but he had to control himself. Being spotted was not a risk he could take.

The large man stopped and looked at the van suspiciously as it pulled away. Moments later, after watching the gas engineer's van disappear around the hedge-lined corner of the lane, he stepped into his own vehicle and pulled out from the small layby.

His suspicion getting the better of him, the man swung the steering wheel round with huge paws and began to follow the van.

The police car heading in the opposite direction indicated he had departed the old lady's place in the nick of time.

CHAPTER 42

Just under an hour after departing central London, a special services helicopter touched down on the open expanse of Staple Plain on the Quantock hills, high above the quaint village of Bicknoller. The spellbinding scenery which usually provided DCI Robson with such solace did nothing to ease the growing feeling of unease in his gut. Indeed, the ride itself had resulted in the predictable surfacing of uncomfortable memories, confirming that those particular demons had not been entirely exorcised.

Officer Wilson was well acquainted with Robson's inner troubles and, in the spirit of professionalism, had fought the strong urge to comfort him during the journey. The urge alone was enough to trouble her. She couldn't allow any distractions – not with the current stakes so high.

A police Land Rover was waiting to escort them from the hill. Robson and Wilson jumped in the back seat together and the vehicle immediately set off down the slope, easily absorbing the uneven terrain as they raced the short distance towards the village. They watched the view of the Bristol Channel disappear as they thundered down the gradient.

The atmosphere inside the vehicle was tense. Robson had spent the entire journey trying to contact his daughter, mother, and Sarah, all to no avail. Wilson was well aware of her ex-partner's anxiety but continued to resist the urge to show any empathy. She welcomed the rumbling sound as they traversed a cattle grid and arrived at the brow of a narrow lane, at which point the young, uniformed constable activated the vehicle's siren. Five minutes later, they arrived at their destination.

Robson looked over the gate on their left and swallowed hard as he took in the sight of the pretty cottage. The well-tended garden was populated with uniformed police officers and a small forensics team, who had apparently already begun an examination of the property.

As they entered the gate, two members of Robson's CID team appeared at the front doorway of the cottage, having been notified by the Land Rover driver of their arrival. Both detectives gave awkward glances in Robson's direction. The fact that one of them had been part of the company that had arrested him at the hospital two days earlier held no relevance to Robson. His mind was dominated by thoughts regarding his family's wellbeing.

The more senior of the two CID officers stepped forward hesitantly.

'Sir.'

Robson saw that his inspector wanted to be delicate.

'Hello, Bannister. What's happened here?'

'I'm sorry, sir. Mrs Robson, your mother, was found half an hour ago by uniform.'

'And?'

'It seems they were looking for something, sir. The place has been turned upside down.'

'Looking for something? That seems odd. How is my mother?'

'She wasn't in a good condition, sir. The ambulance took her away only fifteen minutes ago. She had been tied up for some time, it seems. I'm afraid I can't really give you any reliable information on her medical state.'

Robson heard Wilson breathe deeply next to him as he responded.

'Sorry? Tied up? She's seventy-nine years old! What about my daughter – has anyone spoken to Jasmine?'

'No sir. Your mother was found alone inside.'

Wilson finally gave in to her concern and placed a hand on Robson's shoulder.

'Jack. You go straight to the hospital. I'll stay here with CID.'

Robson hesitated, wanting to be at his mother's side but also feeling a burning desire to make sure that Jasmine was safe. Not to mention ensuring the lowlife responsible for attacking his mother was found, quickly. Wilson continued, preventing Robson from responding. She addressed the uniformed officer who had driven them from the helicopter moments earlier.

'Constable. Would you kindly take DCI Robson to the hospital?'

The young man nodded, 'Yes ma'am,' before politely waiting for Robson to surrender to Officer Wilson's passive instruction. Robson gave his inspector a piercing stare to reinforce his next instruction.

'Keep me posted, Inspector Bannister.'

He nodded at Wilson and followed the uniformed constable back towards the gate.

With Robson out of earshot, Wilson stared firmly at Bannister, who had remained in the doorway of the cottage.

'Inspector Bannister, please listen carefully. I want you to terminate all investigation work here immediately.'

'I ... I'm sorry, ma'am?' the inspector stammered, while his colleague, DC Jenkins, looked on, equally bewildered.

'This is officially a security service crime scene. Kindly remove all your team from the site forthwith. I'd like a scene guard at the house entrance while I await my colleagues. In the meantime, I will be conducting my investigation alone.'

Bannister raised his eyebrows at DC Jenkins in a gesture of surrender. Jenkins duly began to discharge Wilson's orders to clear the site.

As she waited for the property to empty, Wilson paced to the corner of the small garden, holding her phone to her ear. She began speaking softly.

'Things have escalated. Get here as soon as you can.'

She gazed back at the cottage as she replaced the phone in her pocket, and began to replay memories in her mind of more sociable visits to the cottage. Happier, less complicated times, which felt like aeons ago. She returned her thoughts to the current situation, while in the back of her mind she wondered how she would begin to explain the scale of the predicament to Robson.

CHAPTER 43

It felt to Jasmine as if she had been running for hours. Her sore feet pounded the soggy wild grass, and she was certain her jelly-like thighs were going to give in at any moment. The sound of her pursuer's panting breath seemed to have dissipated, but she didn't dare turn back and risk losing speed, or worse, tripping on the uneven terrain.

The distant trees had been the first sight to grab her attention on smashing through the front door of the remote property. Given the openness of the environment between the house and the wood, she had decided that aiming for the tree cover was her only chance of evading recapture – she just had to make it that far.

Up close, her hypersensitive vision plotted a course into the wood. The trees at the wood's extremity ruffled in the wind as she arrived at its entrance and peered into the darkness beyond. The absence of the man's heavy panting behind her provided little reassurance – she realised that, against the noise of the howling wind, she wouldn't have been able to hear her stout pursuer even if he were only a few paces behind. The urge to turn back to check the distance between her and the musky smelling man was compelling.

Before deciding on her next move, she twisted her neck round – she had to. She had to know how close he was. Her relief soon turned to anxiety. It was good news that the man wasn't close, but that he was nowhere to be seen was unsettling. There was nowhere for a person to hide between the wood and the house, yet her pursuer had somehow managed to disappear. The bleak expanse of long grass she had just covered was devoid of any other person. She had lost her hunter. But, somehow, she knew he could not have lost her.

She patted her sides and trouser pockets, desperately hoping to locate her mobile phone. As she removed her hand from her empty pockets, she vaguely remembered her phone being on the sideboard in Sarah and Mark's kitchen before her ordeal had begun – in what now seemed like another epoch of existence.

Jasmine had to decide between the darkness of the wood and the openness of the terrain alongside it. She had to traverse one of them in order to reach the nearest public road.

She swallowed hard as she entered the wood and let out a startled yelp in reaction to the sound. She forced herself to continue, tears streaming down her cheeks as she chided herself unsympathetically for jumping at the noise of twigs breaking underfoot.

CHAPTER 44

The tubby fellow screwed up his nose as he raised his binoculars to his face. Distant birdsong accompanied the sight of the airborne creatures busily delivering building materials for their nests high up in the trees beyond. Beneath the canopies, there existed only darkness.

The man dropped the binoculars at his feet in frustration. They bounced on the overgrown garden, as he acknowledged to himself that the girl must have entered the wood by now. Which meant he would have to follow. He cussed again as he knelt to retrieve the binoculars. The sudden sound of the gate's latch interrupted his cursing. He remained on his knees, frozen, as he watched the man dressed in gas-fitter's attire approach him.

His visitor looked down at him from a yard away. The look on his face was one of disdain.

'Where's the girl?'

Without speaking, the stout man pointed. The sun was beginning to set over the top of the gigantic trees, two hundred yards up the hill.

'You let her go?'

The stout man became irked.

'No, I didn't fucking let her. She's fast. But I know where she is. Now you're here, we can jump in the van and go fetch her. Let's get the old lady inside first though, eh?'

'There is no old lady.'

'What?'

'We've been beaten to it …'

'What do you mean?'

'Someone else got to her first.'

'What? She's been taken?'

'No … I don't think so …'

'Mart, for fuck's sa—'

'Let's just concentrate on the girl, shall we? If we lose her too, this is not going to go well.'

The rotund man sighed heavily as he grabbed the binoculars from the long grass and stood up.

'How many were there? At the cottage?'

'Just one. Some huge guy.'

'It doesn't make sense. What has he done with the old lady?'

'I don't know, but let's deal with one problem at a time. I've got plenty of rope in the car.' He nodded towards the wood. 'Let's get up there before daylight starts to fade.'

*

At the top of the Quantock hill, an imposing figure stood perfectly still as he surveyed the view, although he wasn't there to admire the picturesque surroundings. Seeing the gas van that he had followed park at the remote house, he had decided to take a diversion so he could observe from a distance. Quite unexpectedly, it looked like he was going to be rewarded for trailing the man that had been in Bicknoller earlier. His instinct had served him well, he thought, as he watched the girl enter the wood and nervously try to navigate a route through. It was undoubtedly the girl he'd been briefed about. Robson's daughter.

Just inside the entrance to the ancient wood, he had managed to make himself invisible, despite his colossal frame. The young girl had looked petrified when she arrived at the perimeter earlier. Now, she seemed to be frozen with fear. Crouched behind dense vegetation, he watched her for a moment longer as she stood rooted to the spot. The girl seemed to be captivated by something that had piqued her interest at the northern extremity of the wood, and she continued to gaze in that direction, as though she were planning a route through the trees.

The great man felt confident that he would have plenty of time to deal with the young girl, and he turned his attention to the gas van which was now ambling its way up the grassy gradient towards them.

First things first.

Inside the van, the taller of the two men gripped the steering wheel as it shook with vibrations from the rough terrain. He looked on intensely as his stout companion pointed towards an area of the wood. Not far from the spot pointed at, the man behind the tree gently flexed his muscles in preparation for action.

He unfolded his immense frame but remained behind the cover of the nearest tree, cracking his knuckles as he stepped sideways. Moving stealthily among the vast trunks, the giant almost looked like a tree himself. He took up a new position in preparation for the new arrivals.

Just wait a little while longer, little girl, I won't be long.

CHAPTER 45

Jasmine tried to shake off the sensation of dread as she realised the cause of her déjà vu. Somehow, she instinctively knew that she was standing in the same area where, only days earlier, the person who had shot Mark Connor had been. Her eyes were fixed on the hut in the clearing beyond. She forced terrifying memories from her mind and did her best to concentrate on matters at hand.

There now appeared to be two men chasing her, both of whom had got out of a small van less than a hundred yards away, just outside the southern perimeter of the wood. Strangely, the distant noise of twigs snapping underfoot had died away, leaving an eerie silence interrupted only by the sound of trees swaying in the wind.

A small gathering of wasps started to bother her. The young girl decided to risk waving a hand to warn the annoying insects against venturing any closer but it only seemed to encourage them. She swallowed and began to panic as she realised that she had lost sight of her two pursuers.

*

Just inside the entrance to the wood, two bodies lay a few metres apart from one another on the forest floor.

The head of one was unnaturally positioned on its twisted neck, its face recording a look of surprised terror. The second, taller figure was almost as still, but for a small movement of his chest. The volume of rasping noise which emanated from deep within the throat of the blood-soaked man diminished with each shallow breath.

Seconds earlier, there had been no indication that the gigantic man had harboured plans to attack them so brutally. He had moved with extraordinary stealth considering his bulk. He now moved a good fifty yards away from his recent prey and began to home in on his next target, an altogether simpler prospect.

*

Jasmine scanned the trees. It occurred to her that the two men might have decided to split up to increase their chance of success. She supressed the urge to run, somehow managing to tap into rational thought, despite shaking with terror.

The van remained eerily abandoned at the edge of the wood, and the great, luscious tree canopy swayed in reaction to a sudden gust as the thirteen-year-old once again attempted to dispel the onslaught of stinging insects.

Instinctively, she slapped a hand to the back of her exposed neck the second she felt the needle pierce her skin. Suppressing the yelp that erupted in her throat, she was confused – instead of feeling the soft fur of a small insect at the back of her neck, a peculiar pen-shaped object protruded, before being pulled away. The calm numbness that suddenly swept her body and mind provided a welcome release from her fear. Her eyelids closed as she dropped on to the soft woodland carpet.

The huge man lifted the relatively small bundle as though merely throwing a sack on to his shoulder. He calmly carried his quarry out of the forest before finally exiting the trees at the end opposite from where the white van sat abandoned. He deposited the unconscious girl in the boot of his hidden vehicle before patting her unconscious body and checking all visible pockets. After getting into the vehicle, he made a short call on his mobile.

'It's me. I haven't found it yet, but I have the girl.'

Through the blacked-out windows of the car, the driver's massive head was barely visible to a group of walkers in the car park, as they watched the dark estate car coast past them. It had arrived, peculiarly, from one of the pathways that led on to the Coleridge Way. They all shook their heads in unison as the car wheels let out a screech before speeding out on to the narrow road and flying off across the moor.

CHAPTER 46

Robson had not been allowed to stay at his mother's bedside for long. After an increasingly frantic couple of hours searching for Jasmine, he had now returned to the hospital again hoping that Gwen might have regained sufficient consciousness to shed light on his daughter's location.

Sarah and Mark Connor were both uncontactable, which itself was unnerving. Robson recognised the excruciating wrenching within his gut that threatened to overwhelm him – helplessness. Discovering that his mother had not shown any sign of improvement left him feeling close to despair.

The medical staff had resumed their tests and round-the-clock observations of the unresponsive patient. Having been accustomed to her positive youthfulness for his entire life, even in the difficult recent months, he had never seen his mother looking so sullen and grey.

He continued to pace the empty waiting room, now feeling the warmth of the mobile phone that had been pressed to his ear since becoming aware of the potential threat to his family. Jasmine's jovial answerphone message made his chest hurt each time he listened to it. It was becoming difficult to avoid developing his own hypothesis as to where she might be, and each moment that passed in which he was unable to contact her, the more frightening his theories became.

Robson wondered if, and how, the latest development fitted in to the events of the past couple of days. The information that had recently been shared kept leading him to the same conclusion – this would be no ordinary investigation. But he would be involved, of that there was no doubt. To hell with protocol and 'conflict of interests'.

At that moment, alone outside his mother's private hospital room, the only course of action he could think of was to continue in his attempts to make contact with his missing family and friend, in case he was able to grab a moment when either Sarah or Jasmine might be able to answer.

As Sarah's voicemail message played again, Robson pictured the newly-weds and shook his head, still contemplating what he had been told about 'Mark Connor'. He had got to know the man well over the past year, or so he had believed. And Connor's romance with Sarah, while something of a whirlwind, had seemed as though it were meant to be. The idea of his down-to-earth friend being a spy for the secret service was beyond bizarre. The thought of him being a rogue agent, apparently now on the run with Sarah, and possibly his daughter, was astonishing. But Robson realised that he partially hoped for that scenario to be true, for at least it would have meant that Sarah and Jasmine were together. *Surely Sarah would not have left Jasmine alone?*

Robson's thoughts were interrupted by a sight through the windows in the ward doors. Outside, Wilson paced through the corridor towards him. He felt a familiar tingle down his spine as he watched her, despite the circumstances and her serious countenance.

'How is she?' Wilson asked softly, as she approached him.

'Very ill. But apparently stable.'

'I'm sorry, Jack. She's strong though. '

'Emma, this might come as a surprise, but I'm beginning to struggle with the implications of recent events.'

'Let's grab a drink, Jack.'

She indicated a vending machine standing in the corner of the waiting area. Robson nodded acquiescently and walked alongside her. Steam rose from the hot plastic cups as they sat next to each other in two padded chairs by the machine. Robson looked at her enquiringly.

'Have they uncovered anything at the cottage?'

'Not yet, but they're going through it with a fine-toothed comb.'

'What's happening here, Emma?'

'We don't know, Jack.'

She paused, holding his pleading gaze with a look that he knew was sincere, before continuing.

'Jack. Before the recent events involving your mother, I was going to ask you something else.'

Robson remained silent and sipped at the plastic cup. He suddenly felt so exhausted he could barely taste the liquid.

'The case of Miller's escape is currently being led by Superintendent Grayson.'

'I know. He arrested me two days ago.'

'The thing is, Jack. Given the history behind Miller's conviction and potential contacts, my colleagues and I don't believe he is necessarily the best choice as senior investigating officer, despite being the senior officer.'

'And what concern would it be of yours? If you'll pardon the question.'

'Jack, I'll cut to the chase. This afternoon, we had a long discussion with your senior officers and the commander of Gold Group. Our proposal was to have you take over as SIO for the case, considering your inside knowledge. And because of your skills.'

'Good luck with that one.'

'We have their full support. It's been accepted that security and intelligence services will be involved, because of the fact it appears to be intrinsically linked to our ongoing, rather sensitive investigations.' Wilson paused to study his face. 'But now of course, things are different. And I guess we'll need to rethink.'

Robson raised his out-of-focus eyes from a spot on the floor and looked at Wilson.

'What do you mean?'

'Well, you're obviously emotionally involved in this now, which changes things.'

'Are you saying you believe these events are connected to what's just happened to my mother?'

'No … not necessarily. But if they do turn out to be connected …'

'I accept.'

Wilson sat in silence for several seconds, once again examining his expression.

'You're sure?'

'Yes. Just do me a favour, Emma, will you?'

'What's that?'

'Find Jasmine.'

Wilson nodded.

'We will, Jack. It's a priority.'

A nurse walked purposefully into the room. Robson suddenly became anxious and stood to intercept the middle-aged woman before she entered his mother's room.

'Nurse … sorry, is everything okay?'

'Yes, yes. I'm only here to do Gwen's observations.'

They watched the nurse enter the single room, closing the door behind her. Wilson turned to one side and leant forward to peer into Robson's face, forcing him to turn his attention away from the door to his mother's room.

'What will you do first?'

He looked incredulously at her, before realising he should be glad for her dogged determination.

'Give me a chance … I guess one of the first things will be to examine the list of Miller's known associates.'

'Right. Well, I'd agree with that, for what it's worth. There is actually one associate that we've been keeping an eye on, but we haven't yet been able to identify whether any communication has taken place between them.'

'Who would that be?'

'Do you remember Louise Hart, Thorpe's former personal assistant?'

'I certainly do – 'Loo' as she was known at the station.'

'That's her. Well, she's currently serving her time, or what's left of it, at HMP East Sutton Park. We think it'd be worth paying her a visit, since she's the only known UK-based ex-colleague of Miller's. Still alive, that is.'

Robson nodded while picturing the 'open' facility in Maidenhead. He had visited the prison on several occasions during his time with the Met.

He remembered the judge passing Louise Hart's sentence like it had been last year, rather than eight years ago. He also recalled his reluctant admiration for Hart's competent defence team, which had successfully claimed that to house her in a closed facility would have been a waste of already stretched resources. Her barrister had argued, most compellingly, that Hart's involvement with the Arcam conspiracy had not been of her own free-will. The judge eventually accepted the argument put forward by the defence and agreed that to imprison her in a higher category prison would have caused more harm than good. He believed that Hart had 'demonstrated that she would be entirely receptive to rehabilitation in an open facility'.

As prisons went, Robson recalled, HMP East Sutton Park had been the most pleasant, or least bad, that he had ever visited. As he began to respond to Wilson, he could still picture the scene in the courtroom as the judge passed his verdict on Hart.

The sound of beeping from inside his mother's room had only just registered sufficiently to interrupt their discussion as the double doors at the other end of the room swung open and a small team of medical staff clattered in behind a trolley. Robson looked on, speechless, as they dashed past and into Gwen's room. He noted the wording on one of the medical team member's uniforms as they disappeared inside. *Emergency Resuscitation Team.*

Instinctively, Wilson grabbed one of Robson's hands as they watched one of the members of the emergency team hastily roll down the blind on the inside of the door.

CHAPTER 47

Sarah stared at the phone display as she sat on the edge of her bed, paying no attention to the luxurious surroundings of their chic hotel suite. A feeling of unease grabbed her as she churned over the possible reasons for not being able to contact either Jasmine or Gwen since departing for their honeymoon. And now, for some reason, both of their phones seemed to have totally lost connection with the outside world, so she would have to give up on contacting Jack too.

She pulled at the bottom of her summer dress, the hem resting at the top of her slender, tanned legs, which moved gracefully as she meandered to the window of the lavish, typically Parisian hotel room. She raised the ornate sash and leant out, breathing in the cool, summer air. The grounds were suddenly filling with strollers again, who were seizing the opportunity to fill their lungs with fresh air before dinner following another unseasonal downpour. Even sunny Paris, it seemed, hadn't escaped the misery of extensive summer rain.

*

Beneath Sarah's window, her husband had been trying to make a call of his own.

Hidden from view by the luscious foliage covering the elaborate pergola, Connor perched on the stone seat situated in one of the hotel's cultivated gardens and attempted to make contact again. Neither of his associates had answered, despite him having made several attempts in the past twenty-four hours. Connor began to grow concerned. *I should have heard from them by now.*

Additionally, he was unable to contact either the young girl or her grandmother, which was currently adding to his wife's stress by the minute. He wandered back inside, knowing that if he didn't return to Sarah soon, he might not get away with maintaining the pretence of booking travel arrangements.

Inside the hotel, the pleasantly antiquated sound of a bell indicated the arrival of one of the lifts in the foyer. The elderly woman showed her appreciation of Connor's chivalry as he waited for her to enter the lift before him.

'Merci, monsieur.'

'De rien, madame.'

As the elevator doors began to close, he almost jumped at the sudden warbling sound from his phone. The doors of the lift stuttered to a halt as he held his hands out either side and prevented them from closing. He withdrew the device from his pocket and studied the display while retreating from the lift apologetically.

'Pardon, madame. Continuez s'il vous plait.'

Another couple had arrived for the lift, but Connor was sat in a deserted part of the foyer by the time the elevator had closed its doors. He sat back in a grand leather chair with his phone to his ear.

'Hello.'

'Jeune marié?'

'Bien sur.'

'Sir. Pierre will collect you at 09:00 tomorrow, in the pre-arranged location.'

'Thank you.'

He tried to disguise the intense concentration on his face as he looked up to find Sarah standing only yards away, watching him replace his phone. He knew that she must have noticed his ruffled reaction.

'Sarah. You startled me!'

'Who were you talking to just then?'

'That was Gwen!'

He smiled, hoping that Sarah's expression would change to match his.

'What? Why didn't you put me on? What the hell's happening? Where are they? Is Jasmine all right?'

'Woah, slow down, honey! Had I known you were standing over me I would have gladly passed you the phone. Everything's okay, darling. They were engaged in one of their movie marathons yesterday, and they've been with Jack this morning.'

'Jack? Is he okay?'

'They're all fine.'

'I thought you said you couldn't get a signal.'

'I know. But the queue at reception was huge when I arrived, so I thought I'd give it another go from down here.'

'Oh, thank god, Mark! Can you call them back for me please, darling?'

Tears welled as she rushed towards her husband's outstretched arms. He embraced her tightly, buying himself time to think of a plausible response.

'They were literally about to go out into the back garden. Jazzy claims her phone doesn't get any signal out there.'

'Let's try Gwen's landline then!' Sarah pushed away from his chest and looked him in the eyes. 'Please, Mark?!'

Connor held his best loving gaze as he thought.

'The phone lines are down in the village again.'

'Really? Again?'

'Afraid so, I spoke to her on Jasmine's mobile. I'll try to get through again,' he held his phone out, casually selecting the number for Jasmine while his left hand remained in the pocket of his beige chinos.

Connor silently watched his wife's expression change to one of frustration as she eventually looked up from the device.

'Oh, Mark, for goodness' sake!'

'Sarah! Keep it down!'

'No service again!'

'Oh, really?'

He looked down briefly, feigning an annoyed look as he returned his gaze to Sarah, who had begun to sob.

'I've been so bloody worried!' Sarah's voice trembled. Connor wrapped his long arms around her and squeezed her to him.

'I know, I know. Jasmine says that her phone doesn't work at Gwen's house, except for occasional reception in the kitchen. And to top it all off, Gwen's phone is down! She says the engineers are outside working on the fault.'

Connor raised his eyebrows as he continued to reassure his new wife.

'But listen, the main thing is, they're both okay. Perhaps we can begin to enjoy our honeymoon now, eh?'

'Yes, yes!' Sarah nodded as she wiped her eyes, which glinted as she smiled. 'I think I'll try them again in a moment. I just need to hear their voices for myself.'

Connor presented his best loving gaze.

'Come on, let's go and have a drink before dinner. I want to tell you about a surprise I've arranged!'

Sarah kissed him tenderly and surrendered to his strong arms as he pulled her in again, before releasing her and taking her hand as they walked across the foyer together.

Using his training, Connor discreetly scanned the area for potential threats as he accompanied his wife to the hotel's champagne bar. At the same time, he fingered the device in his left pocket, double checking that he had correctly operated the jamming signal and not the alternative. He couldn't afford to leave his own phone blocked like he had his wife's. As he put his arm around Sarah's slender waist, the feeling underfoot became notably softer as they crossed the threshold to the hotel's bar. Sarah's phone made no sound as it dropped from his jacket pocket and into the deep pile of the luxurious carpet.

As soon as they entered the bar area, a man dressed in a pristine suit rushed towards them and bowed as he offered his greeting.

'Bonsoir, Monsieur, Madame.'

'Bonsoir. Une table pour deux, s'il vous plait.'

The maître d' summoned a junior colleague with a hand gesture as he responded.

'Oui monsieur, bien sur.'

A smart young waiter arrived with a white cloth draped over his forearm as he smiled to greet the couple. While they followed the young man to a table adjacent to one of the huge sash windows, a hotel porter stopped to adjust the pile of luggage on the trolley that he had been pushing towards the elevators. He looked around carefully before deftly swooping to collect the fallen phone from the soft carpet.

The porter peered into the wine bar and watched the Connors as they lowered themselves into plush chairs, aided by the dutiful young waiter. Content that he hadn't been seen, the porter quickly pocketed the phone and walked towards the hotel entrance, abandoning the luggage trolley. *A gift! Naamah will be pleased …*

Soft jazz played inside the bar as Mark Connor confidently placed their order.

'Une bouteille de champagne, s'il vous plait.'

Sarah gazed admiringly at her new husband.

CHAPTER 48

It was a peculiar sight for the others within the small gathering – to see the giant so obviously afraid. The big man seemed to cower slightly as Naamah continued to pace the uneven surface, still choosing not to grace him with eye contact. He considered interrupting the silence but thought better of it, and instead allowed his huge bald head to hang in deference.

'I'm surprised at you, Ben. You have made a severe error of judgement.'

'I'm sorry, Naamah. I thought it'd help us get to him, and the device, if we held the girl.'

'No, Ben!'

A lump visibly formed in the man's trunk like neck as he swallowed hard, his throat feeling suddenly dry.

'What it could do,' Naamah continued, 'is provide a trail to us. Which is why you will remove the girl from here immediately.'

'Yes, Naamah, of course. Shall I return her to the old woman.'

'Unfortunately, it's too late for that. Granny Robson has been rescued and is currently in hospital. Another failure. She gave you no information, but you have managed to draw maximum attention. I understand that even the security services have been on the scene – the inimitable intelligence officer Wilson no less. I hear she insisted on searching the property alone, which means that we cannot be certain if anything has been found. But you can be sure that Wilson and her colleagues now know that we are looking for something.'

'Sorry, Naamah.'

'Let's just hope the device turns up somewhere else, and soon. Listen carefully, I don't care where you leave the girl, as long as it doesn't leave a trail to us. Understood?'

'Of course, Naamah.'

'Carlos will accompany you. Deal with it immediately.'

Naamah had left the small enclosure by the time Ben began walking towards the only exit with Carlos alongside him. Relieved that the immediate tension had passed, his breathing began to slow down again as he watched his other companions replace their firearms.

CHAPTER 49

DCI Robson's mind was a cauldron of emotions.

The uncertainty over the status of his closest family members combined with the likelihood that his friend – and Sarah's new husband – was in fact a rogue spy … it all seemed surreal, even for a man of his experience.

Robson stood alongside Inspector Matthews at the gates to HMP East Sutton and prepared himself for what, from a personal perspective, could turn out to be the most important interview of his life.

Superintendent Grayson had assured Robson that he would be keeping a close eye on the search for Jasmine, having already used his influence to ensure maximum possible prioritisation for the case, but it took every sinew of professionalism and experience for him to focus on the job at hand. He understood that if he didn't, Grayson would have him off the case without hesitation. As he prepared to address the guards at the entrance to the open prison, he paused to clear his mind before continuing.

Access turned out to be swift. The guards had his name on their list of expected visitors, and they were soon escorted from the dull façade of the outer prison entrance towards the less severe interior grounds. Robson had lost count of the number of times that he had had cause to enter a prison in the line of duty, but the comparatively relaxed aura of the open prison at Maidenhead still took him by surprise, despite it not being his first visit.

'Louise is currently working in the garden, Chief Inspector. If you're happy for me to do so, I can take you directly to her there, or I can arrange for her to be brought to one of the interview rooms, if you prefer?'

'I think the garden will be fine, thank you, officer. As long as we can get a little privacy. It'd be a shame to waste such a rare fine day.'

'Absolutely,' the guard chuckled. 'I think you might find Louise to be more amenable in her preferred surroundings anyway. She's been like a bear with a sore head for the past month or so, trying to maintain her pride and joy while the English summer weather does its best to ruin everything.'

'I see,' Robson responded, pensively. 'So, she's become a keen gardener then?'

'Oh yes. Anyway, I needn't accompany you gents any further,' the tall man lifted his rolled sleeve to point towards a lone figure kneeling in the distance while tending a colourful rose garden. 'There's your girl, over there. She's working alone currently.'

Robson instantly remembered the middle-aged, though youthful, secretary to his superintendent in the Somerset CID division, whom he had known for a brief time eight years earlier. The crouched figure that he now approached had been compelled to exchange heels and smart business wear for plain, dungaree style overalls. The well-groomed hairstyle was now roughly tied back, doubtless for practical rather than fashionable reasons.

The female inmate seemed to sense her visitors as Robson and Matthews approached within thirty yards, and she turned her head in acknowledgement. As she rose, Robson noticed the admiring look in Matthews' face. The young inspector seemed surprised to find such a naturally attractive woman in these surroundings, who, despite her age, evidently retained her youthfulness. She also displayed an impressive agility, as she hopped a couple of feet down from the flower bed and moved to greet Robson with a coy smile without casting so much as a glance in Matthews' direction. Her attire may well have been inferior to the elegant clothes she had modelled during her days at Somerset headquarters, but her figure and complexion defied her years. Prison life seemed to be serving Louise Hart well.

'Hello, Louise.'

'Jack, you look well. Still as handsome as ever.'

Robson shuffled awkwardly while Matthews looked on, enviously.

'You're looking rather bright yourself, Louise. Nice to see you looking so positive. You remember my colleague, Inspector Matthews, I presume?'

'Can't say I do actually. Pleased to meet you though, sir.'

She gave Matthews a bland smile as she shook his hand, before turning her attention back to Robson.

'Yes, well. Being in here day in, day out, gives one time to reflect, Jack.'

'I'm pleased to hear that it has helped you, Louise.'

'It has certainly helped. At least, it has ever since I allowed it to.'

'What do you mean?'

'I mean that I've become much happier since acknowledging to myself that being here was actually the best outcome from the whole Arcam situation. Imagine if we'd been successful!'

Matthews, feeling like a spare part, remained silent and allowed his chief inspector to continue.

'Do I take it that you've seen the error of your ways?'

The look in Louise's eyes revealed that she hadn't failed to pick up the scepticism in Robson's tone.

'Let's put it this way. Over time, the psychological conditioning seems to gradually wear off, a bit like the original brainwashing process but in reverse, I guess. But it has been hard, I'll have you know.'

Robson and Matthews both noticed the almost girlish, carefree demeanour that originally greeted them had now cracked a little to reveal hidden depths.

'I'm sure it has.' Robson responded curtly, allowing her to do the talking for as long as she was prepared.

'Imagine waking up one day and suddenly realising your life has been a total con. And that the thing, the principle, that you believed in so passionately is exposed as nothing more than a lie. It took a couple of years, DCI Robson, but when it happened, it was immediate, like an explosion going off.'

'That must have been tough.'

'Tough? Jack, I was totally lost in the wilderness. But I now realise that the dark period had to happen, to pave the way for the rehabilitation process.'

'And now?'

'I now realise that I was taken in by a sickening bombardment of indoctrination, by people who, at the time, I had held in the highest esteem. I now see them for what they really were. I'm just sorry they're not still around, so that I could one day let them know how I feel about them. But anger isn't the solution.'

'Can we go and sit somewhere, Louise?'

The pretty smile returned, raising her cheekbones further and enhancing the flirtatious sparkle in her eyes.

'I know somewhere very private where we won't be disturbed,' she winked, before turning on her heels. 'You can leave your friend here.'

Robson looked at Matthews and gave an embarrassed shrug, before following Hart along a path which meandered round to the left of the rose garden. They were quickly out of Matthews' sight and proceeded towards an archway laden in clematis.

CHAPTER 50

'Roger that, vessel FV21.' The harbourmaster watched the small dot on his radar screen inside the control room as he continued. 'Landing bay two is clear, you may proceed.'

VHF 14 continued to display on the transmission system aboard the approaching boat as the skipper responded.

'Roger. Thank you, control.'

Having switched to the port's channel several minutes earlier, the skipper of the fishing boat immediately reverted to the secure line, as the vessel cruised out of the Irish sea and into the murky Dee estuary. He felt buoyed, not only by the apparently successful progress of the mission, but also by the feeling of being at the helm again.

'Come in, come in. Shem here, over.'

In the silent seconds that followed, the skipper opened the passport on the control panel in front of him, once again studying the name, date, and place of birth. The radio crackled suddenly.

'Hello, Shem. Naamah receiving. What's your status?'

'Now landing at Mostyn Port, Naamah, as arranged. I'll be with you soon.'

'Fantastic news, Shem. Please call again when you're securely on dry land. I might have something else for you to oversee before you arrive.'

Shem raised his eyebrows slightly.

'Understood. Any news on Arkwright?'

'Yes, we have tracked our *Harry*, or should I say *Mark Connor*, to a romantic little hotel in Paris where he is staying with his new bride.'

'I see. Have you ordered to strike?'

'Of course.'

'Good … I will resume contact in approximately one hour. Shem out.'

Having flicked to the back page, he once again admired the likeness in the photograph. Had it not been for his altered physique, it would have been difficult to maintain the deception, but Shem, otherwise known as Jacob Miller, felt confident that, once he had secured his vessel, he would breeze through the minimal security of the private port.

CHAPTER 51

DCI Robson maintained a respectful distance from the slender woman beside him who seemed so at peace, as though she had been practising meditation at a health farm rather than serving ten years' incarceration. In fact, she seemed to have benefited, at least outwardly, from her time in the apparently laid-back surroundings of the institution. There was something decidedly different about the late Superintendent Thorpe's former personal assistant.

From his short time working with her, he remembered that she used to command the attention of several of the male officers, and not just the older ones. Now, though, there seemed to be a new radiance to her, as if prison life had injected her with a newfound youth. Somewhat paradoxically, her face somehow still seemed to record a traumatic history.

She also appeared to have developed an impish side, Robson thought, as he shifted to adjust his position on the bench. He held her unfaltering stare.

'You really are looking well, Louise.'

'Oh shucks, Chief Inspector. Don't overdo the famous Robson flattery, please! Five years is a long time for a girl to be in a female only institution, you know.'

Her eyes glistened with a mischievous sparkle and she seemed to take pleasure from Robson's awkward laugh.

'Don't you mean eight years, Louise?'

'Yes, I suppose so. I only tend to begin counting my time here since my "awakening".'

'I see. Look, I don't want to take up too much of your time. It appears you have clearly formed a different view of the Arcam project since your incarceration.'

'That is correct, sir.'

'You can stick to Jack.'

'But I'd prefer to play the submissive role, sir.'

'Fine.'

Robson wondered if the work shirt beneath her dungarees had been unbuttoned quite so low from the beginning of their encounter, or whether it had been deftly opened when he hadn't been watching.

'So, would it be correct to assume that you haven't been in contact with any of your former … accomplices during your time inside?'

'Why do you ask?'

'I just wondered if you'd managed to stay abreast of how your former counterparts were faring since the conclusion of the court cases. Is there anyone you have kept in contact with?'

'Really, Chief Inspector – are you serious? You may remember that my "colleagues" were blown to pieces!'

'Not all of them.'

'Most of them.'

'In the UK perhaps, yes. But there were many involved overseas, weren't there?'

Louise shook her head.

'You're eight years too late for this interview, DCI Robson. As I've made it clear during several past interrogations, I was not privy to information relating to the other bases. I was a mere minion, which is why I eventually ended up in an open prison, you might recall.'

Robson nodded amicably, but remained silent, allowing Louise to continue.

'What's happened anyway? Why have you come to ask me these questions now? Don't tell me they're at it again?'

Robson noticed for the first time that her elocution seemed now to have lost all traces of its former West-Country accent. He once heard a northern friend tell him how he used to find it quite hilarious how expat southerners lost their accents within such a short time of departing their indigenous regions.

'What about Jacob?'

'Miller?'

Robson nodded.

'What about him?'

'Have you had any contact with him in the last eight years?'

'How? He's in a Category A prison, isn't he?'

'Was.'

'Pardon? Are you telling me he's escaped?!'

Robson knew the identity of the escaped prisoner had been kept from the public, but those with the right connections wouldn't have had too much trouble finding out the truth.

'No. He has been downgraded to Category C.'

Robson wanted to test Hart's knowledge. He remembered hearing about the decision. He had almost choked on his coffee when he found out that approval had been granted to downgrade the 'well-behaved' Jacob Miller to Category C. *And now look what's fucking happened!*

'Oh. He must have been an exceptionally good boy, then?'

'One can only presume so.'

'What's he done, Chief Inspector?'

The teasing smile had returned.

Robson considered offering a snippet, to test her reaction.

'We think he may have been communicating with some of his ex-colleagues. We're trying to find out who else is involved.'

Louise Hart smirked.

'I wasn't born yesterday you know. The girls and I were watching the news the other day about a prisoner escaping while being transferred to Dartmoor. Very daring – did you hear about that, sir?'

Robson remained poker-faced, ignoring the coquettish pose as Hart turned and leant forward with both elbows in her lap, resting her chin on upturned palms.

'I did.'

She sighed.

'Listen, DCI Robson. If I had any information for you, I'd freely volunteer it, you can be sure of that. I have no reason to do anything to assist the crazy bastards who ruined my life. In fact, I've made it my objective to totally eradicate those lunatics and their ridiculous ideas from my memory.'

Robson decided on a different tack.

'Well, at least you are free of them now. It's intriguing really, isn't it? How you came to be embroiled in such a conspiracy, given your feelings on the matter now, don't you think?'

'Not really, Jack, no. I think that's how these things happen. They begin small, and the radicalism slowly builds. I remember when I first encountered Sir Geoffrey Charlesworth. Thorpe had told me about this island out in the channel. I'd always known about Steep Holm, but I'd never visited the cute little island. Well, once I'd been once, I was hooked – it was so beautiful!'

'So, you visited Steep Holm frequently?'

She nodded.

'Was Charlesworth the reason you kept going back to the island?'

'Not really. Certainly not at first. It was the natural beauty of the place, along with the interesting buildings.'

'Oh? Such as?'

She let her head drop but looked up at him.

'I just loved the lighthouse. Such an old building and still standing after all that time. I used to love watching the gulls and other birds gathering at the very top.'

Robson tried to study her face without encouraging further flirtatiousness. She spoke about the island with such passion – she had clearly always been a horticulturalist, perhaps also a botanist at heart.

'Do you think you'd like to go back there one day?'

The smile disappeared from her face as she shook her head.

'Never.'

Robson waited for her to continue, but his last question seemed to make her clam up. Instead, he accepted that the meeting was over and handed her a card.

'Fair enough, Louise. We have to cover all lines of enquiry, as you well know. But would you be so kind as to give me a call if you think of anything relevant – even if it seems trivial?'

She accepted the business card and placed her tongue inside her left cheek as she leant back provocatively, her hair brushing against the clematis overhead.

'You know something? I might just do that ... sir.'

'Thank you, Louise. I'll leave you to it, then. Thank you for your time.'

Robson wasted no time in standing up and setting off down the path after shaking her hand. He didn't turn back as she called after him.

'I'll try to make more of an effort with my appearance next time, sir!'

CHAPTER 52

The cool air felt refreshing on Jasmine's face, encouraging her to finally wake up from her latest induced sleep. Blurred lights danced before her every time she attempted to open her heavy eyelids. Gradually, as awareness of her surroundings increased, so did her concern, as she sensed that her enclosure was in motion. She squeezed her eyes shut to control the stinging.

The noise from the rumbling container in which she bounced seemed to overpower all other sounds. The whirring lights began to settle, and she felt alarmingly disorientated as she looked up at what appeared to be a star-laden sky. She tried to recall the previous hours. She remembered being in the wood … Her heart sank as she recalled that she had lost sight of the two men among the trees.

Damn it! They've obviously recaptured me! But who are they? I was stung by a … wasp?

Craning her neck, Jasmine managed to lift her heavy head off the flat surface to confirm that the remainder of the immediate space around her was empty, except for a coiled rope and a metal box. She couldn't be sure if her hazy memories were accurate, but the voices she had begun to intermittently detect above the rumbling were surely real. She summoned enough strength to lift her head high enough to identify the source of the conversation. Two silhouetted heads wobbled as their vehicle traversed the obviously uneven terrain.

Jasmine attempted to move her arms, gently at first, then gradually increasing the force until she noted the ties across her wrists, fastening them together in her lap. She shook her head, feeling hopeless. She couldn't stop wondering how the two men in the woods had managed to get to her without her noticing. Like ghosts, they were a safe distance away one moment, and then they had simply disappeared.

And then ... the wasp sting?

She had no idea what they wanted with her. But whatever motivated them, they were clearly determined to hold her captive. As if activating a switch, she decided against expending any more energy on trying to guess what couldn't be known and instead forced herself back into survival mode. She turned her thoughts to escaping.

As the vehicle seemed to pick up speed, she tried to raise her head again to get a better view. Her heart sank as it became clear that her cover had already been blown – it was too late to feign sleep. She had chosen to look up the same moment the man in the passenger seat had turned back to check on her.

The man's voice caught her totally off-guard. The West Country accent she had previously heard was now replaced with something more continental.

'Buenos tardes, señorita! Cómo está?'

Jasmine felt panic threaten to consume her again as, for the first time, she began to take in the size of the silent bear in the driving seat. Who are these people? she thought to herself, breathing intensely.

At that moment, she realised that they seemed to be plummeting down a steep gradient. The foreign man nonchalantly turned back to the driver and spoke something unintelligible to her, before both men began to laugh heartily. She resisted the urge to cry with every sinew of her strength.

Oh my god! What am I going to do?!

Jasmine moved her left leg so that it extended off the bed. She managed to bring herself forward by a couple of inches, so that her heel finally touched the metal box. She judged that the noise from the road would be enough to drown out anything that took place in the back of the vehicle, and so she began to draw the metal box towards her, inch by inch.

*

Robson eyed the late arrivals with disdain. He could feel himself about to snap, until Matthews appeared at the doorway behind them and intervened, apparently noticing his DCI's vexation.

'Sorry, sir. We've been working on the prison visits, as you asked. We've just had some information hot off the press, and we thought it would be good to bring details to this briefing.'

The rest of the incident room seemed to let out a collective breath, as they watched the DCI's shoulders begin to relax.

'Okay, DI Matthews, come on in, I don't want this to be too long.'

Matthews closed the door and took the nearest available chair.

'Right, everyone. Thank you for attending our second briefing for Operation Sandstone. I trust that by now you have all had a chance to get yourselves up to speed with the existing leads, regardless of your own current lines of enquiry.'

Robson surveyed the room full of nodding officers before he continued.

'First, some news on resources – the Super has managed to acquire another four officers from the south-west regional force. That means another team, which will hopefully allow us to make some headway poring over the usual bloody details.'

He noticed Wilson's complexion change immediately and decided to correct his faux pas. Ninety percent of the attendees were familiar with the woman who had just entered the room and it showed in their faces as they watched the attractive and businesslike blonde stroll towards the front. Officer Wilson, now of the security service, exchanged friendly glances with several of her ex-colleagues as she took a seat close to Robson in front of the incident board.

'Sorry, introductions. Most of you already know Officer Wilson and have had a little time to catch up with her informally. But before introducing her to you all, let me clarify how this investigation is going to be structured – this will be a joint investigation with MI5, or, sorry, the Security Service. Officer Wilson is obviously representing the Security Service. She will be a permanent member of this team for the time being, and we will see some of her colleagues around from time to time. Needless to say, I need your full cooperation with this. This is a complicated investigation and may well require international cooperation, which is even more reason for us to have Officer Wilson and her team on board.'

Wilson rose from her position at the front of the room and gave a nod, while displaying the faintest of smiles. Most of the faces in the room were familiar to her, which was a good sign, on a professional level. It also meant that many of them had known her personally and were fully aware of her past involvement with Robson.

Robson continued, brushing aside the nagging feeling that, despite his introduction, Wilson didn't seem to be fully appeased.

'Matthews and I went to visit Louise Hart a couple of days ago.'

Robson nodded to his colleague as he spoke. Inwardly, Matthews thought it laughable that his DCI had invited him to brief the room on Hart, considering she had only been prepared to talk to Robson. Standing up, the chair screeched as his legs pushed it backwards.

'Well, there isn't much to tell really. Louise Hart is currently serving what remains of her sentence at HMP East Sutton Park. When we visited, Hart claimed that she hadn't had any contact with Miller or anyone else related to the prior Arcam investigation since her incarceration. We're still going through the official prison records, but so far we haven't come across any visits of particular interest.'

Robson intervened.

'What visitors do we know about, James?'

'Just her solicitor every now and again, and the only family member that appears to have bothered visiting is her younger sister, Melissa. Although, it seems even those visits stopped several years back, according to the records at least.'

'Oh? Any idea why that might have been?'

'Not yet, sir.'

'Right, there's a new priority then – find Melissa and bring her in for a chat please. There's currently no reason to think Louise Hart is involved in any of this, but we need to eliminate her.'

'Understood, sir.'

'So, while we're on the subject of prison visits, DI Matthews …'

'Yes, sir. DS Burford has been leading an analysis into the records for HMP Belmarsh for us, with a view to producing a list of Jacob Miller's visitors.'

Burford responded to Matthews' glance and rose. The other officers watched the stern woman at the back of the room.

'That's correct, sir. We haven't completed our examination yet, but just before this meeting we came across something that might be of interest.'

Robson's eyes narrowed.

'Go ahead, Sergeant Burford.'

'Well, sir. If Louise Hart's visitors appear sparse, Miller doesn't appear to have any friends whatsoever. Up until this morning, the only recorded visits have been his solicitor, which, unsurprisingly, have been quite regular over the past twelve months while he had been negotiating a downgrade of his classification.'

The room was filled with ironic looks, as Burford continued.

'However, going back a little further, about three and a half years ago, Miller was receiving another visitor on a regular basis, for a period of about six months, it seems. A certain Professor Alberto Romano.'

'What was their relationship, Burford?' Robson encouraged his sergeant to get to the point.

'We don't know yet, sir. It is unclear how the two men knew one another.'

'And what about this Professor Romano – do we know anything more about him yet?'

'Yes, sir. Professor Romano is a senior scientist at the HAARP facility in Alaska, it seems.'

Out of the corner of his eye, Robson noticed Wilson shift uncomfortably in her seat. She recognised the name – he could see it in her face.

'HAARP?' Robson probed, still surreptitiously watching his ex-colleague.

'Yes, sir. It's an acronym. It stands for High-frequency Active Auroral Research Programme.'

'Meaning?'

Burford could tell by her DCI's curt dialogue that she wasn't moving fast enough for him.

'Sir, essentially, it appears to be a huge scientific facility related to weather research.'

Robson knew his sergeant had reached the limit of her technical prowess and stared at DI Matthews, as a cue for the young, tech-savvy inspector to fill in the gaps.

'That's correct, sir. It is a weather research facility. It is an extremely well-known programme, certainly in scientific and meteorological circles.'

Robson still had one eye on Wilson as he encouraged Matthews to continue.

'Well, sir, from what I understand, the facility in Alaska houses a vast research instrument, which comprises an enormous site of transmitters. Almost a couple of hundred huge pylons are used to transmit power – radio energy – into the upper layer of the earth's atmosphere, which apparently enables them to study the planet's weather systems and its causes. And it also provides fertile ground for conspiracists.'

'In what way, Jimmy?'

'There are several theories, sir. Some of the more popular ideas relate to weather manipulation, use of the technology as a high-tech weapon, and even mind control.'

'Fascinating, I'm sure. So, who employs this professor?'

'The American government.'

'Not an obvious associate for Miller, you wouldn't have thought?'

'Precisely, sir.'

'Right, let's track him down, James.'

'Sir.'

'I want us to have a word with this Professor. Make it a priority please, DI Matthews.'

'Yes, sir.'

'DC Jenkins.'

'Yes, boss.'

'Let's talk to Miller's solicitor. Who is he?'

Jenkins looked down at a scruffy notepad before responding.

'Chap by the name of Tristan Cumberwell.'

'Okay, set up that meeting.'

'Will do, boss.'

'Right then, people, everyone has plenty to be getting on with. Officer Wilson and I will be paying a visit to Steep Holm island. Forensics have been spread a little thin, but the island is the last place we can be certain that Miller visited before disappearing, so our presence there is overdue. You should also be aware that, immediately prior to setting off for the island from Porlock Weir, Miller is known to have visited the Ship Inn. Within a day of that visit, the landlord, Samuel Peterson, was found murdered. The Inn is currently still sealed off as a crime scene, which I am hoping to visit in person as soon as I can.'

Robson looked around the room for a reaction.

'Does anyone have anything to add to that?'

'Sir,' DI Matthews responded, 'as you say, uniform still have the pub sealed off. We're awaiting the results from forensics, but all that's known so far is that a young bar assistant found his boss in his office late morning. They had been serving breakfast at the pub. Peterson had been bludgeoned across the back of his head and the emergency services declared him dead on arrival.'

'Anything unusual reported by the bar assistant.'

'No, sir. The young lad was interviewed at the scene by uniform – he was in quite a state. We've had him in since. He says it was a quiet day at the pub – no more than ten punters all day. They had just finished the breakfast shift, and the chef had just been sent home. The landlord had disappeared a little earlier apparently, after serving a customer – a man on his own. The lad says that he finally tracked his guv'nor down in the office out the back. The office door had been locked and the landlord was lying in a pool of blood. His skull had been caved in. Pathology say that it was a single blow, with something heavy such as a scaffold pipe. No obvious forensic traces, but they're working on that.'

'Have the premises been searched?'

'Not completely yet, sir. That's why it's still sealed. It'll remain that way until we've been in and been over the place thoroughly. We are also trying to establish the identities of everyone who visited the Ship Inn that day.'

'Okay, thank you, James. Perhaps Officer Wilson and I could incorporate that as part of our visit to Steep Holm.'

Robson watched her nod in his peripheral vision.

'Right, there's lots to do, people, let's go!'

Wilson remained seated as the remainder of the officers filed out of the room. As the last of them left, she looked at Robson seriously.

'Jack, before you go ...'

'What is it?'

'The extra officers that have been seconded – do you know them?'

Robson frowned.

'No ... why?'

'Did Grayson hand-pick them?'

'Hand-pick them? Are you kidding? You are aware of the current resource crisis in the force, aren't you?'

'I don't want them involved in the Miller case.'

'I'm sorry?'

'Jack, listen, for reasons that will become clear, we cannot risk too many people knowing the ins and outs of this case. Let me make a suggestion. Allocate these new personnel to Grayson, in his, erm, case ...' said Wilson, carefully side-stepping the need to mention Jasmine's disappearance directly.

Robson sighed, seeing there was no scope for negotiation in her eyes.

'Fine. I'll have a word with the Super now. Sit tight and I imagine you'll be able hear his response from here.'

'Don't worry, you get back to work. I'll deal with Grayson.'

'As you wish.'

Robson performed a mock bow, before pacing out of the room. Behind him, the furrow on Wilson's brow grew.

CHAPTER 53

Ministry of Defence - Main Building,
Whitehall, London

Michael Underhill cut a diminutive, mild-mannered individual when engaged in a press briefing. But those inside the MOD fortress were regular witnesses to the Home Secretary's intimidating rage. The cabinet wanted answers.

Peter Grant ran his question through his mind once more before voicing it. He knew it had to be handled with supreme delicacy.

'Home Secretary Underhill, if I may, sir ...'

'You may, Director General. What have MI5 got for us? Has your officer ... Wilson, is it? Has Wilson got any further in discovering where Miller has absconded to?'

'Officer Wilson is working closely with CID as part of a joint investigation team. They are beginning to make inroads, sir. But nothing concrete as yet to report, I'm afraid.'

'And what, pray tell, Mr Grant, needs to happen, in your opinion, to ensure that you do not report the same thing to me next week?'

The poker-faced attendees waited silently for Grant's response.

'Sir, if I might be rather frank with you. We believe the investigation should be handed over to the intelligence organisations. CID is surely not equipped to handle such extremely sensitive affairs, which, let's face it, are likely to involve interfacing with foreign involvement.'

'*We* believe?'

The chief of the secret intelligence service, Sir Justin Blanchflower, cleared his throat. Alongside him, his most senior operative, David Vincent, shuffled in his seat.

'Home Secretary,' Blanchflower began, 'MI6 is also of the opinion that the security and intelligence services should be the authority for the joint investigation.'

'Interesting ... on what basis, Sir Justin?'

'Sir. As Director General Grant has already alluded, the investigation is escalating, and it is evident that our enquiries are going to require sensitive coordination.'

Michael Underhill was still.

'Is that it?!

'Sir?'

'Is that your only offering? With respect, Sir Justin, Peter, you have been involved in this enquiry from the outset, and that does not appear to have particularly accelerated our progress, does it?'

'Sir, with respect—'

'No. Let me be clear. We are investigating a domestic crime. The fact that some of the actors may yet prove to have overseas connections is neither here nor there. And, *with respect*, given that one of the key accomplices appears to be an MI6 agent, let's just say that this does not fill the home office with the greatest confidence.'

'Sir, if I might—'

'This is a police matter. CID will continue to lead the investigation, but it will be coordinated with the intelligence organisations. I want SO19 to act as facilitator for information transfer. Commander Gibson is leading Gold Group ... John, I want to discuss this with you immediately following this meeting.'

At the far end of the long table, Commander John Gibson calmly nodded at the Home Secretary.

'Of course, sir.'

'I think that concludes our meeting, ladies and gentlemen. Let's get on with it, shall we? The Prime Minister wants Miller back in custody within forty-eight hours.'

CHAPTER 54

M ark Connor gently closed the door to the honeymoon suite behind him and strolled into the plush corridor, leaving his bride to soak in her luxurious bath. Despite Sarah knowing that they were on a tight schedule that morning, he knew he could be confident that she wouldn't compromise on her usual bathing routine. He would have time.

As far as Sarah was concerned, her aim was to be ready to depart their room by nine o'clock. Connor had told her that their ride would be at the front of the hotel to collect them at nine-fifteen, to begin their 'mystery trip'. What she didn't yet know was that they would be checking out of the hotel for good.

Warm soapy water ran from Sarah's thumb as she lifted her phone from the edge of the bath and wiped the condensation away. She smiled at the time display, which told her that she could afford at least another twenty minutes in the huge tub of bubbles. Replacing the phone on the side, she allowed her slender neck to fall backwards until her head was resting on the edge of the white tub. She thought again of the wonderful lovemaking she had initiated earlier that morning and smiled to herself, enjoying the scent that emanated from the hot foamy water.

Meanwhile, her husband stood calmly at the reception desk, explaining that he and his wife would be moving on.

'Of course, Mr Thomas, we'll be sorry to see you and Mrs Thomas leave us,' responded the pretty young receptionist in perfect English. 'Would you like to settle in full now?'

'Yes, please. We'll be leaving shortly.'

'Of course.'

The receptionist maintained her friendly disposition, privately admiring the handsome guest, and made dutiful conversation while waiting for the invoice to print.

'Are you going home, sir, or moving on elsewhere?'

Connor looked up from his phone and watched her closely. The girl flushed under his examination, oblivious to the fact that he was in the process of assessing her expression and body language for any signs of being an infiltrator. He forced a smile as she plucked the invoice from the printer's out tray and passed it across the mahogany desk.

Connor replied as his eyes immediately studied the bottom line of the bill.

'We're heading south,' he lied. 'My wife and I are great admirers of the Loire, so we thought we'd spend a few days there.'

He handed over a thick wedge of cash to the receptionist, who began to count the notes. If she had been surprised at the use of cash to pay for such a large bill, she didn't show it. The girl placed the money in the safe behind her.

'The Loire – a wonderful choice, sir. Anywhere in particular?'

'Tours.'

Connor turned without waiting for a response, abruptly terminating the conversation. He pulled his phone from his pocket and began to make a call as soon as he rounded the corner to the elevators. Once he reached the stairwell he began to speak.

'It's me. Can you collect us in half an hour? Good. I sense we need to move.'

He replaced the phone and rushed past the lifts and into the stairwell. He began to take the steps two at a time in long even lopes. Sarah wasn't going to be happy with the news that they would be departing earlier than previously announced, Connor thought to himself as he rushed back to their hotel room. The receptionist had unnerved him, and the fact that they hadn't located Sarah's lost phone was another cause for concern. The sex this morning was very pleasant, he thought to himself as he felt his thighs burning, but it had cost valuable time.

Moments later, as he deftly opened the door to their hotel room, he could hear Sarah singing to herself in the bathroom.

CHAPTER 55

Jasmine cringed at the metallic clanging sound, as her foot lost its grip and slipped from the box. She lay frozen on the makeshift bed as the foreign man swivelled in the passenger seat and turned to look back at her. His eyes possessed an unnerving twinkle.

'Sorry about the bumpy ride, princess. We won't be too much longer.'

She felt her bottom lip tremble as she tried to imagine where they might be going. The man turned his shiny, bronzed head and looked out of the windscreen again.

The girl gritted her teeth and tried to control her adrenaline, willing herself to turn panic into anger. She breathed deeply before continuing to slowly execute her plan, if it could be called 'a plan' – for she didn't know what would be in the box even if she managed to reach it, let alone what she might do next. Her Achilles ached as she dug her heel in hard and tried to drag the metal box closer, hoping to minimise the scraping sound against the metal floor. She needed the box to be alongside her left wrist if she was going to stand any chance of accessing it, given the constraints of her bindings.

By lifting her head slightly from its horizontal position, the steepness of the gradient they travelled down allowed her to see a good distance ahead. The view added to her confusion – the surroundings had changed significantly since she was last awake. If she wasn't mistaken, they were thundering down a vast mountain. A lake came in to view deep beneath them, marking a trough in the folded land, before another huge peak soared into the clouds beyond. A couple of sheep scrambled out of the path of the jeep in the nick of time, bleating their disapproval to the amusement of the two men in the front.

Jasmine's stomach churned and she fought the urge to open her bowels, before adjusting her left leg into an awkward bend. The box gently clunked against the edge of her makeshift bed. After double-checking that the tanned man was still focussing on the windscreen in front, she twisted her wrist and stretched as far as she could. The cool metal felt like a precious lifeline, and, with her fingertips, she felt for a way to open the lid.

Her head suddenly smashed hard against the side of the vehicle as she jumped in reaction to the booming voice in the front.

'Where are we meeting General Miller?'

The driver's accent seemed to be of eastern European origin and the voice was deeper than his companion. She looked up and shuddered as she saw the smaller, bald man watching her with interest.

'Did we make you jump? Don't be afraid, my dear.'

He turned back and pointed to a spot in the distance, seemingly at the bottom of the mountain.

'Over there.'

Jasmine watched the driver nod his immense head, before returning her attention to the metal box, the lid of which now lay open.

CHAPTER 56

Sarah checked her watch again – it was late afternoon. Mark had been inside the toilet block for at least ten minutes. Even though they were apparently only a short distance from their mystery hotel, he had insisted that the call of nature couldn't wait, and their driver had duly pulled into the roadside service area.

She was impressed that Mark had remembered her affinity for Brittany, having probably only discussed it with him once. But being the romantic type that he was, he had stored the information away. The surprise deviation from their Parisian holiday had been timed to perfection as far as Sarah was concerned. Vibrant city that it was, it didn't match the beauty of Brittany in her opinion, even though she knew her impression was probably skewed by fond memories of family holidays.

Sarah began to feel exhausted. It had been a long journey and the tranquillity of the empty service area seemed to dull her senses even further. She spoke softly to their driver.

'What can he be doing?'

'Allow me to go and check for you, madam,' the driver offered politely over his shoulder.

'Oh, thank you, Pierre.'

Subconsciously, she had been aware of a clunk, but she was more interested in why the unassuming little man seemed to hesitate, hovering outside their blue four-by-four. Finally, the Frenchman began to walk across to the brick sanitary block. He was halfway across the parking area by the time Sarah became aware of a whooshing sound inside the car.

How can the air vents be operating? I saw him take the keys from the ignition.

She suddenly grew suspicious. Something seemed odd. Panic began to well at the bottom of her throat and, instinctively, she pulled at the handle to her right, but the door wouldn't budge. In a moment of realisation, the earlier sound seemed relevant but her drowsiness was now becoming unshakable.

Realising that neither of the rear doors were going to give way, she began to climb across the handbrake to the front, to try and find a way to override the central locking. She planted her left foot in the passenger side footwell and fell into the leather seat. Her heavy eyelids had reached the point of no return by the time her head slumped backwards.

Sarah didn't witness the calm exchange that then took place between the taxi driver and her husband outside.

CHAPTER 57

Robson felt like thumping the computer screen. He and Matthews both gazed at the frozen image. The woman's high cheekbones occupied the centre of the laptop, eyelids closed because of the latest interruption to the signal. Matthews was the technical whizz, but even he was struggling to address the situation.

'The Wi-fi seems okay our end. It must be them, sir.'

Before Robson could respond, the woman's eyelids opened again to reveal striking cobalt eyes, and an American accent stuttered through the laptop speakers again.

'Hello, can you hear me?'

Matthews was first to respond.

'Yes, Doctor Stevenson. Sorry, we lost you for a minute again there, but we seem to have you back again for now. You were telling us about the last time you saw Professor Romano.'

'Okay,' the woman spoke confidently. 'So, as I was saying – we haven't seen the professor for a couple of weeks. He was supposed to be going away to Venice on holiday for a week, but no one has seen him since. HR haven't been able to locate him so far. It's actually a little concerning. Do you guys know anything of his whereabouts?'

'I'm afraid not,' Matthews responded.

Robson intervened before she could probe further.

'Doctor Stevenson – could you tell us what Professor Romano is working on?'

'Sure … or at least, I could tell you what he *was* working on.'

'What do you mean?'

'The professor is the lead scientist at the facility here. I don't know how much you officers know about our work, but it essentially comprises firing powerful radio signals high up into the Earth's outer atmosphere – an area known as the ionosphere. Our technology enables us to replicate weather systems on a small-scale, with a view to helping us improve our understanding of the causes of weather patterns. But the facility suffered a massive fault a couple of weeks ago, quite soon after the professor departed for his holiday, as it happens.'

Robson leant forward. He could sense Matthews' excitement.

'What sort of failure, Doctor?'

'An electromagnetic event basically wiped out the transmitters and our entire computer systems.'

'What was the cause of the electromagnetic event?'

'We don't know, Chief Inspector.'

Matthews leant into the view of the webcam.

'Doctor – isn't there some form of protection against electromagnetic interference?'

The screen crackled again, and Robson began to curse. After several seconds, the doctor's mouth began to move again, out of synch with the audio.

'… seems the system had been deactivated.'

'Sorry, Doctor – you broke up again. Did you say that the defence system had become deactivated?'

She nodded her head.

'That's correct, Inspector. The antennae were protected by a huge Faraday cage – basically a kind of electrical shield, if you will. There has been no formal report as yet, but I was one of the first on the scene after the incident, and I am quite certain that the protection was not active at the time of the atta—'

'Sorry, Doctor – you were going to say attack?'

'No, no, not at all, Inspector. It's too early to draw conclusions about the cause.'

'But something makes you think this was a deliberate act, I sense?'

'I don't believe it can be ruled out. It was a significant event, but—'

Robson and Matthews stared at the flashing text. *Reconnecting.* Seconds later the laptop went black. *Call Failed.*

Matthews turned to Robson, who gazed at the screen, deep in thought.

'What do you think, sir?'

'I think we need to track the professor down, as a matter of priority.'

*

Police Sergeant Dickson and his colleague approached the open front door with caution. The previous evening, a small group of walkers had reported hearing a young girl's screams in the area. The witnesses' location at the time had been a good quarter of a mile from this spot, but a small-scale search hadn't thrown up anything of interest. The sergeant knew it would probably just have been kids playing, but he was too long in the game to completely overlook such reports, much to the frustration of some of his fellow officers.

Dickson could sense his young colleague's irritation. He had expressed his opinion, more than once, that he felt they were wasting their time. Nevertheless, as Dickson had patiently pointed out to his colleague, it was nice to be out of the car for once, and the Quantocks weren't a bad place to be wandering on such a rare fine day in the course of one's duties.

He had been close to conceding that they might as well return to their patrol car but, noting that the house was the only residence around, it couldn't do any harm to enquire whether the owner had heard or seen anything untoward at about the same time as the reported screams. As they drew nearer, the open front door piqued the sergeant's interest.

'Hello! Anyone home?'

The deep, authoritative voice of the sergeant echoed into the empty hall for a second before the silence returned. The young constable peered through the front window of the property, while his sergeant leant in the doorway and rapped his knuckles on the wide-open door.

'Hello there! This is the police – is there anyone home?'

The constable arrived at the threshold alongside his sergeant.

'What do you reckon, Sarge?'

'Let's go in.'

'Really?'

'Check your procedures, lad. It's perfectly acceptable if there's a chance someone inside requires assistance. Let control know, will you.'

'Yes, Sarge.'

Sergeant Dickson had completed a quick examination of the three rooms on the ground floor by the time his young colleague had finished communicating with headquarters. The plump sergeant was halfway up the stairs as the constable arrived to join him.

The small bathroom gave little cause for suspicion, likewise the modest bedroom with its double bed. But there was something about the view out towards the wooded area that looked out of place. The sergeant stood with his hands on his hips, studying the scene. Then he saw it. Just over the grassy ridge, he could see the top of a vehicle – what appeared to be a van. Perhaps a National Trust patrol, but instinct told him that it seemed out of place.

'Listen, son,' the Sergeant directed his voice to the other side of the small landing, 'can you get some details on the homeowner, please.'

Dickson paced across the landing to search for his young colleague. He stood with his hands on his hips inside the small empty bedroom, perplexed.

'Where is that boy now? Hawkins?'

As he thumped back downstairs, his large, chevroned shoulder caught a picture which seemed to replicate the scenery outside the front door.

'Hawkins! Where are you, lad?'

He only just caught the muffled sound that seemed to emanate from the living room he had run his eye over a few minutes earlier.

'You'd better not be winding me up, lad!'

The sergeant removed his peaked cap, listening again to a muffled shout as he entered the empty living room. The shout from behind made him jump.

'Sarge, in here!'

'What th—'

The deep furrows on Dickson's brow became even more wrinkled as he looked upon the young constable with a mixture of confusion and suspicion. Hawkins was standing in what appeared to be a concealed doorway, which had earlier been covered by a tall bookcase.

'It's another room, sir.'

The constable stood in silence, allowing his sergeant to take in the small, windowless room. The box room was unfurnished apart from an iron-framed bed positioned against the far wall. Dickson moved in closer to inspect a pink-coloured garment that lay on the bed. He removed a pen from his top pocket and carefully used it to lift what appeared to be a girl's hoodie. Something else that, for some reason, seemed at odds with the surroundings. He deftly swivelled the garment so that he could read the label inside. It confirmed his judgement. *Age 13-14.*

The young constable moved in closer, and with his own pen lifted the label and read out a name written on it using a permanent marker. The sergeant lowered his eyes in thought. He felt sure he had heard the name for some reason.

'Lad, get on to control again, will you. Ask them to run a check on *Jasmine Robson.*'

CHAPTER 58

Detective Sergeant Burford paused with her hands on her thighs as she reached the top of the hill. She took another deep breath before marching forward again to join the small team that had gathered at the edge of the wood. As she drew nearer, she noticed the pale complexion of DC Jenkins, who seemed to be a little removed from the scene as he allowed the uniformed sergeant to do the talking.

The intake of breath had not just been down to physical exertion. Burford thought of DCI Robson and how they were possibly going to break the news. One thing was for sure, she was glad her DCI wasn't with them on this occasion.

As Sergeant Dickson spoke, it was obvious that Jenkins was no longer able to look at whatever spot the sergeant was pointing towards – an opening immediately inside the first line of trees. Judging by the look of shock on their faces, none of them were going to like what they were about to witness. Burford tipped her hat to the uniformed sergeant as DC Jenkins began to snap into protocol at the arrival of his senior officer. He pointed into the wood.

'Over there, Sarge. It's a bit gruesome I'm afraid.'

Burford marched purposefully towards a mound of clothing, with DC Jenkins in tow. As they arrived at the scene, Burford noted another, second mound a few yards away from the first. As she stood, gazing down at the carnage, Burford sensed Jenkins looking at her, as though he were waiting for some sort of confirmation that the horrific scene before them was real.

Both officers swung around in unison in reaction to the sudden sound behind them. The two uniformed officers who had found the victims approached them. Burford noted the young, uniformed constable had obviously not been immune to the dreadful sight either, judging by his pale countenance.

It was about as bad as she had ever seen, Burford privately admitted to herself, but she was thankful for being in the open. Despite that, each time a breeze found its way among the trees, it stirred up the familiar, putrid smell of death. No doubt that had contributed to DC Jenkins' sudden reaction, and Burford screwed her face as she watched him out of the corner of one eye, as he leant forward with a hand on either knee, retching. She returned her attention to the scene at her feet and spoke without emotion as she gazed down impassively.

'Get the full CSI team here right away. I don't care where they are or what they're working on. And that includes forensics. Let's go and have a look at the second body over there.'

'Will do,' Jenkins rasped. 'Sergeant ...'

'What is it, Jenkins?'

'Should I inform DCI Robson of the development.'

'Leave that to me.'

Both officers remained with their eyes fixed on the scene for a few more silent seconds, before turning and walking towards the second mound. The other body appeared nearly as distorted as the first but, if anything, the amount of blood in evidence made the scene seem even more dramatic .

Jenkins and the uniformed officers watched Burford with surprise as she knelt beside the body and pressed an ear to the victim's chest, before becoming uncharacteristically animated.

'This man's still alive!'

Burford felt the uniformed constable land alongside her, apparently throwing his earlier shock aside. She rose to address Sergeant Dickson as the young constable performed CPR on the body. She withdrew a cell phone from her pocket as she spoke to the older of the two uniformed officers.

'Sergeant Dickson – seal this area please. We'll start with a half-mile exclusion radius, I think. I'll get the medics.'

'Consider it done, Sergeant Burford.'

*

Half an hour later, DCI Robson stood at the same spot inside the wood with just a small forensics team for company, having decided against exposing any more of his officers to the sight.

He leant against the nearest tree and forced himself to analyse the scene dispassionately. Yet, for the moment, no matter how much he tried to mentally record all the details, his mind couldn't escape the overwhelming desire to understand what kind of people had possessed the strength and will to do this to two fully grown men. Even more incredible was the fact that one of the victims still somehow clung on to life, although it didn't seem feasible that he would do so for much longer. That was now in the hands of medical professionals.

The look of horror recorded on the face of the dead victim had added to the grotesqueness of the image – it was as though the man's head had been installed back to front. Only a limp, twisted neck gave any indication that the body hadn't originally been that way. Robson removed his phone and activated its camera. Once he was finished, he nodded to the forensic team leader and paced away with his phone to his ear.

'Sorry, Emma, I had to take a bit of a detour. There was an incident nearby. I'll be at the harbour in twenty minutes.'

CHAPTER 59

The Mercedes continued to roar along as its driver kept his right foot firmly planted on the floor. The A73 was almost entirely deserted, which itself was a test of Mark Connor's mental stamina.

He had never had a problem focussing, which was what had made him such a powerful weapon to the Secret Intelligence Service. But he understood that, with both the domestic and overseas intelligence services now aware of his deception and his skills, a significant manhunt would be building, doubtless involving the law enforcement of several countries. The stakes were high, in more ways than one.

He noted the advance warning for the motorway toll, signalling his third border crossing of the journey since parting ways with his wife. Connor swung the car into the nearside motorway lane as he approached the German border. The temptation to pull into the motel at the side of the road was overwhelming, but he had a schedule to keep.

CHAPTER 60

The thick tyre tread ripped the grassy surface from the mountainside as the jeep skidded to a halt alongside the narrow, rocky track.

'How the fuck did she get out?' demanded the bearlike man, already imagining Naamah's reaction to the latest turn of events. 'I thought you had tied her to the bench?!'

The dust caused by the abrupt stop still swirled around them as the two comrades stood face to face at the rear of the vehicle.

'You can see I fucking did – look!' Carlos's tanned head was tilted back on his comparatively small frame as he looked angrily into his Herculean colleague's face, indignant. 'It seems someone left a box of tools for her convenience. She cut the fucking ties off!'

'The toolbox shouldn't have been anywhere near her!'

'Forget it now. We'll have to split up.'

'Where do we start? We don't know where she got out!'

The colossus, Ben, was panting, he knew more from anxiety than physical exertion.

'We know it couldn't have been more than a couple of hundred yards back. I've been checking on the little shit regularly. Come on, let's take a radio each, there's no mobile signal on this side of the mountain.'

*

Fifty yards from the two squabbling colleagues, a young girl lay deathly still. Not daring to raise her head to peek in the direction of the shouting men, she made herself as small as she could, huddled inside a gathering of large rocks and vegetation on the mountainside.

Jasmine Robson suppressed the urge to sob. She wiped tears away with a palm while she placed her other hand against her sore ribs. The impact had been nasty. She had leapt from the open rear-end of the jeep just as the vehicle jolted against a huge bump in the track and consequently, her landing had been awkward. Somehow, she had managed to avoid screaming out from the pain that ran down her left side.

She looked down at her torn, blood-soaked clothes, and prayed that the bleeding wounds hadn't left a trail for her two hunters.

*

A short, athletic figure stood in the deserted car park, while looking up at the great mountain. He removed the phone from his ear and cursed his disapproval at the automated message.

What are those pair of muppets playing at?

He grabbed his binoculars again and saw that, not only had the jeep come to an abrupt halt at the side of the dirt track, but it was also now facing up the mountain. What was more, the occupants seemed to have disappeared, from what he could tell in the rapidly fading light. The sun had already dipped behind the massif, and a quarter of the way up the greatest of the peaks, he watched two separate torch beams illuminate in unison, indicating the onset of dusk had already begun to reduce visibility on the mountainside.

Through his binoculars the lone figure watched the two men heading up the mountain on their separate courses. Understanding the implication of what he watched, Miller kicked the car door shut and replaced the binoculars in his lightweight jacket, before trotting towards the nearest gated access.

Fucking incompetent idiots.

He began to jog up the steep gradient to assist his colleagues.

CHAPTER 61

Bristol Channel

Robson was unable to ignore the growing anxiety in the pit of his stomach which had begun to take hold ever since departing the shore. As the dark mound out in the Bristol Channel grew larger, it seemed extraordinary to be once again approaching the island – an ostensibly beautiful environment – yet it was a place which held so many dark memories. The fact that he travelled alongside his ex-partner seemed to intensify the surrealness of the situation. It seemed that the hands of time had been reversed.

Eight years had elapsed since that extraordinary case. Indeed, two years had passed since he had last been in Wilson's company. But he felt that time had been far kinder to his 'ex' than it had been to him. She didn't appear to wear the same signs of ageing on her face and, if anything, appeared more physically attractive to him than ever. It only caused him regret, rather than pleasure. *That boat's sailed.*

Despite his stirred memories, this time it was markedly different. For a start, they weren't alone. The team aboard the large, unmarked police vessel totalled ten, comprising a mixture of CID officers and Security Service operatives.

'So, what do we know about the two victims at Webber's Post?' Wilson asked. 'Apart from the fact they were apparently attacked by savages.'

Robson wondered if the timing of her question had been partly due to her own apprehension as they approached the pebbly shore of Steep Holm island.

'Unremarkable, really. Both have criminal records. Theft, fraud, with a little bit of violence in the mix. Nothing more than average vagabonds – in the business to do any job for the right money.'

'Where were they from?'

'Somerset – both of them. Martin Hudson was renting a house nearby. We are still working on the connection with the deceased – Bradley Morris.'

'Where was Hudson's rented accommodation? The same property where they found Jasmine's hoodie?'

'Yes.'

'That is, of course, Grayson's case, Jack. What made you attend the scene in person? Do you, or any of your colleagues, suspect that this in some way linked to Miller's escape?'

Robson watched her for a moment. He wasn't sure if Wilson was trying to put ideas in his mind or discourage them. Momentarily, he considered voicing his thoughts – *no, it was because at least one of the lowlife bastards knows what has happened to my daughter.* Robson controlled himself before responding.

'We don't know, but not necessarily. I've already spoken to Superintendent Grayson. Their current working theory is that whoever took out the two men in the wood knows of Jasmine's whereabouts.'

As they followed the dark figures down the ramp of their vessel and on to the island's landing beach, both Robson and Wilson drew in the air deeply, each of them momentarily lost in their own memories of their previous visits to Steep Holm.

Almost immediately, one of the Security Service officers sought Wilson's attention. He pointed to an area of vegetation on the eastern perimeter of the rocky shore. The powerful tide could be heard over the distant sound of gulls which came from higher up the island, as they trudged across the pebbled shore. Without shelter from the channel's infamous gusts, everyone adjusted their outerwear to brace themselves. At the far end of the beach, a group of officers congregated among the dune-like greenery, beyond which the terrain became dense with luscious foliage.

Robson turned to Wilson and shouted to be heard.

'Surely, we're looking in the wrong place?'

'What do you mean?' she frowned.

'Well, this doesn't seem an obvious spot for a runway, does it?'

Wilson was about to respond, as a colleague shouted.

'Ma'am! Over here!'

They marched towards a group that had gathered twenty yards away and had to climb a steep bank before they reached what appeared to be the highest point the tide reached. They both paused to examine the sight. A mess of loose bracken and foliage was being pulled away by the other officers. Peculiarly, beneath the detached branches and greenery, the land seemed flattened, as though something heavy had been stored there. They wandered closer to study the newly exposed ground.

The rest of the team hadn't seemed to notice DCI Robson disappear into the trees. Only when he returned, did they note that he'd been on a lone search. The object he held with one hand caused the rest of the team to stop what they were doing immediately. Robson sniffed at the open aperture of the container, before passing it on.

'Aviation fuel?'

The officer who now held the container nodded in agreement.

'Avgas, I'd say.'

Robson noted Wilson had raised her eyebrows, seemingly in recognition of the name. She spoke, before he could query further.

'Let's split up into pairs and search the area. We will only have a few hours until we lose the last of the daylight, so we'll meet back here at seven – okay?'

Everyone nodded, before splitting up in different directions. Having travelled a good few-hundred yards from the spot where they had found the fuel, Robson stopped to ask Wilson a question.

'You seemed to recognise the fuel? Avgas, was it?'

Wilson nodded.

'That would be consistent with the use of a modern seaplane.'

'Makes sense, I suppose. But surely it can't have travelled far?'

'Perhaps not. Although, you might be surprised at the range of some modern light aircraft.'

'Did you not track them?'

Wilson displayed a wry smile at his directness.

'Only for a bit. They hadn't even travelled a mile when we lost them.'

'How?'

'Both aircraft flew out into the Irish sea, before ducking down beneath the radar.'

'Both?'

She nodded.

'We suspect that whoever met them here left in their own craft. We've extracted a sunken seaplane just off the coast of North Wales.'

'When?'

'Only a couple of hours ago.'

Robson paused to think.

'What happened to the boat they arrived in?'

'They abandoned it. We recovered it from further up the channel, where it had travelled on the tide.'

*

A few hours later, white foam developed on the grey sea and rose to meet the vessel, as it cut its course towards the mainland in the remaining dusky light. Robson and Wilson both understood what was going through one another's minds as they watched the weakening sunlight gradually disappear behind the dark cliffs. Robson smelt her familiar scent as he leant in to speak.

'Emma, I've been meaning to ask, do you recall there being a lighthouse on Steep Holm?'

'Erm, no, since you ask. In fact, I'm pretty sure there isn't one. Why?'

'Just something Louise Hart said to me the other day when I interviewed her. I thought it was odd at the time.'

'What did she say?'

'I'd asked her what is was she'd liked so much about the island, back in the

188

early days when Charlesworth was still in the process of seducing her. And she mentioned how fond she was of the lighthouse on the island.'

'Hmm, odd. I don't remember there being a lighthouse ...'

'There isn't.'

'I suppose it isn't surprising to find that her memory is a little corrupt.'

'No, I guess you're right.'

'So, Jack, are you still planning to visit the Ship Inn?'

Robson nodded.

'I'd like to have a good look around in person. Do you fancy a trip in the morning?'

He watched his ex-partner gently push her hair, which had been blown by the wind, back behind her ear – the way she always used to do.

'How could a girl refuse?'

CHAPTER 62

The following morning, yet more memories were evoked as they pulled into the car park at Porlock Weir. Robson and Wilson slammed the car doors and walked towards the Inn. Steam rose from disposable coffee cups held by the small gathering of uniformed officers outside the building, who had cut short their apparently jovial discussion as they watched Robson and Wilson approach.

It had been an early start. The investigative team had been given a stark reminder of the DCI's driven nature when he requested they attend a briefing at five o'clock that morning. Robson had wanted to get several new wheels in motion. They currently had no idea of the destination of one of the two seaplanes which had departed from Steep Holm island several days earlier. Robson insisted it had to have left a trace somewhere. He had also dispatched two officers to North Wales, to liaise with the local constabulary regarding the discovery of the second seaplane off the coast of the Irish Sea. At the same time, an MI5 team, under the direction of Officer Wilson, were at that very moment undertaking an extensive search of Sarah and Mark Connor's property.

Robson inhaled the aroma as he ducked inside the entrance to the Inn. The uniformed constable replaced the cordon behind Wilson as she joined Robson inside. The normally pleasant smell of hops and alcohol had been tainted by a stale, lingering aroma. The boarded-up windows stole most of the daylight from the inn, giving the place a derelict, haunted feel.

Robson flicked the light-switch to illuminate the familiar little bar. Glasses containing leftover beverages remained strewn across stained bar towels, as well as being scattered across several tables. Some still contained days-old liquor, revealing one of the odours currently attacking their sinuses. The yellowish light from the ceiling lamps reflected off the wooden floor, highlighting several untended beer stains.

The sight of the bar struck a slightly melancholic chord. They both imagined the ostensibly pleasant landlord tending the pumps, while a group of larger-than-life fishermen indulged in noisy exchanges at the far end of the bar. It made Robson recall their first visit, one which had been hosted by the harbourmaster at the time – none other than Jacob Miller himself – the man they now hunted. Robson shuddered at the thought of the conspiracy.

Out of the corner of his eye, he noticed Wilson's lithe figure glide past and turned his head slightly to watch her disappear out of view, to the right of the bar. He followed her out through the rear staff entrance and marched past another uniformed constable who stood outside the office door, still holding the key after unlocking the door for Wilson. The young WPC smiled politely at Robson. He acknowledged her briefly before stepping through the doorway.

Inside, Wilson was focussed on a dark stain on the floor which appeared to have come from the same source as a similar one on the desk. Seeing the small LED illuminated at the corner of a laptop on the desk, Robson tapped the keyboard to bring the screen to life. A message was displayed, requesting a password.

'Looks like he was hit hard,' Wilson commented from behind.

'Yeah, well, a scaffold pole is a pretty hefty weapon.'

'Are forensics done in here?'

'Just about. We're waiting for confirmation before the place gets cleaned up. There was no shortage of samples, but whether they've managed to recover anything that relates to anyone other than the deceased remains to be seen.'

Robson wandered towards a large shelving area at the back of the room.

'Well, whoever smashed the landlord's head in didn't appear to be looking for anything,' he mused.

'Or, if they were,' Wilson offered, 'perhaps they didn't have to look too hard. You wouldn't know anything had happened in here, if it weren't for the stains.'

Wilson looked over her shoulder when she didn't get a response and muttered under her breath.

'We've finished that conversation then, have we?'

She shook her head before turning back to examine the contents of the desk drawers.

Meanwhile, Robson continued to finger his way through a stack of paperwork and invoices stored on the shelves, apparently in chronological order.

'Who do you think did this?' Wilson asked.

'Miller?' Robson shrugged, disinterestedly.

'What would be his motive?'

'Who knows – to silence the man?'

'And risk drawing more attention? I can't really see that. Anyway, the time of death, while approximate, almost certainly confirms that this took place when Miller had already left.'

'When I say Miller … it didn't have to have been carried out by his own fair hand. I mean – he doesn't seem to be working alone. Tell me, Emma. Do you think this is linked? And, if so, where does Connor fit in?'

Wilson thought she detected a crack in his voice. She knew Robson well enough to understand how hard this was for him. But she also understood that it would be harder for him to do nothing, which is why she had persuaded Superintendent Grayson to ensure he remained assigned to the Miller case. Aside from the fact he was without equal in terms of available detectives – especially SIOs – she could also be confident that he would exercise the appropriate level of discretion.

'Jack. I think it is unlikely to be a coincidence. Don't you?'

Robson remained focussed on the paperwork in his hands. Wilson raised her voice in frustration.

'Jack?!'

'Hang on, just a second.'

Wilson wondered if the time was right to share further confidential information with him. It didn't feel entirely normal to be working so closely with her ex-lover. But it wasn't like they hadn't worked together before, and under somewhat strenuous circumstances. The fact was, Emma Wilson had become involved in a world of lies and corruption and, while she relished the challenges that the job brought, she no longer knew who she could trust or, indeed, whose side she was on. Apart from Robson. But her current predicament was determining whether she could possibly bring herself to burden him further.

'Jack, why don't we go and get something to eat? We could have the team commandeer the contents of this office so that everything can be gone through methodically.'

'Yes, yes, of course. This is the first time I've been to the scene myself. I just wanted to …'

'Are you okay, Jack?'

Robson wandered over to her, without raising his head from the paperwork that currently held his attention.

'What do you make of this?' he murmured into his chest.

She leant in awkwardly across his right shoulder, taking care not to make physical contact. The coloured text of the headed paper was the first thing to catch her eye, as it had Robson's. The lettering *RYA – Bill of Sale* seemed out of place in a pub landlord's financial files.

'I didn't know he owned his own boat,' Wilson commented.

'Look further down. Look at the name of the boat.'

Wilson scanned the bill until her eyes stopped at the name of the item of sale – *Shangri-La*. She remembered it as the identity of the boat which had been used to transport Miller to the island.

'Well, it's no great surprise, is it?' she said. 'I mean, it's not the obvious place to file one's boat ownership paperwork perhaps, but it's no surprise the landlord owned a boat, is it?'

'The landlord didn't own the boat,' he said, flipping the sheet of paper over to reveal the sum of the sale, along with the details of the buyer and seller.

Wilson's flawless brow furrowed a little as she noted the names on the docket.

CHAPTER 63

Somerset Police Headquarters

'Robson. We've got every available resource on this.'

'With respect, sir, that doesn't appear to be enough, does it?'

In the silence, Robson noticed familiar shapely legs being crossed out of the corner of his right eye.

'Superintendent. I don't mean to be disrespectful, but she's been missing for two days. Considering her age, let's both acknowledge what territory that leaves us in.'

Superintendent Grayson had known his DCI for seven years, after accepting the promotion opportunity to step into the shoes of his predecessor, the infamous Superintendent Thorpe. Therefore, he wasn't surprised by Robson's frankness. Yet, despite the typical display of stoicism by his colleague, he couldn't allow him what he craved.

'DCI Robson. Just take a step back and realise that what you're asking from me is beyond any possibility. You are, understandably, too emotionally involved for me to allow you to get involved in Jasmine's disappearance.'

Noticing Grayson flicker his eyes in Wilson's direction, Robson also switched his gaze. Wilson seemed to wear a somewhat guilty expression.

'Gold Group has confirmed that this is a major crime investigation. If you're sure you're up to working, then I'm happy to leave you on Operation Sandstone, for now, subject to ongoing review. And that is only because you've been asked for. But that's got to be it I'm afraid.'

'Sir, if we don't pool resources, then you and I both know there is no Miller investigation. Most of our manpower is currently working under you in connection with my daughter's disappearance.'

'I know. That's why I wanted to see you.'

Robson sat back and braced himself.

'We want to appoint officer Wilson as your assistant SIO, officially. How would that be for you?'

Robson shrugged.

'It's fine, I guess. Isn't that how this investigation has already evolved anyway?'

He noted Wilson shifting awkwardly as Grayson continued.

'Precisely. Despite the fact that this is a police-led investigation, it remains a joint investigation, and MI5 have made strong representation for you be assigned to the Miller case because of your knowledge and experience. Not to mention discretion. The Security Service is keen that we don't involve more non-intelligence staff than we have to. However, I've agreed to allow you an additional team of officers to work under your command and Officer Wilson's. Can you see any problems with that?'

Instinctively, Robson glanced over his shoulder. For the first time since being reunited, Wilson briefly displayed the playful grin with which he had once been so familiar.

'I'm sure that would be fine, sir.'

'Good. You will remain the SIO, but Officer Wilson should be consulted on all strategic decisions. Understood?'

'Certainly, sir.'

Both men looked up as Wilson abandoned her chair.

'Superintendent,' she said, 'having established that DCI Robson is happy with the arrangements, I really need to report to my superiors. So, if you would both excuse me.'

'Of course. Thank you, Officer Wilson.'

Wilson marched to the door.

'Not at all.'

Her eyes seemed to linger on Robson's for an extra couple of seconds as she backed out of the room, before closing the door behind her. Robson adjusted his position, realising, as the Superintendent began to speak again, that he had perhaps paid too much attention to Wilson's exit.

'I hope I didn't put you in an awkward position then, Jack. We just need to ensure the lines of authority are not blurred.'

'It's fine, sir.'

'To tell the truth, Wilson wanted to be present. I got the impression she felt she needed to gauge your reaction for herself. Any idea why that might have been?'

'No, sir. Like I said, it's fine.'

'Seems the intelligence community has been making a case for taking over the Sandstone, so I don't think it's a coincidence that the Chief Superintendent has asked for Wilson's role to be formalised.'

Robson gave a knowing nod.

'If it becomes too much for you, Jack, you must tell me. It wouldn't be unexpected.'

Robson rose, and nodded, somewhat wearily, to his superintendent.

'Thank you, sir.'

'Jack.'

'Yes, sir?'

'We'll find her.'

Robson nodded curtly as he rose.

Outside the station, Wilson held her phone to her ear as she paced to her car.

'Where is he? Right, get me on a flight within the next two hours.'

CHAPTER 64

Robson entered the gates of HMP Sutton Park for the second time in a week. Alongside him, DC Lyons continued to make polite conversation, as he had for most of the three-and-a-half-hour journey.

'Tch, do you know, I wouldn't mind staying here myself, boss. The place is more like a bloody hotel!'

'I don't know if I'd go that far, Tom. I can think of plenty of other places I'd rather be.'

Lyons seemed finally to sense that his DCI, seemingly deep in thought, was not in the mood for small-talk.

Robson continued to mull over the facts of the case, but too often his ability to think laterally was invaded by concerns about Jasmine, Sarah and his mother. He also continued to wonder why Wilson had dropped out of the prison visit at the last moment. She had been coy over the development that had suddenly demanded her attendance elsewhere, and it was still obvious that she was being economic about the information she was choosing to share with him.

Their escort at the prison was the same bulky man that had chaperoned Robson and Matthews on their previous visit. DC Lyons, a sporty man himself, wondered mischievously what physical activity the overweight guard had engaged in to cause his limp. It seemed that physical fitness was not an essential quality the prison officers needed to possess at this establishment.

'Hart will be in her room now, officers. The lunchtime chaos has just finished.'

Robson nodded, allowing Lyons to respond.

'Thank you, officer.'

They walked along a corridor with several doors, some of which were closed, while others sat ajar to reveal occupants engaged in various activities. Most incumbents lay on their beds, seemingly wiling away the remaining hours of their boring incarceration. Several others were reading or playing cards, while some sat transfixed in front of their own personal televisions. Lyons watched wide-eyed as one woman sat seemingly in a meditative state focussing on the knitting arrangement before her, while deftly operating the two potentially lethal weapons in her hands.

'Here we are.'

The guard limped along until they reached the final door, at the end of the corridor.

'The penthouse suite,' said the guard, dryly.

Lyons chuckled politely. Robson noted to himself that, compared with the regular spacing between the other doors they had passed, this one seemed to be spaced further away from its neighbour.

'Oh? I didn't realise prisons incorporated VIP accommodation these days,' Lyons said.

'Well, there you go.' The guard breathed heavily with one hand resting on the wall. 'It wasn't constructed for that purpose, put it that way. But our Louise seems to know how to play the Guv'nor, so she was upgraded to this specially converted room a few years back.'

He rapped the door with his knuckle, while continuing to indulge in sarcastic banter with Lyons.

'I'm sure you'll be impressed.'

A female voice answered after a few seconds.

'Who is it?'

The response was faint, giving the impression that the woman on the other side of the door was some distance away. Yet an impatient, almost frustrated, tone could be heard in her voice.

'Hart, I have your visitors – a little earlier than planned.'

He glanced at Robson as if to emphasise his none too subtle message about keeping to appointment times. After several silent seconds, the door began to open, before almost immediately slamming shut again. Before it shut, Robson observed a security chain through the gap. He couldn't believe what he had seen – a cell door that could be secured on the inside. The prison guard responded to Robson's exasperated expression.

'The chain is more a token of protection than anything else, Detective Chief Inspector. A long story, but it was provided to appease certain fears Louise harboured a while back.'

Robson raised his eyebrows, as the guard paused to control his rasped breathing.

'Like I say, it is a long story. But don't worry, if we ever needed to get inside in a hurry, the chain wouldn't stop us.'

At that moment, the sound of a metal cover could be heard scraping across the other side of the door's spyhole, before the woman spoke again.

'I didn't agree to this!'

For some reason, Robson felt as if the woman inside the room had been addressing him. Noting that the prison guard did not appear to be in a hurry to negotiate, the DCI stepped forward slightly and maintained an even tone.

'Hello Louise. We're really sorry to bother you again. We just wanted to ask you a few more questions. I was told that you had agreed to seeing us. It won't take long, I promise.'

Her tone seemed to change slightly.

'I said I would meet you, Jack. I didn't agree to an inquisition party. Who's this?'

'This is my colleague, DC Lyons.'

Lyons took his cue, a little too overexuberantly. As usual, Robson thought.

'Hello Louise. It's Tom to you!'

Robson thought he heard a cynical snigger.

'Fuck off, Tom. There's a good boy.'

Lyons flushed just a little and chewed the inside of his cheek. The guard decided to rescue him.

'Now, now, Louise. A little impolite, don't you think?'

'It's okay,' said Robson, signalling to the guard that her request for a one-to-one meeting was not insurmountable. Lyons backed away as if trying to fade into the background. Robson turned to the guard.

'Perhaps you wouldn't mind taking DC Lyons for a cuppa while I go in and have a quick chat with Ms Hart?'

'Sounds like a good idea to me,' the guard responded, while Lyons nodded in silent agreement. Robson patted his colleague on the back before he wandered off with the guard. The guard turned briefly.

'You know where to find us, don't you, DCI Robson?'

'Yes. I shouldn't be too long.'

The chain could be heard disengaging on the other side of the door.

CHAPTER 65

Jasmine Robson wasn't sure if it was the cold, or simply her terror, that made her entire body tremble. Her arms wrapped around her knees, she squeezed them towards her shaking ribs, too terrified to move. The large rock before her seemed to have little effect in breaking the wind, and the foliage that surrounded her swayed violently, surrendering its leaves to the gusts.

It had been a while since Jasmine had last heard a voice, but that offered little reassurance. The sound caused by the harsh weather overpowered most other noises. The last thing she had heard, some ten minutes ago, was an unfamiliar voice. She couldn't be sure, but it had almost sounded as if someone else was shouting angrily at the other two men.

She began to feel like a sitting duck and considered peering out of her rocky cover. Then, behind her, the foliage seemed to rustle out of synch with the power of the wind. Her instinct was to freeze, but the sound behind her grew unmistakably louder. She wondered if she were being paranoid, but she also knew that if she were to make a run for it, the decision would have to be made quickly.

She risked peering through the bush and poked her head through the branches overhead as she rose slightly. Outside her shelter the overcast sky blocked out all starlight, leaving the remote mountainside in almost total darkness. The torchlight evident earlier had disappeared, which suggested that the men must have moved on to search another area.

The rustling noise returned, this time even louder. As Jasmine twisted her head in the direction of the sound, the sight nearly made her jump out of her skin. As she tried to control her breathing, she allowed herself to chuckle inwardly, even though such a reaction seemed totally incongruous in her situation. Her heart was still pounding as the fluffy creature nearby let out another bleat. Her eyes could now pick out the outline of a lone sheep. A faint glow of moonlight, which had pierced a gap in the cloud cover, suddenly reflected in the animal's eyes.

'Ssh. Move along little one,' she whispered to the animal. 'We don't want to alert the nasty men!'

Talking to a sheep seemed ridiculous, yet, at the same time, felt somehow soothing. It provided her with the courage she needed to make her next move. She became aware of herself shivering again as the temperature continued to drop. She realised that she wouldn't be able to withstand a night on the mountainside. She needed to get away, although she had no idea where she was, or what she would do even if she made it off the mountain.

Nonetheless, after a quick prayer to her mother, Jasmine Robson decided to start moving in what seemed the only logical direction – downwards.

CHAPTER 66

Robson hesitated inside the entrance to Louise Hart's accommodation, holding the door behind him with one hand.

'Louise?'

He felt slightly foolish, having waited for a good minute to be invited inside the room of inmate A2514AA. He was intrigued by what he might discover inside the 'penthouse suite', complete with its own security chain, but even those who held the most cynical views about the effectiveness of HMP's correctional facilities might have been stunned by the sight that confronted DCI Robson as he finally entered the room.

He forced himself to ignore the extraordinary comfort of his surroundings and focussed on his immediate priority of locating the inhabitant. Louise Hart was obviously in an obnoxious mood, having refused to allow Lyons inside. Now, apparently, Robson had been left to navigate his own way in.

'Hello … Louise … Is it okay to come in? It's Jack … I'm alone …'

A female voice came from another room.

'I'll be there in a moment, Jack. Just make yourself at home. Have a seat.'

Having satisfied himself that he was there by invitation, Robson relaxed and began to study the room again. A three-piece sofa suite grabbed his attention, and he shook his head as he took in the large, flat-screen television on the wall. He walked across to the entrance of a short corridor. The nearest door was ajar, revealing a small but modern kitchenette. Robson was astounded to discover that a prisoner had been provided the benefit of self-catering facilities. He decided to postpone his exploration and returned to the main living area.

'You clearly have some influence around here, Louise!' he shouted, while lowering himself into the armchair facing the entertainment system on the wall.

A further silent minute passed while he took in the comfortable facilities, until the sudden proximity of his host's voice made him jump.

'It's what you get for being a good girl, Jack.'

Robson rose from the soft armchair, partly out of instinctive chivalry, but partly in an awkward attempt to cover his embarrassment. He swallowed hard at the sight of the delicate figure gliding past him. The dungaree-wearing gardener from a few days ago had now swapped her muddy workwear for black lace. The nightdress she wore barely covered her behind as she passed unnecessarily close to him. She stopped to deliver a peck on his cheek, before sitting next to him, close enough to touch thighs. Aware of the nearness of those shapely legs to his, Robson decided to begin their conversation immediately.

'How have you been, Louise?'

'Really good, thank you, Jack. How about you? You certainly look well.'

As Robson inhaled more perfume-infused air, he judged that there seemed to be a little more than harmless mischief behind those twinkling eyes. In fact, to Robson, she seemed to be away with the fairies.

'Thank you for seeing me, Louise—'

'It's Loo, Jack, to you.'

'Thank you, Loo. I was hoping to ask you a few more questions, just to follow up on our chat the other day. Would that be okay? It shouldn't take long.'

'Oh, there's no rush, Jack. Can I get you a drink?'

As she rose, the hem of the skimpy nightie ruffled tantalisingly, only just covering her dignity. Robson watched wide-eyed as she walked towards the entertainment system. He noticed the small drinks cabinet for the first time and, astounded, realised that she wasn't offering coffee.

'I'm fine, thanks all the same, Loo.'

'Oh, go on, Chief Inspector. I always find it's easier to exchange information if one is able to loosen up first, don't you?'

She winked at Robson, allowing him to consider the transaction, before turning her attention to the small cabinet and pouring from an already-opened bottle of red wine. Robson observed that Hart seemed to move with such effortless grace as she glided towards him carrying a couple of filled wine glasses. She delicately handed one of the crystal glasses to Robson, before resuming her previous position on the sofa. He decided to play along for now, tilting his glass to let the warm red liquid touch his top lip and holding Louise's gaze as she also drank, while she held the stem of the glass delicately between her thumb and two fingers.

'Do you get many visitors these days, Louise?'

Hart's coquettish grin remained as she shook her head.

'Alas not, Jack. I'm a very lonely girl.'

'What about your sister?'

Robson watched carefully for a reaction.

'I haven't seen her in a long time actually, but why do you ask?'

'I just wondered really. I understood that she used to be a regular visitor of yours. What was her name again?'

'Melissa.'

'Yes, that was it. Do you know where Melissa is living now?'

She shook her head again, but this time the smile had faded.

'She doesn't share anything regarding her life with me these days, Jack.'

'Oh? Why would that be?'

'We fell out. Some years back. That is why she stopped visiting me, I guess. She just doesn't make any contact whatsoever.'

'That seems a shame. Can I ask what the disagreement was?'

'I'd rather not talk about that now. Family stuff that I'd rather forget.'

The statement confirmed what Robson had already seen in her eyes. *We'll come back to this, Louise.*

'Fair enough,' he responded nonchalantly, as he pulled a folded piece of paper from the inside of his jacket.

'So, Louise. I wanted to ask you a little more about your involvement in Arcam and I'd also like to find out what you know about Jacob Miller.'

'Okay, Jack. Why don't you *try* me?'

Robson coughed before continuing, ignoring the subtle innuendo.

'Forgive me for going over old ground – but are you certain that you haven't had any contact with Miller since the court case?'

'That is correct.'

The silk negligee rose a little further as she crossed her right leg over her left. Robson had to admire the woman's youthful figure. She must have been ten years his senior, but prison life seemed to have reversed the aging process in Louise Hart's case. He looked around the room again. It seemed that her easy prison-life had contributed to her apparent well-being. Although, judging by the increasingly vacant twinkle in her eyes, he began to wonder if her mental health matched her physical appearance.

'We found some information relating to you recently, in the course of our enquiries.'

He handed the paperwork to her. Hart uncrossed her slim legs, balancing the wine glass carefully while accepting the documentation in her other hand. She examined the photocopied invoice. Moments passed while she studied the proof of sale.

'Does that invoice look familiar, Loo?'

Robson watched a hint of confusion pass across her face.

'Why, yes. It was quite a while ago, but of course I remember. It was for the purchase of a boat, as you can see. Where did you get this?'

Robson noticed that, despite appearing somewhat inebriated, she didn't slur her words. She appeared to be more spaced out than drunk.

'We found it among the files at the Ship Inn, at Porlock Weir.'

'Oh, really?'

'Any idea why it would have been there, Louise?'

'No.'

'Where is the boat kept moored up these days?'

Her shoulders rose inside the delicate silk.

'How should I know, Jack?'

'You don't know?'

'I've been inside for eight years, Jack. And I'm going to be in here for a long while yet. I have no interest in keeping tabs on property that I don't even own any longer.'

'Oh … so, you've sold the boat?'

'I honestly don't remember. Why is this so important, Jack?'

'Because the boat was recently used in a crime.'

'Really?!'

As far as Robson could tell, she seemed genuinely shocked.

'I could really do with some help here, Louise.'

Louise Hart rose, placing her glass on the coffee table before her.

Robson noticed the pristinely painted toenails at the end of her bare feet. She wandered to the other side of the room, then stopped with her back to him. Her hands rested on the curve of her hips as she replied.

'And what makes you think I can help you, DCI Robson?'

Robson stood up. It seemed more appropriate for him to be level with her. He knew well that eye contact was key to any negotiation.

'Louise, your boat – or *ex-boat* – has been used to escort an escaped prisoner off the North Somerset coast. The person who had been in possession of the invoice from your original purchase was found with his skull caved in, in his own office, not long after the boat was used to carry the escaped convict away. The same convict was supposed to be serving time for being a part of an organisation that had been intent on creating genocide. The same organisation that you, yourself, were a part of Louise. Indeed, the same organisation that you now claim to loathe, isn't that right?'

Robson replaced his glass on the table and turned to his right on hearing a click. Louise faced him now. Her smirk had morphed into something more alarming, more menacing. In her hand, she held a key that she had extracted from the cell door, having apparently locked them both inside.

Robson watched her silently.

Hart, too, remained silent as she began to approach him slowly, maintaining a peculiar stare with her now crazy-looking eyes. As her hand disappeared inside the parting in her nightie, Robson prepared himself to respond at the first sign of a weapon. The weapon that was suddenly revealed was not what he had expected. So much so that it took several seconds for him to process the situation. He looked down at Louise's feet, which were now wrapped in the silk negligee that had slid down her body.

He momentarily lost control of his gaze as it climbed upwards over her naked body. He swallowed hard and realised that his actions had already betrayed his feelings. Hart watched him, smiling confidently, and looking entirely satisfied with herself.

This woman has really looked after herself.

'My memory just isn't what it was, Jack. I think it's down to my monotonous existence inside these walls ... perhaps it would help me remember if something exciting were to happen? You know, something to stir my adrenaline ...'

Robson realised that speaking might be his only defence, but he found himself lost for words. He abandoned his thought process and opened his mouth to speak, not knowing himself what he was about to say.

'Louise. I don't think this is appropriate. I really think you ought to get dressed.'

She displayed a teasing smile, and Robson suppressed a shudder as she approached him. Up close, it looked to him as though she were about to feast on some indefensible, cornered prey.

'Okay. This has gone far enough, Louise. I think I'd better leave.'

With only millimetres between their noses, he felt her warm breath on his face. Then, warmth of a different kind presented itself on his hand, as she began to guide herself up and down, in a slow but firm motion.

'DCI Robson, you're going nowhere. Not until I've had you.'

CHAPTER 67

Connor deposited his room key in the slot provided at the reception desk and slipped out of the tiny, shabby foyer unnoticed. Outside in the narrow side-street the air felt cool, which was unsurprising given the relatively early hour. After the sour, musty atmosphere of the cheap city hotel, the fresh breeze felt pleasant on his face. His stubble had already turned to dark, short whiskers but he had no intention of shaving. The further from his normal appearance he could look, the better. More importantly, the next passport identity he intended to use required him to sport a beard.

He had been careful to avoid checking into a hotel with a staffed reception to minimise the number of people he would have to come face-to-face with. Therefore, the automated two-star facility had been a godsend, given that the only interaction necessary had been between the hotel's computerised, self-service check-in point and the bank card for one of his alias accounts.

In the distance, the faint rumble of vehicles and human voices indicated that the cafes, restaurants, and shops were about to open for another day of trading in the historic marketplace. Despite the distant hustle and bustle, the narrow alley he stepped out into from the hotel seemed to be entirely deserted.

A minute later, he approached the junction to a slightly wider road. He peered along the street on his left. At a glance, it seemed the same as it had late the previous evening: parked cars on both sides stretched out along its entirety, leaving just enough room for a vehicle of average size to pass between them.

Satisfied by the scene before him, he turned into the wider street and walked on until he saw the innocuous-looking Volkswagen Golf – one of several vehicles of the same make and model parked along the street – while keeping a cautious eye on his surroundings.

Before he reached the dark hatchback for which he had paid an inflated price, in cash, the previous evening, he noted a young couple in a vehicle some fifty yards away. Connor pretended not to notice the man and woman, who both appeared to be in their early to mid-thirties. They sat together in a silver BMW, talking, but not appearing to be in any rush to go anywhere. The attractive young couple seemed too wrapped up in one another to notice him approaching.

Being careful not to pay any special attention to it, Connor passed the Golf he had purchased without stopping, before slowing as he arrived at another, a few cars further along. He stopped at the random vehicle and pretended to fumble for keys in the pockets of his lightweight jacket. After putting on a show of frustration, he turned and began jogging back along the road to give the impression to anyone watching that he was returning to retrieve his misplaced car keys. At the end of the street, he darted right, briefly heading back towards the hotel, before doubling back behind a parked van. Connor sprinted to the end of the alley and tucked himself out of sight around the corner.

Moments later, he withdrew a phone from his jacket and deftly activated the camera's 'selfie' mode. Pretending to hold the phone aloft as though attempting to gain a signal, he watched the BMW carrying the young couple crawl into the alley and head away from him towards the hotel. Connor replaced the phone in his pocket, before taking in his new, unplanned surroundings.

He found himself in a large, sparsely populated area, which continued in a wide street that stretched some distance ahead. The surrounding gothic-style arches told him he was in the market square – the Prinzipalmarkt. He visualised the street map of the area which he had committed to memory the previous evening while lying on the single bed in his box-like hotel room.

As he planned an alternative route to his car, the distant sound of screeching tyres grabbed his attention, like an animal suddenly sensing a predator was nearby. He held his phone out to peer around the corner again. The silver BMW was moving towards him. The female passenger had got out for some reason and now ran alongside the vehicle.

Instantly, Connor turned on his heels and sprinted towards the shopping quarter in search of crowds.

*

Wilson picked up her pace as soon as she spotted Connor disappearing into the square. By the time she reached the main street, he had disappeared. *Damn! We should have moved sooner!*

The volume of shoppers was still thin at such an early hour, allowing her a view as far as Drubbel Square. She watched for any conspicuous movement but saw nothing apart from a few people milling around casually, ambling between the arched entrances to the shops. Cafe workers were putting the finishing touches to their attractive outdoor seating areas, ensuring tables were equipped with cutlery and that all parasols were erected. She spoke into the microphone attached to her coat lapel.

'Stavros here. I've lost visual. Target has possibly entered one of the stores or cafes. We're going to need cover on both rear sides – west and east. I'm on the main street.'

The responses came into her earpiece immediately.

'Roger, Stavros. Echo 1 is complete, currently covering west.'

'Echo 2 heading towards the eastern flank now.'

Wilson leant into the microphone again as she walked, still slightly breathless from running.

'Be as quick as you can, Echo 2. Echo 1, since you're already in position, please coordinate the local plods. Make sure they are clear about the target's identity and get them in the shops as soon as you can.'

'Yes, ma'am.'

As she reached the early morning shadow cast by the ornate church spire, Wilson eyed the sergeant of the Munster police force. The man's broad moustache bristled as he barked commands to his team, dispatching his officers into as many storefronts as they could cover simultaneously. The

British officers seemed to appear from nowhere as she arrived at the church, now at the northern end of Prinzipalmarkt street.

'Split,' she commanded.

The officers immediately divided into three groups and began to cast their net. Wilson paused, looking back along the street towards the bottom end. It was only a fleeting sighting, but she was certain it had been their target – only some thirty to forty yards away, discreetly slipping out of one store and into another, wearing his jacket collar as high as it would reach.

One of the German police teams had noticed Wilson sprinting and joined her as she reached the shop entrance. A dark-haired man with a short beard turned as she reached out, looking somewhat alarmed as he felt a hand grip his shoulder.

'Excuse me, sir …'

Wilson held her hand up as a signal to the officers behind, who she knew had come to join her, before addressing the man at the shirt rack.

'I'm sorry, sir, I have the wrong person. Forgive me.'

'No problem, madam,' came the response, in perfectly spoken English, albeit with an unmistakably German accent.

She spoke into her discreet microphone again as they burst out of the store.

'Echo 1, Echo 2 – any joy?'

'Echo 1 – nothing to report.'

'Echo 2 – nothing yet, ma'am. We're closing in.'

'Shit! We're running out of time!'

CHAPTER 68

Robson remained frozen to the spot for several moments. He was torn between following the sobs coming from the bathroom or simply taking the opportunity to make a dash for it, and so evading a potentially damaging situation. But he needed information.

He bent over and picked up the door key from the floor where Louise had thrown it as she ran from him, seemingly unable to deal with his rejection. Robson imagined the prison officials were probably not quite so difficult for her to seduce.

He stopped in the doorway of the modern bathroom and tried to avert his eyes, while at the same time checking that she was okay. The sobbing had stopped, and the naked inmate was kneeling at the toilet. At first Robson thought she had been vomiting, but he now noted that the toilet seat was closed, and realised it sounded more like hard snorting than vomiting. The mess of white powder next to the sink confirmed his suspicions.

'Louise ...'

'Are you still here, DCI Robson?' she hissed.

'Louise. Can we just talk?'

'Chief Inspector, if you know what's good for you, you'll get the fuck out of here right now.'

She leant back over the toilet, resuming her indulgence. Robson fetched the towelled gown from the hook on the back of the door and walked the short distance to the toilet basin.

'Here.'

He dropped the pure white garment on to her back, covering her dignity. Louise Hart turned as she spoke.

'Do I disgust you that much, Jack?'

Robson saw that her eyes were bloodshot. Mascara had run down her moist cheeks and a little saliva escaped her mouth as she spoke.

'You don't disgust me at all, Louise. I'm a police officer, on duty. Be realistic.'

She let out a sardonic chuckle.

'I haven't got any information.'

She stumbled as she stood, wrapping the large, luxurious towelled robe around her. She smacked Robson's arm away almost as soon as he offered it.

'Quite the gentleman, eh, Jack?'

Her voice sounded full of bitterness.

'Can I make you a brew?'

'Fuck off, Jack.'

She suddenly toppled, as though she had been taken out by a sniper. Robson winced as her head hit the side of the bath and she slumped awkwardly across the floor. His immediate instinct was to check for a pulse so he rushed over to her and held her slim wrist between his thumb and two fingers. He felt relieved to detect a beat, albeit a rather slow one.

He grunted as he extended his thigh muscles and cradled the unconscious body while he began to walk towards an open door which he hoped would lead to a bedroom. The towel had fallen open and dragged along the floor as he carried the comatose woman. He looked away from her naked body, feeling awkward despite being the only conscious person in the room. Inside the bedroom, he let her down gently on the double bed and checked her pulse again once he had restored her dignity.

Then Robson set to work.

CHAPTER 69

The slight man peered over the top of his half-moon spectacles as he hurried across to the changing rooms to attend to the gentleman now exiting one of the booths.

'How is the fit, sir?'

The tailor spoke in good English. Even though his patron had spoken in flawless German ever since entering the specialist fitters, he had judged the origin of his customer. The little man could always tell these things – he had spent his entire career observing people. However, the confident man seemed irked by the tailor's decision, apparently preferring to speak in the native Munster tongue.

'Perfect. I'm going to keep them on, if you don't mind,' replied the customer continuing to speak in perfect German. 'I have a meeting to attend right away.'

'Of course, sir. Please, if you will be so kind as to come to the till with me.'

The diminutive German tailor had reverted to his native tongue, privately admiring the debonair look the gentleman carried as he adorned his new suit, despite sporting a short, slightly scruffy beard.

'Here, keep the change,' said the bearded man. 'Sorry, I'm in a rush.'

The man adjusted his small spectacles as he beheld the generous wad of notes in his hand, which clearly exceeded the cost of the clothing and shoes that his customer had bought. The frown on his face grew as he realised the man had not taken the clothes he had been wearing when he entered the store.

He dashed to the changing cubicle to confirm, then shrugged his shoulders. He addressed the young girl on his way back to the cash register.

'Angela, please tidy up the clothing in dressing room two.'

'Of course, Sebastien. Which section are they from?'

'None. Put them in the charity bag.'

Sebastien left the girl looking confused, as he carefully counted the cash in his hand. After pocketing the excess, he made his way to complete the transaction at the till – for a suit, shirt and tie, plus dress shoes. The flat cap was an unusual addition to the ensemble, but who was he to judge?

*

The prison governor rose as his guests were escorted in by one of the guards.

'Officers, please have a seat.'

'Thank you for agreeing to see us at such short notice, Governor Morrison.'

'Not at all, DCI Robson. I am sorry about Louise. She has been taken to the infirmary. No doubt they will have her back to normal in no time. I'm sure it is nothing too serious.'

Robson raised an eyebrow at the governor's nonchalant tone. It was as if he was implying that Hart had been a victim of nature, rather than suffering the self-inflicted consequences of stoned face on drugs.

Morrison nodded to the prison guard.

'Thank you, Watkins, that will be all. Please let me know as soon as there is any update on Hart's condition.'

'Sir.'

The guard nodded at Robson and Lyons as he closed the office door, leaving them inside with the governor.

'So, how can I help you with your enquiries, officers?'

'Governor,' Robson responded, 'I'll come straight to the point. We'd like to understand how Miss Hart has come to be rewarded with such extraordinary accommodation. How long has she been in such a luxurious room?'

Morrison rested his chin on his steepled fingers, his face expressionless.

'I think we moved her in only this year, as it happens.'

'I see. And is it normal protocol?'

'Is what normal protocol?'

'Governor Morrison, I am no expert on the prison system, but from what I understand, the accommodation that Miss Hart currently resides in is not commonplace. Would this be correct?'

Lyons shifted uncomfortably in his seat.

'I guess that would be a reasonable generalisation, DCI Robson, yes.'

'Who authorised Hart's "upgrade"?'

Morrison's brow furrowed.

'Who authorised it? I am the governor of this facility. The responsibility ultimately lies with me. But the decision to relocate her was the result of a joint decision with the parole board. It was viewed as a positive step in her rehabilitation programme, given that she is close to a potential release date.'

'Sorry … I wasn't aware. She had been given a release date?'

'Not a date, DCI Robson, no. But her progress and recent communication with the board has given us a strong indication that it probably will not be too far away. I believe she was awaiting a hearing date.'

'I see.'

'I'm sorry officers, will that be all? I do have another appointment.'

'Sure, we are sorry for taking up your valuable time at such short notice. Just one final question if I may. Were you aware that Louise Hart had access to class A drugs?'

Morrison's face became unreadable as he leant back in his chair.

'DCI Robson, like every prison up and down the country, we do our very best to prevent unauthorised goods and substances coming into our facility, but we cannot catch everything.'

'Understood. But were you aware that Miss Hart had access?'

'No.'

'Will Miss Hart be tested?'

'We will be guided by the medical staff as to any procedures or testing Miss Hart may require. Now, if you will excuse me, officers.'

Robson remained seated as Morrison rose from his desk. As he approached the door it was DC Lyons that spoke for the first time during the meeting.

'Governor … who was the previous inhabitant of Miss Hart's new room?'

Morrison pulled the office door open as he answered.

'I don't recall, Constable. But if you would like to get in contact with a member of staff, I'm sure we can get that information to you – if it is relevant to your enquiries.'

Robson extended his right hand as they left.

'Thank you, Governor Morrison. You have been most helpful.'

CHAPTER 70

The British Secret Intelligence officer flew across the mall and past the boutique tailor's, in response to Wilson's command. Several shoppers gingerly stepped out of his path as he raced past them. Some of them, disgruntled, appeared shocked at the thoughtless man careering through the public area, but most shook their heads in disapproval – except the smart, suited gent who did not seem phased at all, even tipping his flat cap to the MI5 man.

As the rest of the bystanders resumed their window-shopping while discussing the incident, the bearded gentleman in the cap walked out into the main square, whistling the tune of *Deutschlandlied*.

CHAPTER 71

The incident room had fallen silent to listen to DCI Robson's update. Robson was in his familiar position at the front of the room, with his office manager and senior detective, DI Matthews, alongside him.

'Both of these plans were found at the Ship Inn's office, buried amongst reams of paperwork. Both represent accurate, up-to-date plans of two operational prisons – HMP Belmarsh and HMP/YOI East Sutton Park.'

With his thumb, Robson indicated the drawings pinned to the wall behind him. He knew the prison names would grab his officers' attention.

'You will not need me to highlight the relevance of this material. Belmarsh is the facility where Jacob Miller was being detained prior to the transfer that went wrong. Sutton Park is the facility at which Louise Hart currently resides.'

Robson sensed DI Matthews alongside him and paused to allow him to speak.

'Sir, do you think they were planning to break out?'

Robson shrugged.

'We must assume that was a possibility. However, Louise Hart is still an inmate – if that is the correct term, given her somewhat privileged surroundings. And, as we all know, Miller managed to engineer a different kind of escape to that of breaching the walls. But in answer to your question – I don't know. Could be a coincidence.'

The room stirred with ironic murmurs, interrupted by a loud voice from the back of the room.

'Sir, with respect, surely not?'

DC Jenkins leant back and stretched out his legs. Robson folded his arms.

'Miller didn't escape from Belmarsh. He escaped from a bloody van.'

'And Hart hasn't escaped—' added Matthews.

'Yet,' said Robson.

The murmuring rose again. Directly in front of Robson, DS Simpson crossed her legs and adjusted the position of her notepad.

'Sir, what do you propose to do?'

'I propose to find out who acquired such detailed plans, Mary,' Robson responded. 'And to start with, I want you to get up to Sutton Park to see Louise Hart. Take DC Lyons. Louise likes to see a familiar face.'

Lyons forced a grin, as DCI Robson continued.

'A further, somewhat contradictory element worthy of note is the fact that, according to the Sutton Park Governor, they were expecting Hart to be granted parole sometime soon.'

The officers exchanged more confused looks.

'I want you to take the plans and confront her. Speak to Governor Morrison first and request an immediate appointment. And demand they ensure she's clean when we arrive. No cosy meetings in the garden or in her room. Get her into an interview room this time. Understood?'

'Yes, sir.'

DS Simpson immediately rose to get to work. Robson continued.

'I have also gained authority for a drugs test to be carried out on Hart, so you will be accompanied by a forensic medical examiner. And just one more thing before you go – Simpson, Lyons. As you know, I had the privilege of being in Ms Hart's company yesterday.'

He waited for the sniggering to die down.

'I took the liberty of carrying out a brief search of her room while she took a nap in her bedroom. It didn't turn up anything of interest, apart from this.'

Robson handed a slip of paper to Simpson. He waited for signs of recognition as she studied the details scribbled on the sheet.

'Sir – it appears to be a list of contact details.'

Robson nodded.

'Read them out, would you?'

Simpson cleared her throat, before proceeding.

'Dennis Teasdale. 0740—'

'Just the names will do, Mary,' Robson interjected, 'the telephone numbers won't be necessary.'

'Sir ... Tristan Cumberwell. Jacob Miller. Louise (Sis). Alberto Romano. Carlos Fernandez. Jack Robson ...'

Robson watched the faces of the silent officers.

'Any ideas, people?'

After several silent seconds, Simpson spoke.

'Sir. Does Hart have another sister with the same name, Louise?'

'Not as far as we know,' Robson responded.

'More to the point,' Burford intervened, 'what the hell is she doing with access to a telephone inside?'

'We don't know that she has, DS Burford,' Robson said.

At the front of the room, DI Matthews looked stunned. Robson knew that he would have recognised one name in particular.

'Sir – Alberto Romano? As in, Professor Alberto Romano?'

Robson remained impassive.

'It would seem so.'

Matthews sat down, appearing to take stock of the implications. As the others in the room caught up, Robson continued.

'Matthews. I think that brings us neatly on to your recent research – into Professor Romano.'

Robson stood aside slightly to allow DI Matthews to take centre stage. Matthews nodded to his DCI as he stood at the front and pointed at a large photograph of an elderly, grey-bearded man.

'Okay. As you are all aware, Professor Romano is a physicist who specialises in atmospheric studies. In simple terms, he's into the weather – a renowned meteorological expert. As reported at an earlier briefing, he works at the High-frequency Active Auroral Research Program, or HAARP, as it is known, which is based in Gakona, Alaska. We know that Professor Romano has visited Miller in prison, albeit several years ago. We also know that the professor left work over two weeks ago, supposedly to go on a ten-day holiday, but he has not returned, even though he was expected back a few days ago.'

'Has anyone heard from him?' Lyons queried.

Matthews shook his head.

'Bearing in mind that, essentially, he works for the American military, it has been very painful, to say the least, trying to get anything from them. The best they could offer was that they would contact us when they hear from him. Other than that, they refused to give us any further details. So, we found out a bit more for ourselves.'

The room waited patiently as Matthews got into full flow.

'We spoke to one of Romano's colleagues at HAARP – Doctor Jilly Stevenson. She told us that Professor Romano hadn't seemed himself for a while—'

'What does that mean, exactly,' interrupted DS Burford.

'Apparently, he never was much of a social animal and was pretty much devoted to his work. But – according to Doctor Stevenson, who considers herself to be a friend as well as a colleague – the professor had become something of a recluse over the past few months.'

'Did she know where he was supposed to be going on holiday?'

'That's something else that is peculiar, actually. He had been a little cagey about it, according to Stevenson. A few weeks ago, after a degree of prying, she managed to get his intended destination from him – Venice, Italy. Apparently, Romano was somewhat reluctant to talk about it. Doctor Stevenson left it eventually, as it was clear the conversation had been bothering him.'

'Perhaps he simply doesn't like discussing his private life.'

'Perhaps, sir.'

'Do we know if he has returned from Venice?' Robson asked.

'He didn't go, sir.'

'Pardon?'

'He didn't go to Venice, sir – we've checked with passport control. Some forty-eight hours after leaving work a couple of weeks ago, he flew into Heathrow. The same day, he flew from London to Cardiff, and then picked up a hire car.'

'Where did he go?'

'We don't know yet, sir. He rented the car for four weeks.'

Robson nodded pensively and looked around the room at the detectives' faces.

'Okay, before I let you all get back to your investigations, I have one final bit of information for you. As you all know, we've been examining the visiting records for Belmarsh over the last eight years, to check who Miller's visitors have been. We already know that the professor, somewhat peculiarly, visited Jacob Miller only once, as far as we are aware. The only other visitor was Miller's lawyer, who had been working tirelessly for his declassification almost from his first days inside. Apart from that, it seems Miller didn't court friendship. We have been trying to track the lawyer down, but he is no longer with the partnership, and has recently relocated to the United States, it is reported. We're working on finding him.'

'Sir, is it really worth the effort?'

DC Lyons immediately felt embarrassed by his own crassness and looked sheepishly at his DCI – Jack Robson, possibly the most thorough CID detective any of them had ever met. Robson stared at his detective constable for a moment, before addressing the entire room.

'The lawyer's name is Tristan Cumberwell.'

He waited. Matthews was first to pick up on the name.

'Sir – as in, one of the names on Louise Hart's list of contacts?'

Robson nodded.

'It would seem so, Inspector. The very same.'

Robson allowed the excited murmurs to die down before continuing.

'We have done a little bit of digging into the lawyer's background. It's pretty bland to be fair, but there is a lot more research to do,' he looked pointedly at DC Saunders, who smiled in understanding.

'But there is one detail that, I'm sure you'll agree, is rather interesting. Mr

Cumberwell has recently completed the purchase of a property in the UK. He has sold his luxury apartment in central London and has just bought a small cottage in Snowdonia, North Wales. Which is interesting, since, as far as his ex-employer is concerned, he had emigrated to America.'

'Perhaps he just wants to retain a base over here, sir?' DS Simpson mused.

'Really?' Matthews said. 'In the middle of nowhere? It doesn't exactly lend itself to convenient commuting, does it?'

Matthews pushed his spectacles up on to the bridge of his nose.

'Precisely, Matthews,' said Robson.

'Hang on a moment,' DS Burford spoke. 'Is his new base anywhere near the location where the sunken seaplane was discovered?'

Robson felt pleased at the sergeant's recognition.

'Now we're getting somewhere, thank you, Burford. DI Matthews – I want you to pay a visit to Snowdonia. Let's get a look at this cottage, perhaps we might find something, or someone, of interest there. Contact the local bobbies first and let them know in case they have any useful intelligence before we get started.

'Yes, sir.'

'Sergeant Burford,' Robson continued, 'I want you and DC Jenkins to pay another visit to the house near Webber's Post. Forensics are done, so let's get in and have another nose around, eh?'

'Will do, sir,' Burford spoke from the back of the room, as Jenkins nodded alongside her in his typical military pose, arms behind his back and chest out.

The mention of the house where, evidently, Jasmine had been held, reminded everyone in the room that DCI Robson had troubles of his own – personal worries that would render most people too paralysed to think. They knew Robson was extraordinary, but the room suddenly fell into awkward silence, each wanting someone else to ask the question they were all thinking. Robson observed his team's discomfort and decided to rescue them.

'So far, the only item of interest from Grayson's investigation has been Jasmine's hoodie. The superintendent has agreed to allow us to take a look just in case there is a crossover between the two investigations. We have to remain open-minded.'

One or two of his officers still did not seem to want to make eye contact, as Robson continued.

'We have also got a DNA match for the survivor in the woods – Martin Hudson. Mr Hudson remains in hospital and is still in a critical condition, apparently showing no signs of recovery yet. There is every chance that it will never be possible to interview him. Given the links that are forming, I want to get in there and take the place apart.'

Robson watched the officers in the room shuffle awkwardly.

'It's okay, I know what you're thinking. Conflicting responsibilities, right? To put your minds at rest, Superintendent Grayson is fully aware of my proposal and has agreed that we cannot rule out a potential link between the two cases. In fact, it seems to be growing ever more likely by the day, wouldn't you all agree?'

CHAPTER 72

As DS Burford studied the map on her phone, the boss's instructions still echoed in her mind. DCI Robson had said to be thorough, and that they had. Typically, Burford had made sure of it, diligently discharging her commanding officer's orders.

She had scolded DC Jenkins earlier, for nearly dismissing what appeared to be an innocuous-looking slip of paper. The postcode represented a rather remote-looking area according to his map. It summoned up an unavoidable parallel with a previous investigation eight years earlier – the now historical case which seemed to be growing in relevance as the current investigation progressed. It could have been just a coincidence, but Burford knew that her DCI didn't believe in such things.

At first, Robson's reaction had seemed a little odd when Jenkins rang in the information moments earlier. But the DCI seemed to become more interested in the postcode as their conversation proceeded. It seemed possible that Robson was going to consider extending the boundaries of their enquiries. That would suit me, Jenkins thought, still studying the map. *Could be worse places to visit.*

The stolid constable suddenly became aware of the relevance of the location and chided himself for his own insensitivity, now realising the dark significance the newly extended area of investigation held for his DCI. *Snowdonia ... shit!*

DS Burford interrupted Jenkins' thoughts.

'Jenkins, looks like we have company.'

Jenkins lifted his head to look at his sergeant. She wore her usual serious countenance as she stood perfectly upright looking out of the living room window of the seemingly deserted property. As Jenkins approached the window, he watched a blue four-by-four stop abruptly, as though the driver had been discouraged by the sight of the small, uniformed police presence at the front of the property.

'Come on,' Burford spoke hurriedly, and they both rushed out of the front door.

As they arrived to join the uniformed officers at the front gate, the blue Land Rover had already turned around and was now skidding away from them.

'Did you get the VRN?' Burford asked the two constables.

'Too far away, Sergeant,' one of them answered.

'Then get after them, will you!'

'Ma'am, we're supposed to—'

'Constable, I don't fucking well care what you're supposed to be doing. I'm telling you to get after that car. And woe betide if you lose them! Understood?'

'Yes, Sergeant.'

Both constables jogged the short distance to the police Land Rover, and blue lights began to flash as they sped away from the house, but the blue four-by-four had already disappeared.

*

Pierre Marchand adjusted his round-rimmed glasses with a thumb and forefinger. With the other hand, he gripped the wheel tightly as he guided the blue Land Rover off the moorland, the vehicle leaping on to the narrow access road. Inside the vehicle, Mark Connor's voice resounded through the car speakers.

'We need to make this quick, Pierre. We'll only have a minute, tops, before they triangulate the signal.'

'Of course. We have a problem, boss. I've just been to the house – there were police there.'

'Shit. Which house?'

'Webber's Post.'

Marchand listened to Connor's deep breathing, waiting for a response.

'Have you had any contact with either Hudson or Morris?'

'No. Both their phones are dead and have been ever since we departed the ferry at Plymouth.'

'Fuck it. Listen, did anyone see you?'

'Yes, I'm currently in the process of losing them.'

'Do you think they got your number plate?'

'Probably not. I didn't get nearer than a hundred yards from the house.'

'Change the car as soon as you can and go straight to the other safe house. Send me a message when you arrive. It'll take a while for me to respond as this is going back offline, but if I can get hold of a burner phone in the meantime I will get the details to you.'

The car phone went dead before Marchand could respond.

Inside the modified boot of the Land Rover, a blonde woman in her thirties began to awaken, encouraged from her stupor by the way in which the vehicle bounced on its suspension. From her lying position, she was unable to get any sense of bearing looking through the large rear window, but Sarah Connor was certain she could hear a siren in the distance.

CHAPTER 73

Mud sprayed from the spinning tyres as the police four-by-four climbed out of the shallow valley. The blue Land Rover had almost disappeared again, but they caught a glimpse of its tail end every now and again – just enough to register most of the number plate. PC Bryant bounced around in the passenger seat as he communicated with the control room.

'Blue four-by-four, French plates. Last two letters – X-ray Delta. Driver appears to be male – IC1, average build. No passengers. We are in pursuit, currently heading south from Webber's post, Exmoor. The occupant arrived at the house and appeared to flee when he noticed us.'

The control room inspector responded.

'Roger, Foxtrot one. Is the suspect believed to be armed?'

'Negative, control, not at this stage.'

'Continue with your pursuit, Foxtrot one. We are dispatching a response vehicle and your progress is being tracked, please keep us updated.'

'Affirmative, control. Subject vehicle has just turned left – left on to Mill Lane, travelling at approximately eighty miles per hour.'

Alongside PC Bryant, PC Gardener remained unemotional and focussed on his target. Seconds after the blue four-by-four had veered from view, the police Land Rover was expertly manoeuvred on to the same course. The narrow road straightened as they rounded a corner, giving a good half mile of visibility. Both officers looked on in astonishment as they observed that the route ahead was devoid of any other vehicle.

'Shit!' PC Bryant hissed, before raising the radio to his mouth again.

'Control, this is Foxtrot one.'

'Go ahead, Foxtrot one.'

'We have lost visual. How's our support coming along?'

'Roger, Foxtrot one. Your support vehicle is still approximately ten minutes away. Airborne support can be dispatched within five.'

PC Gardener suddenly slammed his right foot down hard, causing the Land Rover to screech to a halt. Bryant looked across at his colleague, wide-eyed, as the police vehicle's tyres screeched again before the vehicle began to race backwards along the narrow road.

'What are you—'

Bryant suddenly noticed the opening to the field which they had flown past seconds earlier. He was quietly impressed by his colleague's awareness.

As they left the road, evidence of a former gated entrance laid either side of their vehicle. Both officers bounced inside as the car rumbled through a waterlogged ditch. Gardener began to manoeuvre through the gears, and the vehicle's powerful torque could be felt as they raced across the overgrown field. In the distance up ahead, a blue four-by-four was nearing the wooded perimeter of the meadow.

'Control, Foxtrot one has visual again. Requesting immediate airborne assistance.'

*

Sarah Connor continued to slowly regain consciousness.

The ride had become noticeably rougher, but perhaps that was down to her growing awareness, she thought. She began to sense that her carriage appeared to be travelling at high speed across some particularly rough ground. Her vision moved in and out of focus as she tried to take in her immediate surroundings. Someone, it seemed, had taken care to ensure that she would be comfortable in the large boot, having laid her out on a mattress and surrounded her with pillows. The bindings around her wrists and ankles, however, were at odds with her soft bedding.

*

In the driving seat of the blue four-by-four, Marchand's alert little eyes flicked between the terrain ahead and the rear-view mirror. Seeing flashing blue lights in the distance behind him, he pressed his right foot down as far as it would go. Connor had given clear instructions.

Do not get caught – at any cost.

CHAPTER 74

Inmate A2514AA inhaled another neat little line of white powder from the side of the bath. She let her head drop back and slid down into the hot water, semi-consciously enjoying the liquid warmth on her slender shoulders. An empty pill container fell from the corner of the bathtub, and her naked body jerked as it lost traction with the bottom of the tub. Bubbles began to rise to the surface as her face became immersed, leaving only the top of her head above the water.

The last fix of the evening had been enough to send her well on her way and, as she had hoped, the lethal cocktail of opiates would ensure she remained that way. Her supplier had been clear, her time had arrived. She understood that it was best to end it this way, totally numb and unable to feel any pain. The alternative intervention would not have been without pain, of that she was sure. In fact, her sister had as good as told her so.

The water continued to sway in reaction to her sunken body, but the last air bubbles had now disappeared from the surface.

*

Wilson eyed the driver inside the stationary Mercedes halfway along the growing queue of vehicles that were awaiting embarkation at the ferry port. She had to admire the man's stamina. It had only been twenty-four hours since he had managed to give them the slip at Munster, but he had already managed to cover five hundred miles to reach the northern tip of Denmark. But even

Mark Connor was not perfect. He had used his phone just long enough to allow them to triangulate the signal to within a few yards.

Even from several hundred yards away, Wilson could tell the commander of under-cover police was close to boiling point. He had been furious when Wilson, somewhat sternly, instructed him to allow the suspect to continue with his journey. She had explained that it was imperative that they were able to establish Connor's intended destination.

The radio crackled into life.

'Charlie-Nine-Zero has control of the target. Arkwright is one vehicle away from passport control. Standing by for further orders.'

'Roger, Charlie-Nine-Zero, you have control. I repeat my earlier command – do not intervene. Request radio silence until Arkwright has boarded the ferry.'

The fact that she already had a hunch about Connor's destination did not change a thing – she had to be sure. But finding Connor at Hirtshals had served to strengthen her suspicion. She noted her colleague shuffle in frustration alongside her.

'Are you sure we didn't ought to grab him now, ma'am? He has already shown his ability to elude us.'

Wilson merely shook her head, indicating that she had no intention of explaining herself again. The man rubbed his hands together as the icy breeze picked up, before trying a different tack.

'Why do you think he wants to head for Norway?'

She turned to face him, looking severe.

'What makes you think he's headed for Norway? That's the queue for the ferry to Iceland.'

'Iceland?! Why would he be going there?'

Wilson shrugged.

'Who knows? Perhaps that isn't his ultimate destination. Either way, we have him.'

*

Connor watched the Scandinavian woman in the passport control booth with interest. He knew from her excessively laid-back demeanour and from the way her eyes scanned the phony passport that his cover was blown. Yet his pursuers weren't on him and, instead, had chosen to remain at a distance for the time being. Which could only mean one thing – they wanted to know his destination.

He glanced in the wing-mirror and watched the unusual manoeuvre taking place four cars behind him. The stewards, in their high-visibility jackets, allowed the dark saloon with blacked-out windows into the queue.

Hello guys.

Connor smiled confidently at the pristine blonde as she stretched an arm out of the booth, releasing the aroma of cheap perfume into the car. He thanked her in French, stubbornly maintaining the façade, and took the passport from her. She, too, seemed to find the whole exchange rather comical, and politely spoke to him in his supposed native tongue.

'Voila, Monsieur Leblanc. Merci, et bon voyage!'

'Merci, madame.'

You're fooling no one, princess.

CHAPTER 75

A new voice crackled from the radio inside the police four-by-four. 'Foxtrot one, this is Whisky Five Zero, DCI Robson speaking. We are approximately two miles south-west of your current 20. Update your status please.'

Bryant held the radio to his mouth. 'Foxtrot one remains in pursuit. Sir, the subject vehicle has increased its lead.'

'Just ensure you keep him in sight. We're nearly with you, heading in from the east.'

'Roger Whisky Five Zero. We'll do our best, sir.'

'Come in, Control, this is Whisky Five Zero.'

'Control, go ahead DCI Robson.'

'Where is our air support, Control?'

Another voice echoed over the secure channel before the control room inspector could respond.

'This is X-Ray Alpha Nine Five. We're with you, Whisky Five Zero. We have you in our sights, DCI Robson.'

The occupants of both police vehicles looked up and, despite not being able to see one another, watched the same helicopter swoop into view over the roof of the forest.

'Foxtrot One - PC Bryant, stand by, your target has just turned east. There is a river crossing approximately three quarters of a mile between you both.

DCI Robson – if you can get to the crossing first, you should be in a position to block the suspect's course.'

'Whisky Five Zero. Roger that, X-Ray Alpha Nine Five,' responded Robson.

Alongside him, in the driving seat, DC Saunders pushed her right foot down and deftly whipped the steering wheel to swerve around a small truck. The vehicle's engine screamed as she took it to maximum revs.

*

Sarah Connor had no idea where she was, but she knew the car was travelling far too quickly for the terrain. The vehicle felt like it had left the ground momentarily after an especially fearsome bump. She screamed out as the hard landing made her smash her head against the metal interior, causing her to inadvertently bite her bottom lip. She began to panic as she recognised the voice of the driver cursing in French, as she sensed the car being suddenly manhandled on to a different course.

*

Aboard the MS Norrona, the suited gentleman stretched his long frame inside cabin 202, before removing his jacket. He removed his flat cap to reveal a dark military crop which matched the colour of his newly grown beard, and stood with his face pressed against the door, eyeing the comings and goings outside in the corridor. He watched the English couple giggling arm in arm outside his door, before finally disappearing out of the small viewing aperture's field of vision.

Connor smiled to himself as he heard the door of the adjacent cabin clunk open, and the same giggling transfer to the other side of the thin cabin wall.

Bingo! The stars appear to be in alignment.

He strolled the short distance to the narrow bunk and laid down on the bottom bed. He would rest until the time was right.

CHAPTER 76

Jasmine's chest burned as she ran down the dark mountain, feeling relieved that the gradient had become less severe for a moment. She tried to push negative, intrusive thoughts aside, but they were becoming overwhelming. *Why is this happening to me? What have I done? Where are my family?* Tears welled in her young eyes as she fought to control her fear.

Her senses once again reported the sound of footsteps behind her. For a dozenth time, she tried to resist the urge to turn and told herself it was simply the sound of blood pumping in her ears. Despite her legs wanting to stop, she forced herself on.

She had begun to grow accustomed to the faint lunar light which illuminated her path just sufficiently to make out large obstacles when she was close enough to them, but she could see little beyond her immediate footsteps. Consequently, tripping was almost inevitable, but the heavy fall that occurred at that moment took her completely by surprise, Jasmine having believed she was on a clear section of her route.

Her immediate assumption was that she had caught another tree root – goodness knows she wasn't exactly on a particularly well-trodden path. Seconds after falling, something landed on top of her, and suddenly she found it difficult to breathe. Everything was dark and she began to panic, realising that, not only was she unable to move, but her senses also seemed disabled, leaving her totally disorientated.

Have I fallen into a lake?

Slowly, Jasmine tuned into her surroundings again, shaking off the initial shock of the fall. She trembled as she listened to someone breathing. It sounded like they had undergone physical exertion, but the breaths were controlled. She fought to draw breath herself but found it difficult to inhale. There seemed to be a huge pressure being applied to her lungs and her head began to swim from lack of oxygen.

When the moment of clarity arrived, she wished it hadn't. With terrified eyes, she watched the outline of a large, strong hand being placed firmly over her face. To the petrified young girl, the strength of her oppressor seemed supernatural.

Why is this happening to me? Who are these people?

With one final flurry, she tried to explode upwards, but the huge weight covered her entire body, preventing her from moving a single muscle. Just before passing out, she heard the sound of other voices.

*

Robson focussed on the old wooden bridge ahead as DC Saunders applied further pressure on the accelerator. They raced towards the river crossing, intent on reaching it before the blue four-by-four which approached from the opposite direction, followed by the police Land Rover in the distance.

On the northern bank of the Exe, the progress of the blue four-by-four was remarkable, seemingly swallowing up the terrain between it and the gushing river. The timber deck of the bridge rumbled violently as the suspect vehicle began to thunder across and sped on to the southern riverbank, seconds before the CID vehicle arrived alongside the riverbank.

Saunders accelerated, knowing that they had only seconds before the target would be back out into open terrain. Moments later, as they leapt off a grassy bump, the wheels spun as their vehicle struggled to gain traction alongside the riverbank. The route narrowed as they sped towards the bridge, the line of trees on their right meaning there was only room for a single vehicle.

Within moments, the police land rover arrived at the northern end of the wooden crossing. Robson spoke over the radio as Saunders began to apply pressure to the brake pedal.

'Whisky Five Zero to control. We have visual on the suspect and we are blocking its path. Foxtrot One is covering the rear. Hold your position Foxtrot two zero. There is nowhere for our mystery guest to go.'

'Control. Roger that, Whisky Five Zero. X-Ray Alpha Nine Five, are you complete?'

'Roger, control, this is X-Ray Alpha Nine Five, we have visual. Confirmed that Whisky Five Zero and Foxtrot One have the suspect vehicle blocked.'

*

The French chauffeur did not flinch as he watched the unmarked CID vehicle approach them head-on. Noting the police Land Rover at his rear and the dense forest on his left, Pierre Marchand knew he had to make his decision fast. He acknowledged to himself that the roaring river on his right was too wide to contemplate crossing and he had no way of estimating its depth.

Desperate times require desperate measures ...

Marchand operated the electric window controls.

'Hold on!' he shouted to his passenger. There was no response.

*

DC Saunders shuffled uncomfortably in the driving seat. She wasn't overly eager to engage in a game of chicken with a four-by-four and, as the suspect's vehicle began to accelerate towards them, she braced herself, anticipating an order from her commanding officer any second. Saunders glanced to her left and recognised the steely determination on her DCI's face, providing all the confirmation she required that she was to hold their position.

As the four-by-four came within twenty metres of them, it had to be travelling close to seventy miles per hour, which seemed double on the narrow, sodden terrain. Saunders closed her eyes instinctively, anticipating the impact.

'Reverse!'

The shout came from the passenger seat.

Saunders reacted immediately, releasing the clutch milliseconds after throwing the gearstick into reverse. It took several seconds to gain traction on the moist riverbank and they both looked on wide-eyed as the four-by-four bore down on them, before suddenly flying from the riverbank.

'Shit!'

Seconds later, the wild river erupted to their left as the blue four-by-four came to a halt at the midway point and immediately began to sink.

*

For a split-second, Sarah enjoyed the respite from the effects of the rough terrain and tried to adjust her position as far as she could within the constraints of her bindings. But her relief was short-lived as, almost immediately, they encountered what felt like a huge obstacle.

Lured into a false sense of security, she hadn't braced for the impact. The back of her skull smashed against the interior metal shell. Her senses swam as her ears detected the noise of gushing water.

*

From the riverbank, Robson tried to see inside what remained visible of the submerged vehicle. A crack had appeared in the top right-hand corner of the windscreen from the impact with a large tree branch just before the four-by-four had flown into the water. The vehicle had surrendered its buoyancy and was threatened to disappear entirely as its metallic blue roof sank closer to the surface.

Slightly further along the bank, PC Bryant was busy removing his boots and outer clothing. Moments later, the young officer leapt into the cold river. Robson followed his lead and dived in after the constable, causing minimal disturbance as he pierced the water surface.

PC Gardener scrambled from the back of the police Land Rover with a rope. Seeing that two of his colleagues had already gone into the fierce river, he struggled to remain upright as he ran along the sodden riverbank. Soft clay squelched beneath his feet as he approached DC Saunders. He stood alongside her, rope in hand, and together they watched the action in the river unfold.

The heavy blue vehicle sank with surprising speed. Large bubbles exploded on the surface as the roof finally disappeared, expelling the remainder of the air from inside the car.

'Bloody hell!' exclaimed DC Saunders.

PC Gardener nodded absentmindedly, summoning a memory of the river from a previous visit.

'Yes,' he responded, 'must be over ten foot deep. Up until recently, it was never more than three feet here.'

'I know,' Saunders murmured, thinking of the recent extraordinary rainfall. Now, though, she was more concerned by just how many casualties might result from the incident unfolding before her.

Seconds later, PC Bryant appeared as he broke through the water surface, gasping while wiping water from his eyes. Gardener tossed the rope towards his exhausted colleague.

'He's not here!' Bryant gasped.

Saunders frowned.

'What? Where's Robson?'

Bryant appeared immediately confused and began to scan the riverbank.

'Shit! Did he come in here? I haven't seen him!'

Bryant took a deep breath and immediately manoeuvred to dive in again.

'No!' Saunders screamed. 'The current's too strong. Let us pull you in.'

At first, the soaking wet constable appeared to submit to the CID officer's command. Then, in an instant, Bryant cast the rope aside and disappeared back beneath the surface of the water. Saunders rushed past Gardener and shouted as she leapt into the water.

'Leave the rope in position!'

A second later, she disappeared underwater, leaving Gardener alone on the riverbank.

The constable stood helplessly for almost a minute, until both Saunders and Bryant surfaced together and began to swim towards Gardener on the southern side of the river. There was still no sign of either the four-by-four's driver or DCI Robson.

CHAPTER 77

A private plane screeched to a halt on the wet runway. The freak storm had brought many of the commercial airlines to a halt that morning, but such events did not tend to prevent the military from staying airborne.

On board the Piper PA-31 Navajo that morning was a single Security Service operative. Officer Wilson had left her colleagues in Denmark with strict instructions to tail the rogue SIS agent for a little while longer. Given Arkwright's training, it was a high-risk strategy, but there was little possibility that the spy would speak the truth under interrogation, and Wilson was determined to establish Connor's intended destination before they struck.

The aircraft door opened to a mighty gust, revealing a dark saloon at the bottom of the steps. The driver opened the car window slightly and gave Wilson a brief wave, evidently deciding that a formal greeting was unnecessary, given the inclement conditions. Wilson pulled her coat around her tightly as she descended the steps. She threw her hand luggage on to the back seat of the waiting vehicle and swiftly joined her bag inside. As usual, she wore no makeup, but she still dabbed at the raindrops that dripped on to her face from her hair.

'Don't stand on ceremony please, Richard. Let's move.'

'Of course, ma'am.'

The driver sneaked one final glance at his attractive passenger in the rear-view mirror before speeding off the runway and heading towards the destination for her meeting.

Wilson made herself comfortable for the short journey ahead. She watched the twin-engine aircraft manoeuvre further from the runway towards the waiting fuel tanker, while she composed herself for the meetings ahead. She knew that they were running out of time. MI6 hadn't eased their pressure to assume responsibility for tracking their rogue agent and it had required her best powers of reasoning to persuade them to allow Arkwright to board the ferry last night. She hoped she wouldn't live to regret that decision, in the same way her opposite number in MI6 had lamented his part in allowing their agent so much slack, resulting in the murder of two innocent prison officers.

For Wilson, there was also the added problem of the information she held – explosive knowledge that could have irreparable consequences if it were not treated with the utmost delicacy. The trouble was, she had to tell someone. However, paradoxically, the information was such that she no longer knew who she could trust.

Apart, perhaps, from one man. But even that would not be straightforward, for Robson was more than just a colleague. She had been in love with him and, despite them no longer being together, her innermost feelings towards him were complicated. It was, therefore, a question of whether she would be prepared to burden him with such dangerous information, considering what he and his family had already been through.

Twenty minutes after landing, they passed through a security checkpoint and approached the iconic building fondly referred to by its staff as 'The Doughnut' – one only had to view the building from the air to appreciate why. After parking close to the entrance, Wilson entered GCHQ alone. She was immediately recognised by the receptionist, who called for his colleague to escort Wilson to her destination without delay. Efficient, Wilson noted, even for Government Communications Headquarters.

As she was escorted along the familiar, soundproof corridors, she wondered what information her superiors had to share that had been quite so important to justify temporarily plucking her from a live operation. She wondered if they had discovered what she and Mark Connor both already knew.

CHAPTER 78

The driver of the now submerged blue four-by-four knelt, hidden in the lush green vegetation on the opposite side of the river from the police vehicles and watched the distracted trio of police officers as they frantically scoured the muddy water.

The chopper roared as it lowered just a few yards behind the officers on the ground, its crew evidently having decided to land so that they could support the search for DCI Robson. It was a pleasing sight to the diminutive Frenchman, and he hoped it would allow him to confidently break cover once the time was right.

As the helicopter personnel arrived, they all seemed interested in a certain spot in the river. Pierre Marchand took his chance and departed the cover of the bushes on the northern riverbank. After an early sprint to gain some distance between him and the police officers, Marchand reduced his speed a little to conserve energy. The run had warmed his body sufficiently to stop the shivering, allowing him to pace himself until he could make sufficient contingency arrangements. He knew that the latest development would mean that he would have to escape at all costs – as soon as the officers finally recovered the young woman's body from the boot of the car, he would be the subject of a serious manhunt.

Several minutes later, he ducked down beside a group of bushes to take a breather. Looking back, he was pleased to see he had made it a good quarter of a mile from the river and, most importantly, no one appeared to be in pursuit. Looking down at the device in his hand, he felt satisfied by his decision to acquire a waterproof phone. Yet the phone call he needed to make would not be in any way comfortable. He had to tell his employer that he had just lost their prized asset. He replaced the phone, deciding that the call would wait until he was out of the woods.

Checking again that nobody occupied the expanse between him and the gathering down at the river, he rose to embark on the remainder of his journey just in time to see the whites of his attacker's eyes bearing down on him.

*

Robson had decided that he had to take the opportunity to strike there and then. His opponent was significantly smaller than him, yet he did not appear to be in any way intimidated as Robson elevated his frame and braced himself for confrontation.

'Freeze!' DCI Robson slipped instinctively into official protocol. 'You're under arrest. Turn around with your hands on the back of your head!'

Water dripped from his elbows as the short, stocky man slowly obeyed Robson, who wasted no time in moving in closer with a set of cuffs. As the metal touched the suspect's right wrist, his elbow flew back at lightning speed, cutting into the DCI's ribs. Robson stumbled backwards, wheezing as he watched the bespectacled suspect begin to sprint away, while Robson fell to the ground, winded and momentarily paralysed.

After running fifty yards, the soaked Frenchman looked back and was surprised to see he was being pursued again.

Robson felt he had a psychological advantage, having gained significant ground on the suspect so that he was now only a few metres behind. Then, moments later, the Frenchman seemed to find another gear.

Robson felt the energy sapping from his aching legs and being absorbed by the soft ground. He judged he was just within tackling distance and threw himself towards his prey's flying legs. In mid-air, his fingertips briefly connected with a stocky calf muscle, before he found himself desperately grabbing at thin air. He shouted in pain as his ribs smashed the rock concealed beneath him among the otherwise soft wild grass. Seconds later, expletives could be heard coming from elsewhere. Evidently, he had done just enough to topple the Frenchman.

Robson was on him immediately, placing a hand around his throat. He fumbled to get a tight enough grip around the suspect's wet neck to immobilise him, but it was like trying to catch a desperate animal as the nimble man thrashed about beneath him, displaying extraordinary power for his size. Suddenly, Robson felt his nose sting as he was caught by the Frenchman's right uppercut. Robson's eyes watered heavily and, with his vision momentarily lost, he could feel the suspect wriggling free. Blindly, Robson threw himself forward and managed to deliver a powerful hook beneath the man's diaphragm, making him double over. He didn't give the Frenchman time to recover. Robson's feet left the ground before he brought his elbow down on the back of the man's neck with almighty force, causing him to collapse.

Gasping heavily, Robson wiped his bloody nose with his sleeve and took a few seconds to regulate his breathing while his opponent lay face-down, spread-eagled, and lifeless on the wet grass. Robson knelt on the fallen man's back and wrenched his arms behind his back, before hissing into his upturned ear.

'What were you doing at the house?'

The man groaned beneath him.

'Listen, fuckwit. You may believe that we British plods always play it by the book, but trust me, it doesn't always apply. It's just you and me out here pal, and who knows what kind of accident could happen?'

He tightened his grip further.

'I know nothing!' the man screamed in his Gallic tone.

The response was hoarse and seemed slightly docile. But he screamed again as the DCI increased the pressure on his elbow bending his arm backwards as far as the joint would allow.

'Last chance. Or I break this one before moving on to the left.'

'What do you want to know?'

The panic was detectable in his voice.

'Where is she?'

'This wasn't my idea, I swear. I was just doing as I was told!'

'Where the fuck is she?!' Robson screamed in his ear and positioned himself vertically above the elbow, bracing himself to apply the final, arm-breaking jerk.

'She's in the car!'

'What?!'

'In the car – the boot!'

'You fucking scumbag!'

Robson powered his left fist into the man's jaw and began to race back towards the river.

CHAPTER 79

The exhaustion felt by all the police officers gathered on the riverbank was exacerbated by the hopelessness of the situation. They each cut forlorn figures as they paused in their frantic search. Then, one by one, each of them registered the remarkable sight of the dishevelled man running in their direction.

Blood appeared to be streaming from Robson's face as he raced towards them. Despite his appearance, they all felt relieved to see him alive, until he got sufficiently near for them to notice the horror in his face. His scream was close to sounding hysterical.

'She's in the boot! Jasmine's in the boot!'

By the time Robson had leapt back into the river, three of the other officers were submerged, searching with even greater desperation than before. Beneath the surface, PC Bryant swam into the open driver's side window and, inside the four-by-four, through to the rear of the submerged vehicle. The others watched Bryant gesture from inside before he swam clear and they all surfaced. Robson felt hopeless as he gasped air into his lungs.

'The rear window's been removed!' Bryant panted.

Robson stared at the constable.

'What?!'

'There's no one inside the vehicle, but the rear window has been broken open!'

'Spread out!' Robson commanded.

Robson took another glance at the small area of incongruous colour in the long grass at the northern edge of the water, which seemed out of place. He swam towards the area on the riverbank, picking up speed as he got closer to the strange bundle. Initially, it had appeared to be discarded clothing, but what suddenly perplexed Robson was, though he recognised the attire, it did not relate to his daughter. Seconds later, he recognised the casualty as he shouted to announce his find to his colleagues.

'Over here!'

As the other officers arrived, they found Robson administering CPR, not to a child, but to an adult female. The woman had apparently managed to reach the riverbank before losing consciousness. Robson worked on her for twenty seconds before she began to splutter. As he moved her on to her side and adjusted her limbs to the recovery position, she vomited filthy river water on to the grass. Shivering violently, the woman was now breathing on her own. Saunders returned with a blanket from the car and threw it over the casualty, before wrapping it around her body. Robson gently moved a sodden clump of long hair away from her face, before addressing the drenched woman.

'Sarah ... what's happened?!'

*

PCs Bryant and Gardener both wore frowns as they scanned the wild grass. They were certain that they were standing in the spot described by DCI Robson. There were no other trees in the immediate vicinity, so they had an obvious marker, and the abandoned handcuffs confirmed they must have been at least approximately in the right place. But the suspect had disappeared.

Both constables returned to the patrol car. Bryant lifted the radio to update Robson and Saunders, as Gardener started the engine and began to drive towards the main road.

As the car began to move, the man hidden in the back prepared himself. Just as the vehicle lurched off a large bump in the terrain, a thick forearm suddenly appeared in Gardener's peripheral vision. To his left, Bryant thrashed in the passenger seat as he desperately tried to wriggle free of the length of rope that had been aggressively wrapped around his neck. Gardener felt an almighty jolt ripple through his body as he brought the vehicle to an abrupt halt.

Beside him, Bryant began to make a hideous rasping sound from deep inside his throat. Just before a final attempt to draw breath into his suffocated lungs, his final desperate thought was to wonder why his colleague hadn't come to his rescue.

Moments later, Gardener was aware of the rear door being opened. Yet, despite being conscious, he was unable to adjust his position to watch the uninvited passenger exit the vehicle. He was also unable to look at his lifeless, blue-faced colleague alongside him. Just before paralysis had set in, PC Gardener had felt the muscles in his body spasm violently. Now, he slumped helplessly in the driving seat, unable to move, nor control his dropped jaw.

The driver's side door was wrenched open and two strong hands clawed him, seeming to drag his slightly overweight frame effortlessly out of the vehicle before dumping him unceremoniously on the damp grass. Still unable to move, Gardener sensed another body being dumped beside him, before feeling an almighty impact at the side of his head.

The wheels span beneath the police Land Rover as they churned up the damp grass and began to speed away from the two bodies. Inside the vehicle, the French driver shivered and threw the taser into the back seat before cranking up the heating.

CHAPTER 80

All three suited men were expressionless as they watched Officer Wilson enter the room. The Director General remained impassive as he spoke.

'Thank you for joining us at short notice, Emma.'

'No problem, sir.'

She cast her eyes over the other attendees. She required no introduction from any of them. The man to her left, Adam Fields, was a familiar face at GCHQ. But only recently had she had cause to work closely with the tall, thin man alongside Fields.

Salutations, as ever, were on hold until they entered a secure environment. They all turned their attention to the man who had been Wilson's escort as he began to open an immensely thick door, providing access to another room. The Director General gestured with his hand and they all passed through the new opening into a soundproofed chamber. Understanding the protocol for the spy base, they all remained silent until the escort had sealed the door behind them and locked them inside. The Director General began the meeting, suddenly speaking as though someone had operated a switch to turn him on.

'Right, time is of the essence. Do take a seat everyone.'

He continued as Wilson pulled herself up to the table alongside her boss, so that she and the Director faced the other two men.

'Okay. Introductions. I am Peter Grant, Director General of Her Majesty's Security Service, MI5.'

He looked to his left. Wilson took her cue.

'Officer Wilson. Senior Operational Intelligence Officer, Security Service.'

'Adam Fields. Senior Data Analyst, here at GCHQ.'

'David Vincent. Secret Intelligence Service. Head of counter-terrorism.'

'Thank you, everyone. In accordance with the usual protocol, this meeting is classed as top secret. The reason for the short-notice gathering is to update you all on the ongoing search for the missing MI6 agent, Arkwright, also recently known as Mark Connor, and his suspected connection to the escaped convict, Jacob Miller.'

David Vincent coolly helped himself to some water from a jug in the middle of the table. Wilson watched his warm smile guardedly as he offered the jug to her. She poured a glass of the clear liquid as Peter Grant continued.

'Officer Wilson. Could you appraise us on your progress, please?'

'Certainly, sir. As you will already be aware, we located Arkwright in Munster, Germany, a couple of days ago. He managed to evade us, but we were able to pick up his trail again. He had managed to cross several borders before arriving in Denmark. He has operated under several passport identities, the names of which have already been reported, although at this time, none of this information has been shared with Interpol.'

She took a sip from her glass, before continuing.

'This morning, I left the investigation team at the Danish port of Hirtshals. We have allowed Connor – or Arkwright – to board a ferry bound for Iceland. Our operatives are under strict instructions to follow only, and not to attempt to intercept until we can be sure of his intended destination.'

'Have we any idea where that might be?'

'No, sir. We don't know whether his movements are planned or if they are random. Which itself would be somewhat perplexing.'

The suave MI6 man intervened.

'Perplexing? In what way, Officer Wilson?'

'Well, Mr Vincent, given his training, and what he's managed to accomplish this far, one wouldn't expect him to panic. I would find it hard to accept that there isn't a preconceived motive behind every move.'

The Senior MI6 officer nodded in apparent agreement, allowing the chair to continue.

'Quite,' said the MI5 Director General. 'Thank you for the update, Wilson. David, would you mind sharing your information?'

'Certainly, Peter. Our intelligence officers have been pooling recently gathered data obtained in collaboration with our American counterparts, who, incidentally, seem to be developing a growing interest in our rogue agent. We have agreed to share our information with them regarding Arkwright and, in return, they've briefed us regarding an incident in the Arctic circle that's been troubling them.'

Wilson displayed her usual poker-face, showing no sign that the apparent relevance of the area had piqued her interest. The room remained silent, allowing the MI6 officer to continue.

'The CIA have informed us that, only a couple of weeks ago, they experienced an extraordinary attack on one of the American government's most fiercely guarded outposts, in Gakona, Alaska.'

'What's driving the theory that such a significant event is linked to your man?' Wilson interjected.

'The timing,' Peter Grant added to the conversation, before allowing David Vincent to continue.

'The incident happened only forty-eight hours after Connor, or Arkwright, was shot.'

'Connor was shot in error. What is the relevance?'

'Was he? With respect, that has not yet been established as far as I am aware, Officer Wilson.'

'Sir,' Wilson addressed the MI6 representative directly, deciding, for the moment, to conceal what Robson's CID team had already uncovered, 'which US military establishment has been attacked? And how has such an event been kept under wraps?'

'That's the interesting part, actually. It wasn't an attack in the sense of what you might be imagining. In other words, it didn't involve destructive firepower. This was a much more sophisticated attack, which targeted one of the most advanced technological sites anywhere in the world.'

Wilson pushed any immediate queries to the back of her mind for the present – such as when had they planned to share their theory that DCI Robson had not necessarily been the bullet's intended recipient at Webber's Post, as previously assumed. She believed them to be wrong anyway, but she couldn't risk showing her hand. *Not yet.*

Wilson allowed her slender body to fall back into the chair and allowed the MI6 man to continue.

'Officer Wilson, have you heard of a facility known as HAARP? Spelt H-A-A-R-P.'

She shrugged.

'I believe I might have.'

'The acronym stands for *High-Frequency Active Auroral Research Programme.* It is the US ionospheric research programme.'

'I see. Yes, now you come to mention it, I think I might have watched some conspiracy documentary on it a long time ago. What is the relevance?'

'That is the site that was targeted in Alaska two weeks ago. An unknown attacker launched a pair of technically advanced e-bombs which, apart from wiping out all power over a fifty-mile radius, also totally incapacitated the IRI and the central computer, which have still not been possible to reinstate as yet.'

'An attack on Alaska? That must be among the most heavily guarded US airspaces, surely. How on earth did the attackers manage to get that close?'

'The missiles were launched from a sub off the north Alaskan coast, some eight hundred miles from its target. The devices were intercepted by two F-16 fighter jets. The bombs were detonated directly above Gakona and the resulting explosion knocked out all electronic equipment over more than a fifty-mile radius, including, unfortunately, the controls on both fighter jets. Neither of the two pilots made it.'

'Sir, with respect, the incident you've just described sounds more akin to an attack by a hostile state, rather than one by some two-bit fanatic, even if it were supported by someone with the skills and experience of Connor.'

'Two-bit, miss Wilson? Surely you know better than anybody not to underestimate the resources of certain organisations?'

'What *organisation*? Apart from Miller, who is left from the Arcam conspiracy?'

Wilson was testing their knowledge to establish how much they actually knew – or how much they would be willing to divulge that they knew.

'Perhaps not in the UK. The Americans' first instinct was, naturally, to accuse the Russians of an act of hostility against a US state. But the CIA has intelligence – which it has recently shared with us – that potentially connects Miller's escape with this event. They also believe that Connor's actions are no coincidence.'

'What would the motive be? It just sounds like mindless vandalism, albeit on a rather large scale. Do the Americans think there could have been a financial incentive?'

'That's what they'd like us to help them establish. Finding both Connor and Miller are objectives which now have a global significance, I can assure you. Since Miller disappeared, the only current link to him is our evasive MI6 agent, so we are all very keen to ensure that we do not lose him … again. Which brings me on to the next point …'

Here it comes, thought Wilson.

'Officer Wilson,' the spy boss continued, 'up until now, your strategy of trying to establish Connor's intended destination has been supported on the basis that, if we were to intercept too early, it might not be possible to extract crucial information from him. But I'm afraid we have run out of time. If we do not take him immediately, we will all find ourselves under unimaginable pressure …'

Wilson noted the exchange of glances between the MI6 officer and her boss, the Director General of MI5. The latter displayed a slightly sheepish look under Wilson's gaze, before reaffirming his authority and confirming his agreement.

'Wilson, as you have said yourself, we do not believe his current journey is without objective. But I'm afraid we cannot take the risk of him evading capture again.'

They all waited for Wilson to react.

'Do you think he might be on his way to Alaska?' she asked.

Her blunt response seemed to disarm the others for a moment.

'It's possible,' said Vincent, after taking another sip of water, 'but not certain. The HAARP facility is more closely guarded now than ever. But of course, we can't be sure who he's working with.'

'Or for.'

'Quite,' Vincent agreed.

'Officer Wilson,' Grant intervened gravely, 'your orders are to have Connor taken into custody immediately.'

'Understood, sir.'

'Before we let you go, Fields is going to brief us on recent research that GCHQ here have been supporting. Adam …'

'Thank you, sir. Okay, to cut to the chase, there is an area in North Wales that is currently interesting us. We picked up a brief coded communication at Mostyn port approximately twenty-four hours ago. The person initiating the conversation used the handle 'Naamah', which alerted us immediately, because it is a term that has recently come to our attention. We have interviewed the harbourmaster to establish which vessels had been admitted to the port around that time, of which there were several. But the least significant was a small fishing boat that had apparently travelled across the Irish Sea. We have requisitioned the vessel in question and our own people are carrying out a discreet DNA analysis as we speak.'

Wilson nodded thoughtfully.

'Mostyn port – is that anywhere near where the second seaplane was found?'

Fields nodded as the other two men looked on, both poker-faced.

'Indeed, it is. The plane sank a mile away. But that's not all.'

'Oh? Go on …'

'For about a week now, we have been aware of an unexplained increase in electromagnetic activity in North Wales.'

'What does that have to do with anything?'

'Perhaps nothing. Our telecommunications team have been examining the activity and have just reported that the levels of radio signals picked up would have to have been produced by a rather large transmitting device. Or several working in unison.'

'And?'

Wilson frowned as she watched Vincent, the senior MI6 officer, hand his electronic tablet across the table. He spoke as she took the device from him.

'Officer Wilson, let me show you a photograph.'

Wilson looked at the screen. It was displaying an aerial shot of what appeared to be thousands of pylons. As she looked closer, she could see that the towers were in fact radio transmitters.

'Where is this?'

'Alaska. Gakona, to be precise. You're looking at a recent photo of the HAARP facility.'

Fields spoke again.

'We believe that the strong activity detected in North Wales would require infrastructure not too dissimilar to that which you are currently viewing.'

'Oh … I see. And exactly where in North Wales has this activity been detected?'

'Snowdonia.'

The Director General watched her reaction for a second before adding to the conversation.

'So, in addition to the capture of Arkwright, we would like you to arrange for the joint investigation with CID to spread its wings slightly and extend the investigation to Snowdonia.'

'Sir, with respect, the investigation team barely has enough personnel to cover the existing boundaries of the investigation, let alone incorporate an additional area.'

'Ask for more resources. And if they are not forthcoming, let me know, and we will make it happen. But we will let you consult with the SIO first – we wouldn't want you stepping on his toes now, would we?'

'Sir. Will that be all?'

'I think so, Wilson. Good luck, and don't forget to let me know if there is anything you need.'

'Will do, sir.'

CHAPTER 81

Seydisfjordur, Iceland

On either side of the MS Norrona, thin ribbons of water cascaded down volcanic cliffs, as the ferry was carefully navigated through the fjord.

Several bleary-eyed travellers stood at the large window in the ferry's main concourse, still confused as to why they had been asked to depart their accommodation an hour before arriving at Seydisfjordur, but the majestic view began to lift their spirits as they drew closer towards the dramatic backdrop.

Two floors below deck, the security services had managed to evacuate an entire corridor, apart from one cabin. With the corridor now secured at either end, one of the special service operatives held a portable battering ram and waited for the command. The team leader had tried knocking for a third time and, once again, there had been no response from inside Cabin 202.

Despite their numbers, a degree of tension ran through the team as they wondered what their target could possibly have in mind. The cabin had been watched ever since the suspect had entered the previous evening – he had no means of escaping the force that awaited his exit. Yet there remained a tangible aura of uncertainty among the special agents. They were dealing with one of their own. An agent that had defected. The sooner this was over, the better.

On hearing the command, the helmeted operative smashed the sturdy ram against the cabin entrance. The door shattered on impact and the operative dived to one side as multiple firearms were trained on the messy hole that used to be a door.

'Agent Arkwright, this is Captain Borthwick of the United Kingdom security service. We have you surrounded. You are under arrest. Come out immediately with your hands above your head or our armed officers will be instructed to use lethal force!'

After another few silent seconds, the captain spoke into the transmitter on his lapel and at the same time signalled to the armed personnel to his left.

'Charlie-Nine-Zero, we are IN, IN to Arkwright's cabin. Stand by.'

Five armed personnel burst into cabin 202 as the remainder of the team took up formation outside to maintain cover on the shattered entrance.

CHAPTER 82

The noise of the incident room began to reduce as DCI Robson entered, partly out of empathy for what the man must have been going through, but mainly out of the same natural respect they had felt towards their boss ever since his arrival from London eight years earlier. A few of the officers in the room were incredulous that the man could do his job at such a time, but most were simply in awe of the way he still appeared to be his usual, focussed self.

The fact was that Robson needed to keep his mind focussed. It was the only way he could deal with the situation. It was also the only chance he had of making a positive contribution towards reuniting with his daughter. In a way, although Robson would not allow himself to believe it, things were perhaps starting to move in the right direction. They had Sarah back and it seemed she was going to be okay, physically at least. Unfortunately, she hadn't been able to offer any clues about what had happened to her since she last saw her husband.

Robson paced to the front of the room, exchanging a polite smile with some of his colleagues, before turning to address his team.

'Hello everyone. We'll speak in a moment about how our search for the elusive Frenchman is going. But first, let's catch up on the other developments.'

Most of the team remained seated at their desks, with a handful of officers choosing to stand. Robson pressed on.

'DI Matthews and co have been to North Wales in search of the lawyer's house. I think it's fair to say, James, the visit was rather fruitless, correct?'

Robson felt a degree of satisfaction from Matthews' palpable frustration. He wanted to work with people who cared.

'Correct, sir. We called on the house and stuck around all day, but there were no signs of any comings or goings.'

'Has Cumberwell been seen by the neighbours?'

'There aren't really any to speak of, sir. The nearest are about half a mile away. We went to see them, but when we asked, they weren't aware that anyone had moved in yet, although an elderly man seemed to think he had seen a car in the area a few times.'

'Description?'

'White Range Rover, sir.'

'VRN?'

Matthews shook his head.

'Sorry, sir.'

Robson looked directly at Saunders.

'Trudy, remind us what type of vehicle Professor Romano picked up from Hertz car rentals at Cardiff airport last week, please.'

'It was a white Range Rover, sir.'

'I think Snowdonia demands a slightly more intensive presence,' Robson said, casting his eyes around the room. 'What about the local force, James?'

'They have no knowledge of the homeowner. But we have found out a little more information for ourselves – we checked who the lawyer, Tristan Cumberwell, bought the cottage from ...'

'And?' Robson asked rhetorically, for the rest of the team's benefit.

'The house previously belonged to a Miss Louise Hart.'

Robson watched the reaction of his team, most of whom were staring at the front of the room, while others murmured to one another.

'So,' he took over again, 'any doubts about a connection between Hart and the escape seem to be fading. It seems that Louise was perhaps more embroiled in this than she has allowed us to know.'

'And ever will know,' DC Jenkins murmured.

'Thank you, Jenkins. Let's have some faith in ourselves, shall we? As you will all be aware, we have, unfortunately, lost access to any more information from Miss Hart, due to her recent death. The coroner has confirmed that her death was a result of a huge overdose of some pretty potent substances, but he has stated there are no suspicious circumstances, so that is our working theory.'

'Except,' Matthews intervened, 'the fact that she appeared to have had almost unlimited access to Class A drugs while inside.'

'And the rest, James. So that brings us back to our recent encounter with the Frenchman. Anything for us, DS Burford?'

The woman stepped forward and pinned a large photo on the wall at the front. They all looked at the blue roof of a car just protruding above the water surface of the River Exe, alongside the photos of Sarah and Jasmine which were already hanging nearby.

Robson had been sure to give Detective Sergeant Burford the responsibility of interviewing Sarah in hospital. Superintendent Grayson was keeping a close eye on DCI Robson's state of mind, but he had to acknowledge that, to date, Robson had somehow managed to retain his usual steely focus. Interviewing his closest friend, however, would have been a step too far.

'Well, there isn't really a great deal to report, unfortunately,' started Burford, cautiously. 'Sarah, Mrs Connor, reports that she and her husband started their honeymoon in Paris as planned, albeit in a different hotel, due to some mix up with the booking. It had been tough for Sarah, because she hadn't been able to contact either Jasmine or her grandmother … that is … DCI Robson's daughter and mother …'

The officers in the room all moved their eyes towards the DCI, keeping their heads perfectly still. Burford continued after an awkward pause.

'Sarah Connor remembers that her husband, Mark, had seemed a little preoccupied at the beginning of their trip, but she had put that down to recent events and thought that he, too, had been concerned about having to leave Jasmine alone.'

Most of those in the room continued to do their best to avoid eye contact with Robson. The huddle of tense faces remained focussed on Burford, who maintained her typical military posture at the front of the room.

'But, perhaps ominously, she remembers thinking that Connor had seemed back to himself on their last day together. Apparently, he had claimed that he had finally managed to contact Jasmine. The same day – in fact, immediately after his alleged telephone conversation with Jasmine – Connor apparently told Sarah that he had organised a surprise trip for them. Early the following morning, they were collected from their hotel in Paris and driven all the way to Brittany. The last time Sarah remembers seeing her husband, they were in a wooded service area on the rural outskirts of Caen. She seems to think that she passed out in the vehicle.'

'When did she wake?' The voice came from DC Kelly at the back of the room.

'It's a bit unclear. Her consciousness seems to have been somewhat sporadic since then. As far as she can recall, she never left the vehicle once. At least, not until it landed in the River Exe.'

'How on earth did she get out of the river?' DC Lyons enquired.

Robson stepped to the front and motioned to Burford that she was relieved from her mini briefing.

'That, my friends, is nothing short of a minor miracle. But the fact is, she did escape. Unfortunately, so did her chauffeur, and we have had very little success so far in tracking him down. As you are all aware, a young police constable lost his life in the process. So, the driver is wanted for murder.'

The room took on a sombre atmosphere. Burford relaxed her military poise slightly, remembering the day she had spoken to the two constables at Webber's Post, instructing them to pursue the Land Rover. She hung her head slightly. Robson sensed the mood and continued in a sanguine tone.

'The police vehicle that was stolen from the two officers was found abandoned at Simondsbath. A motorbike was reported stolen from that area around the same time, and it hasn't been found since.'

'Another disappearance,' added Matthews.

'Indeed,' Robson responded, 'but we have managed to come up with a possible name, thanks to the help of our French counterparts in Paris. This is not yet conclusive, but the French authorities are keen to speak to a man named Pierre Marchand. He is wanted in connection with a fraud case, and he has previous convictions, including robbery and their equivalent of GBH. The same day that the Connors embarked on their little trip to Brittany, a man fitting the description of Marchand boarded a ferry alone, using a passport that turns out to have been fake. Can you guess what sort of vehicle he was driving?'

'Blue four-by-four, sir?' Saunders responded.

'Precisely, Trudy.'

Robson waited for the talking to die down again.

'Now, one final thing about the Connors' honeymoon,' said Robson. 'Why was there a mix up with their original booking? Any ideas, DS Burford?'

Burford lifted her head and looked at her DCI seriously.

'There wasn't, sir. As far as we can tell, Connor never booked the so-called original hotel.'

'And what about the second? Did he use his own name? Or, should I say, did he use the name Connor?'

'No, sir.'

They all turned in unison at the sound of a door and watched Wilson enter the incident room.

'Your timing's perfect, Officer Wilson, we were just about done. Would you like to address the team?'

DS Burford moved aside respectfully to allow the new arrival to pass. Wilson appeared typically businesslike, her keen eyes piercing the audience, although the loose skin around them betrayed a lack of sleep.

'Before I begin,' Wilson started, 'I'd just like to remind you of the obvious, if I may. What we discuss in here is strictly confidential, as always. However, in this case, there is a level of sensitivity that means we must demand utter observance of this rule, which also means that the case should not be discussed with any colleagues apart from those currently in this room, and certainly not with family or friends.'

She looked around at the nodding, serious faces to ensure her message had sunk in, before continuing.

'We are in pursuit of two extremely dangerous people: Jacob Miller, an escaped convict who was serving a life-sentence; and the man being referred to as Mark Connor, whose SIS codename was 'Arkwright', but was known by the official identity of John Harry Reilly. I am aware that several rumours have been circulating, and I would encourage you not to indulge in any unhelpful speculation. I can confirm that Arkwright was, until recently, in the employment of Her Majesty's Secret Intelligence Service. Again, I must remind you that this information is strictly classified and must not be discussed outside of this room. We strongly believe that Arkwright is linked to the house near to Webber's Post, where Jasmine Robson's clothing was found. Arkwright, or Connor, as you are all aware, was close to the Robson family, and he is currently our number one suspect as the kidnapper.'

While Robson nodded in agreement, the others in the room felt staggered at his ability to detach himself from such a deeply personal situation. Many in the room had begun to feel emotional as Officer Wilson continued.

'As for Jacob Miller, it is now strongly believed that he has reunited with his former, international comrades from Arcam. We have reason to suspect that he has been hidden in North Wales, but, of course, we cannot be certain that he hasn't moved on again.'

She paused, watching her temporary team members, several of whom were ex-colleagues.

'The search for Arkwright is now global and we are working closely with our foreign counterparts. And, as the Superintendent has recently advised DCI Robson, it is expected that this team will still predominantly focus on the search for Miller. MI5 will be heavily involved in this search and are also interested in the kidnapping investigation. These two cases are essentially now merged. It is believed that both cases are intrinsically linked and can no longer be treated as being independent of one another.'

In the silent pause, she looked across at Robson.

'DCI Robson ...'

'Thank you, Officer Wilson. Unfortunately, the death of Louise Hart means we have lost our only potential, albeit tenuous, lead to Miller. However, as alluded to by Officer Wilson, recent intelligence shared by MI5 suggests that we will need to expand our search.'

Eyes were rolled by some of the officers who filled the room, as they planned how they were going to break it to their families that they had another residential trip coming up.

'I will be dividing this team into two. I would like four of you to remain here, to work with additional personnel to be supplied, so that we can maintain our enquiries in the immediate area and try to plug the gaps in Miller's journey since departing the shores of Porlock Weir. It is possible that he has more allies out there, people that are not currently known to us. My preference is that the following officers remain here: DI Bannister, DS Simpson, DC Jenkins, DC Kelly. That means I'd like the following team to join me in North Wales: DI Matthews, DS Burford, DC Saunders, and DC Lyons.'

He looked around for a reaction.

'Does anyone think they might have a problem with that?'

Resigned head shakes indicated to Robson that there was not going to be any resistance to his proposal.

'Thank you everyone. We all have lots to get on with, so let's get cracking. The five of us that are heading for Snowdonia will aim to be ready to depart by ten in the morning. Obviously, let me know if there are any problems. We will also be taking our own forensic support with us, for now.'

The detectives filed out of the briefing room, leaving Robson and Wilson alone.

'I see they're still loyal to you,' Wilson smiled, leaning her willowy frame against the wall.

Robson shrugged modestly.

'I'm guessing they all feel a little sorry for me at the moment.'

'Understandably. How are you doing, Jack?'

'Fine.'

'You know the only reason the Super is keeping you on this is because he thinks it's your only way of surviving the current situation.'

'I think he's probably right.'

Robson retained his determinedly impassive exterior.

'I know. And how's your mother?'

'Not great. But she's a stubborn old sod, she's hanging in there. She might even be allowed home in a day or two.'

'Stubborn, eh? Just like her son.'

Robson would normally quickly suppress any analysis of his 'other' life. His private life. His family. But Emma Wilson had already breached that barrier a long time ago. There was nothing sacred left to defend when it came to her. Nevertheless, he was keen to steer the conversation back to the job.

'So, when we spoke on the phone earlier, you seemed quite enthusiastic about the proposal to dispatch a team to Snowdonia. Anything specific I should know about?'

Wilson shrugged her neat shoulders.

'It's currently the strongest lead, isn't it?'

'Still, it could be construed as being rather tenuous ... unless there is any additional compelling evidence that points to that area?'

Her smile, while brief, was warm.

'Perhaps. GCHQ have picked up some out-of-the-ordinary activity in the atmosphere in that region, apparently.'

'Out-of-the-ordinary activity? Sounds like something from a *Bourne* movie. What kind of 'activity'?'

'Electromagnetic activity.'

'Implying what?'

'We don't know yet. But the security services are keen for you to investigate the area further, while, in parallel, they remain focussed on the search for Connor.'

The sound of his friend's name still seemed surreal. A couple of weeks ago he was eating curry with him on the eve of his wedding to his best friend – indeed, Sarah was closer to being a sister. And now, having been identified as a rogue spy, this man was the focus of an international manhunt.

'Emma, there's obviously a desire to reveal only what is absolutely essential, and clearly I can appreciate that. But it'd still be nice to understand what it is that we are investigating!'

Wilson held Robson's interrogative stare. Her cobalt eyes sparkled with complete understanding, yet she suppressed the urge to tell him everything. It wasn't the only urge she had been suppressing.

'All I can say is the signals that have been picked up are consistent with an increase in other regions, internationally, all of which appear to have coincided with Miller's escape and the disabling of the HAARP facility in Alaska.'

Robson frowned.

'Don't the military have far more sophisticated means of investigating such things, rather than simple boots on the ground, as it were?'

'They do, and they've been exercised, hence your involvement now. Drones were dispatched in the areas of the most intense signals only last week.'

'And?'

'And ... they were all destroyed. By the very electromagnetic interference that they were there to detect.'

'How many?'

'In Snowdonia alone, three separate flights all met the same fate.'

'Anything in common with the locations where they came down?'

'Oh yes, I think you could say that.'

'Okay, good. So, what's our target?'

'They all came down above Mount Snowdon.'

Wisely, Wilson chose not to insult him by dressing the news up in an attempt to soften the impact. Robson was suddenly aware that her hesitation hadn't simply been down to clandestine protocol. She had been protecting him, in a way. Not only was he, essentially, searching for his own missing daughter. The enquiry was going to lead them to the most distressingly poignant location in the world for DCI Robson. The place where he had lost his beloved wife.

Wilson watched the emotion pass over his eyes, feeling the sadness that she knew, so well, still existed deep within him.

'Do your colleagues believe Jasmine to be in danger?'

'No. They ... we ... think she's been taken for a reason.'

Robson nodded.

'Jack, I've told you that I agreed that you should remain on this case. But you must throw the towel in if it doesn't feel right. The job will still get done.'

He nodded again, knowing himself that he would have been part of the investigation whether officially assigned or not. He suspected that Wilson and his own superiors understood the same, and that it was part of the reason he remained as SIO. He knew that he needed to be a part of it, and that it kept his mind from wandering off into all sorts of terrifying thoughts. The sleepless nights he'd suffered were testimony to that.

'Will you be accompanying us to Wales?'

She shook her head gently.

'No. Not yet anyway. I'm going to rejoin the search for Connor.'

The search! she thought to herself.

We know where he is. And potentially where he's heading. We just don't know why …

CHAPTER 83

Captain Borthwick had begun to sweat as he spoke into the intercom. 'Charlie-Nine-Zero to control. Arkwright is not inside the cabin. We have lost the suspect.'

There were a few silent seconds before the response crackled in the field team members' earpieces.

'Officer Wilson here, Charlie-Nine-Zero. How can we have lost him? His cabin has been under continuous surveillance. He must be hiding.' Wilson had joined the closed communications channel from the back seat of a dark saloon, currently transporting her to catch another flight to join her colleagues in the field.

'Negative ma'am. We have conducted a full search. Not that there is much to search ...'

The captain darted through the narrow space between the two bunks as a shout echoed from an adjacent room.

'Captain, we have something here!'

As Borthwick burst into the tiny bathroom, one of the special agents held a towel rail away from his body, which was still draped with large white towels. The captain did not blink as he took in the space on the wall where the rail had been removed. A rough hole, about half a metre in diameter, had been cut from the thin wall that separated the room from the adjacent cabin. Wilson's voice sounded in the team member's earpieces again.

'Update please, Charlie-Nine-Zero.'

Before the captain could respond, another voice came from somewhere the other side of the hole in the wall.

'Sir, there's someone in here!'

As his colleague dived through the hole, the captain spoke into his transmitter.

'Standby, ma'am.'

By the time the captain joined his two colleagues in the adjacent cabin, they were removing the gag from a terrified-looking young man, whose hands and legs had been bound tightly behind him. The man's voice broke as he screamed at the captain.

'Help us please! He's taken my wife!'

Immediately, the captain barked into his transmitter.

'Charlie-Nine-Zero to control. SHUT DOWN, SHUT DOWN the ferry! Nobody is to leave. Arkwright is missing. Suspected that he has taken a hostage. Seal all exits – now!'

The response was swift.

'Control, disembarkation is already underway, Charlie-Nine-Zero.'

'Terminate disembarkation immediately and inform passport control! Nobody leaves this ferry terminal!'

*

The passport control attendant smirked as he returned the passport. The driver withdrew his outstretched arm and closed the car's electric window. His right arm hadn't moved from his young wife's midriff the whole time. Obvious newlyweds! thought the attendant cynically.

As the vehicle drove away from the line of new arrivals, all eager to get away from the port and begin to sample the island's natural beauty, the phone rang inside the booth. Protocol dictated that the officer was obliged to take the call before dealing with the next passengers.

As he lifted the handset, the passport control officer noticed for the first time that the queue for passport control seemed oddly short, as though there had been some sort of delay at the ferry. And, as he listened to the urgent command through his earpiece, it appeared that his colleague in the adjacent booth had just received the same instruction – to advise the frustrated travellers in the cars outside their booths that they wouldn't be going anywhere for a while.

Two vehicles which had recently passed through passport control now ambled up the slope towards the port's exit. The second vehicle, containing the newlyweds, drove immediately behind the bumper of the first car, which seemed to make the driver of the front vehicle drive even slower. The driver in the second vehicle spotted the gathering presence up ahead and knew immediately what was happening – they were going to lower the barriers.

In an instant, Connor hit the throttle and roared alongside the first car, which had also noticed the activity taking place before them and began to slow even further. As the barriers began to lower, armed officers moved into the path of the approaching car and began waving their hands, displaying the universal signal to halt. The car's engine shrieked as Connor dropped a gear and raced towards the exit. Alongside him, the terrified young blonde screamed as her captor dragged her down by the hair, her head resting on his right thigh. Seconds later, several bangs were followed by the sound of shattering glass, but the vehicle did not slow.

After ten minutes, the young woman remained in her awkward position beneath the height of the dashboard. She continued to shake but was otherwise paralysed by fear as she continued to feel a gun barrel against her ribs. The vehicle suddenly came to an abrupt halt, tyres screeching, and the man spoke to her again for the first time since departing the ferry.

'Out! Get out of the car … now!'

Her captor leant across her, operating the door lever as he shouted. Seconds later, she backed out of the vehicle.

As the car tore off, quickly performing a three-point turn in the narrow street, she slumped on to the pavement and curled up in the foetal position, sobbing.

CHAPTER 84

Jasmine Robson shook in bewilderment as she listened, desperately trying to discern the conversation above the noise of the jeep as it continued to hammer down the steep gradient. Her wrists and ankles were once again bound, this time more tightly. As extra security, the colossus now sat beside her.

The great man had not spoken or acknowledged her presence in any way since he had unceremoniously bundled her into the back of the van earlier. It almost seemed like he was trying his best to pretend she wasn't there. To Jasmine, he seemed tenser than his two colleagues, who continued to talk in the front.

Until that moment, Carlos had been genuinely interested in hearing about General Miller's journey since escaping prison, but the question he had been putting off had to be asked sooner or later.

'What are we supposed to be doing with her, Jacob?'

The lingering silence told Carlos all he needed to know. However, Miller finally spoke.

'The girl's too much of a risk to us now.'

Carlos considered his response carefully.

'She has certainly caused us a few problems,' he agreed. 'But for all that, she doesn't really know anything, does she?'

'Maybe not. But, for as long as she's around, she's a liability to us.'

'Agreed, but can we not simply let her go once we're far enough away from here? Or perhaps take her to the gypsies?'

Carlos allowed himself a glance at his superior, briefly looking away from the bumpy mountainous terrain. He felt a cold shiver descend his spine as he watched the cold intent unmistakable in Miller's eyes. It was Miller who broke the silence.

'You're not going soft on us now, are you, Carlos?'

'Of course not. I just wouldn't like us to draw any further, unnecessary attention.'

'Precisely.'

Carlos swallowed, understanding that the debate had ended, and began to steel himself for the task that lay ahead.

'So, where are we headed?'

'The coast. A place called Devil's Point. It can be dangerous though. Someone can disappear if they don't exercise appropriate caution.'

Carlos felt the tingle in his spine again. His knuckles went white as he squeezed the steering wheel.

*

Connor calmly watched the procession of immigration police vehicles roar off in the distance as they steadily climbed away from the ferry port. Meanwhile, normal activity appeared to have resumed at the port and the detained passengers began to pass through passport control.

Nonchalantly, Connor wandered out into the open and approached the rental vehicle, an all-terrain Navara off-roader which had been left in accordance with his instructions. Moments later, he pulled out, joining the line of vehicles all making their way out of the ferry terminal, and approached the small town, towards the distant sound of sirens.

Connor double-checked his rear-view mirror and began to relax as he watched the spectacular wooden buildings of the town come into view again beneath the backdrop of mountains on either side. For a second, he wondered if his previous passenger had been reunited with her poor fiancé, before once again focussing on the job ahead. Patiently, he followed the car in front as it wound its way along the mountain road. Connor glanced down as he crossed the Fjardarheidi pass, briefly taking in the magnificent view more than six hundred metres below, a view that many might have considered hair-raising.

The sight of kayaks navigating the mountain lake far below made him cuss in irony at the contrast between such a serene scene and the last impending leg of his own adventure. He returned his attention to the narrow road as he arrived at another tight bend. A reindeer darted back into the trees in response to the arrival of more traffic on the road.

CHAPTER 85

The handsome, professional-looking couple clearly wanted to be left alone. Having finished their squid starters, they had requested a twenty-minute interval before the main fish course was brought out.

Jakop, their waiter, was more than happy to comply with their requests, including their somewhat peculiar desire that the nearby tables were not occupied. The generous wad of cash which had been discreetly thrust into his palm as he collected the empty starter dishes had helped. Intelligence officer Kline allowed the sycophantic waiter to move out of earshot before addressing his female companion again.

'What are the chances of finding Robson's daughter now?'

Not many people witnessed that the impassive, senior intelligence officer Wilson was unable to hold eye-contact. She looked troubled and filled with emotion as she looked away from Kline and gazed out of the floor-to-ceiling window. The lake below seemed to convey its own mystery, doubtless amplified by the more distant sight of steam rising from the lava fields that occupied the vista all the way to the horizon. Wilson chose to respond by asking her own question.

'Tell me, Giles, what is your personal theory about Arkwright's destination? Is he on his way to Alaska?'

'I think he's leading us on a merry goose chase and enjoying every fucking second of it.'

Wilson nodded, turning her attention back to the volcanic landscape. She glanced at her watch and began to tinker, remembering she had not yet switched to Icelandic time.

'I agree. Our orders are to arrest him, immediately. Despite the risk that it might not be possible to get him to talk. Are we tracking him?'

'Yes, we have a device on the hire car that was left for him and we've already picked up his trail.'

'Good.'

'So, what next?'

'We just follow for now. I can understand the nervousness around allowing his freedom—'

Kline raised an eyebrow.

'Allowing?!'

'Obviously, this isn't quite what we had planned. But he still hasn't evaded us, has he?'

'Wilson … As long as he remains at large, we have no way of predicting his movements. We don't even know what level of risk he poses.'

'I know. I just have a feeling there's another dimension that we don't yet understand.'

'Let's make our move and get the slippery bastard first. You can leave the problem of acquiring information to me. We have people who will be able to help us with that, despite his training.'

Wilson suppressed a shiver as she looked back at the frozen lake outside.

CHAPTER 86

Typically, DCI Robson used the long car journey to North Wales to mentally catalogue the events to date. Ostensibly, someone seemed to have it in for him. There had been three direct attacks on his family, yet, despite the evidence, his intuition told him that those occurrences had been somehow secondary.

Alongside him, Inspector James Matthews suppressed a yawn as Robson negotiated yet another hairpin turning. As they climbed even higher up the massif, the view became increasingly enchanting. A sea of red heather dominated the foreground, before giving way to fields that climbed the hills beyond in a patchwork quilt of green, yellow, orange, and brown.

At that moment, Robson did not, for some reason, feel his recent, typical aversion to silence. He was aware of this sudden and inexplicable change to his psyche but could not fathom its cause. Sure, it could have been down to the serenity of their new environment. Perhaps it was his subconscious mind sensing the area they were approaching – a place that spoke only of sadness to him, yet at the same time would forever hold a shrine-like importance.

But there was something else he could not quite place – something far less illusory. He put it down to the simple fact that they were taking action, and as far as DCI Jack Robson was concerned, that almost always brought results – eventually. He felt sure the investigation was heading in the right direction. The only question was whether it was going fast enough.

Glancing in the wing mirror, Matthews saw that their colleagues had remained in tow. They began to descend the other side of the mountain and, as they passed through another small hamlet, witnessed a reminder of Welsh patriotism, the first house proudly displaying a huge, metallic red dragon on its roof.

The satnav display informed them that they were within half an hour of their hotel. Robson settled back, adjusting his position in the driving seat just as Matthews stirred him from his private analysis.

'So, what is our plan of attack, sir?'

'Let's get checked in, have a quick lunch, and then we'll go and introduce ourselves to our hosts,' said Robson, referring to the local constabulary. They had agreed to provide them with an incident room for the duration of their investigation, along with any necessary support, although Robson knew they would not be overwhelmed with resources.

'Okay, great ...'

Robson managed the faintest of smiles, knowing all too well how his young colleague would be thirsty for information.

'Let's save it for the incident room shall we, Jimmy? I'd rather not give two separate briefings. As I said earlier, I think we should make an immediate start around the massif, but I want to see if the local bobbies have any interesting intelligence for us before we start sniffing around properly.'

'Yes, sir.'

CHAPTER 87

Benjamin Vladescu had always been a firm believer in fighting for what he believed in. Several years earlier, it was that mantra which had ensured his loyalty towards the inimitable Sir Geoffrey Charlesworth. It had been nearly a decade since he first met the man who had eventually become a father figure to him, if not a deity, and not a day went by when he did not miss him. He knew he wasn't the only one that grieved for the great visionary.

Vladescu knew that many regarded him as fortunate. It was a wonder that he had escaped the raid on the Arcam establishment on Exmoor eight years earlier. The fact was that, given the chance, he would have gladly given his own life to have saved their leader. But there was nothing he could have done.

Almost every night, he remembered the moment the authorities burst into the secret bunker in the Exmoor wilderness, just at the time of reckoning. Ben had been close to the exit when the incendiary device blew the door that formed the secondary opening to the underground bunker. The special forces had flown past him in large numbers, totally missing the great bulk that remained hidden amid the dark, chaotic scenes. Ever resourceful, he managed to remain hidden on the moor for weeks, until the police and military presence finally dissipated almost as suddenly as it had materialised.

Survival had never been a problem for Ben Vladescu, given his background. He knew that 'The Principal' would have known that he was alive. And sure enough, they eventually came for him, giving him a new, false identity for everyday life. One which, once again, gave him the liberty to live what appeared to anyone else to be a normal existence, while maintaining his clandestine association with the movement.

His loyalty had never wavered. First-hand he had witnessed the rise and fall of communism, and, he believed, he was now witnessing the decline of capitalism. There was only one way – their way – and he was committed to helping them reach the metaphorical promised land, whether he personally made it or not. What they aspired to was for the greater good of all humankind.

The Principal had wasted no time in appointing a new leader for their mission, and Naamah had proven to be a wise choice.

The irony of how events had come full circle had not been lost on the huge man. Eight years ago, DCI Robson and his associates had managed to foil their mission. Now, on the cusp of creating their future again, it was Robson who was suffering. The unfortunate DCI had been wrongly imprisoned after almost being shot. Then his frail mother had been kept prisoner in her own home. Most incredible of all, Vladescu now sat on a makeshift bed alongside Robson's only kin. Just a young girl, yet she was making her final journey.

He took no pleasure from the situation. However, he knew that his superiors would not expect any leniency that might risk compromising their mission. All the same, this would be his greatest test yet. He had never expected to have to dispose of a child, and the truth was, it seemed to him to be so at odds with their core principles.

Gargantuan fingers interlocked on his lap as he tried to meditate, with stern eyes focussed on the contrasting, beautiful scene outside. No one spoke as the jeep was brought to a stand, now perched only ten metres away from the edge of the cliff top.

*

Connor checked his rear-view mirror again as he swung off Route One and joined the F88, suddenly altering his course from northwest to due south. It had been two hours since he had left Seydisfjordur and he had only encountered a handful of other vehicles in that time, most of which had been heading in the opposite direction, apart from a couple of trucks he had overtaken long ago.

He had been driving at a relentlessly fast pace so nothing could catch him, yet in the distance he was sure he could make out another vehicle.

There was nowhere to hide in the barren wilderness of the Icelandic desert, which began to take on a slightly sinister quality the darker it grew. Peculiarly, if it was a vehicle about three-quarters of a mile to his rear, then the occupant had chosen not to activate any headlights, despite the onset of dusk.

Connor decided to slow his pace significantly and studied his wing mirrors. In every direction, the vista comprised flat, rocky terrain interspersed with patches of pale green, behind which there stood a backdrop of dark, menacing peaks signifying his arrival at the highlands. A blanket of grey and white cloud cover created a distinct dullness.

As he watched the vehicle behind turn on to his course with its headlights still extinguished, he knew that his suspicions had been accurate – he was being followed again.

*

Miller felt satisfied that the elements had worked in their favour, without requiring any intervention or manipulation. Not that they had the power to control the tide – yet. The high tide would mean that any object dropped into the strong current would be certain to get dragged out into the Irish sea, and, with any luck, would likely never be discovered.

Miller was not tuned in to the discomfort felt by his colleague who sat alongside him in the jeep. The usually rock-like Carlos seemed frozen in anticipation of what they had to do next. It was the colossus, still sat in the rear with the girl, who seemed to Miller to be unmoved by the prospect of the task at hand.

Good. I think we'll give the big man a chance to redeem himself.

CHAPTER 88

Connor's destination was finally in sight, despite it being another hour's drive away. He took another glance in the rear-view mirror and saw the now familiar dark saloon. Despite the fading daylight, he knew there was no way of evading them now, the constant sound of chopping rotor blades from above confirming that he was also being tracked from the air. He could only hope that they would maintain their distance for long enough. One thing was for sure, he could not afford to play any more games – Connor was running out of time.

As he continued his course across the bleak, volcanic landscape, it seemed a comical game of cat-and-mouse. The terrain was uninhabited as far as the eye could see, apart from himself, the three vehicles half a mile at his rear, and the chopper chugging away overhead. Nevertheless, he would gladly lead them to his destination if they would allow it.

He had one more trick up his sleeve.

*

While the vehicle had been moving, Jasmine Robson's overwhelming emotion had been that of anger. Anger at the fact that she had managed to escape twice, only for a new face to arrive each time and spoil her short-lived freedom. However, since the vehicle had become stationary, there had been a discernibly tense atmosphere. No one had spoken for several minutes and she sensed her captors were, for some reason, struggling with their next move, whatever that was going to be.

The new man in the front – the athletic 'General Miller' who apparently possessed authority over the other two – seemed utterly impassive and without emotion, but it seemed the tanned man in the driving seat hadn't moved a muscle since parking the jeep. Perhaps if she knew where they were, it would help her to understand the atmosphere. Perhaps I don't want to know, she thought as she felt herself begin to tremble again.

The big man who still sat in the back with Jasmine finally looked away from the side window and turned his eyes to lock on to hers. For the first time, she saw his uncertainty. Fear, even.

What are they going to do?!

They both looked in the direction of the firm voice that came from the front.

'Okay, Ben. Let's get this over with,' said the leader, casually.

The big man nodded before turning his head towards the side window again, almost, it appeared, in disgust, as the young girl alongside him began to weep.

CHAPTER 89

Connor waited patiently in the shadow of the great mountain. It was not difficult to find a quiet spot in the sparsely populated plateau. The Icelandic highland roads were not traversable for ordinary vehicles and the evasive agent had bought himself time once his route had begun to involve several river crossings.

He eyed the steep slope before him and pondered what might be happening at that moment, out of sight. He would soon find out – as soon as darkness descended fully, he would begin the final leg of his journey.

The forces that trailed him had been wise enough to arrange for air cover, but, unfortunately for them, the helicopter would not be much use to them. He knew it was still there somewhere – every so often, he could hear it pass overhead – but he detected it was gradually increasing the radius of its search. *Good … They are beginning to panic.*

For a fleeting moment, Connor thought of the life he had left behind and of the people that he had so ruthlessly deceived. It gave him no pleasure and, he had to admit to himself, the pretence of marriage could possibly have been avoided, but the honeymoon guise had been an invaluable asset. Only now, when it was too late, would people be finally connecting the dots that linked him, John Harry Reilly – Agent Arkwright, to his alias, Mark Connor. And soon enough, after enough digging, they would uncover his *true* identity. But they were too late now.

He felt confident that his pursuers could not possibly have been able to see him deposit his vehicle in the deep lagoon and now, given his comprehensive cover, they wouldn't have been able to spot him even if they were to drive right past him. Once the onset of dusk arrived, he would make his move, and then it would be near impossible for them to reach him.

Almost there, he thought, drawing his thick, fur-lined coat around his cheeks.

*

Robson was not surprised by the apparent range of opinion regarding their presence. It was clearly generational, and he had witnessed the same thing many times. Despite the initial appearance of cooperation, the older heads did what they could to ensure their engagement with the 'foreigners' was kept to a minimum, while most of the younger members of the team seemed to perceive the invasion as an opportunity to be part of something other than investigating small-time drug dealing, or a tussle down in the town on a Saturday night.

Unperturbed by the less convivial section of his hosts, Robson selected those he wanted to be part of his briefing based on who, on initial indications, was likely to be most useful. He did not care whether they were reluctant or otherwise – he had been given carte blanche by the chief constable, and he was going to use it. Sergeant Griffiths was one of the old-timers – a seasoned expert in looking like he had something more important to do, even though he rarely did.

'So, what is all this about, Chief Inspector?'

'Well, first of all, my colleagues and I would like to thank you for your hospitality. I understand it is less than convenient having us descend on you like this.'

'Not at all, sir. The accommodation isn't the problem. It's if you start taking my officers that it could become a problem frankly, sir.'

Robson ignored the brusque tone.

'Of course. We have no intention of stealing your officers unnecessarily, but we are very much counting on *some* local support, certainly in the early stages of our presence here.' He watched the message sink in, before continuing. 'But what I'd really like to begin with is simply a little local intelligence.'

'Oh?'

'I won't beat around the bush. We are interested in a certain area, at least to begin with, and I wondered if you could give us a local perspective.'

'The area being, sir?'

'Mount Snowdon.'

'Can I ask why?'

'We have intelligence to suggest that there has been, and continues to be, unauthorised and possibly criminal activity in the area.'

'What sort of criminal activity?'

'Unauthorised use of radio frequency equipment.'

Robson noted Griffiths' thoughtful expression as he responded and continued to watch the plump sergeant's body language as he continued.

'Clearly,' Robson said, 'we're aware that the mountain is something of a tourist hotspot, so we need to work out the best way to tackle the investigation.'

Griffiths' brow became wrinkled.

'Not at the moment it's not, boyo.'

'Oh?'

'The National Trust and National Park Authority sold their shares to a private trust last winter and it has been closed to the public ever since. The new owners have secured European funding to renovate the seriously worn paths, after someone dropped off the edge of one of the routes last year and fell to their death.'

'Really? Interesting. Would that mean that the only people on the mountain currently are the workers?'

'As far as I'm aware, sir. It hasn't been particularly good for the local economy this year, but it's been a nice peaceful summer, until now.'

Robson rewarded the quip with a brief grin. He needed the sergeant on side for the time being. Robson's smile disappeared at the sound of a mobile phone and he prepared himself to deliver his patent death stare to the owner of the noise, until he felt the vibration in his own pocket. Robson muttered a half-hearted apology, almost to himself, and held his phone up to read the display.

'Okay everyone, let's take a break. Could we all be back in twenty minutes, please?'

Robson turned his back on the room to answer the call. Despite knowing the caller, he announced his name.

'Robson.'

'Jack. Hi, it's me.'

'Hi there.'

The exchanges between them still felt a little awkward.

'How's it going, Jack? Have you settled into your new home yet?'

'Just about. How can I help?'

'Jack, I'm just about to board a flight to Cardiff. I should be with you this evening.'

'Okay, see you then.'

*

Half an hour later, Officer Wilson looked out of the window of the Boeing BBJ and peered down at the white peaks below. It seemed that Agent Arkwright had led them to a spot specifically for the purpose of losing them.

The conversation with her superiors had been difficult, to say the least, but Arkwright wasn't going anywhere. With a little help from the local special force, as well as the Americans who had, somewhat unusually, insisted on having a presence, no one was getting in or out of the cordon they had set up, which formed a ten-mile radius around its centre – Connor's last known location. It had not been difficult to secure the area, given that the terrain was among the least habitable in all of Iceland.

Now that they had Connor ringfenced, Wilson was keen to reunite with DCI Robson and his team. The FBI had also shared some additional information resulting from their intensive background checks, meaning that her new priority was the investigation now getting underway in Wales. Recent intelligence had convinced her beyond all doubt that DCI Robson and his team were in the hotspot, and she intended to be there when Miller was hauled back into custody.

CHAPTER 90

DC Trudy Saunders's boots sank into the boggy grass, increasing the effort required to traverse the hundred yards from the road to the cottage. She began to curse to herself, privately lamenting the adverse conditions that welcomed them on their second visit to the cottage, which, she suspected, would turn out to be as fruitless as the first. It was presumably why her senior officer had pulled rank and decided to remain in the vehicle, on the premise that he didn't wish to abandon it.

Under normal circumstances, DI Matthews would have been able to park immediately outside the property, but the narrow road had been churned up beyond all recognition due to the recent flooding, meaning that the only way of accessing the remote property was via the sloping meadow that separated it from the main road.

In the layby, Matthews felt a fleeting pang of guilt as he watched his colleague from the warm interior of the car. While Robson and the rest of their colleagues were at the local station coordinating the investigation on the mountain, Matthews and Saunders had been dispatched to have another go at tracking down the resident of the home supposedly belonging to Jacob Miller's solicitor, who, as they had recently discovered, had recently purchased it from the late Louise Hart.

As Saunders finally reached the short pathway leading to the front door of the quaint property, Matthews peered up at the magnificent landscape beyond the stone cottage and wondered whether it did indeed hold any relevance whatsoever to their investigation. The cottage was located as close to the mountain as it could be without resting on its actual slopes.

Matthews looked away again and began to access his emails on his phone in an effort to do something constructive. Although he hadn't said as much to Saunders, he held next to no confidence that they were going to discover an inhabitant. Therefore, when he looked up from his phone towards the giant mountain again, with the little cottage nestled against its foothills, Matthews was surprised to see the front door closing. Saunders was nowhere to be seen.

The hollow feeling that DI Matthews suddenly felt in his gut was inexplicable, but it told him to get up to the cottage as a matter of urgency. He bolted from the car.

He pressed the remote car-locking fob as he hurdled the stile, not noticing his mobile phone drop from the top pocket of his shirt as he leapt on to the boggy field. He began to trudge along the waterlogged ground toward the isolated cottage.

*

Jasmine shivered violently despite being firmly gripped on either side of her bound arms. The ties on her ankles dug in deeper as she struggled and thrashed her feet, which dangled several inches from the ground. Despite her efforts, she was unable to generate any force with her kicks.

As they arrived at the cliff edge, she brought herself to look down at the scene beneath her. Her body went rigid at the terrifying sight. Huge white crescents smashed and churned against the dark, jagged rocks and she suddenly understood her destiny and the reason for the dark atmosphere.

She screamed through her chattering teeth.

'Please! Why are you doing this?! Please, just let me go – I haven't done anything!'

Behind them, Miller gave a calm and assured nod to the other two men as they looked back towards their general, apparently seeking absolute confirmation. The general appeared unmoved by the girl's pleas. They had chosen the location well. Nobody would survive such a drop, let alone the freezing ocean, which, if all went according to plan, would dispose of the body for them.

The girl's screaming reached a hysterical pitch as they edged her forward and she realised she was unable to provide any resistance against the strong hands that held her.

'Please, no! Help me, someone!'

The two men stopped and allowed her feet to touch the ground, before each of them released a hand from either arm to reposition their palms at the small of her back, ready to push. She closed her eyes and began to vomit as she felt the firm shove.

A second later, she felt weightless as her feet left the cliff-edge and her body flew towards the intimidating arms of the ocean.

CHAPTER 91

Matthews panted as he leant forward to place his hands on the doorframe and began rapping on the solid oak door, having finally arrived at the cottage. Halfway up the slope, he had realised his phone was missing and went back to retrieve it from the car, but his search had been in vain.

After half a minute of receiving no response, he turned the doorknob. The heavy door moved a centimetre before coming to an abrupt halt and the bolt inside held. He tested it with his shoulder to find that it was solidly in place. He retreated and began to assess the premises for an alternative means of entry.

The largest window on the ground floor was obscured by a large overgrown mess of brambles and every other window within reach appeared to be barely large enough for a child to fit through. Off-white paint flaked from the worn frames and inside each portal there hung a set of net curtains, preventing any glimpse of what might be going on inside.

Matthews leapt into the thorn bush and began to make his way towards the nearest and largest window, wishing that he had been wearing more than a short-sleeved shirt and lightweight coat. Razor-sharp barbs ripped at his arms as he tried to make his way through the vegetation.

As he leant forward to reach the window, he felt a large bramble rip at his knee and, as he tried to wriggle free, he stumbled and instinctively threw his hands out in front of him. There was a loud thud as his palms connected with the pane and he stared through the window, still unable to see anything through the nets.

The window was firmly closed, so Matthews began to force his fingers inside the rotten frame. The decrepit wood began to splinter and come away immediately under the force of his finger, as he wedged his hand further inside. So intent was Matthews on the task at hand, he did not notice the click of a rifle barrel behind him, and it was only the gun bearer's voice that finally got his attention.

'Stop right there, or I will shoot you.'

CHAPTER 92

Pierre Marchand watched the pandemonium at the cliff-edge from a distance, using the dense vegetation as cover for both himself and his newly acquired car. There weren't many things in life that shocked the sturdy Frenchman, but the scene that unfolded before him had him flummoxed. These people meant business – *what sort of ruthless bastards would throw a young girl from a cliff-top?*

It was too much for him to watch, and he dropped his head into his hands, dismayed by his lack of options. By the time he forced himself to look again, it seemed that something unexpected had occurred after the girl had been pushed over the edge. Only two of the three men remained standing, seemingly engaged in an angry exchange. Seconds later, he noticed a third body lying on the ground a few yards from the other two.

*

Carlos had done his best to ignore the sinking feeling in his stomach when he shoved firmly at the girl's back, releasing her arm as she left the cliff edge. Instinctively, he screwed his eyes tightly shut as their actions reached the point of no return. Even though it had been by his own hands, the event, and its speed, had shocked him. Gravity hadn't given them a chance to reconsider – its force seemed to have literally sucked the girl from their arms.

When he opened his eyes again, the sound of screaming disorientated him even further. But it wasn't a scream of terror, but of anger. He turned to face

General Miller, who seemed to be almost foaming at the mouth, like a rabid dog.

'Ben!'

Carlos edged away from the clifftop, not understanding what had occurred. As Miller moved towards him and Ben, Carlos could see that his eyes burned with anger.

'Do you mind telling me what the fuck you're playing at?!'

*

Jasmine's eyes had been tightly closed as she braced herself, anticipating the sensation of freezing seawater, hard rocks, or both, at any moment. But she had expected the feeling of weightlessness to last longer. Sure enough, a hard landing came, followed, bizarrely, by the feeling of being lifted into the air, before once again becoming motionless. Am I bouncing? she wondered. She laid perfectly still, unable to move, but, peculiarly, she was still aware of voices somewhere nearby.

'Nail the fucking idiot!'

Hearing the shouting, Jasmine opened her eyes to watch the scene. She was still at the top of the cliff.

Their leader, 'Miller', was screaming at the smaller, tanned man, trying to snap him from his apparent disorientation. It worked. The Mediterranean man drew a gun from his jacket pocket and lifted it towards his other colleague, the colossus. However, before the firearm had reached shoulder height, the huge man, moving with surprising speed, covered the few yards between them and flew at his comrade with a giant fist.

It was clear that the single blow had been enough to knock Carlos out, his weapon flying off the cliff edge. Had he been conscious, he might have had a chance to grab one of the rocks or tree roots and stop the momentum of his fall. As it was, the last any of them saw of him were the soles of his size nine walking boots as he descended hundreds of feet towards the sea.

Within a split second, Miller was wielding his own firearm, but as he began to take aim, he felt his wrist break under the impact of the big man's kick. Despite the searing pain, Miller's reaction was swift. For five years he had pushed himself to the limit, following the most intense training regime while inside the fortifications of his captive prison walls. It would not be for nothing.

His opponent was twice his size and possessed great strength, but Jacob Miller knew what he was doing. He evaded the hammer uppercut and, while his right hand hung limply at his side, delivered a precise jab into his opponent's thick neck, catching Ben's windpipe with pinpoint accuracy. A grotesque gargling noise followed, emanating from deep within the big man's throat as he staggered backwards, both hands clawing at the bulging veins in his neck.

Ben's eyes were wide-open and increasingly blood-shot, his bright red face fixed in a horrified expression. He crashed to his knees and watched, helplessly, as Miller advanced. Paralysed, Ben could not avoid the kung fu kick that connected with his temple just before the lights went out for good.

Miller watched his former colleague disappear off the cliff edge. Not waiting for the landing, he turned his attention back to what had been their primary objective. But the girl was no longer in the spot she had been deposited by the giant after he had rescued her at the last moment, swinging her back from the precipice. The only evidence of her being there were the severed ankle ties that were now discarded.

He turned towards the sound of a car door in the distance, and, beyond a small area of trees and bushes, he watched a man throw the girl – *his* prey – into the rear seat of another vehicle. Miller began to sprint towards them as the small, spectacled man dashed around the car and leapt into the front.

Miller knew he wasn't going to make it in time. Abruptly, he changed course and was back at the helm of the jeep by the time the other vehicle had spun its wheels and torn away from the car park. The jeep's engine screamed as Miller put his foot to the floor, the high revolutions allowing him to pull away in second gear.

He ignored the pain from his right wrist, which he placed on the door's armrest, and gripped the steering wheel with his left hand. The engine continued to wail as he dipped the clutch, briefly removing his one functional hand from the wheel to jump up another two gears.

CHAPTER 93

The cuts on his arms began to sting as Matthews held them aloft and spoke to the elderly gunman.

'I'm a police officer – where is my colleague?'

'Bullshit,' the old man responded, with an accent indicating foreign shores.

'It's the truth! Let me show you my warrant card ...'

'Leave your hands where they are! Trust me, you will not be receiving a second warning. Now, I will ask you once, and only once – who are you and what are you doing snooping around my property?'

'Your property? You mean ... you're Tristan Cumberwell?'

The gunman's reaction was brief, but it was enough for Matthews to notice his apparent surprise at hearing the name. The old man lifted the rifle to his face and closed one eye, taking aim through the sight. Matthews closed his perspiring palms and opened them again in a disguised signal. The gunman seemed to have reached a point beyond negotiation but Matthews could see the anxiety in his eyes. He clearly regretted wielding the firearm, but that didn't mean he wasn't going to use it. His trigger finger was trembling as he began to squeeze.

There was a loud thud as the blow from behind connected with the back of the man's neck. Matthews exhaled heavily as he watched the gunman fall into a clump on the overgrown lawn. Behind him, DC Saunders replaced the baton on her belt and knelt to treat the fallen man.

DI Matthews tried to ignore the stinging sensation from his arms as he sat opposite the grey-bearded man, while DC Saunders briefed the local uniformed officers who had been summoned. Saunders tried to remain matter of fact, but the absurdity of their tale wasn't lost on her. It had been embarrassing even explaining it to Matthews, let alone these two rural plods, who would simply relish hearing about the calamitous CID operation.

She remained focussed and deadpan as she explained that there had been no response when she had first knocked at the door of the cottage, so she had opted to check the rear of the property. Evidently, on disappearing round the back, the homeowner had answered the door. Meanwhile, Matthews, it seemed, had only witnessed the door closing and had rushed to support DC Saunders, assuming that she had entered the property. After spending a couple of minutes banging on the front door of the old cottage, Matthews had approached the living room window to try to find another way in, ripping his arms and legs to shreds in the overgrown front garden in the process. The homeowner – an overweight, grey-haired and slightly crooked old man – had finally arrived again to answer the door to find someone apparently trying to break in, and promptly produced an air rifle to defend his property.

As Saunders and the two officers joined Matthews and the homeowner in the small, cosy living room, she felt another pang of guilt for striking the man. He appeared to be well over sixty years of age and was clearly suffering from impaired mobility. Indeed, it had been quite an effort for her and Matthews to escort him back inside, one under each arm, like carrying a dead weight as the old man's legs occasionally buckled beneath him.

One of the uniformed officers offered Matthews a tube of antiseptic cream from a first aid kit for his own injuries, as Saunders sat alongside him and looked, somewhat sympathetically, into the aged man's eyes. She was relieved to see that his face, which had been decidedly grey a few minutes earlier, had begun to regain some of its natural colour and he had regained enough strength to lift a mug of sweet tea to his lips. Her voice was level and polite as she addressed him.

'How are you feeling, sir?'

The old man held her gaze with intelligent eyes but displayed a look of disdain. Matthews winced as he applied cream to the last of his cuts and joined the conversation.

'Sir, DC Saunders regrets having to use force earlier. However, with respect, she found you aiming a firearm at a police officer, and therefore took her only available course of action.'

The man coughed, and his hand shook as he returned his mug to the small coffee table alongside his armchair.

'How was I to know that you are police?'

A distinct Latin tone was evident in the man's croaky voice, Matthews noted, before ignoring the question and continuing with his own.

'What is your name, sir?'

Matthews saw in the man's worn, brown face, a reluctance to answer before clearly deciding to give in to his own hesitance.

'Romano. Alberto Romano.'

Matthews and Saunders kept their eyes fixed firmly on the man. *Bingo!*

'Would that be ... Professor Romano, by any chance, sir?'

Romano grunted slightly as he nodded.

'Professor Romano, we'd like you to accompany us to the station for questioning.'

CHAPTER 94

Alone in the barren, windswept landscape, a pair of eyes squinted from inside a heavy, thermal hood. The figure had dressed well for the environment and the fur-lined outer clothing formed a robust shield against the bitter wind that howled on the lower mountainside.

The Eskimo-like figure stopped briefly to validate his bearings. It wasn't that the route was unfamiliar to him. Indeed, it was a pathway well-trodden not only by him, but also by his loyal, if naïve, comrades.

As he gazed towards his destination, he prepared himself mentally, running through the remaining itinerary in his mind. The large gathering of police and special forces that surrounded him at a distance was no cause for concern. He had already reached his final stop.

However, despite having traversed the route before, he knew the first point he sought was going to be difficult to locate if he did not concentrate fully. But this MI6 operative would not be susceptible to any miscalculations.

Agent Arkwright – aka Mark Connor – pocketed the electronic navigational device and began to head up the final few hundred metres towards the secret entrance.

CHAPTER 95

Flanked by Matthews and Saunders, DCI Robson commanded the interview. He gently pressed the professor in his own inimitable style.

'You see, Professor, if you try to see it from our point of view, it simply doesn't add up, wouldn't you agree?'

The old man lifted his grey, bushy eyebrows, but remained silent, apart from coughing intermittently.

'You left your place of work over two weeks ago, supposedly to take a one-week holiday. Nobody has heard from you since, and we find you living in a totally different part of the world. And you cannot give us an explanation? When were you planning to return to Alaska?'

The professor shrugged.

'As I've already told you, Chief Inspector – I decided to take an extended break.'

'But you didn't feel inclined to notify your employer?'

Another shrug.

'Who owns the house that you're staying in over at Snowdon?'

'I don't know. I rent it through an agency.'

'Really? Who?'

Watching the old man shrug his rounded shoulders again, Matthews fidgeted in his seat, feeling frustrated at the old man's lack of cooperation. His DCI remained stoically unaffected.

'For the benefit of the recording, Professor Romano shrugs. Professor, does this mean you do not know who you are renting the house from?'

Romano began coughing. A cough that indicated many years of cigarette smoking. Saunders stepped in, opting to play 'good cop'.

'Professor, can I get you another glass of water?'

The man nodded his wrinkled head, while pushing his empty glass across the table. He managed to clear his throat to croak a response.

'And a cigarette break would be nice.'

Robson stared into the professor's eyes for a few seconds before responding – just long enough to silently inform the professor that he had been present at enough interviews to be able to recognise delay tactics when he witnessed them.

'Sure, Professor. Interview suspended at 15:25.'

CHAPTER 96

Two unmarked CID vehicles followed a police car into an empty car park, each taking a space between the barely visible white lines. Given the early hour, all the parking bays still sat in the shadow of the mountain. Robson, along with DI Matthews, DS Burford, and DC Saunders, all lifted their heads instinctively to take in the vast peaks that surrounded them. Sergeant Griffiths watched the visitors patiently.

'It's actually hills in every single bloody direction,' Matthews observed.

'Mountains, they are, boyo. Each one is well over six hundred metres to the peak, mostly over nine hundred. Except for Yr Wyddfa – or, Snowdon, as most people know it – she's over a thousand.'

Matthews could tell the sergeant was proud of his heritage.

'Of course. I'm sure I'll soon pick up the correct terminology.'

Robson would normally have been all over such an exchange, jibing his colleague over his slip, but, while his indomitable spirit allowed him to push on with the job, he couldn't face humour at that moment. He could feel his mental state deteriorating with every day that passed that separated him from his beloved daughter. He understood that he was close to the brink, and now he had to fight against the growing melancholy he felt as he looked upon the glorious terrain he had visited previously with his late wife – the place where he had also lost her.

'Right, lead on officers, if you'd be so kind. I'm keen to get started.'

The local uniformed officers led them out on to the quiet road, where they faced a featureless youth hostel.

'The entrance to the ranger path is just by there,' declared the stocky sergeant, pointing a thick finger towards an opening on the left-hand side of the hostel. 'It's a good three and a half hours to the top.'

'Right, thanks. We might not make it to the top today. Matthews, has anyone spoken with the owners of the hostel there yet?'

'No, sir, I don't believe so.'

'You'll have a job, my friend.' Sergeant Griffiths intervened. 'Like I said earlier, the tourist season has been cancelled this year, so the hostel hasn't been open.'

'I see. Are you coming with us?'

'No, I'm afraid not, sir. We need to get back to the station. We'll leave you lot to explore.'

'Fine. Will we have any problems gaining access?'

'No, lad. Sorry ... sir. It's not that secure. Just be prepared for the uneven paths. It is going to be quite precarious given the amount of rainfall we've had this summer. I can see you've all got sensible footwear. I wouldn't recommend deviating from the paths, or what's left of them – just remember that and you'll be fine. The higher you go, the greater the chance that you'll lose visibility.'

'That it?'

'I think so, sir. Oh, just watch out for the plant machinery.'

'Thanks.'

The two constables turned and returned to the car park behind their sergeant, leaving the four CID officers to cross the narrow road. They began immediately to climb the gradient towards a farmhouse.

'Let's have a little wander, then perhaps we'll call in there,' Robson spoke as he strode ahead, remembering treading the same path a decade ago, hand in hand with his fiancé. It had been an infinitely more enjoyable trip than their return visit a couple of years later, when they had chosen to see the mountain from the air.

Robson swallowed the horrific memories, then strode on in front of the others.

CHAPTER 97

The young receptionist adopted his best professional pose as he stood to attention behind the front desk of the Royal Goat hotel. The attractive lady who had just breezed through the front door seemed to have minimal luggage with her and the newly arrived guest's allure was not, in the virile young man's opinion, in any way impaired by her apparent weariness.

As he mentally prepared his most charming greeting, he was disappointed to find that the lady's attention appeared to have been distracted. She stopped on her way to the small reception desk and gazed though the open archway to her right.

Inside the bar and restaurant area, DCI Robson reacted to a tap on his shoulder and turned his back to the bar. As Wilson entered, wheeling a small case behind her, he felt the usual tingle down his spine as he raised his hand and smiled at his ex. Robson strolled towards her, smiling.

'Here comes the weary traveller.'

'Hello, Jack.'

Unlike Wilson, Robson wasn't aware of the sudden awkwardness experienced by the small CID team behind him, as he leant in to kiss her cheek. But he soon sensed her embarrassment, as she stood like a statue with her arms straight at her sides. He stepped back, awkwardly.

'Can I get you a drink?'

She shook her head as her face broke into a listless grin.

'No, thank you. I'll check in and freshen up.'

'Fine, shall we meet for something to eat later?'

'Sure.'

She turned and, to the delight of the young man at reception, left the bar and approached the front desk. Robson frowned. He had hoped that he was over the disappointment of his failed relationship with Emma Wilson. Evidently his ex-partner had made more progress moving on than he had.

It wasn't only that though, he thought to himself, as he went to rejoin his colleagues at the bar – she was keeping something back from him, he felt sure of it.

CHAPTER 98

Sarah Connor placed a tray of drinks on the coffee table with as much enthusiasm as she could muster, while her elderly companion sat watching her in the armchair. Despite the grey and purple bruise marks visible on her flabby arms and one side of her face, the elderly woman radiated a genuine smile as she looked maternally at her younger companion.

'You don't have to put on a brave face for me you know, Sarah darling.'

'I know. I'm not – it's for me.'

Sarah began to pour Gwendoline Robson's tea.

'Okay, fine. But don't be afraid to talk to me, Sarah. I'm not quite as fragile and helpless as you might think.'

Sarah shook her head. This time, her amusement was genuine. In collaboration with the hospital staff, they had managed to persuade Mother Robson to remain on the ward, but it had only lasted a couple of days. The doctors and nurses had insisted that she would need care for the next few weeks as a minimum. It wasn't going to be a chore as far as Sarah was concerned – she knew that she would benefit from the company as much as her convalescing, adoptive mother, if not more.

'Oh, I know that, Gwen. It's just a lot to take in, that's all. Shall we put the TV on?'

Gwen's eyes became slits.

'What are you hiding, young lady?!'

Sarah chuckled and took a sip of her tea.

'Don't be silly, Mum!'

She adjusted the volume which did the trick – Gwen became instantly engaged in the quiz show. Sarah felt relieved – she wasn't confident she could have withstood too much interrogation. Perhaps from the police, but not Gwen – she had a way of peering into one's soul.

And that wouldn't do. She didn't know how relevant the information she had gathered would prove to be, but, given where it had been hidden, it seemed certain that her estranged husband hadn't wanted anyone else to find the documents – including her.

An hour later, Sarah woke to the sound of her phone ringing. She looked down at the display and then at Gwen, who had her head tilted back in the chair, with her eyes closed and mouth wide open. Sarah answered the call.

'Hi, Jack.'

'Hello, Sarah. I haven't got long, I'm meeting someone in a bit. How are you both?'

'We're fine, Jack. How are you?'

'I'm okay, but I haven't been driven into a river, or tied up in a cupboard.'

'Jack, we're safe, alive, and well. And if you don't believe me, I can place the phone closer to Gwen so that you can hear the snoring!'

'I'll speak to you again soon. Take care, both of you.'

'You do the same, Jack. See you later.'

'Oh – Sarah?'

'Yes, Jack?'

'I presume you've been home?'

'Of course.'

'Good. Now that you're going to be at my mother's place for a while, I'm getting the team to go in and carry out another search, in case Mark left anything behind that might be of use to us.'

'That's fine. I kind of expected as much.'

'Okay, good. I don't suppose you've come across anything you think we might be interested in?'

'I don't think so, Jack,' she lied, 'oh, except for a passport ...'

'Oh? Whose?'

As Sarah spoke the name, Robson felt his heart rate quicken and was momentarily paralysed.

'Jack? Are you there?'

'Y-yes, yes, thanks, Sarah. Just leave everything as you found it, okay?'

'Of course. Goodbye, Jack, take care.'

'Bye, Sarah.'

Sarah put her fingers to her lips and watched the elderly woman sleep, as she struggled with her conscience.

Am I doing the right thing?

She needed to find out more about the information she had retrieved before she shared it with anyone. Especially Jack Robson – he had enough on his plate. Sarah made her decision there and then.

CHAPTER 99

Robson approached the table and took a chair opposite his dinner companion. He noticed that Wilson seemed to have regained some of her natural vitality.

'Good evening, Jack,' said Wilson, as the waiter placed a napkin on Robson's lap.

He sat awkwardly under the attention and watched the waiter pour a deep red Rioja into his glass from the bottle Wilson had ordered for them. The waiter carefully positioned the bottle on the table and left them.

Robson relaxed into his soft seat and looked out at the tranquil setting. Across the quiet road, a stream flowed gently on the other side of a row of mature trees, which swayed in the shadow of the great mountain.

'You're looking refreshed.'

Robson planned on treading carefully, after their earlier, slightly awkward engagement.

'Thank you. I feel it.'

Robson sipped the wine, trying to read her cobalt eyes. She had pulled her hair back from her face in a neat bun, the way he had always preferred it, revealing defined cheekbones and her thin, smooth neckline.

Definitely holding something back ...

'So, I understand you've been to the mountain already, Jack, is that right?'

Robson shook off any romantic notions, having received the clear indication that they were there to talk shop. He allowed the waiter to take their orders, noting his companion still couldn't resist the temptation to order duck when it appeared on a menu.

'Briefly, yes. Just a recce.'

'And?'

'And – the place is still rather barren. Perhaps even more so nowadays. There were plenty of tyre prints, which isn't surprising, although we didn't see any of the plant machinery. But then, we didn't get far.'

She nodded thoughtfully.

'Nothing out of the ordinary, then?'

'We spoke to an elderly couple that live in the farmhouse at the bottom of the ranger path. According to them, there have been no vehicles on or off the mountain in quite some time.'

'Why would that be unusual?'

Robson shrugged.

'The tyre marks were fresh, and they continued to the bottom of the mountain. So, something has recently arrived, or departed, the mountain. But I guess the old couple weren't there to witness it.'

'Anything else?'

'Not really. We're going out again tomorrow with a larger team, so we can simultaneously cover all of the main, traditional paths up the mountain. We'll also have forensics with us to carry out a more thorough search. The only thing we observed was the odd formation of the tyre prints.'

'What do you mean?'

'Well, they weren't indicative of a continuous journey. There was one area in particular where ...'

'What?'

'Well, it's almost like someone has been 'doughnutting' up there!'

They both locked eyes as their meals were slid on to the table. Robson salivated at the aromas, preparing to tuck into the liver dish before him.

Wilson looked up from her plate. He could tell she was disappointed.

'I think we're going to have to go higher, Jack.'

'I wouldn't be surprised, but what makes you say that?'

'Well, as we discussed the other day, there has been some unusual, unauthorised electromagnetic activity detected up there.' She glanced out of the window at the cloud formation that had moved in, obscuring their view of the mountainous peak, before returning her gaze to Robson. 'And, as I have also already stated, several drones have been dispatched to carry out reconnaissance, and each one was destroyed, more or less as they passed above the summit.'

'Why haven't Special Branch been called in to deal with this?'

'It's too early. The activity was only detected a week ago. So far, we haven't been able to contact anybody from the company that's responsible for the repair and renovation work on the mountain. My bosses are keen for the investigation to proceed on foot, and they are prepared to support the investigation in any way necessary, with the support of Special Branch, if necessary.'

Robson took a sip from his wine glass, inwardly pleased that Wilson had ordered his favourite tipple. They had spent many an evening together sharing a bottle of the very same variety of Rioja. He glanced out of the window at the raw serenity before them. The sound of the stream trickling on the other side of the trees was accompanied by a lone bird singing from somewhere in the tops of the giant conifers. The mountain rose ominously in the distance before it disappeared into the clouds.

'I see. Who is the company responsible for the renovation project?'

'Gonzales Partners.'

'Never heard of them. Do we know anything about the company?'

Wilson shook her head.

'I was hoping to leave that with you to deal with, Jack.'

They looked across the table at one another in silence as the waiter collected their plates. Robson still felt there was something else. Despite her new, secretive demeanour, he could still tell when she was holding something back,

'Do we know who we're up against?'

She shook her head and pushed her near-full plate of food to one side.

'That's what we're hoping you will be able to establish, Jack,' she smiled.

'What did you manage to get out of Professor Romano?'

'Not a great deal.'

'Nothing?'

'He has basically refused to answer any questions.'

'Have you kept him in custody?'

Robson shook his head.

'He's too unwell.'

'Keep an eye on him, Jack.'

'I know, we intend to. He's on bail.'

'Based on what charge?'

'Possessing a firearm without a licence. And obstruction.'

The faintest of smirks passed across her face, as Wilson slowly rose from her chair.

Instinctively, Robson stood in response.

'I'm bushed, Jack. Early breakfast?'

He nodded.

'Go ahead. I'll take care of the bill.'

They exchanged a brief embrace as she passed his chair, and Robson remained standing as he watched her depart the dining room, before taking his seat again. Suddenly alone with his own thoughts, Robson turned his attention to the half-full bottle of red. For a moment, he contemplated drowning his melancholy, but he remained sufficiently sober to make the right decision.

He abandoned the table and instructed the waiter to charge the bill to his room before leaving the restaurant. Robson nodded to the young receptionist as he passed the desk and began loping up the stairs, two at a time. He felt a degree of pity for the young man, who must only have been in his late teens, for having to endure his long shift duration.

*

The sound of the telephone brought Robson out of his comatose state. He looked down at his own body, confused to see himself fully clothed. His mind still a cacophony of unfinished dreams, he remembered leaving the dining room some time ago – what seemed like an age – but now he was lying on his bed, fully dressed.

He noted the time on his phone – 23:35. He'd only left the restaurant an hour and a half ago. Even more surprising was the displayed caller ID. Robson cleared his throat before answering.

'Hi. You okay?'

'Hi. Yes, fine. Are you alone?'

'Yes, of course, why?'

'Someone's been trying to get in here … into my hotel room.'

Robson's drowsy brain was suddenly alert.

'Are you sure?'

'Positive.'

'I'll come. Which room?'

'Twent—'

Within seconds of the line going dead, Robson was flying along the corridor, jabbing at his phone and desperately trying to reconnect with Wilson.

CHAPTER 100

Miller focussed his attention on the road ahead, mentally shutting down another surge of throbbing pain from his wrist, which was dumped on the armrest of the door. With his left hand, he dragged the steering wheel to the right and hammered the jeep around a large lorry. The girl and her new chauffeur were only a quarter of a mile ahead.

The ex-harbour master had learnt many useful skills during his incarceration. The ability to control pain was but one. Inwardly, he was proud of his achievements, considering how close he had been to ending it all during his earliest, darkest days inside. He had devoted himself to the movement and he had been unfailing in his belief that they would be there for him. But, after the death – the murder – of Sir Geoffrey Charlesworth, and in the months after the judge had delivered his sentence eight years ago, Miller had felt more alone than ever before. He thought he had been abandoned.

Often, he remembered his first day as a Category-A inmate on Block 1 at HMP Belmarsh. He had only been granted a day in Block 3 to 'bed in' to prison life. In his own room, he had pondered whether they had really abandoned him – he, Jacob Miller, after all he had done for the movement.

The next day, he got his answer. As soon as he was escorted through the gates to his new, permanent residence – Block 1 – he knew he had not been given favour. It had been immediately clear that the sight of the overweight harbourmaster would provide the other long-serving prisoners with malevolent

316

amusement. The look on each of their faces was unmistakable – they were going to have great fun with their new companion.

For the first few days, the abuse was psychological. But he knew it was only going to be a matter of time before things escalated. The assaults started the moment he attempted to decline their first carnal advances. On the whole, they were always careful not to inflict too much damage, for the last thing they wanted was to lose their new plaything to the prison hospital.

And so it continued for the unfortunate Prisoner AB6794AA. The insatiable inmates would always use just enough force to coerce their dumpy new toy into compliance. After only a few weeks inside those formidable walls, Miller had felt utterly forsaken. On one occasion, when the animals had taken things a little too far, they had left Miller with a fractured jaw, not to mention severe rectal trauma.

While recuperating in the hospital's infirmary, one of the more compassionate guards began to visit him regularly. He seemed to read what was going through Jacob Miller's mind. The concerned guard had been right – in the temporary peace of his hospital bed, Miller was planning his suicide.

The lifeline offered by the guard seemed futile and a little far-fetched. But Miller agreed to give yoga classes a go, at least until he could acquire the equipment he needed to finish himself.

Six months after moving to his new home, he met Bingwen Liu for the first time. His new yoga teacher was ostensibly a quiet, unassuming man. But beneath the pleasant exterior there hid a lethal weapon. Bingwen Liu was a master of more than simply yoga. A diminutive, second generation Chinese man, Liu was an expert in martial arts.

Over the first few weeks of his new training programme, Miller began to feel fitter and more confident. And, thanks to the privacy they had been entrusted with, Liu had also made him feel wanted in a way Miller had never experienced before –the ex-harbour master began to appreciate the small man's exotic beauty.

On experiencing such promising changes over such a short space of time, Miller took Bingwen Liu's advice and also began to use the prison gymnasium.

The attacks still came, and Miller stood no chance of holding his own against a gang of burly men. The sick bastards turned up wherever he went, including the gym, in which there was one particularly gruesome assault on him, his naked body mercilessly fastened to a piece of apparatus by its steel cable while it happened.

But as well as his improving physical condition, Miller's mental toughness was growing exponentially – Bingwen Liu also taught him how to meditate. The inmates saw Miller daily and, perhaps for them, the transformation was gradual and less noticeable. What, in fact, eventually happened to Miller over the next eighteen months was nothing short of a metamorphosis. Bingwen Liu had created a new being and, two years after beginning his incarceration, Miller knew he was ready.

He began to face his aggressors one by one, and he enjoyed each encounter equally.

For his first act of revenge, Miller killed the fellow inmate inside his own cell, effectively snapping his tree-trunk of a neck. The next two retaliations resulted in paralysis for one, and instant death for the other, from a precisely delivered jab to a vital pressure point. At this point, the attacks on Miller stopped.

Although Miller now had the skills to defend himself, his regular visits with Bingwen Liu continued, partly to carry on honing his skills, but predominantly because he couldn't get enough of his new male lover.

The entire prison watched the ex-harbourmaster in awe. The coroner's verdict for Miller's two deceased victims at that point was 'accidental death'. That was when Miller knew for sure. He had not been forgotten after all.

But that had already been confirmed, for it turned out that Bingwen Liu was more than a martial arts teacher; he was the movement's man on the inside, and he was there to rescue Miller. Or, at least, to equip Miller with the means to rescue himself.

Miller began to radiate an aura of invincibility, a reputation which was sealed when he eliminated another two of his tormentors at the same time, in full view of a prison audience.

Like the rest of the group, his opponents were not small men, but Miller made both muscle-bound thugs look like children in the prison's dining hall. The two had appeared nervous but clearly felt they could take Miller together. In the end, neither of them managed to land so much as a single blow on inmate AB6794AA, who showed the entire block 1 community the level of savage skill he had become capable of. Henceforth, his power was indisputable, amplified further by the fact that the guards had looked the other way, only eventually arriving at the scene to clear up the mess and recover the two corpses.

Two former tormentors remained. Miller had deliberately saved them until last, knowing full well that they were the group's ringleaders. Both men lived in fear, knowing their day would arrive. The day they both arrived at his cell, Miller enjoyed every moment as, together, they begged for his forgiveness. It had been quite pathetic.

The day before the two men had arrived to make their pleas for absolution, Miller's bent solicitor, Tristan Cumberwell, had been to visit. After several months of planning and negotiations, the end to his incarceration was in sight. There was a date for his hearing, which, his solicitor assured him, would result in the approval of their application for him to be reclassified as a category C prisoner, due to his 'impeccable behaviour'. Incredibly, his solicitor was even able to inform him of the week in which he would be transferred.

Miller knew then that he had four weeks left to enjoy himself with the two apologetic men, his only surviving tormentors. He was to have his fun before he departed.

Both men did as Miller commanded for the next four weeks. It had been hard on them for sure, but at least they were surviving. When Miller's last day arrived, they knew they had to conceal their elation. He could still get to them if he wanted to, right up until their cell doors were locked.

Upon hearing the clunking of metal doors echoing along the corridor on Miller's final night, his two former tormentors could not resist the impulse to celebrate. The guards had to visit Miller's two slaves twice to tell them to keep the noise down. They knew they couldn't push it any further. And they knew that Miller would have heard what he had needed to. But they were free again … in a prison sense …

Later, as they played cards under the light of their headtorches, both men looked up in surprise from their poker hands when the cell door clunked again. They had never been interrupted in a card game before then – the guards knew better – and they had been quiet since the last request. Surely the governor hadn't been summoned for such a minor misdemeanour.

Then they understood.

They saw the embodiment of their fate standing in the doorway of the cell and it was suddenly clear why they had been allowed to live. Miller had simply wanted to make them sweat for as long as possible. But their stays of execution had now expired.

*

Miller waited until he hit another straight stretch of road before releasing his grip from the steering wheel. After deftly operating his phone, he swiftly replaced his only functional hand on the wheel and waited for the voice to sound on the jeep's stubbornly basic audio system.

It was just about the only voice left in the world he felt any veneration for, and he wanted to please Naamah more than anything.

'Jacob. Tell me you have some better news since we last spoke.'

Miller knew he would not be immune to the organisation's ruthlessness if he failed. Earlier, when he had telephoned headquarters, he was careful to ensure the blame for the girl's escape could only lie with Ben, who, conveniently, should by then have been somewhere at the bottom of the Irish Sea. But now there was no one left to blame. Not even Carlos.

'Yes, Naamah. I have visual on the car. I won't lose them.'

'Make sure you don't. Do what you must, Jacob. Ideally, I'd like to know who the getaway driver is.'

'Of course. I'll do my best.'

'But that is not your priority. As you are well aware.'

Miller smiled at the callousness implied by Naamah's words as he overtook another car. They were approaching narrower mountain passes now and the vista became more dramatic the higher they climbed.

*

Inside the saloon car, Jasmine continued to tremble. She turned to face forward again, having seen that the jeep at their rear was getting closer. She watched the little spectacled man's reaction, desperately hoping for some sign of assurance. But reassurance did not arrive.

He hadn't spoken since screaming at her while throwing her into the back seat of the car half an hour ago – 'stay there, if you want to live!'

She thought there was a foreign accent to his voice. *Perhaps Italian ... or maybe French?* The man had remained icily calm throughout the journey, until now. Now, he looked rattled.

He shouted over his shoulder into the back of the vehicle.

'Jasmine!'

Definitely French, she decided privately, while remaining silent, too frightened to speak.

'Listen to me, Jasmine. This is important. I need to explain why I rescued you, we don't have much time.'

CHAPTER 101

The receptionist could not have been much older than nineteen or twenty. He seemed pleased at first to be called into action. But the chief inspector had suddenly become rather intimidating. Robson held his warrant card aloft in front of him, so that it nearly touched the young lad's nose.

'I do not fucking well care about the hotel's privacy policy. This is a police matter and, unless you wish to be arrested for obstruction, give me Ms Wilson's room number.'

'S-sir, it's twenty-four. First floor.'

Robson replaced his identification and held out his palm.

'Key!'

The young man was perspiring. He retrieved a key from one of the hooks behind him and handed it to Robson, who was halfway up the stairs again by the time the receptionist had lifted the phone.

The brass room numbers on the door were showing signs of age and rattled slightly as Robson knocked.

'Emma!' he hissed.

There was no response. He noted there were no obvious signs of forced entry as he turned the key in the lock and threw the wooden door open.

'Wilson!'

Robson ran to the crumpled figure in the middle of the worn carpet, instinctively placing his fingers on the side of the casualty's neck, hoping to find a pulse. The groan which emanated through swollen, bloodied lips gave Robson sufficient confidence to momentarily leave the casualty and dart towards the open window, which faced out of the front of the hotel.

He stared at a dark saloon in the lay-by below which represented the entirety of the hotel's parking facilities. Despite not being able to see through the car's blacked-out windows from that distance, somehow, he knew that Wilson's attacker was staring back at him. Dust filled the air for a moment as the vehicle span out into the road and disappeared.

Robson made a mental note of the registration plate before turning back to the room. His surprise at finding that Wilson's hands had been bound behind her back was surpassed only by the unexpected sight of the figure in the doorway.

'What are you doing here?'

'Sir,' the young receptionist's voice trembled, 'I came to ask if you needed help. I've called the police.'

Robson frowned again at the sight of Wilson's bound wrists. Despite her incapacitation, she had now managed to move to a seated position, in a demonstration of her core strength.

'Son, we are the bloody police. I tell you what, you want to be useful? Go fetch me a pair of strong scissors please.'

'Of course, sir.'

The young man could be heard running along the corridor as Robson spoke into his phone.

'Matthews. Get yourself over to room twenty-four immediately. First floor.'

He wandered over to the bedside table and grabbed a handful of tissues, before crouching beside her and dabbing her lips with the soft paper.

'You okay?'

She stared at the blood-soaked tissue and nodded.

'Emma, who was here? And what the hell were they after?'

He noted the open, discarded case at the side of the bed, and rose to inspect the mess further. The contents had been strewn across the floor. A trail of belongings led into the dated bathroom. A broken bottle of perfume teetering on the edge of the avocado green sink. Absentmindedly, he noted from the aroma that she still wore his favourite scent.

He re-entered the bedroom to discover that the receptionist had let himself back in and stood awkwardly in the doorway holding a pair of scissors. Impatiently, Robson indicated towards the dishevelled casualty with his eyes. He watched the young man as he knelt close to Wilson and fumbled with the scissors. His thin arms shook as he squeezed the scissors together. The boy seemed to be intimidated by being so close to Wilson. There was a clunk as the thick ties finally gave. Even from his standing position, Robson could see they had already left angry, red marks on her wrists.

The receptionist rose with a guilty expression, feeling the DCI's inquisitive stare.

'Who did you allow past the reception desk?'

The young man gulped, beads of sweat showing on his brow.

'They were undercover police officers, sir.'

'Did they have identification?'

The young man hesitated.

'What's your name, lad?'

'I-it's Owen, sir.'

'Owen. Do you like working here?'

'I-I suppose so, sir. It pays okay.'

'Then I strongly suggest that you tell me everything, all right?'

The boy nodded. His cheeks looked flushed.

'Did they have identification?'

'Yes, sir.'

'How many were there?'

'Two.'

Robson looked up at DI Matthews, who stood in the doorway looking concerned as he surveyed the scene. Wilson, who was now laid on the bed and making the most of being able to move her arms again, did not acknowledge their colleague's arrival. The receptionist looked relieved at being given a temporary reprieve from his inquisition as the DCI addressed his colleague.

'There was a break-in. They escaped in a dark saloon.'

Robson then reeled off the memorised registration plate, wondering all along if the same people knew of Jasmine's whereabouts.

'They have ten minutes on you. Go and wake Burford and Saunders and get after them. Let me know as soon as you track them down. And get hold of uniform – the receptionist has already called them. Tell them not to waste time coming here and that we are dealing with it. They'll be more use to you in tracking down the vehicle.'

'Yes, sir.'

Matthews left without hesitation, very much aware of the signs that told him the boss wasn't taking questions. Robson resumed his inquisition.

'What were the officer's names?'

'I can't remember, sir.'

'Think hard, my friend. This is important.'

'Sorry, sir. They only flashed their identification cards. I only noticed the titles.'

'What were the titles?'

'Special Branch, I think, sir.'

Robson glanced at Wilson, who now looked back at him, while Owen remained frozen to the spot, looking petrified. Robson felt his pulse quicken as he handed a card to the young receptionist.

'If you think of anything else, call me.'

'Yes, sir.'

'And Owen …'

The lad turned back, standing in the doorway.

'You tell nobody else about what has happened, including your boss, is that understood?'

He nodded and left.

Robson moved his fingers through slightly greying hair as he sat on the bed. Wilson was staring at a spot on the ceiling while continuing to hold blood-soaked tissue to her mouth.

'What were they after, Emma?'

Silence.

Robson turned to look at her. She was still beautiful, he thought, even with a split lip and bruised face. But he could never remember her behaving so secretively. Nor ever being this quiet.

'Do you think they were going to kidnap you?'

He began to feel frustrated at the silence.

'Emma, I can't help unless—'

'Lock the door, Jack.'

Robson realised, from her impeccably calm demeanour, that she was still in control. He did as she asked and pulled the seat away from the bedside desk so that he could sit facing her. Wilson sat up again and slid to the edge of the bed until her legs flopped over, the two of them only a foot apart.

'Jack, they think I have information.'

Robson waited, then became impatient.

'What information?'

'Incriminating information.'

'Incriminating for who?'

She seemed to be about to speak, then suddenly her frozen exterior cracked. Her head fell into her hands and she began to sob. Robson got up and sat next to her on the bed. Instinctively, he wrapped his arm around her, pulling her in tight. It no longer felt awkward, but perfectly natural.

Their embrace lasted for a minute and when Robson gently pushed her away, his shirt was slightly damp with her tears, along with the odd trace of blood.

'I knew there was something. What is it you've been trying to tell me, Emma?'

He could see that her moment of weakness had passed as quickly as it had arrived, and she once more wore her resolute exterior. Robson had always been amazed at how quickly she seemed to recover from such incidents. Wilson instantly appeared to be in full control of herself again, so her next, impulsive move, was entirely unexpected.

The kiss came without warning and, at first, Robson froze in shock, as

Wilson pressed moist lips against his. After a few seconds, her familiar taste and smell was too much to resist. He grabbed her head firmly and squeezed her hard with his long fingers as they began to fall back on the bed together.

It seemed like the passion between them was more electric than ever before, as though the years apart had generated a renewed sense of longing, despite their familiarity, resulting in a level of excitement that was pulsating. They panted together, oblivious to the mess that surrounded the bed, the contents of her raided case now jumbled with the clothing they had ripped from one another's bodies in their desperation to once again be with one another.

For the next fifteen minutes, everything else was forgotten as Robson experienced the thrill of being with her again and the scintillating feel of their naked bodies together.

Once it was over, Robson's only thoughts were of Wilson's new fiancé. He laid on his back next to her and neither of them spoke. It had been almost too wonderful for words, but it had also been awful and became more torturous as his sense of fulfilment faded. Their parting, years ago, had been painfully sudden and without any formal farewell. In that moment, Robson sensed that this was it. The belated goodbye.

He had never liked goodbyes.

CHAPTER 102

Detective Inspector Matthews looked around at the weary faces in the briefing room. He knew this would be a tough shift. Robson had instructed them to gather at 5 am for the briefing, so they could get an early start on the mountain. Even the DCI himself seemed a little out of sorts compared to his usual standards, but everyone knew the reason for that, or at least they thought they did.

Matthews had already briefed them that they would be split into four teams of eight. Each team would cover a quadrant of the mountain, and would comprise a CID representative, uniformed support provided either by the local constabulary or drafted in from the wider south-west force, forensics, and mountain specialists.

DI Matthews now looked towards his DCI for approval.

Robson felt dizzy as he rose to address the packed room. He had left Wilson's hotel room at three o'clock that morning and collapsed into his own bed shortly after. When his alarm sounded at four, the memories of the previous night had seemed surreal. He took a large swig of water and addressed the officers.

'Thank you, DI Matthews. Right, you all know your teams. I'd like you to spend the next half an hour familiarising yourselves with your allocated territory. Your mountain specialists will take the lead on that. One further point – we don't know what, if anything, we're going to find up there. I want you all to have open minds. If there is the faintest sniff of forensic evidence, we work on it there and then, understood?'

Heads nodded to accompany the murmured affirmations in response to the DCI's searching look.

'If a forensic officer thinks they have something that justifies more comprehensive analysis, then that will be our priority, and support will be provided by the other teams if necessary. Any questions?'

He noted the jaded looks around the room. He knew several of them would be inwardly questioning what they had done to deserve this reallocation. At least his own detectives appeared to be chomping at the bit.

'No? Good. In addition to the resources inside this room, we have Special Branch on standby should they be required. Right then, let's get on with it. Our next rendezvous will be over the secure radios. Let's say 6:15.'

As the officers began to file out of the busy room, a young constable flew in through the open door. DC Saunders gave the young man a disapproving look, having narrowly escaped the swinging door.

'DCI Robson. Sir, I'm sorry for the intrusion.'

'What's the problem, Constable?'

'Sir, I thought you ought to know – we've just received communication from the coastguard. They've found two bodies washed up on the peninsula. They are saying they think that it must have occurred quite recently.'

Robson frowned at the young officer, as Wilson suddenly appeared behind him and squeezed past to enter the room. The room fell silent as a bruised version of the normally vibrant-looking woman walked into the middle of the room. Wilson's swollen lip protruded involuntarily as she focussed on the constable. Robson swallowed, ignoring the attention.

'And what relevance is this to me, Constable?'

'Sir, the coastguard also received a report yesterday evening from a passing vessel. They reported seeing what appeared to be a fracas on the clifftop at Devil's Point at approximately six o'clock yesterday evening. They reported witnessing two bodies falling into the sea. There was a spring tide, so they couldn't risk getting any closer to the rocks. They reported it to the coastguard.'

Robson let out an impatient sigh as Wilson intervened.

'Have the bodies been identified, Constable?'

He shook his head.

'No, ma'am, not yet. However, the on-duty patrol went over to Devil's Point late yesterday evening. There aren't many residents within the locality, but our officers spoke to the inhabitants of a property just off the coast road who reported witnessing some unusual behaviour sometime after 6 pm yesterday.'

'Go on,' encouraged Wilson.

'Apparently, the residents were in the garden having a barbecue when a car raced past them at excessive speed. They reckon it must have been travelling at eighty or maybe ninety miles per hour. Then a few minutes later, a jeep went past doing a similar speed. Both vehicles heading inland.'

Robson took over.

'This is all very interesting, Constable, but we are about to embark on a strategically vital operation. Can we leave this to you and your colleagues, do you think?'

The young man began to look sheepish as his sergeant arrived on the scene. The sturdy Sergeant Griffiths immediately took over the constable's difficult task.

'DCI Robson, we sent a car over to Devil's Point early this morning to have another look around in the daylight. They found tyre marks and footprints. We currently have the area cordoned off …'

Robson noted that even the sergeant seemed to enjoy prevarication. *Will no one just come to the bloody point?*

'Sir, our officers also discovered a student ID card. It belongs to a female secondary school student, sir – Jasmine Robson.'

Seconds later, with the news still sinking in, DI Matthews interrupted the silence with a commanding voice.

'Okay everyone. We've only got another hour before our next rendezvous. Let's go!'

Most officers seemed to be looking anywhere but at DCI Robson as they departed the briefing room. Every officer from Somerset CID fought to hide their true feelings, with the exception of Matthews and Robson. DCI Robson cast his inspector a steely look.

'Thanks, James. Please proceed without me, we cannot afford any delay. I'm going to the mortuary and will catch you up later. Get a forensic presence over to Devil's Point immediately.'

Matthews nodded. He desperately wanted to put an arm around his DCI's shoulder.

'Of course, sir.'

Wilson, who had been fighting off her own emotion, noted Matthews' doubtful expression.

'Carry on, DI Matthews. I will accompany DCI Robson.'

As Matthews left, Sergeant Griffiths stepped in.

'Sir, we'll take you up there ourselves ... as soon as you're ready.'

*

The crackle of the radio was a welcome interruption to the silence as far as Sergeant Griffiths was concerned. Not that he didn't understand the reason for the silence – the whole force was aware of DCI Robson's incredibly tragic situation – but the tension in the patrol car had become unbearable.

Peculiarly, the DCI himself had seemed quite calm, even focussed. But his colleague, the MI5 woman, seemed oddly far more on edge than him.

Anyone would have thought it was her daughter that was missing.

'Griffiths,' the Sergeant responded on the squad car's radio.

'Sir, it's control. I don't know if you've arrived at the mortuary yet, but we have more details.'

Griffiths saw the alertness in Wilson's eyes. DCI Robson continued to look out of the rear side window adjacent to her.

'Go on.'

'Both corpses are confirmed as adult male. We're still working on their identities.'

'Okay, noted, thank you, control. Out.'

They were only one turn away from the mortuary. Before they reached the turning, Wilson began to sob. Griffiths surreptitiously eyed the rear-view mirror and watched Robson wipe the back of his hand against his own watery eyes, before putting his arm around the MI5 officer.

*

The pathologist was a tall, lean man. His white lab coat appeared pristine, and Robson wondered if the man remembered that he had at some point placed a pencil behind his ear.

Sergeant Griffiths had introduced Robson and Wilson to Doctor Fraser but elected to remain in the background for the remainder of the visit. He stood behind them as the doctor slowly peeled the sheet away from the first body. Griffiths screwed up his face, as though trying to discern whether the mess that lay on the slab was even human. Robson leant in, ignoring the deathly scent.

'Like I was saying,' Doctor Fraser looked at Wilson as he spoke, leaving the DCI to inspect the carnage, 'the bodies have been pretty badly smashed up. Dental records are the only way we're going to identify this one.'

Robson nodded, showing no emotional reaction to what he was viewing.

'Are there any signs of damage that could have been inflicted by anything other than rocks, Doctor?'

The pathologist adopted a pensive frown.

'It's going to be fairly difficult for us to determine that, Chief Inspector. As you can see, this guy has been smashed about a bit, so if any trauma was incurred prior to him ending up in the sea, then it is going to take time for us to be able to identify it.'

Wilson nodded in understanding. Inwardly, she still felt relieved that neither of the bodies were child-like in stature. Especially not the second, judging by the shape beneath the blanket a few yards away.

'What about the other one?' she asked.

'Well, it's taken a hammering too. But, as you will notice, the second specimen is a rather more robust sample and has, consequently, remained a little more intact. Even the face, somewhat surprisingly.'

Doctor Fraser covered the first corpse and moved across to a second slab, where Wilson already stood. Robson joined them and Griffiths moved to the rear again, letting out a whistle.

'Good grief, I see what you mean!' exclaimed the Welshman. 'What a colossus!'

After a few seconds, both Griffiths and the pathologist noticed that the other two had become totally absorbed by the image before them. Robson and Wilson each looked momentarily shocked.

'Erm, if you don't mind me saying … You both look like you've just seen a ghost, officers,' said Fraser.

Robson didn't react.

'I believe we have, Doctor,' Wilson gasped.

'You both know this man?'

'Let's just say we go back a bit,' she continued. 'Although we certainly never expected to see him again, did we?'

She looked at Robson. Robson shook his head as he considered the evidence, which provided perhaps the strongest indication yet that the Arcam community was alive and well. But the question that remained unanswered was – what did they want with Jasmine?

*

Robson gazed down at the sea. He wondered which of the jagged rocks the two unfortunate fallers had been broken against. Despite being surrounded by a wild bleakness, the place, to Robson, still seemed to possess beauty on a certain level. Dark beauty. *Perhaps that was where the name came from.* Devil's Point certainly didn't seem to be the sort of place one would come for a picnic.

'Jack.'

Robson turned at the familiar voice. Wilson stood a couple of feet from him, in from the cliff edge.

'Are you okay?'

He nodded.

'Fine. You?'

She rolled her eyes at his stubborn stoicism.

'You are allowed to be emotional you know?'

He shrugged.

'And how will that benefit me?'

'Jack, when we found out neither of the bodies was Jasmine in the car earlier, you almost seemed like you already knew ... '

He looked thoughtful.

'I suppose I did.'

'How?'

'The student card – why, out of all the possessions that could have been left behind, would there be such an obvious means of identification?'

'What do you mean? You think that Jasmine left us a clue?'

He shrugged again.

'Possibly.'

Wilson spoke to the nearest member of the forensic team.

'Where was the girl's ID card found?'

The man remained crouched low, and his white suit ruffled slightly as he raised an arm to point towards a group of rocks immediately next to a small area of foliage which circled the blackened, charred remains of a fire that someone had previously built. Robson and Wilson both wandered over to the spot.

'On these rocks?' Wilson shouted again.

The same forensics officer rose this time and decided to join them.

'Yes, right here,' the man nodded, hands on hips.

'How had it been left, exactly?' Wilson probed.

'It was wedged beneath a couple of the stones.'

'I supposed there's no way of knowing when it would have been left?' she continued.

'Well, actually, I think there could be. You'll notice the emphatic tyre marks on the ground here,' he pointed to the ground immediately to their left. 'I'd suggest, as a working theory, that the identification was left deliberately, just before they left in quite a hurry. The way the card had been forcibly wedged in so that it was easily legible, certainly appeared deliberate. And there was also this ...'

Robson frowned at the area highlighted by the forensics officer. He stood to get a better vantage position and gradually made out the rough shape of an arrow. The symbol was pointing towards the small mound of rocks that had housed the ID card. He buried his hope and walked towards nearby tyre marks. The forensics officer stood behind Robson as he crouched to inspect the dirt again.

'Just a standard saloon?'

The forensics officer nodded.

'Seems so.'

Robson remained low to the ground, studying the area as he spoke.

'Was anything else found here?'

'Yes, sir, as a matter of fact. Further writing etched into the dirt. You can barely make it out now because we've had a shower since arriving earlier, but I can show you a photo. We think it must be a name.'

Robson and Wilson both leant in to look at the forensic officer's phone display. The officer swiped a gloved thumb across the phone's screen to skip from the photo of the arrow beside their feet to reveal the next image in the gallery. A second image appeared on the screen. Robson and Wilson both stared in silence at the single word that had been scraped into the ground - MILLER.

CHAPTER 103

Thirteen-year-old Jasmine Robson watched the small man's eyes in the rear-view mirror. This must be what they mean by Hobson's choice, she thought. Which of her would-be kidnappers seemed more insane? *The guy that wants to throw me off a cliff, or the man that seems hell-bent on driving us both off one?!*

The girl suppressed a scream as her chauffeur took another hairpin bend too quickly and momentarily seemed to lose control. The tyres screamed and let out a ripping sound as the stocky little driver fought to retrieve the car from a ditch at the side of the road. The wheels span furiously, distributing wet mud all over the sides of the vehicle. Suddenly, the noise of their own vehicle was overpowered by another roaring engine. Jasmine jerked her head round to look out of the rear window and saw the jeep she had previously occupied flying towards them at high speed.

She braced herself for impact as the front tow bar of the pursuing jeep grew menacingly close. The axle of their vehicle groaned as its spinning front wheels finally gained traction and drew the vehicle from the ditch. She screamed at the impact from the rear as they snaked back on to the mountain road. Beads of sweat had formed on Marchand's forehead. He fought to regain control but did not dare to release his right foot even a millimetre from the accelerator. The engine yelled at him for a higher gear.

In the small car park on their right, a small gathering of people was engaged in enthusiastic conversation, evidently enjoying the enchanting mountain vista after an enriching hike. Focussed on the approaching bend, Marchand paid them no attention and therefore didn't see them looking in disapproval at the two apparent maniacs that screamed past them on the narrow mountain road. The onlookers knew the boy-racers were dicing with death – one false move would be all it took. The walkers shook their heads in unison before returning their attention to Mother Nature. A few returned binoculars to their faces, while others preferred to behold the panoramic view unaided.

A hundred yards away from them, the driver of the jeep saw his chance. His prey had been unable to open a lead on him and, despite the first car's additional power, the driver couldn't quite match the dexterity with which Miller handled the treacherous route. Miller had forgotten all about his distorted wrist. He eyed the next bend ahead and made his decision.

In the front car, Marchand drew a little confidence from the additional lead he had been gradually building. He touched the brake gently as they reached another ninety-degree bend. As the car slowed in response to his late brake application, his heart thumped on hearing the jeep's engine screaming up behind them.

Marchand's horror-filled glance into his rear-view mirror would be his last. The impact of steel on steel echoed between the threatening mountains on either side, but the sound paled into insignificance compared with the explosion to come. The car shook from the impact and flew from the road sideways, immediately beginning to roll down into the deep chasm below.

Miller paused and drew breath. From his high vantage point inside the jeep, he watched the scene unfold below. The smoke that rose seemed to be a mixture of dust and mist, but the explosion was music to Miller's ears. He watched the fireball with a sadistic grin.

Two birds with one stone.

The group of enthusiasts in the car park looked at one another with shocked expressions, their disbelief increasing as they witnessed the jeep crawl away until it disappeared around the bend.

Inside the jeep, the driver nonchalantly made a call which was answered swiftly. This time, as though anticipating a parent's approval, he was looking forward to breaking the news.

'Hello, Jacob.'

'It's done.'

Miller understood the long pause was no indication of doubt. He heard Naamah let out a sigh of satisfaction.

'Well done, Jacob. Now let's get on with this, shall we?'

'I'll be back within the hour.'

'Good. See you soon, Jacob. I have some news about our friend Mr Connor for you.'

CHAPTER 104

Robson and Wilson sat facing one another in a secluded corner of the bar. Things seemed more intimate between them again, yet at the same time, more distant. Robson was in no doubt that she thoroughly regretted their recent physical encounter and was doing her best to avoid acknowledging it. She might not have felt the same love for him any longer, but he knew she cared about him and he also understood she was probably trying to spare him any further heartache. He observed her with a hollow feeling in his gut as she determinedly steered the conversation towards the job.

'So, there's nothing to report from the investigation on the mountain today, Jack?'

Robson's head pounded. He knew the stress was catching up with him, but he couldn't let it show. If he revealed any hint of the fact that the situation was becoming too much for him to manage, he would be removed as SIO, as a minimum, that much he knew for sure.

He took a final swig of whisky, emptying another tumbler, and savoured the mouthful of liquor as he gently replaced his empty glass on the table. His throat burned pleasantly, his anxiety lessening with every drink. Nonetheless, his mind was becoming an unpleasantly dark place to inhabit and he was thankful to be given any opportunity to stay away from its frightening speculations. He swallowed the whisky and shook his head in response.

'Not yet. They've been working late to recover as much forensic evidence as possible. I believe we're expecting another downpour tonight.'

Wilson nodded, her eyes displaying sympathy and unmistakable compassion.

Robson's head was scrambled. His mother had been assaulted in her own home, and his best friend – his daughter's surrogate mother – had been duped by a dangerous spy. And now his beloved daughter was missing. The circumstances should have overwhelmed him, but he was determined not to let that happen. The memory of his wife lived on in his soul. Her spirit had become his lifeblood, and he would not let Isabelle down, especially not regarding their daughter. Yet, despite his extraordinary troubles, he felt a fervent desire for Wilson. Last night hadn't been enough. Not anywhere near it. Suddenly, he was consumed with the need to be with her again. He made a conscious effort to control his breathing before he spoke.

'You know what? Since our reunion, we haven't spoken about ourselves, have we?'

Wilson shrugged. She recognised the look in his eyes. She wasn't offended, in fact she would have loved to nurture it. Yet she was concerned – last night had been a mistake. One big mistake, and it had been entirely her fault. She offered him a non-committal response.

'I don't suppose we have, but aren't there more important issues to discuss?'

Robson gave her a sad smile. Wilson thought he suddenly appeared a little intoxicated. There was a subtle glint in his eyes as he spoke.

'What's your story, Emma?'

Time for diplomacy, Wilson thought to herself.

'That's top secret, Jack.'

Robson had always admired her dry sense of humour. It was one of several personality traits they shared.

'Why don't you tell me about you, Jack?'

'There can't be anything you don't already know,' Robson snorted slightly, as he downed another Scotch seconds after a waiter had deposited it on their table.

'What do you mean?'

'Well, you're the secret service, aren't you? You knew about my arrest and you knew about my personal circumstances.'

Wilson forced a conciliatory grin.

'I knew what I needed to, Jack. Nothing more.'

'Whatever. Anyway, never mind me. You're the mysterious one. Do you want to tell me about that ring that was on your wedding finger when we met in your little underground base? It seems to have disappeared since.'

Wilson glanced at her left hand, self-consciously.

'It's early days. His name's Michael. We met—'

'At work?' Robson indicated to the barman for another Scotch.

'No,' Wilson admonished. 'We met in a jazz club. He's an IT engineer.'
Robson nodded.

'I hope you'll both be happy.'

The conversation had hit a height of awkwardness. Wilson exhaled at the sudden noise from the bar.

'Last orders please, ladies and gentlemen!'
Saved by the bell.

Robson waved to the barman again and held up two fingers, doubling his previous order.

'Take it easy, Jack. Haven't we got an early start back on the mountain tomorrow?'

He shrugged.

'One for the road. You feel free to go on if you like.'

Wilson ignored the comment.

'Have you spoken with Sarah?'

'Why?'

'Jack!' she gasped. 'I just wondered how she is!'

'She's okay, under the circumstances. She's looking after my mother.'

'What's her take on Connor?'

'That he's a total fucking scumbag, I should think. An audacious scumbag though, you have to say.'

'Has she been able to provide any useful information?'

Robson shook his head silently, accepting the double whisky from the barman.

'Why don't you just tell me what you already know that I know.' Robson's speech was becoming slurred. 'Or, better still, let's talk about who it was that broke into your hotel room and assaulted you the other night. And how the vehicle possessed an untraceable VRN – what do you say?'

Wilson was sitting perfectly upright and looked at him seriously. She had hoped this moment wouldn't arrive, but Robson was, quite understandably, losing his ability to remain objective. She began to feel nauseous but managed to maintain an even tone.

'Jack, what do you mean by *what you know*?'

'Let's not play games, Emma.'

Robson regretted slamming the empty tumbler down a little too hard, attracting the attention of the few remaining customers.

'As you are already aware, Sarah found a passport.'

'That's impossible, Jack. We examined the house ourselves and removed pretty much everything that looked like it belonged to Connor. There were no identity papers, which wasn't unexpected – we know he has enough material with him to enable him to assume several aliases.'

Robson's eyes pierced hers. Wilson was good. Anyone else would have been fooled into believing that she was being truthful.

'Tut, tut,' he mocked cynically, 'so you mean I might know something that you don't, Officer Wilson?'

'Jack, seriously, I understand the pressure you're under, but – not to put too fine a point on it – let's cut the fucking crap. If you know something, then you need to tell me.'

'Sarah knew of a little garage that Connor rented, just around the corner from their home. He obviously believed he had managed to keep it a secret. I guess he didn't realise that Sarah had found out about it. She told me there wasn't too much of interest inside there – tools and security paraphernalia he needed for the job, items that Sarah wouldn't have wanted in the house. But she also found a passport containing Mark Connor's mugshot – but guess what? It didn't belong to any Mark Connor.'

'Then who?'

'Harry Charlesworth.'

The name seemed to hang in the air. Robson immediately realised he had been wrong. Wilson had turned pale – she hadn't known. By the time he had staggered to his feet, she was rushing out of the bar, with her phone pressed to her ear. She spoke into the device as she leapt up the staircase.

'Yes, it's me. I need you to run an urgent check on someone. And please inform our people in Herdubreid to stand by for orders. We're going to have to close in on Arkwright.'

CHAPTER 105

Robson was feeling a little better than he had several hours earlier, at the beginning of their early-morning trek. The fact that Wilson had decided to join them provided a curious comfort. His headache had begun to subside, thanks to an earlier concoction of painkillers, and now the fresh air seemed to be helping to clear his head from its whisky-induced sluggishness.

As predicted, heavy rainfall had destroyed any remaining strands of forensic evidence and Robson had instructed that they focussed on extending the boundaries of their search, given the worsening conditions. The frustration he felt at the loss of forensic clues was, in part, compensated by the feel of the cool raindrops on his haggard face. Every so often he could still taste last night's Scotch.

Wilson had been cagey since the previous night and she seemed to be very reluctant to discuss the discovery of the passport. No words were necessary to confirm the significance of the find. If it turned out that Connor's real identity was in some way connected to the Charlesworth clan, then things suddenly appeared to be slotting into place, with frightening connotations.

Robson saw their expedition lead, the mountain specialist, rolling his eyes before turning in reaction to what was becoming a familiar sound. Officer Wilson answered her phone for the fourth time of their hike and, once again, she ensured that she was out of earshot before conversing.

Wilson listened carefully as the caller proceeded in his familiar monotone.

'Ma'am, we have discovered that Harry Charlesworth – son of Mary Gibbons – had been living with his mother in the United States. It appears his mother reassumed her maiden name after leaving her husband about ten years ago.'

'Was the husband Harry Charlesworth's real father?'

'Affirmative, ma'am. The parents split up ten years ago. Harry went to live with his mother from the beginning of the split, while his father, Sir Geoffrey Charlesworth, returned to the UK after relinquishing his role as a UN weapons inspector. Apparently, he sought custody of his son, Harry, who had been fifteen years of age at the time.'

'Was Connor, or Harry Charlesworth, ever in touch with his father?'

'I'm afraid we don't have sufficient intelligence to be able to assert one way or another yet, ma'am.'

'Okay … anything else?'

'We know that he trained as a US Marine.'

Wilson nodded to herself thoughtfully, noting the younger Charlesworth had opted to follow in his father's military footsteps, albeit for a different nation.

'Has anyone made contact with Mary Gibbons?'

'She died just over seven years ago, soon after the fallout from the Arcam case, it seems. Our sources have advised that Harry Charlesworth reacted badly to his mother and father dying within such a short timeframe. He moved back to England shortly after his mother's death, ostensibly to deal with his father's estate. Evidently, he decided to sell everything and was living off the proceeds in various parts of the UK. Then, eventually, he joined the British army, and, within a year, was selected to train with the SAS. It seems he had become an elite commando by the time he disappeared off the grid and hasn't been seen since.'

'How long ago was this?'

'Around two years ago, ma'am.'

Wilson was suddenly distracted. She watched Robson, some distance away from her, as he climbed on to a new path. He had gained a good couple of hundred yards advantage while Wilson had been on the phone, but now he adopted a crouched position, seemingly studying something of interest on the ground. Wilson returned to her phone conversation.

'Right, thank you, that's incredibly useful, please call again if you discover anything else.'

'Sorry, ma'am, there was something else actually.'

'Oh?' she returned her attention to the call.

'We've also looked deeper into John Reilly's background, as you requested.'

'Go on.'

She marched forward so that she could begin to make up ground on Robson as she talked. She noted that the DCI was now sitting.

'John Harry Reilly joined the Secret Intelligence Service – MI6 – approximately two years ago. He underwent on-the-job training, during which time he was involved in live assignments, as far as we have been able to establish. It is very difficult to obtain information on serving agents, even for us, as you know, but we have been able to establish that MI6 were keen to take Reilly and did so with open arms, given his specialist background.'

'Which was?' Emma was now within a hundred yards of DCI Robson, who remained slumped on the wet mountainside. The rain suddenly grew more intense and the sky was almost black.

'As an SAS commando and former US Marine.' Wilson froze. She already knew what was coming next. 'He was given the identity of *Arkwright* on joining MI6, with a new persona John Harry Reilly, enabling him to lose his existing identity, Harry Charlesworth.'

'So Harry Charlesworth, Harry Reilly, and Mark Connor are one and the same person – would it be normal practice for the intelligence community to turn a blind eye to a person with such questionable connections?'

'Only if it's in the interests of the service, and then only if they want the person badly enough. It seems they wanted him to infiltrate Miller's organisation, hence the desire to lose the "Charlesworth" surname.'

She listened in silence, bemused to see that Robson was still sat on the ground. As she approached, she could see he seemed to be reaching out to something. The voice on the phone reminded her that she was still involved in a call.

'Thank you, Graham, I'll get back to you in a bit, thanks for the update.'

As she drew nearer to Robson, she was shocked to discover that he appeared to be sobbing, while the rest of the team continued to inspect another area, about fifty yards further up the mountainside. The sight was all Wilson needed to confirm to herself that the situation had finally, and quite understandably, got to him. Having been so close to Robson for a while, she was one of the very few ever to have witnessed him display emotion, but never before had it been witnessed while he'd been on duty.

'Jack?'

She stood a respectable distance from him.

'It's okay, we'll find her,' she offered unconvincingly, crouching alongside him.

Tenderly, she placed an arm around his shoulders. Wilson only spotted the inscription on the rock as she began to rise again, attempting to pull Robson up with her. As she began to understand the cause of Robson's sudden distress, she instantly dropped down again and replaced her arm. She felt tears forming in her own eyes.

'Oh, Jack, I'm sorry.'

She could hear her own voice cracking. Robson shook his head, as though he were attempting to dispel the pain.

'It's okay, it's fine. I hadn't ever expected to see this again. Not in my wildest dreams.'

For nearly an entire decade, the rugged mountainous climate had attacked the huge boulder that sat stubbornly before them. No doubt the rock had been worn to a small degree, but the inscription remained almost as clear as when he had first etched it using the small chisel that he'd carried with him for that sole romantic purpose. They both looked at the message.

Isabelle. I Love You. Will you marry me? Love, Jack x.

He had never been much of an artist, so had quickly abandoned the idea of carving a heart shape all those years ago, instead settling for the simple 'kiss' sign. On seeing his written proposal again for the first time, there was no way he could have stopped the memories. He remembered Isabelle's reaction, how she had been initially flummoxed, bizarrely turning into a giggling girl, her own antithesis, before reverting to her default exterior. Robson heard her response in his head all over again.

Jack! I thought you'd never ask?! Still can't bring yourself to speak the words though, eh darling?!

He had always enjoyed the teasing and banter they shared.

Is that a yes or no?!

Isabelle had simply thrown her arms around his neck, just as a mountain bike flew past them on the path.

As Robson reminisced involuntarily, a voice suddenly interrupted his nostalgia and brought him back to the present.

'Come on Jack,' said Wilson. 'Let's get to the bottom of this.'

CHAPTER 106

A large group of intelligence officers stood among an even larger gathering of security force personnel at the foot of Herdubreid mountain, looking up towards the vast table-topped plateau. If their man had ventured on to the tuya, then he had left no signs.

The mountain team had also arrived and had already briefed them on their journey. Upon hearing the plan, it had sounded arduous, but achievable. But now, as they stood at the foot of the mountain and took in the huge flat summit, their challenge felt even greater.

Nevertheless, their recent orders were unambiguous – they had to close the net on Arkwright now. The threat level had been raised.

*

DCI Robson took another sip of hot coffee, before returning the lid of the thermos flask to Wilson.

'What do you think Charlesworth's objective is? Is he avenging his father's death?'

'Perhaps,' Wilson responded.

She had pondered the same thing. Eight years had elapsed since they foiled Sir Geoffrey Charlesworth's outlandish attempt to change the world order, by 'reinventing humankind'. They may have shut down the UK operation, but Charlesworth's cult had achieved a global reach, which had been essential, given the project's objectives. The security community had feared the re-emergence of remaining cells although there was almost no intelligence to support such a fear, other than the hunch of probability. But they hadn't factored in the threat being reignited from unknown or forgotten kin. How could Charlesworth's son have been able to get so far, completely beneath their radar?

Robson looked directly into her eyes, searching for information.

'But why join MI6? Seems a bit of a curveball, doesn't it?'

'Not really, the more access the group has to the top, the easier it becomes to access classified information.'

'And to pollute that information?'

'Precisely. To be able to control the flow of information is to hold great power.'

'I just can't understand why the secret service would take someone on with such a background.'

'On the contrary, he must have come from the perfect background, in their eyes.'

'In a military sense, yes of course. But what about his close connection to someone who had recently been such a major security threat?'

'He must have been good,' she said, smiling wryly. 'And I wouldn't mind betting that there was a hope that he might have been able to infiltrate the remaining network.'

The walkie-talkie on Robson's breast crackled.

'DCI Robson, DI Matthews here, do you read, over?'

'Go on, Inspector Matthews.'

'Sir, we've found something here that you might find interesting.'

*

Wilson should have realised that an ordnance survey map wasn't necessary when Robson had asked Matthews to describe the view from where his team currently stood. She knew well that he and Isabelle had explored Mount Snowdon extensively. They had both loved every inch of its wild beauty.

Sure enough, within half an hour of receiving Matthews' message, they rounded a vast rock face and saw an investigation team standing in the middle of what appeared to be a newly constructed road. As Robson and Wilson both climbed down to meet Matthews' team, rainwater sprayed off the long grass as they waded through the luscious green blades. The cloud covering had thinned considerably, allowing the rays of the climbing sun to reach the eastern face of the mountain. As they approached Matthews, a large lake glistened far beneath, as if enjoying the rare sunshine. Robson spoke without taking his eyes off the man-made construction.

'Hello, folks.'

'Hello, sir. Officer Wilson,' said Matthews, as he nodded to the new arrivals. Robson pursed his lips, deep in thought.

'This is quite a construction.'

'It is, indeed, sir. Hence we felt it worth bringing to your attention.' Robson turned his attention to one of the local bobbies.

'I thought you said they were renovating the paths.'

'Aye, sir, that was my understanding.'

'So, what is your take on this construction?'

'Looks like a service road to me, sir. Possibly so they can get the machinery on to the mountain?'

'Are there any more roads like these?'

'I've no idea, sir.'

'Okay, let's carry on. Team Zulu,' Robson looked at Matthews as he spoke, 'I'd like you to swap quadrants with us. I want to take a closer inspection of this myself, so Team Yankee will continue from here.'

Matthews nodded and everyone began gathering their respective rucksacks. Some took swigs of water before beginning to walk, while Matthews removed his hood to speak.

'Sir, I know we are maintaining radio contact. But what is the plan if we can't communicate – should we nominate a rendezvous point?'

Robson looked around the expectant faces, before responding.

'Good point, DI Matthews. Our rendezvous point will be the summit. Take plenty of fluid on board as you go. Let's check in with one another at least every hour. Can you communicate the same to the other two teams please, Matthews?'

'Will do, sir.'

'Good. Any more questions?'

Seconds later Robson acknowledged the silence, although he also observed that most of his colleagues already appeared too exhausted to speak.

'Let's go.'

CHAPTER 107

On the Icelandic highlands, the assembled team of mountain specialists had fought against the harsh elements for several hours in their effort to establish any sign of human activity on the tuya. Morale was not aided by their awareness that they hadn't even reached the midway point in their climb.

The seasoned mountaineers among the group were accompanied by only a handful of intelligence officers and special police – those officers considered to be the fittest – while the remainder had been left at the temporary base camp. At four hundred metres above sea level, the team of hikers stopped in a huddle and attempted to brace themselves against the arctic wind while they discussed their next course of action.

'It'd take weeks for us to be able to confidently state that we've examined every inch of ground,' affirmed the expedition lead. 'I've requested another team to come and assist the search.'

Officer Kline attempted to control his chattering teeth as he responded.

'Agreed. That's good news. Tell me, have you seen anything in your opinion that might suggest the faintest hint of human activity?'

'I wouldn't say so, no. But the weather here does a good job of covering tracks rather quickly.'

A couple of hundred metres below the special police force, the entrance that Connor had accessed nearly twelve hours ago had once again become completely hidden from view as a result of the fresh snowfall. It was a portal that led inside the dormant volcano and represented the only viable access to the top in such conditions – where another world existed that no one else would have believed.

*

Robson blew the chilly air from his lungs as they climbed higher. It had always required a degree of exertion to climb the steep eastern flank of Yr Wyddfa, but it should, under typical conditions, have been the easiest time of year to do so.

The extraordinarily wet summer had left the underfoot conditions especially treacherous and what remained of the paths had to be walked with care. Even the newly constructed route was hazardous, evidently acting as an artificial water course. Robson and his team followed their experienced mountaineer's lead as they waded through the gushing water that had chosen the new road as its easiest route from the sodden mountain.

Team Yankee had been walking the new road for almost an hour when the divergence appeared. Robson decided to dispatch the remainder of their team along the left fork, while he and Wilson took the course to the right, thinning their numbers further. Looking at the view ahead, there was still quite a way to go.

DCI Robson watched Officer Wilson pull her hood tight around her face to provide further shelter against the wind, which continued to grow in strength. However, that did enough to muffle the noise emitted by the vehicle approaching them from behind, just out of sight around the previous bend in the empty road.

Robson gazed at the concrete road surface as he allowed his hearing to tune itself into the growing rumbling. He looked back in the direction from which they had travelled and saw nothing but an empty, sodden road surface. But the incongruous rhythm grew, as though competing with the pitch of the blustery wind, which continued to ruffle the vegetation on the mountainside.

Wilson was only a few yards in front of Robson by the time the front of a jeep came into view, jolting and bouncing over the rough terrain as it appeared above the brow. Robson plunged forward, shouting as his thighs worked to drag him along the steep road.

'Get off the road!'

Wilson didn't move from her course, her senses severely compromised by the sides of her hood flapping in the wind. Robson leapt forward. He was in mid-air as he caught hold of her middle and pulled her off the road. The two of them tumbled into the deep ditch on the right-hand side of the newly laid concrete.

Robson was on top of Wilson and held his right hand firmly over her mouth. He felt guilty at the sight of blood trickling from the fresh wound above her eye, but even worse was the panic with which she looked at him. In that moment, he could see how far apart they had drifted – to a point where she could bring herself to believe that his actions, although spontaneous, could represent something other than honourable intentions.

'There's a vehicle coming. Stay low.'

Wilson nodded, wide-eyed. Robson moved off her, leaving her lying on her back, before rolling over on to his front. He crawled towards the ridge above them which formed the edge of the crudely carved road. Rocky debris was dispatched in their direction as Robson stayed just high enough to see the thick tread on the jeep's tyres as it bounded past. He sensed Wilson's presence alongside him, but avoided turning to acknowledge her. Together, they watched the green, military-style vehicle climb the steep terrain. They both laid motionless, apart from heaving chests, until the rear end of the open-back jeep disappeared. Their recent, unexpected physical contact seemed to have inserted a virtual wedge between them. Robson spoke first, adjusting his position to disguise the awkwardness of the moment.

'Sorry about that. I'm sure there's a less than exciting explanation for the jeep, but I thought it wise not to reveal ourselves yet. Just in case.'

Wilson pulled herself back on to the road before Robson had a chance to offer any assistance. They dusted themselves off in silence. Seconds later, without either uttering a word, they proceeded silently in the direction of the green jeep.

CHAPTER 108

The lake below them continued to shimmer in the sunlight, which had begun to warm the mountain to a more pleasant temperature.

Wilson sat watching the water in silence as Robson paced in a small circle, holding his mobile phone to his ear. He pondered the news as he replaced the device in his pocket. At the same time, Wilson answered an incoming call on her own phone.

Once again, to Robson's frustration, she did not attempt to disguise her desire for privacy as she moved far enough away to be out of his hearing before continuing. On several occasions during the call, Wilson looked across the distance that separated them. Robson tried to fend off his growing paranoia – he knew he was not in the best mental condition of his life – but there was no mistaking the dark look on Wilson's face as she returned. Something in her troubled eyes informed him that he needed to steady himself for whatever news she had. It came as something of a surprise when she began with a question of her own.

'What's the latest?'

Robson studied her, his eyes finally resting on the cut above her brow for which he had been responsible. He became aware of the urge to comfort her and cleared his throat, again demanding clarity of thought from himself. He shrugged as nonchalantly as he could muster.

'It seems this isn't the only access road. They've found another three.'

'Really?'

Robson nodded.

'That seems like a lot of excavation work simply to provide access for construction traffic.'

Robson nodded again, before responding.

'Perhaps. But the local bobbies did say they were carrying out renovations on every route, didn't they?'

'What have you instructed?'

'I've asked them to join us. We don't have the resources to investigate all four routes simultaneously, and given that we've witnessed that this one, at least, appears to be operational, I think it'd be worth our while focussing on this route as a priority, don't you?'

Robson watched her activate her poker face as she nodded.

'What about you? Any news from Iceland?' he asked.

'No.'

'Who were you just on the phone to?'

'My team in the UK. I've asked them to join us for a while, to bolster our numbers.'

'Oh. When?'

'Immediately.'

Robson watched her closely as she lowered her eyes. It suddenly seemed to require great effort for her to look at him. She raised her eyes to meet his and continued.

'Jack, there's been an accident.'

'What kind of accident?'

Robson saw the suppressed emotion in Wilson's face.

'A car has driven off a road through one of the other mountains on the massif.'

'Whose car?'

'It was the vehicle that was stolen from uniform, when you were rescuing Sarah from the river.'

'Have any bodies been found?'

'No. They are saying that they don't expect to find much – the vehicle fell a couple of hundred feet before going up in flames. There wasn't a lot left by the time we got there, apparently.'

'So how can they be certain about the vehicle?'

'They got lucky. One of the first things they managed to recover was a part of the chassis containing the VIN. I doubt it matched the number plates, or the bodywork.'

'Any other evidence?'

Wilson thought carefully. She had already decided not to give him the full details yet. Not there.

'A few items of clothing and personal belongings apparently. Nothing has been identified yet. They're still searching the crash site.'

Robson felt he should be relieved.

'Okay. Shall we continue?'

'There's one more thing, Jack ...'

'Go on.'

'There were eyewitnesses. Four out of the six witnesses claim it didn't appear to be an accident.'

'In what way?'

'The car seems to have been involved in a high-speed chase. There was a collision that caused it to spin off the road. The impact was a sideswipe at high speed. The eyewitnesses believe it was deliberate.'

'Have we got an ID for the other vehicle?'

'Only make and model, no VRN. Apparently, the other vehicle was a green, open-backed jeep.'

CHAPTER 109

Miller drew up over the final brow, knowing that he was near the end of his journey as the rocky incline levelled off abruptly. He drove the jeep through the lowered section of the vast steel perimeter and proceeded inside the great perimeter wall. Almost immediately, the entrance began to close automatically behind him.

The concrete road beyond him continued for another quarter of a mile on an incline, until it terminated at a large steel perimeter fence. Miller proceeded slowly, warily inspecting the terrain around him. As he approached within fifty yards of the fence, he saw there were people waiting on the other side.

He abandoned his vehicle and stretched his athletic body, before approaching a gated entrance. The fence itself was a high-security, eight-foot high steel enclosure. Horizontal steel bars reinforced the upright spikes, forming an altogether formidable barrier.

An armed man peered at Miller from inside the entrance. The man's dark eyes studied the ex-harbourmaster, seemingly wary of the unfamiliar face. As Miller drew nearer, a spark of recognition seemed to be invoked in the guard, whose sudden relaxation was visible as soon as the visitor spoke the agreed password. Inside the gate, a tall, African man moved alongside the guard, as his colleague began to unbolt the gate fastenings.

'Welcome, General Miller,' said the guard. 'It's good to see you. My word you've changed!'

'Thank you, Samuel. You haven't,' Miller responded, stony-faced.

The guard noted Miller's strength as they exchanged a brief handshake, then quickly recovered to summon his colleague.

'Emanuel, this is General Miller. Please escort him directly to Naamah's quarters.'

'Of course. Please follow me, sir.'

Miller addressed the senior guard one final time before walking away with his escort.

'Once you've moved the jeep, make sure you secure the fence again. As quickly as you can. I've a feeling we could have company soon.'

'Will do, General.'

Miller and Emanuel had reached the far side of the small courtyard by the time the guard had brought the jeep inside a wider opening and finished ensuring that the bolts on the gate were secured.

'The main entrance is just through here, General Miller.'

Miller paid little attention to the toned African man, instead taking in the huge field of pylons that came into view as they walked through the opening at the far end of the courtyard. He had been told about the vastness of the field of transmitters, but he had to admit that seeing them in person sent a tingle down his spine. He watched the huge, dark cloud formation gradually move in from one of the high mountainous peaks in the distance. *Is that one of ours?*

They turned and followed a well-defined, man-made path that clearly led towards the highest peak, some 1085 metres above sea level.

Nearly ten minutes later, Miller and Emanuel were immersed in the same cumulus that had been moving towards them earlier. The sudden reduction in visibility meant that Miller was only aware of their destination when they were on top of it. Miller paused to take in their new surroundings. Many years previously, the building had started life as a large wooden shack, but had clearly been extended to something far vaster, its size apparent even in the reduced visibility.

The door before them slid open moments after Emanuel had spoken on the keypad's intercom and they were greeted by a slight, East Asian man, who smiled at them. Miller felt suddenly stirred, unable to take his eyes off the host that greeted them. Instantly, the ex-harbour master's mind was awash with passionate memories.

'General Miller, how exciting! Welcome, sir.'

'Thank you, Bingwen Liu. It's always Jacob to you.'

Liu bowed his head submissively, before turning to the guard.

'Thank you, Emmanuel, I will escort General Miller from here.'

The guard nodded respectfully at them both, before disappearing back into the fog outside. Miller followed his former, diminutive companion and trainer, watching his silky black ponytail swish slightly as he nimbly turned on his heels. It had been almost a year since Miller had last set eyes on his prison lover, and his desire took hold of him as he remembered their experiences together.

Liu led them into a large hall and Miller was distracted from lustful thoughts as he took in the unexpectedly high ceiling. The wall on their left was entirely paned with thick glass, which created a spectacular vista and ensured that no one could not forget that they were situated at the top of the highest mountain in Wales. However, the view at the far end of the room gave him even more pleasure. He stared ahead now, eyes fixed on the newcomer to the room. Naamah held his gaze and grinned triumphantly.

Reunited at last.

Naamah retained a lopsided grin while addressing Miller.

'Jacob. How wonderful to see you at last! And my, how you've changed, for the better I might add!'

'Likewise, Naamah. But before we indulge in pleasantries, we need to prepare for company.'

'I know, Jacob. It's okay, I know.'

CHAPTER 110

Professor Romano was sweating profusely.

He had been so relieved the previous day when DCI Robson had had no choice but to release him from custody, even though he had been instructed to remain in the area. And anyway, that wouldn't be a problem – Romano wasn't planning on going far. The main thing had been that he had survived the CID questioning, despite the intense, albeit hands-off, nature of the DCI's interrogation.

But this new batch of suits seemed a different prospect altogether. He couldn't pinpoint what was more intimidating – the fact that there wasn't a uniformed officer in sight, or the unequivocal confidence with which they addressed him, seemingly unaffected by protocol or interview regulations.

There had been no physical contact – yet – but their questioning was becoming unmistakably aggressive. Judging by their accents, the professor had detected that his uninvited guests comprised two Englishmen, a huge Scotsman, and an American. The transatlantic team member seemed to be the most senior.

'Professor Romano. I don't think you quite realise what sort of trouble you're in, sir. You see, we *will* know when you've told us everything. And believe me, *Alberto*, we won't be going anywhere until that happens.'

The American man paused to ensure the message had sunk in. He watched the old man's hand trembling on the arms of the soft chair and nodded at the silent confirmation.

'Good.' He briefly glanced at the other three, who had moved in closer so that all four men surrounded the professor. 'I do believe he's starting to understand, fellas.'

Romano felt a shiver run down his spine as he took in the seemingly wicked grins on the four faces before him and gulped before speaking hoarsely.

'P-please, I'm not well. I-I need water ... please, could I get some water, gentlemen?'

The American cocked his head to address his colleagues.

'What do you think, men? The professor is thirsty. Should we get him some water?'

The largest of the men responded in a broad Scottish accent.

'Of course.'

Despite being the farthest away from the living room door, the big Scotsman walked across the narrow space between his standing colleagues and the seated professor. The professor let out a dry yelp as the man's size ten stomped across his big toe. The man stopped and turned.

'Ach, I am sorry, professor. I am a clumsy clot. Goodness me, I hope I don't do anything else to hurt you.'

Romano tried to ignore the call from his bladder and took a few deep breaths in the uncomfortable silence. They listened to the nearby sounds of a cupboard being closed heavily, a rattle of glasses, and a tap being turned on and off, before the man returned.

The professor watched in bewilderment as the large man appeared again in the doorway and held a litre jug out to the American. It had been filled above its maximum so that water slopped over the edges and dripped on to the professor's trousers as it was held out for him to collect. As Romano held a quivering, wrinkled hand out, the American leant forward and tipped the jug. The professor began to panic as the cold tap water ran down his face and chest, spluttering and wiping his eyes and face with the back of his cardigan sleeve. Every time he tried to respond, his cough prevented him from speaking.

The sound of the heavy jug shattering against the wall shocked him into silence.

Romano's eyes opened wide to look towards the area of the wall that had been the crash site. If he had been able to see that far, he would have noted that, apart from the glass shards now lying around the sofa and carpeted floor, a large piece of plasterboard was missing from the wall. Instead, he saw only two crazy eyes and the outline of a face just an inch from his. He felt the American's warm breath on his cold face as the man hissed at him. His tone was now filled only with aggression.

'Okay, Professor. You've fucked us around for long enough. You are going to tell us everything, including where the missing key is …' the professor jerked as he felt the American's large hand wrap around his jugular, '… or things are going to get pretty bad for you, pretty quickly.'

The American turned to address the big man, who had remained in the doorway.

'Jock. Put the kettle on, will you?'

The professor couldn't see past the American's face to see what the big Scotsman's reaction was, but seconds later, he heard his heavy footsteps crossing the tiled kitchen floor as the American spoke, almost into his nose.

'Okay, over to you, and make sure you don't forget anything, Professor Romano. You have the time it takes for the kettle to boil. Otherwise, the next bit really isn't going to be pleasant for you at all.

CHAPTER 111

'Extraordinary,' Robson exclaimed, feeling slightly dizzy as he looked down into the abyss.

After spotting the jeep, Robson had ordered the rest of Team Yankee to rejoin him and Wilson in their pursuit of the vehicle. Having reassembled and hiked another hundred metres in the direction the jeep had travelled earlier, they had arrived at a bridge.

Now, they all stood on the concrete structure and looked down into the cavernous space beneath them. A wide concrete trough passed beneath the bridge and continued in either direction for as far as they could see. The huge trench also appeared to have been manufactured from concrete and was a good twenty metres wide, and at least another twenty metres deep.

Up ahead, just at the end of the bridge, the road terminated at a ten-metre high, steel wall. Robson was reminded of the typically dreary façade of a prison as he looked up at the sturdy perimeter. He began to think of Louise Hart and her recent, unfortunate end as, evidently, the latest, unsuspecting casualty of the strange cult and their radical utopian vision.

The look on the Welsh sergeant's face confirmed to Robson that the vast construction was as much a surprise to the locals as it was to him and the rest of the CID officers.

'I take it you had no idea about this?' Robson asked.

The sergeant appeared slightly dumbfounded as he turned his broad head from side to side.

'No, sir.'

'Who is responsible for the current renovation work?'

'The contract was awarded to a foreign consortium, I believe.'

'Who regulates the project?'

'Erm, good question. Ultimately, it's the Welsh government, but I believe a third party has been employed to oversee the work.'

Robson looked across at Wilson, who was still studying the apparent fortification. They exchanged glances, both disbelieving at the thought that they might be witnessing history about to repeat itself. Wilson looked at the weary sergeant, who had decided to rest his sturdy legs and was sitting on a nearby boulder.

'Would you happen to know the names of the organisations involved, Sergeant Griffiths?'

'I did, although the name escapes me at this moment. But it's no great secret. They have done a lot of PR engagement with the local community. Do you remember the name, constable?'

'I don't know about the construction contractors, sir. But I remember the management team was an acronym of some sort.'

Robson decided to interrupt their casual gossip, seeing that it was going nowhere.

'I wonder if there could be another entrance in this wall?'

'Sir, what are those?' the sergeant answered, while pointing a stubby finger towards what looked like a hatch at the bottom of the trench. As they moved towards the edge and inspected it more closely, they could see several others, seemingly evenly spaced at about thirty metres apart, running along the floor of the vast trench.'

'Hmm, no idea. Drainage perhaps?' Robson pondered.

They all turned in unison, as another group of people appeared unexpectedly from around a green verge. Robson and the others watched Matthews and the rest of Team Zulu approach. At first, the young Detective Inspector appeared excited, as though he had something to report, but his expression changed on glancing at the wall's entrance.

'Wow! There are more of them, then?' Matthews gasped.

'More?' Robson countered.

'Yes. We've just left a similar looking installation.'

'Really? How far away?'

'Took us about half an hour to walk it.'

'Right. I want to get a full and extensive search carried out, urgently. I don't care what resource it takes. Let's make it happen. I'm calling in Special Branch. Matthews – alert firearms that we need them to be on standby.'

*

Over two thousand miles away from Mount Snowdon, Arkwright knelt on top of an elevator roof and listened to several disgruntled voices outside the big steel doors above him. From the tone of the voices, it seemed that they were close to accepting defeat. Moments later, the volume of the group's chuntering decreased. Connor could just about make out some of their parting statements as their voices grew distant.

'Incredible. We can create a high-tech facility at the top of a mountain, and we can control Mother Nature, but we can't get a fucking elevator to work!'

'Stop bloody moaning. It'd do you good to lose a few pounds!'

'A few pounds?! I'm likely to have a fucking heart attack! You do realise how high we are?'

'I do indeed.'

Arkwright listened carefully to the subsequent sounds. He had studied the area enough on his previous visits to be able discern the meaning of each vibration. As soon as he could be sure that the workers had all disappeared into the emergency stairwell to return to their living quarters, Arkwright rose to fully stand and retrieved a crowbar from his bag. With a quick shove, he inserted one end between the steel doors that gave access to the top floor of the installation and began to wrench them open. Once he had prised them a few inches apart, the electronic control took over and the doors opened fully under automatic operation.

Arkwright was swift. He leapt from the elevator shaft and on to the floor, before grabbing another implement from his backpack. Lying on his front, he leant out into the lift shaft with the huge bolt cutters and began to apply great strength to squeeze the handles together. A loud twang echoed deep inside the lift shaft as the steel pulley finally gave. Having already disabled the emergency braking mechanism, the elevator car submitted to gravity. A growing echo of vibrations and scraping metal was emitted from the open lift doors.

Arkwright scrambled to his feet and ran ten metres to the stairwell entrance. Swiftly, he threw the large bolts across at the top and bottom of the thick door to secure it closed. Next, Arkwright withdrew a welding torch from his holdall, swiftly igniting the oxyacetylene, and then setting to work on sealing the bolted entrance permanently.

CHAPTER 112

DCI Robson and Intelligence Officer Wilson stood side by side at the front of the incident room. There had been a tangible shift in the mood of the team. Not least because, suddenly, the locals were visibly keen to become more involved. Robson was tuned into the change and allowed himself a wry smile as he contemplated the catalyst for the apparent emergence of their enthusiasm – someone was messing with their national treasure – 'The Mountain'.

Many of the CID staff currently present were familiar with the Arcam operation eight years earlier – some to a greater degree than others – but every one of them knew enough to understand the frightening relevance of Mark Connor's true identity once it had been revealed to them. To the others, the name Charlesworth meant nothing, but, to the CID officers, it served as a cold reminder of the radical nature of the organisation they were, apparently, in pursuit of once again.

Robson himself was still struggling to come to terms with the fact that a man who had become his closest friend had not only turned out to be a secret service agent – a double agent at that – but was also the son of his ex-nemesis, Sir Geoffrey Charlesworth.

'What's the news from the operation in Iceland?'

Matthews's question reminded the team that their investigation was only part of an overall, coordinated hunt. Wilson was first to respond.

'Arkwright has been surrounded at Herdubreid mountain, which is a remote area in the highlands of Iceland. It is believed that he may have actually ventured on to the mountain, but his precise location is currently unknown.'

'Is it a coincidence that we are currently searching two separate mountain ranges in connection with the same enquiry?' Robson intervened, in an effort to create openness in the briefing.

'It is unlikely to be a coincidence. There is a growing belief that both locations are somehow connected.'

'Okay everyone, but our focus is, of course, to find out just what is going on at Mount Snowdon, even if it is to eliminate it from our enquiries. Although a clear link cannot be denied. Therefore, our priority is to get inside the newly built perimeter wall up there as a matter of urgency.'

At that moment, DC Saunders burst into the room looking energised and holding a piece of A4 paper. She held the sheet in front of her as she rushed towards Robson at the front.

'Sorry for the interruption, sir,' she handed the printout to Robson before continuing. 'We've got some information on the firm that has the contract to oversee the renovation work on the mountain.'

Robson's eyes widened as he speed-read the data in front of him. Wilson filled the silent void.

'Would you care to share the information with the rest of us, DC Saunders?'

'Of course, ma'am. Gonzales Partners were founded four years ago, in Spain. The director is a certain Señor Carlos Gonzales.'

'Okay, what do we know about this outfit? What it the size of its workforce?'

'Well ma'am, it seems that there are no permanent employees.'

Matthews picked up on the peculiarity immediately.

'No employees? How does a company comprising a workforce of one director win a prestigious construction contract?'

Saunders swept a curled lock behind her ear and nodded.

'Quite, DI Matthews. That contract alone is reportedly worth over twenty million euros. The company uses a workforce entirely comprising subcontractors.'

'The modern world of employment,' Matthews pondered.

Robson remained silent, allowing his detective constable to deliver the final bombshell, having already read and reread the final sentence at the bottom of the piece of paper, which he continued to stare at.

'That's not the only contract either,' continued Saunders. 'Gonzales Partners have also recently been engaged in another large-scale construction contract in Iceland.'

An excited cacophony of low whispering filled the room. Saunders allowed it to linger for a second and die away, before continuing.

'The company recently acted as one half of a joint consortium to oversee the construction of a fully accessible route to the top of Herdubreid mountain in Iceland.'

Robson looked up from the printout for the first time since receiving it.

'Who's the partner?'

'A US based company – Geoclimate Incorporation. We're running a search on them as we speak.'

Wilson recognised the name immediately from her recent briefing at GCHQ. She turned to Robson and spoke just loud enough to be heard above the rising commotion.

'DCI Robson, could I have a private word with you, please?'

Robson found he could still, evidently, read what was in her eyes.

'Okay, everyone, can we get organised for the operation please. I want to get back on the mountain very soon.'

'Will there be air support, sir?'

'Not yet. Every attempt to send surveillance drones into the area has resulted in the destruction of the devices. We don't yet know what technology is in use up there, but it appears there is some kind of powerful radio transmission that is being used to jam electronic devices. Only last night a military helicopter approached the mountain, but once it came within half a mile radius the pilot almost lost control.'

As the team filed out of the room, Robson and Wilson sat together at the nearest desk.

'Jack, I know that company.'

'You do?'

'They are responsible for the management of the HAARP facility in Alaska.'

'The facility that was recently sabotaged?'

'Yes. I'm going to have to report this immediately. Can you wait for further instructions before you act?'

'My orders were that this is a CID-led investigation.'

'Jack, this could be vital.'

'I'll give you twelve hours – tops. In the meantime, I think we'll get a certain Professor Romano in for a chat again. Given the latest connection, I feel confident that we can go to work on him properly.'

'Jack, a team of intelligence personnel has been sent out to see him. Let's await their report before taking any further action.'

'Why wasn't I informed of this?'

'The decision was taken yesterday, while we were on the mountain. I've only recently found out myself.'

Robson began to shake his head in frustration.

'Officer Wilson, this collaboration thing is a two-way fucking street, you know. I'll give you a few hours, then I'm sending the teams back to the mountain again. We have Special Branch on their way to join us, along with firearms and officers from SO15 counter-terrorism command. I'm not having them hanging around with their fingers up their arses. And I suspect that before too long, I will have Commander Gibson breathing down my neck now that SO15 are involved.'

'I understand.'

Wilson knew there was more motivation than ever for Robson to track those involved in the construction work on the mountain. She decided she had to share the latest evidence with him, even though it could well mean that DCI Robson would be unable to continue with the investigation.

'Okay,' Robson looked at his ex-lover with a serious countenance. 'You've got twelve hours. By which time we will have a significantly larger force available to move on to the mountain. Therefore, I propose that we reconvene at six tomorrow morning.'

As Robson instructed Matthews to oversee their preparations for the morning, he noticed the anxious look on Wilson's face as he returned to her.

'Is everything okay, Officer Wilson?'

'Jack. I need to talk to you about the crash earlier. Involving the jeep.'

Robson immediately felt anxious at her expression.

'Go on …'

Robson's phone shook on the table in front of them as it buzzed, causing them both to look down. They both recognised the caller ID.

'I'm sorry.' In truth, Robson was glad of the interruption. 'I ought to take this.'

Wilson sighed, before nodding politely and getting up from the desk, leaving Robson alone to answer his call.

'Hello … are you okay?'

'Hello, Jack. Yes, I'm fine. I'm so sorry to disturb you.'

'It's okay, Mum. What's up? Are you okay?'

'Yes, yes, I'm fine. I just wanted to make you aware of something …'

'Go on.'

'I'm sure it's nothing to worry about, but Sarah seems to have gone missing.'

'What do you mean?'

'I mean, I haven't seen her since we said goodnight to one another yesterday evening before bed. As far as I'm aware, she hadn't planned to go anywhere today. But her car has gone, and she seems to have taken her luggage bag.'

'How can you be sure?'

'About what?'

'How do you know she's taken her luggage, Mum?'

'I suppose I don't. Not for sure, anyway. But I remember it was on the side in her bedroom last night. She had it opened out to dry, after being retrieved from the river. I told her just to bin it, but she seemed hell-bent on preserving it for some reason.'

Robson held his temples, trying to stop the room from spinning around him.

'Okay, Mum, thanks for letting me know. There's no need to worry, I'm sure she's fine. I'll track her down and let you know what's happening, okay?'

'Okay, darling.'

'Bye, Mu—'

'Jack, dear?'

'Yes?'

'Is there any ... any news from your end?'

'Not yet.'

'Okay, my love. Take care, Jack.'

'And you, Mum.'

Instantly, Robson began tapping the phone to locate Sarah's number from its directory. He held the phone to his ear and, after a minute, listened to Sarah's pre-recorded voice message before recording his own.

'Sarah, it's Jack. Mum called me, she's worried. Could you let us know what's happening please? Ta.'

*

Naamah looked at the phone display and smiled.

'Sorry, Jack,' she whispered to herself. 'I can't take your call right now.'

Seconds later, the device vibrated again to indicate that a message had been left. Naamah touched the display to access the voicemail and listened to DCI Robson's message on the loudspeaker. A young man of average build entered the room as the message ended. He forced his gaze above the silk negligee and looked into his boss's sultry, piercing blue eyes.

'You asked to see me, Naamah?'

'Yes, Samuel. Would you speak to General Miller, please, and ask him to ensure he is ready. I believe DCI Robson and his team will be on their way soon.'

'Yes, ma'am.'

CHAPTER 113

As his ordeal progressed, it became clear to Professor Romano that this was not an official interview. He winced as the American spoke again.

'For the last time, Professor, we would like you to tell us everything that you told CID, and please make sure you don't leave anything out ...'

Romano was gasping as his breathing had become shallower, but his weak heart continued to thud away inside his chest. As he sat at the kitchen table, naked and cold, he could only foresee two potential outcomes, and neither was particularly palatable.

'Like I told you, I haven't told them anything, you must believe me!'

'Then why have they been all over the mountain since they met you?!'

'I-I don't know, perhaps they have found some other form of evidence!'

'Like what?'

Romano's groin and abdomen burnt with pain as he adjusted his position in the hard chair. He tried his best to stop shivering, each vibration further intensifying the pain coming from his damaged ribs. The chill he felt throughout his body contrasted perversely with the burning sensation coming from his blistered feet.

'Perhaps they have aerial footage of—'

'Impossible!'

'Then, I don't know. P-please. Could I have some clothes ... or a blanket?'

The American grabbed the chair opposite him and sat, leaning forward so that his mean eyes were an inch away from the Professor's.

'We'll see if we can afford to be a little kinder when you tell us the fucking truth, Professor! Now, start talking. So, let's park your CID meeting for a while and get back to Connor and the missing device. Tell us what you know.'

The professor heard the click of the kettle being turned on behind him again. Instinctively, he looked down at his raw feet which were trembling violently with the pain from the previous serving of boiling water.

'I know nothing about that!'

A string of phlegm escaped the Professor's trembling lips. He fought back sobs as he listened to the kettle bubbling.

The sudden knock at the door seemed ominous. The three suited men exchanged brief glances.

'Shit! Turn that thing off,' the American hissed to his colleague nearest the kettle before grabbing Romano by his wrinkled throat.

'Who are you expecting?!'

'N-no one, I swear!'

The leader twisted his neck round at the sound of footsteps entering the kitchen. The big Scotsman, who had sprinted upstairs to take a look outside, looked pale as he stood in the doorway.

'Who is it?'

'I don't know. A couple of suits and from what I can make out, two armed police officers …maybe Special Branch?'

'Fuck it! Security Services.'

'What shall we do?'

'Nothing, let's just sit tight.'

'Sir – the window!'

An armed officer stood perfectly still outside the property as he watched the group inside the house through the kitchen window. The American reacted swiftly.

Outside in the garden, the police officer was speaking into his radio as the bullet smashed through the kitchen window and tore through his chest within milliseconds.

'Let's move!' commanded the American.

As they abandoned the shocked professor and departed through the rear door, another gunshot could be heard at the front of the property. Seconds later, Romano's three tormentors arrived at the narrow driveway behind the house and made a beeline for the dark saloon they had arrived in.

'Shit, they've fucking blocked us in!' shouted the Scotsman, as he looked at the two newly arrived vehicles. Both the unmarked saloon and police car seemed to be unoccupied.

'No, they fucking haven't, just get in the car, now!'

The wheels of the dark saloon span, spraying sodden mud and grass behind it, as it slalomed across the overgrown rear garden. Shots were fired from the house and ripped into one of the car's rear wheel arches as they disappeared through a six-foot privet hedge and span on to the narrow access lane that led to the property in a tangle of hedgerow and smoke.

Back at the cottage, the security services operatives continued administering CPR to the fallen Special Branch officer, while the other armed man reported the dark saloon's registration plate to his control room.

Inside the kitchen, the professor lay on the hard kitchen floor, grey and alone.

CHAPTER 114

Ysbyty Gwynedd General Hospital

D S Gail Burford continued to make small talk with the nurse as she escorted them through the quiet corridors. Immediately behind, Wilson spoke softly to Robson.

'Why did they have to bring the professor here? Isn't there a hospital closer to Snowdon?'

'Yes, but this one is the nearest with a plastic surgeon.'

The gruesome image of Professor Romano's raw, blistered feet occupied Wilson's mind as she nodded. A second later they arrived at the entrance to a single room and followed the nurse and DS Burford inside.

'Hello, Professor. Are you up to visitors?' the nurse asked cheerfully.

The patient slowly turned his face so that the pipe of the oxygen mask drooped off the bed slightly. Romano appeared grey and seemed to stare beyond the new arrivals. The nurse had moved alongside her patient to carry out further observations in the silence. Gently, she pulled the mask from the professor's face while her other hand rested on his shoulder.

'These people are very keen to speak with you, Professor. Do you think you could manage just five minutes? I will come back to make sure they don't outstay their welcome.'

Romano's eyes shifted to the side and he gave a faint nod. The nurse addressed Burford as she departed the single room.

'As you can see, Professor Romano is still very frail, so it has to be five minutes tops, I'm afraid.'

'Thank you,' Burford smiled.

As the door closed behind the nurse, the three officers approached the bed. Burford displayed a concerned smile.

'How are you feeling, Professor?'

Romano gave an ironic scoff, which quickly escalated to a sickly cough. Robson stepped alongside his sergeant.

'Hello, Professor Romano. We know you just want to rest, so if you can give us the information we need, we will be able to leave you in peace. Does that sound okay?'

Romano nodded.

'Excellent. Well, first of all, what can you tell us about the people that did this to you?'

The professor cleared his throat as he shrugged.

'Not a great deal I'm afraid. There were three men. They knocked and asked if they could come in for a chat, but they were very intimidating, and it was clear that their question had been rhetorical.'

'Who did they introduce themselves as?'

'Police.'

'Did they provide you with any identification?'

Romano nodded.

'Can you remember their names?'

'Davidson, I think, was the name of the main man. The other two didn't show their cards.'

'I see. Can you remember anything else about Davidson's identification?'

'Just that it said Special Branch.'

Robson paused briefly to catch his own breath. He glanced casually at Burford to give the impression he was allowing sufficient time for her notetaking. He sensed Wilson's eyes burning his back.

'What did they want to talk to you about?'

'They wanted to know about, erm, well, they had technological questions.'

'Such as?'

Romano tried to disguise his attempt to delay for time by applying the oxygen mask. Robson could sense Wilson's shocked response as he snatched the mask from the Professor's face, causing his eyes to open wide.

'Listen, Professor. You may feel comfortable under the protection of your nurse, and so you should. But we have to think about the protection of others too, don't we? And don't be under any misconception that I do not have the ability to pull rank and outstay our welcome if I must. So, I'll repeat my opening statement, that if you give us the information you have, then we can leave you alone. Do you understand, sir?'

Romano gave a resigned nod.

'Good. What did the men from Special Branch want?'

'They pretended to want to know about the mountain ...'

'What do you mean by pretended?'

'Because, after a while it became clear that they were actually looking for something.'

'Oh? What would that be?'

'A key.'

'A key to what?'

'An electronic key. A multi-factor authentication key.'

'Which does what, precisely?'

'It gives access to a computer system.'

'Whose system?'

Romano reached across for the plastic cup to his side. His frail, wrinkled hand trembled as he sipped the lukewarm water.

'Professor. Why don't you save me having to ask a multitude of questions and just tell me what is going on? Like I say, the sooner you do, the sooner we are out of here.'

Suddenly, the door to the room opened and the nurse walked in confidently.

'Okay, that's five—'

'We will require more time unfortunately, nurse. Could you leave us alone please?'

'I'm sorry, DCI Robson, but my patient needs rest, I must insis—'

'DS Burford, kindly escort the nurse from the room. Sorry about this nurse, but this is a confidential enquiry.'

'The nurse blushed as Burford awkwardly escorted her from the ward and closed the door.

'Right, Professor,' continued Robson, 'please feel free to continue in your own time.'

'Wh-what do you want to know?'

'Everything, Professor. Perhaps you could start by telling us a little more about the capability of the infrastructure. Like, how does it compare with HAARP in Gakona?'

'The intention for Snowdon was always to replicate HAARP, but on a larger scale.'

'Larger? How much larger?'

'Well, the HAARP facility comprises a field of a hundred and eighty radio transmitters, across an area greater than thirty-three acres. As a result, the facility is capable of transmitting 3.6 megawatts of energy into the upper atmosphere and the ionosphere. It is cutting edge technology, but it is directly based on the research of the incredible Nikola Tesla.'

'Sorry, who?'

'Tesla was a genius. An inventor who possessed extraordinary prescience. He was a Serbian-American scientist, and a futurist. The technology employed at HAARP is a direct application of his research from the very beginning of the twentieth century.'

'Didn't he also invent cars?' Burford asked.

Romano sighed.

'No. But I believe the electric car manufacturer named their company after him.'

Robson ignored the professor's brusque tone towards his colleague and continued.

'How does Snowdon compare to the installation in Alaska?'

'The facility up on Snowdon is roughly double in size.'

'And why would they want to do that, Professor? What is the purpose of this new, larger facility, and why was HAARP sabotaged?'

'Despite the various conspiracy theories, HAARP is and always has been used to provide vital research into weather and climate patterns on Earth. Whereas the facility on Snowdon is designed to modify weather, instantaneously.'

'How?'

'That is not a simple question to answer. But, in the simplest possible terms, enough energy can be generated to steer whole weather fronts, and to even modify the jet stream.'

'So, do you mean that it would be possible to create any weather at any time?'

'Essentially, yes, within certain constraints.'

'Within what range?'

'Range?'

'Yes, Professor, range. How far from Snowdon can the facility influence the behaviour of the weather?'

'Sir, there is no limit, at least not as far as the habitable planet is concerned. The facility of Snowdon is, in theory, capable of controlling the weather anywhere on the globe.'

'Extraordinary. Does HAARP have that power?'

'Not on its own.'

'What do you mean? Are there other facilities?'

Romano sipped from the plastic cup as he nodded.

'How many?'

'Three, in total.'

'So, am I right in surmising that all three can be combined to provide one overall force?'

'That is correct, yes. The facilities have been configured so that they can be interconnected, in order to provide one overall cumulative transmission system.'

'Where are the other two stations?'

'One is in Iceland ...'

Robson heard the door swing open and smash against the wall. He looked around in time to see Wilson darting into the corridor.

'And the other?'

'Alaska ...'

'What? HAARP?'

Romano's trembling seemed to increase as he nodded again.

'I thought HAARP had been incapacitated?'

'It can be reactivated. The e-bomb that was used to attack the facility only destroyed the control station. But the raw infrastructure, that is, the IRI and the transmitters themselves ... they were still protected. A secret, additional control station has been installed onsite which, once activated, will be capable of operating the facility once again. So essentially, the attack on HAARP was merely to deactivate the local control facility for long enough to allow it to be controlled remotely.'

'Okay, but surely it would be possible for engineers on site to reverse the situation and destroy the remote-control capability, wouldn't it?'

Romano appeared ashamed as he dejectedly shook his head.

'Once they have taken remote control, nobody will want to be in the vicinity of HAARP, trust me. It will become too hazardous for human inhabitancy.'

Robson felt himself becoming more bewildered the more the scientist described the conspiracy. 'Why? How?'

'Simply because of the radiation power it is capable of. If in the wrong hands, HAARP can be used as a weapon, both short and long range.'

'How is it going to be reactivated?'

'Remotely ... using a highly secure multi-functional authorisation key.'

'The missing key?'

Romano's eyes displayed his terror, before his head sank into his chest. Robson turned as Wilson re-entered holding her phone and looking serious.

'Who has the key?'

'I don't know.'

'So whoever has the key be able to control the facilities, is that correct?'

'If they know the password.'

'Do you know the password, professor?'

Romano nodded, while Robson held his gaze in a silent command.

'Diluvian. D-I-L-U-V-I-A-N.'

'What does that mean?'

'I understand it is a term from the book of Genesis, in the Old Testament. It literally means *The Flood*, in reference to the biblical flood.

'As in, Noah's Ark?'

Romano nodded again.

'Professor, you mentioned conspiracy theories earlier. What theories?'

'There are several, Chief Inspector ...'

'Such as?'

'Such as, for example, HAARP is a secret weapon used for weather modification rather than research. Also, that it can be used for electromagnetic warfare, and even mind control.'

'And what is your view on those theories?'

Robson and Wilson both spotted the anxiety on the professor's face. Wilson spoke.

'Perhaps we should ask the professor what his view *was* before he became involved in this ... project ... Professor?'

Romano appeared forlorn. He began to shake his head.

'This was not what I signed up for ...'

'What precisely did you sign up for, Professor?'

'They said they wanted expert assistance for a top-secret programme ... a revolutionary experiment in combatting climate change.'

It seemed to Wilson that Romano was on the verge of sobbing and she decided to offer a few words of encouragement, detecting the DCI beside her was out of patience.

'Go on, Professor. Can I get you another glass of water?'

Romano shook his head.

'You see, officers, I have dedicated my life to climate research. And during that lifetime I have witnessed utter betrayal by the world's governments – a lifetime of hearing empty promises while mankind continued to systematically and irreversibly ruin our planet.'

'What motivated you to believe in *this* organisation?'

'Frankly, it was the fact that they were nothing to do with any government, just a group of philanthropic, albeit rich entrepreneurs, ostensibly at least, who wanted to do the right thing. People that wanted to take responsibility for their planet, rather than leaving it to the deceitful, greedy superpowers.'

'Who did the organisation claim to be exactly?'

'They said their organisation was Geoclimate Incorporation, and that they had an exciting new project taking place in the Welsh highlands that they wanted scientific support with.'

'And you agreed, right away?'

'No, no, of course not. But they were very persuasive. They sent a party to Alaska to meet me, and after a few weeks, they had me believing in their vision. I really was taken in.'

'And what is your view of the organisation now?'

'That they are not what they claimed to be. They aren't interested in taking control of climate change. They are only interested in the same thing as everyone else ...'

'Being?'

'Power. Power and control.'

'And how do they propose to achieve that?'

'Officers ... I believe you now know about the power that HAARP holds. And I take it that your research has enlightened you as to its conspiracy theories?'

Robson nodded.

'We've learned bits I suppose, but why don't you fill us in.'

'Well ... frankly, the conspiracy theories are true.'

'Sorry? Are you suggesting that HAARP is used for more than just observation?'

'No, no I am not saying that at all. As I have already stated, HAARP has always been used as it was intended – as a non-intrusive testing facility. A facility that has provided us with great insight into the behaviour and causes of weather patterns and how they are influenced by activity beyond our own horizons, in space. But that is all it has ever been, despite the conspiracy theories. It has not been used as a military weapon, it is not used to modify the weather, and it most certainly has never been used to attempt population mind control.'

'Mind control? Is it really capable of mind control?'

'Theoretically perhaps, But just because it is possible, it does not mean that it is happening.'

'So, are you suggesting that Geoclimate Incorporation is using the facility on Snowdon to modify the weather and to use it as a weapon?'

Romano gave a dejected nod. 'And perhaps more, as I alluded to earlier. With the right, or wrong … settings, the HAARP facility can be dangerous to life.'

Romano looked up from beneath his brow, his eyes displaying great anxiety.

'And what is more, they have the power to jam any attempt to sabotage their infrastructure.'

Wilson gazed into Romano's eyes as he continued.

'I fear that what the conspiracy theorists have long said about Nikola Tesla's invention is coming true …'

'Meaning what exactly?'

'That, like Frankenstein's monster, HAARP should never have been invented…'

CHAPTER 115

Robson felt a renewed vigour as he watched the body of officers swarming on to the massif in their respective teams. They had been gathered not just from the south-west region, but from various locations throughout the UK. He understood that having influential friends had helped his cause, and it was without doubt that his ex-boss, Commander Gibson of SO15, had ensured that the case was now being afforded serious priority, given the growing interest from Counter Terrorism Command.

The crack of several hundred boots could be heard as the company marched across the tarmacked road and on to the first of the mountain routes they would be navigating. Despite the time of year, a steamy mist emanated from the group as they split away from the crowd and exhaled the cool air. Judging by the thick cloud that covered the top portion of the mountain, visibility wasn't going to be good. But DCI Robson would not tolerate any further delay.

He had delivered what had become their customary early-morning briefing at the foot of the mountain to save wasting time at the station. And a vast audience it had been, comprising several fresh faces, as well as the familiar bleary-eyed detectives, uniformed officers, and mountain specialists from their previous treks. The entire body of investigators had already been briefed by Matthews on their respective routes, to enable some advance detailed research.

Robson had opted to join the roadway that represented the former Llanberis

Path. He watched from the car as Matthews delivered their final instructions. Alongside Matthews, Intelligence Officer Wilson looked around, searching for Robson. The moment she spotted him, she rolled her eyes. Through the tinted car windscreen, she could just make out that he held his phone to his ear. Robson held a finger aloft to indicate the estimated duration of the call and she turned to join the rest of the team.

Wilson was fighting an internal battle of her own. She felt torn. A large part of her regretted not informing DCI Robson that some of his daughter's belongings had been found in the vicinity of the car wreckage in the mountain valley only a few miles away. But, having missed earlier opportunities to break the news, she had recently agreed with Matthews and Superintendent Grayson that it wouldn't be beneficial to do so. Not yet.

The consensus was that the only reason any evidence had been available must have been a result of it having been thrown from the vehicle during its calamitous descent. Anything still inside the vehicle at its moment of impact had been incinerated and it would be several days before they had anything close to DNA clues, if at all. Wilson certainly knew that she couldn't tell him now. Every time she thought about it, which was often, she had to fight against her own emotions. They had to get on with the job.

Inside the dark saloon, the recipient finally answered Robson's call.

'Jack. How're you doing?'

'Hello, sir. Not too bad, thank you.'

'Any news on Jasmine?'

'Not yet, John.'

'I'm sorry, Jack. Hang on in there. It'll turn out okay. We're all praying. What of the investigation?'

Robson knew that, despite his former colleague's exponential rise in the force, he was always available as a personal counsel. Commander John Gibson was one of the few remaining people that Robson trusted, and for good reason.

'I feel we're closing in.'

'Have you managed to get anything from that professor yet?'

'Yes, sir. It seems there is some extraordinary technology being housed on the mountain. And, if Professor Romano is to be believed, it isn't the only installation.'

'I heard. Listen – are you still in Snowdonia, Jack?'

'Yes, sir.'

'Are you sure you're up to this?'

'Of course. I need to be involved, John.'

'I understand. Is there anything I can do to help?'

'You've already been a great help, sir. But there could possibly be something you might be able to speed up for me ...'

'Go on.'

'We've identified a private construction company that we'd like to get more details on, but we seem to have hit a brick wall. MI5 are looking into it, but the information flow isn't proving to be particularly effective, at least not in my direction. I wondered if your guys might be able to uncover something for us.'

'Okay, we'll certainly try. What's the company?'

'It's Geoclimate Incorporation. Apparently registered in the United States.'

In the silence that followed, Robson wondered if his ex-boss was going to work his magic then and there.

'Leave it with me, Jack. I'll get our people on to it immediately.'

'Thank you, sir. And thank you for your help in securing the extra manpower.'

'Anything I can do, you know you only have to ask. As you know, Counter Terrorism Command is taking a keen interest in how this one unfolds. Take care, I'll be in touch if there's any news.'

Robson locked the car and jogged after his colleagues. A row of multi-terrain vehicles sat waiting at the foot of the mountain. He jumped in the frontmost four-by-four, alongside Wilson.

CHAPTER 116

'Who was the important phone call to?'

Wilson's voice shook with vibrations from the ride as their vehicle led the short convoy, tearing up the terrain as they thundered up the mountain.

'John Gibson, actually.'

'Oh? What did he want?'

Robson looked at her quizzically.

'He wanted to discuss our progress. I've asked him for assistance in getting some intel on the construction company.'

'Okay, good idea.'

Robson could see she didn't mean it. She had evidently developed an affliction against sharing information since joining MI5. It stood to reason, Robson supposed. They were called the Secret Service for a reason. What was more perplexing was the apparently mutual distrust between the police divisions and the security service. One thing Robson was certain of – it would have been of far more benefit to the operation if the two forces had worked together.

Inside the all-terrain jeep at the front of the company, the two mountain specialists sat in the front seats in silence, their narrow eyes scrutinising the route beyond. The driver was a young, athletic woman with dark cropped hair. She seemed to Robson to be the type unfazed by anything. Much like his ex-wife. Much like his ex-lover. He seemed to be drawn to strong women –

perhaps it compensated for his own weaknesses, he thought to himself.

Behind them, the convoy comprised another three four-by-four vehicles, each of them equally equipped to deal with the harsh environment. Three more convoys of the same size had been dispatched at roughly equal distances apart, such that they divided the great mountain into four distinct quadrants.

Robson and Wilson began to settle into the rear seat of the forward vehicle as it rumbled along the uneven terrain. Almost immediately, their concentration was interrupted by the sound of distant thunder, as intense as an explosion and so enormous that the mountain itself seemed to quiver in response. The driver of the lead jeep brought the vehicle to a stand and leapt out. Her three passengers followed.

With a strong breeze in their faces, Robson and Wilson exchanged confused looks. It felt unnervingly as if the ground beneath their feet rumbled. The incredible sound, combined with the ominous sight of the dark cloud overhead, told them that they were in for one almighty storm. Robson had to shout to be heard over the growing cracking of thunder and increasing wind.

'Better get back inside the jeep!'

He waved to the others behind, who had also chosen to stand outside their vehicles. But the look of horror on their faces belied more than mere anxiety over a thunderstorm, however severe. Robson hadn't seen what they had, but a sense of deep foreboding grew as he looked upon his colleagues.

Before he could turn of his own volition, Wilson grabbed him by the arm, knowing that it would be almost impossible to be heard above the increasing sound. Robson noticed that Wilson's pale expression matched the others that he had just turned away from. He allowed his eyes to look beyond her, finally seeing the cause of the shocked expressions for himself.

Evidently, the darkness that had rapidly descended on the mountain summit was being caused by more than just a gathering of thick cloud. They watched the scene that was taking place several hundreds of metres away, high above them. Rocky, muddy debris was being hurled into the air by some great force. Even from such a distance, they could see a melee of dark objects and spray grow larger as it hurtled down the mountainside towards them at an alarming rate. The driver of the lead jeep sprinted past Robson and Wilson, screaming as she wrenched at the door to the driver's seat.

'Get in … now!'

Seconds later, all four vehicles made abrupt three-point turns before beginning to scream back down the mountainside. Robson and Wilson, now in the rearmost vehicle, turned to watch thousands of gallons of water gushing down the vast mountain behind them. They were a good half a kilometre away from the entrance at the bottom. Robson found himself calculating their chances of reaching the bottom ahead of the immense body of water.

*

The mountains appeared even more gigantic from the depths of the craggy valley. A lone figure had spent two hours combing the former crime scene but hadn't found anything other than the remains of a charred bumper. The forensics officers had already recovered everything else, hoping to recover a meaningful trace. He was almost certain that the investigators hadn't found what he had come for. In which case, he now concluded that the little electronic device had not been amidst the wreckage in the first place.

The man gave a hand signal to his colleague high above, who stood outside the car parked on the side of the winding mountain road. The man above held a mobile phone to his ear while continuing to peer down at his colleague. He relayed the meaning of the unmistakable hand-signal to the person awaiting an update at the other end of the phone line.

'It's a negative, General Miller. He can't find it. You can deactivate the tracking alarm.'

He heard a loud sigh before the gruff response came.

'Hmm. There's only one other possibility.'

'Really? It's like looking for a needle in a haysta—'

'No! No … the tracking alarm would be unmistakable in that valley. It was purposely designed to be capable of giving out a maximum sound of a hundred decibels. If you can't hear it, then it isn't there.'

'Then where, sir?'

'She has it.'

CHAPTER 117

Rescue boats, having been drafted in from all quarters, were still arriving at the foot of Mount Snowdon, and now totalled eight. The rescuers worked frantically to help the locals from the various old homes and farmhouses scattered around the perimeter of the great mountain.

Mercifully, the roads had been unseasonably quiet at the time of the flash flood. A flood the likes of which hadn't been witnessed in generations. There had been no warning – the water had begun to gush from the mountain half an hour ago and only now seemed to be showing signs of slowing. But the damage was already done.

Cars and other vehicles had been effortlessly swept aside by the water. One rescue team watched a jeep appear above the surface of the water. Instinctively, the team reacted as one and began to make their way across to the shipwrecked vehicle. From fifty yards, the area surrounding the jeep appeared eerily devoid of life.

*

Robson and Wilson held each other in an awkward embrace, each using an arm to lock themselves together against a great tree trunk which stubbornly remained standing, while its smaller cousins had been ripped up by their roots.

The water had finally finished rushing down the mountain, leaving a scene of filthy carnage. Vegetation, which had been ripped from the mountainside, was deposited at random spots, and the mud churned up by the roaring flood covered almost everything in sight.

Robson turned, his nose nearly touching Wilson's wet cheek. They both continued to cling on, resisting the call from burning muscles to release their grip, despite them both being breathless, shocked, and disorientated. It was as if they had been snatched from the planet they knew and dumped into another, hostile world. Wilson twisted her neck round to face him, her arms gripping what seemed to be the only remaining tree in the area. As she turned, the tips of their noses touched briefly before she spoke in a breathless hiss.

'What the fuck happened?'

Robson removed a hand from the tree and squeezed his thumb and forefinger into his closed eyes to rid them of accumulated water.

'The water level seems to be draining fast. I'm going back up.'

Wilson looked incredulous.

'Pardon?!'

'I think we'll be able to get through the barrier now.'

'How?'

'I've a hunch the structure we saw yesterday might have something to do with this sudden release of water ...'

'Jack, even if you're right, the barrier will have been raised again by the time you get there.'

'Maybe. But they won't be expecting us to return for a while, will they?'

'How will you get there?'

'On foot.'

CHAPTER 118

Llanberis Police Station

The desk sergeant eyed their new arrival with wonder. She was drenched and so covered in dirt that it was impossible to determine her age. She could have been anywhere between fourteen and thirty-four by his reckoning. One thing he could see, as clear as the view from the Welsh hills on a spring day, was that she had been in trouble.

The mystery female shook as she approached the desk, her teeth chattering as she opened her mouth to speak to the stunned sergeant. Up close, the sergeant could see from her slightly vacant eyes that she was young, perhaps even younger than his previous assessment. Being a grandfather himself, his paternal instinct kicked in and seeing that she couldn't manage any words, the Welshman took over.

'Now then, my dear, what's happened to you?'

'I-I-I …'

Recognising that the girl appeared to be close to collapse, the sergeant rushed around his desk to lend some assistance.

'My goodness. I tell you what, let's get you a warm cup of tea and a dry blanket and we'll talk after that. How does that sound, my dear?'

The girl grimaced as she fought to control her vibrating jaw.

'D-D-DCI ... R-R-Robso—'

As the girl attempted to communicate, a harassed-looking DC Trudy Saunders led a couple of uniformed officers into the room.

'Sergeant, there's been an incident at Snowdon, we're— Oh my goodness!'

Saunders did a double take and stood open-mouthed as she looked at the dishevelled girl.

'Jasmine?!'

Saunders ran across the room and embraced the girl tightly, lifting her off her feet as she did so.

'Oh, my darling! What's happened?!'

The police sergeant frowned with confusion as he looked between the two females.'

'Jasmine?'

DC Saunders pressed her cheek against the girl's as she looked towards the sergeant.

'Yes, Sergeant. Jasmine Robson. The daughter of DCI Jack Robson.'

CHAPTER 119

CI Robson paid no attention to the noise of sirens, which seemed to emanate from all directions beneath them. His fingertips burning as he dug them in, Robson was determined to claw his way forward, hoping that this would turn out to be the most difficult part of the route.

Ahead of him, the muddy figure of Intelligence Officer Wilson fought her way up the bank with equal vigour. They had both agreed – with the former paths having been seemingly washed to oblivion – that aiming for any visible rocky terrain would be their best chance of making progress.

Minutes later, the surface began to become decidedly more rugged. They had no way of telling whether the more solid ground they had arrived at had been like that prior to the flood, or if it had been exposed by it. They both dared to stand upright and, breathing heavily, instinctively looked beneath them to assess their progress, before turning to examine one another. Together, they made quite a sight, and each thought to themselves how intriguing it was that they could still recognise their opposite number. Wilson swallowed hard.

'How much further do you think it is?'

'I reckon we must nearly be at the eight-hundred metre point. Which means we should be close.'

As he spoke, their attention was drawn to another sound which seemed to be coming from nearby, although, as he knew well, the source of such sounds was difficult to pinpoint in the acoustic environment of the mountain. Robson turned in response to his ex-partner tugging on his soaked shoulder and followed her stare. They both watched on in silence at the breathtaking scene a hundred yards away, as the huge barrier they had witnessed previously now began to reappear, as it slowly rose from inside the ground.

'Do you think they know we're here?'

Wilson looked at him squarely.

'Who knows? Let's get over there before we're too late!'

'Jack. Think about the devastation behind us. We need back-up, but we don't stand a chance of getting it any time soon.'

'We need to take our chance.'

Wilson recognised the recklessness in his dialogue and knew she had to somehow make him see sense, despite his current emotional turmoil.

'Jack, we do not know what we are facing. Let's not simply play into their hands!'

'There's no time to think about it. We've faced similar odds together before, as I recall …'

Wilson knew at that moment that his position was non-negotiable. She also knew that there was no way she was going to allow him to venture forward on his own. So, seemingly dragged along by fate, they ambled forward on tired limbs, doing their best to use the remaining vegetation to provide them with sparse cover.

*

As Robson and Wilson continued to navigate the sodden surface of the mountain on all fours, a hundred metres beneath them, inside the mountain itself, steel ropes within the colossal lift shaft whined as they heaved the enclosure upwards. Few knew about the extraordinary access inside the mountain, which had been built to make it possible to access the mountaintop establishment in a matter of minutes, and regardless of the weather or prevailing environmental conditions. The intention had been that only a select few would ever know of its existence – the inner sanctum.

Since her recent, unplanned excursion into the river Exe, the woman now soaring upwards inside the mountain had known that the next time she came face to face with Jack Robson, he wouldn't be expecting it. The thought of their reunion spurred her onwards. She felt no fear at that moment, perhaps because of the feel of the cold steel in her right palm, but also because she was crystal clear about what she had to do.

The woman was also well aware of the tragic devastation below and of the rescue operation currently taking place at the foot of the mountain. But she was confident that DCI Robson would find a way of reaching the top, despite not having the knowledge that she possessed.

CHAPTER 120

DC Saunders suppressed the urge to hug the young girl again and watched her sip from a mug of steaming milk, ready to pounce to rescue the vessel from her trembling hands the moment it fell.

'So, you didn't recognise any of the men that took you, Jasmine?'

She spoke in soft, maternal tones, observing the colour returning to the girl's cheeks as she shook her delicate head in response.

'And there were, in total, six different men involved?'

Jasmine swallowed another gulp of the slightly sweetened, hot milk. She realised she would have to elaborate verbally to answer the latest question. It felt peculiar that, despite being in familiar, ostensibly safe company, she still felt uneasy and somewhat insecure after her experience of the past week. She felt the need to be with her father at that moment, more than ever before. Or, if not, Sarah.

'Yes, I think so,' Jasmine croaked in response. 'But they didn't all seem to be on the same side.'

'Okay. So, tell me again, in your own time. The man that took you in the first instance – you never saw him again, after you had managed to run off?'

She shook her head abruptly and sniffed as tears finally began to appear and run down her cheeks. Saunders wrapped both arms tightly around the girl.

'I'm sorry, Jasmine. You're okay now. I just want to find out if there's anything that might help the officers that are out in the field right now.'

Saunders leant forward and cupped both of Jasmine's hands in hers, noting that they still felt ice cold.

'And the big man ... you said that he was with the other two that drove you out to the headland?'

She nodded, trying hard not to think about what the men had planned to do with her on the cliff. Saunders continued to probe as gently as she could, knowing that the young daughter of their DCI might well possess information that could have the potential to save any further tragedy.

DCI Robson's daughter!

Saunders realised the sooner she could get the information to her boss she would be preventing further unnecessary pain. But was Robson himself okay? They had lost all contact with their colleagues who had ventured on to the mountain early that morning.

'What about the guy that drove you away from the cliff – you think that he seemed to have been working against the three men with the jeep?'

'That's right.'

Jasmine inhaled deeply as she spoke, mustering her 'Robson strength'.

'How can you be sure?'

'Because the other guy chased after us.'

'Other guy? What about his two friends?'

'They fell off the cliff.'

Saunders searched the girl's face, expecting it to crack with emotion again at any moment, as she privately considered what she had been through and witnessed. But the meltdown didn't arrive. Instead, the girl seemed to have suddenly adopted a renewed resolve. DC Saunders rubbed the girl's shoulder.

'I'm sorry, Jasmine, but you're safe now, okay?'

The girl nodded dutifully, as Saunders continued in a soft voice.

'We believe that the car you were being chased in crashed off the mountainside. Some of your belongings were found inside.'

'What happened to the driver?'

Saunders' hesitation was enough to answer the query. Jasmine let her head drop.

'This sixth guy, the Frenchman – you said he let you get out of the car, just before the collision, is that correct?'

'Yes.' She wiped her nose before replacing the well-used tissue. 'We were stuck in a ditch at the side of the road. The jeep was chasing us and had nearly caught up. He told me to hide behind some trees until I was sure the man chasing us had gone, and—'

'And?'

Saunders couldn't imagine what the girl was keeping back.

'Where did you go, Jasmine? Where have you been ever since?'

'He gave me an address. A map. It was a cottage in the mountains. He told me to wait until—'

'Until what?'

'Can I see my dad now?'

PC Jones entered the room again.

'Sorry, ladies. Just to say, we haven't been able get through to DCI Robson yet. The phone signal on the mountain is famously poor, but we'll keep trying and I'll let you know as soon as we have made contact.'

Jasmine watched DC Saunders exchange a peculiar look with the man as she responded.

'Thank you, Constable. I think it's time I went to join DCI Robson and the rest of the team. Will you look after Jasmine for me, and make sure she gets fed, please?

'No!'

Jasmine was on her feet. Both officers looked at the girl in surprise.

'What's wrong, Jasmine?' asked Saunders.

'I'm coming with you. I need to see my father immediately.'

'All in good time, Jasmine. Your dad's working at the moment. He'll be overjoyed beyond words to learn that you're safe, but he is currently in the middle of an operation.'

'Where is he?'

The officers exchanged awkward glances.

'He's nearby, miss,' offered Jones in a deep Welsh brogue. 'Let me take you to our canteen and get you some proper grub, is it?'

She shook her head in frustration.

'Listen, Jasmine. I really can't take a child – sorry – young girl, to an ongoing investigation and potential crime scene—'

'Are they on the mountain?'

'What makes you say that?'

After a few more seconds of silence, Saunders rose and gave the girl another hug.

'Have something to eat. I'll go and fetch your father. Okay?'

Jasmine nodded and withdrew eye contact from both officers.

If you won't take me, I'll find my own way.

CHAPTER 121

Wilson looked up at the ten-metre high steel wall as she spoke on her mobile.

'Are you sure he's even on the mountain?'

Robson turned his attention from the metallic structure, one eyebrow raised as he appraised his colleague.

'Okay, keep me posted. Arkwright cannot be allowed to escape. We need to bring him in urgently.'

Seconds after replacing the phone in the rear pocket of her filthy jeans, it began to sound again.

'Wilson.'

'I believe he lost his phone in the flood. Yes, back up would be very useful, but I think you might find resources hard to come by right now. We have already requested further support from Special Branch, but I doubt that anyone will be able to get through for a while. There is currently a full-scale emergency rescue effort taking place at the foot of the mountain.'

Losing interest in Wilson's telephone call, Robson had returned his attention to the empty concrete trench they had discovered the previous day. It was wet at the bottom and the hatches were now open. He eyed the ladder to his right, which provided access to the bottom of the trench. He had his back to Wilson, so he didn't notice her staring at him, and was only vaguely aware of the conversation taking place on the telephone.

'Yes, yes, he's with me now.'

It was the detectable emotion in her voice that made him turn back. Robson eyed her with interest. He saw that her normally steely eyes had begun to show the faintest sign of glistening, and her voice now started to wobble as she spoke again.

'I'll let him know, thank you, DC Saunders. Hopefully, we'll see you soon. Try to get as close to the mountain as you can, you're the only member of the team that knows our current 20 until our support arrives. We must assume that air support is still inadvisable.'

For the second time, she replaced the phone, not taking her eyes off Robson, who was now showing an interest in her conversation.

'What is it? Is Saunders okay?'

She knew from experience that his apparent concern for a team member was genuine. The knowledge made her swallow down the lump in her throat before she dared attempt to respond.

'It's about Jasmine.'

'Go on.'

His eyes betrayed the panic that suddenly pervaded his veins.

'She's okay, Jack. She's at the station. Saunders has just left her!'

Wilson's voice broke with emotion.

They both embraced. It was instinctive, but it also gave Robson the short time he needed to compose himself. He held Wilson's shoulders as he spoke, inches from her face.

'I'm sure this trench must be connected to some sort of reservoir. It seems to be drying up again now, but I would wager that we might be looking at the source of the floods, or at least a part of the infrastructure that was used to deliver it.'

*

Constable Jones's bottom lip protruded as he looked around the empty rest room. He placed two mugs of tea on the table and took a seat, presuming the girl was visiting the lavatory. Despite the slight awkwardness of the situation, Jones did not mind babysitting. At least it provided a brief interlude from the sergeant's paperwork pile.

While Jones was sat waiting for his guest to return, the station sergeant looked up from his newspaper and watched a young girl nonchalantly walk past the front desk. He knew it must have been the Robson girl who had arrived a couple of hours ago, but she certainly appeared different after having cleaned up and eaten.

'Everything okay, my love?'

The young girl continued walking towards the building's entrance as she turned her head to respond.

'Fine, thank you. I'm just going out for some fresh air.'

The sergeant's paunch wobbled as he chuckled.

'I would have thought you'd had enough of that by now, eh? I must say, my dear, you're certainly looking better than when you came in, already.'

'Thanks, I feel it.'

'Good. Well, I'll let you carry on then. Judging by the colour of the sky, you won't want to be out there for long.'

He chuckled at his own joke again, before returning his attention to his newspaper. Jasmine forced a polite smile and strode outside. She immediately looked up towards the grey sky and placed both hands in her pockets, feigning a casual stroll around the car park.

Once out of sight, she darted in the direction of the high street to meet the taxi which she had ordered five minutes earlier in the station's rest room.

CHAPTER 122

It was becoming clear that the steel construction was more than just a robust barrier – it also seemed to be acting as a floodgate. Furthermore, it appeared to be capable of being operated remotely.

However, the manual override on the outside of the wall was sufficiently similar to a canal lock gate to enable Robson and Wilson to decipher its operation. They half-expected another torrent to flood through the gates, but it became apparent soon after they began to open that whatever source had previously unleashed its contents down the mountain had either been entirely drained or was being kept at bay elsewhere.

The mechanism groaned as it was operated, but the effort required on Robson's part was surprisingly small. A twenty metre-wide section lowered into the ground where it stood as Robson continued to wind the handle. As the top of the steel section disappeared, he stopped turning and joined Wilson, both looking slightly dumbstruck by the sight before them. Beyond the wall, there was another bridge. It crossed a second canal-like trench, that was at least twice the width of that outside the wall and was filled with water.

Neither of them spoke as they stepped half a metre to cross the lowered section of wall and made for the bridge beyond the metal barrier.

*

Matthews drew the blanket around his shoulders tightly as he continued to shiver on the back step of the ambulance. He went over the events in his head again, remembering how one minute they were on the mountainside and the next, they were being thrown back down towards the bottom, courtesy of the miraculously appearing rapids. If that wasn't enough to contemplate, the apparition that appeared before him now threatened to tip him over the edge. He closed his eyes and shook his head for a fifth time, but still the vision drew nearer, and the resemblance became too strong to deny.

He felt confusion wash over him, wondering what psychological damage the flood must have done. Suddenly, a paramedic stepped into the path of the oncoming visitor, who continued to wade through the standing water, seemingly ignorant of its presence.

'Excuse me, miss. Where do you think you're off to?'

'Hello. I just need to have a chat with DI Matthews if that would be okay.'

The words entered Matthews' head and rattled around for several seconds, before he finally accepted that the voice validated the image and, contrary to all logic, Jasmine Robson stood before him, alone.

'He's not quite himself at the mo—'

'It's okay,' Matthews interrupted the paramedic. 'Let her through, please.'

The paramedic considered warning his patient that he was not in any fit state to make decisions. But by the time he opened his mouth to speak again, it was too late, the girl had already walked past him and stood close to Matthews, who still fought to understand what was happening.

'Jasmine? H-how …'

'Hi Jimmy. I need to see my dad.'

'I – we – don't know where he is, Jazzy. There's been a bit of an incident here, as you can see.'

For a few seconds she took in the scene of devastation, which extended as far as she could see. Thanks to the extraordinary effort of the emergency services, and to good fortune for the proximity of the vast lake, they had managed to reduce the water level to about six inches. It was quite miraculous, especially to those who had witnessed the amount of water dispatched by the great mountain only a short while ago.

'I can see. I need to find him urgently. Will you help me?'

The paramedic had remained within earshot of the conversation and reacted indignantly.

'No, he will not, young lady. And you won't be going any further either. There's still a rescue operation taking place here. Trust me, we don't want any additions to our list of missing people. You will have to stay put I'm afraid and leave the rescue to the experts. If your father, whoever he may be, is out there, then we have the best people looking for him, my dear.'

This time it was the paramedic that didn't wait for an answer and he turned away from Jasmine to attend to his patient again. He watched, horrified, as Matthews got up and wobbled past, throwing off his blanket.

'Come on, Jasmine.'

'I really must advise against this, Inspector!'

'It's fine. I'm not going to let her place herself in any danger. Which is why I'm going with her, otherwise she'll go alone. Trust me on that.'

One of the paramedic's colleagues joined him as he placed his hands on his hips.

'Unbelievable ...'

'Just leave it, Nick. Some people just don't want to be helped. I could do with a hand over here. We've got more broken bones than we have pairs of hands.'

Fifty yards ahead, they watched a somewhat unstable Detective Inspector Matthews hold up the police tape with one hand to allow the girl through, while he displayed his identification with the other. One of the uniformed officers broke away from the large group that manned the cordon and accompanied Matthews and his young friend. The uniformed officer seemed excited, repeatedly pointing in the direction of the entrance to one of the eroded pathways on to the mountain.

*

Sarah Connor watched Jacob Miller and his small group of assistants walk stealthily around the perimeter of the forecourt, all of them focussed on the uninvited guests down below, who were currently traversing the inner canal and approaching the inner security fence. She turned away, not wishing to watch the ambush for herself, and walked back across the empty room.

CHAPTER 123

After crossing the bridge, Robson and Wilson jogged alongside one another for a hundred yards up the steep, barren expanse of soaked land towards a gate in the security fence ahead, before they both threw themselves to the ground on seeing the activity taking place in the distance. Robson turned to Wilson, who panted alongside him. Her hair had begun to dry in blond waves. Robson nodded in the direction of the single-storey building a hundred yards away. Wilson frowned in acknowledgement.

'It's a bit exposed.'

'I know,' Robson pondered. 'The grass is longer over there.'

He indicated towards an expanse of long grasses and wildflowers. Wilson appeared vigilant as she nodded. They both began to crawl to their right but froze on hearing a mechanical sound behind them. The noise was immediately interrupted by a voice – a voice which confirmed that they had been outmanoeuvred.

'DCI Robson and *Intelligence* Officer Wilson, it's been a while.'

They both turned slowly to find three men between them and the canal, each one pointing a pistol towards them. The man that did the talking seemed familiar somehow, but neither of them were sure why.

'I'm glad you came to see us at last. We've been wanting to ask you a few questions!'

It was the accent that seemed familiar to Robson. Then he recognised the eyes.

The eyes never change.

There was no other physical similarity to the man they had been pivotal in putting behind bars eight years earlier, supposedly for life. The ex-harbour master had, it seemed, obtained a new shell in which to live.

'Jacob. You've changed.'

Robson kept his voice even, suppressing his anger. Wilson raised her eyebrows as she made the association herself.

'Neither of you two have. Well, perhaps a little grey hair showing DCI Robson, but otherwise both of you seem to be still as beautiful as ever! I did hear you were an item, is that still so?'

Neither of them reacted to Miller's teasing smile.

'Aw dear. Don't tell me it hasn't worked out for Somerset's golden couple?'

'What's going on here, Miller?'

Robson fixed him with a stare, while he fought to control himself. He deliberately pushed thoughts of his daughter from his mind.

Leave it. She's safe now.

'Let me show you, DCI Robson, let me show both of you. Would you both be so kind as to follow me. I'll be glad to give you a guided tour, but first, I want to introduce you to someone.'

The panoramic view from that altitude was stunning. In all directions there were peaks and troughs, lakes and forestation. Nature at its finest, Wilson thought to herself as she looked ahead at the newly built infrastructure which tainted the otherwise natural magnificence of the scene. There were still three guns directed at them as they moved gingerly through the entrance in the security fence. Boots and heavy breathing were all that could be heard above the wind and bleating sheep in the distance as they climbed the steep incline towards the buildings a few hundred yards ahead. Wilson broke the silence.

'Tell me, Jacob. How long did you think you were going to evade us for?'

'Am I not still evading you, my love?!'

'Hold on to that thought, Miller,' Robson entered the conversation. 'You may not be surprised to learn that we didn't come alone.'

Miller let out an annoyingly carefree chuckle.

'Let your colleagues come, Jack, let them come.'

Robson glanced across at his partner as they approached the brow of the gradient they had been climbing. The building began to obscure the view down the opposite face of the mountain.

'What do you think? He's even beginning to sound like Charlesworth!' Robson hissed, trying his best to display a confident smirk, despite his concern.

Wilson was distracted anyway. Her wide eyes had locked on to a distant sight which nearly made her freeze. Almost a year of seemingly random intelligence and loose strands suddenly came together in a horrific realisation. The facility that sprawled across seemingly endless acres of mountainous terrain was even more vast than the professor had recently described.

She regained her poker expression as she and Robson stood aside to allow one of the others to move ahead to open the entrance to the building. Robson gave a brief, enquiring look in Wilson's direction, having noticed the change in her demeanour.

*

Over a thousand miles away, Arkwright finished ensuring that all the entrances to the Icelandic facility were sealed at the top of the tuya mountain.

In some way it seemed a little tragic, sacrilegious even, to put an end to such an engineering marvel. But other, more important principles were at stake than scientific advancement. He understood that, given their likely increasing numbers and expertise, those pursuing him would eventually track him down. It was only going to be a matter of time. But he knew he did not need much longer.

Arkwright stood in the doorway for a moment and surveyed the control room. Looking around, he saw he was alone, everyone else having evacuated in response to the alarm he had initiated earlier. He stared at the only equipment he needed, confirming to himself that, along with the data that was held only inside his mind, he now possessed nearly everything he needed to complete his mission.

He turned his phone back on, which had only been activated once since leaving his fiancé in Paris almost a week ago. He watched the screen light up and the display confirmed, extraordinarily, that it was receiving a signal. In his mind, there had been no doubt that sufficient network coverage existed on the mountain, due to the installation of several concealed masts scattered across the highlands. He felt a chill run down his spine as he placed his phone on the desk before him. The moment had finally arrived, against the odds.

He really was a Charlesworth.

The device vibrated incessantly for over a minute, signalling the delivery of missed messages and a queue of failed incoming communications. His thoughts initially turned to Naamah, Miller and the others, and he wondered about the current situation on Snowdon. He had resigned himself to the fact that his communication with his comrades had been severed, perhaps permanently.

He returned his focus to his own work and tapped the keyboard on the desk before him, while he watched the large VDU screen illuminate in response.

CHAPTER 124

Robson, Wilson, and their hosts stood in a large reception room. It could almost have passed as a hotel foyer, but with an armed security guard rather than a receptionist at the front desk.

Robson cast his mind back several years and noted how the current surroundings contrasted with the bland, military environment of the underground base located in the Exmoor wilderness – Arcam. Wilson, too, noted the contrast and drew an early conclusion. *A woman's touch?* The tanned security guard eyed them suspiciously while his general engaged in mock hospitality.

'DCI Robson and Officer Wilson, I'd like to introduce you to our new head of operations. Our new leader …'

'Surely there can be no replacement for Sir Geoffrey Charlesworth?' Robson mocked.

Adrenaline-laced blood surged through his veins. Undoubtedly, his spirits had been lifted by the news that Jasmine had been found safe, but he knew it was his anger that now further energised him. In fact, he felt like he might explode. Jacob Miller showed no outward sign that he had been affected by the jibe and continued in an even tone.

'It's a fair point, Jack, really it is. But we do have a worthy successor. Actually, I believe you both may know her?'

The statement had barely registered with Robson and Wilson as the door to an apparent stairwell opened. They stood wide-eyed and watched Sarah Connor enter the room, pointing a firearm at them.

CHAPTER 125

D etective Inspector Matthews did his best to ignore his exhaustion and
the pain from his injuries.

He turned to look behind as they rumbled their way up the steep, now waterlogged, terrain once again. He thought to himself how incredibly efficient the hastily assembled response team had had been at draining the flood. Despite the recent heavy rainfall, the great lake, Llyn Cwellyn, had still possessed enough capacity to absorb the sudden and enormous volume of water. The speed with which they had managed to disperse the water had been largely down to efficient distribution, but the vastness of the two hundred-acre natural reservoir had certainly played its part.

Matthews had managed to persuade the local sergeant to dispatch what seemed to be the only mountain jeep in the area that remained functional. He leant forward from the rear passenger seat, pointing at a spot in the distance. He didn't exactly have an accurate idea of where they were headed, but the message from Officer Wilson recently relayed to him indicated that they needed to approach the wall somewhere on the southwestern slope of the mountain.

Feeling Jasmine's presence alongside him, Matthews allowed himself another regretful glance at the child. He still did not know what she had been through. She was famous among the Somerset CID family for being resolute, but there seemed to be an even steelier determination about her since her recent ordeal. Incredible, Matthews thought. Instead of breaking her, it appeared to have made her stronger. Unquestionably, a true Robson. The thought did not, however, ease his regret at having allowed a thirteen-year-old to talk him into accompanying him on official police business. The only possible glimpse of nerves seemed to be the way she was fiddling with the zip on her jacket pocket, as though she were guarding something of value.

Matthews grunted as his head thumped against the seat in front and turned to look out of the window, tuning in to their surroundings once more.

*

'Sarah?!'

Wilson sounded as poleaxed as Robson felt.

'Hello, Emma.' She appeared nervous as her eyes darted between those gathered, before acknowledging Robson, almost apologetically. 'Hi, Jack.'

Robson noted that Sarah's default, warm smile had disappeared and been replaced by a new expression, one he hadn't witnessed before. It was certainly odd to see her holding a firearm, although, Robson noted, she didn't appear particularly comfortable doing so. The curious angle at which she pointed the gun had attracted both Robson and Wilson's gaze, distracting them from the fact that another female had joined the party.

The new voice startled them both.

'Now then, Sarah, put the gun down, there's a good girl.'

Robson's mind swam as he looked upon the new arrival. His shock at seeing Sarah had been temporarily superseded.

How could it be her?

Sarah's hands trembled as she moved the firearm away from Miller and his colleagues and pointed it towards the graceful woman in the corner of the room. Her elegant demeanour seemed somehow in harmony with the decor, as though by design. In fact, her appearance seemed almost ethereal, Robson thought, as though she were an apparition, a sense undoubtedly fuelled by his belief that the woman who now stood before him should be dead.

Miller began to chuckle at the scene, then pressed his gun against Robson's temple.

'What do you think, Jack? Do you think Sarah will shoot?'

'Back off! Or I'll shoot her!' Sarah's voice trembled.

'I think you'll find you're outnumbered, my dear. Fire one shot and you won't last another second.'

Wilson intervened.

'Sarah. He's right. Drop the gun.'

Sarah switched her wild eyes to Robson for guidance, whose expression confirmed that he agreed with Wilson's advice. She began to sob as she lowered the gun.

Miller approached her slowly while his colleagues continued to aim their weapons at Robson and Wilson. The ex-harbourmaster's outstretched paw dwarfed Sarah's hand as he confidently prised her firearm away and smiled, before turning back to the room. In a flash, his left arm flew back, his clenched fist connecting with the side of Sarah's face. The cracking sound of knuckle against cheekbone seemed to echo as Sarah crashed on to the hard floor.

Robson fought to suppress the fire that burned inside him as he met Miller's provocative stare. He knew full well what the sparkle in the other man's eyes meant. He was willing him to surrender to his emotions and attack.

Miller also watched Wilson's reaction with amusement. She was clearly relieved to see Robson's shoulders drop acquiescently. Miller released his gaze, still confident that he would have his moment with DCI Robson. *Sooner or later …*

'Jack, Emma. As I was saying, I'd like to introduce you to someone. Meet Naamah, our leader.'

The room fell silent again as Robson and Wilson looked at the woman Miller had introduced as their current leader. They both felt relieved to hear the groaning sound coming from the lump on the floor. At least Sarah was conscious. Robson broke the silence.

'Hello, Louise, this is unexpected. Back from the dead, I see.'

'Hi, Jack, long time no see. I knew you'd be surprised. I believe you might have become recently acquainted with my dear, late sister.'

CHAPTER 126

DI Matthews winced again as he adjusted his position on the rocky, makeshift seat, while holding a phone against his ear to listen to the voice on the line.

'Okay, James, we've got your position. Stay put and do not let the girl out of your sight.'

'Affirmative, sir.'

Matthews had begun to regret his decision to allow Jasmine on to the mountain almost as soon as they had set off. But explaining his actions to his superintendent had really served to confirm how stupid he had been.

'I still can't quite believe you allowed her to go. It is a most imprudent decision, Matthews.'

'I know, sir. She insisted she has something she has to give to Robson directly, sir, but she won't say what it is. She doesn't seem to trust anyone else except her father.'

'Well, she certainly can't be blamed for that, after what she's been through. Do not, under any circumstances, attempt to breach the perimeter. Your priority is the safety of the girl. And your own, for that matter. The first thing we need to do is get you both the hell off that mountain. Sit tight, we have people on their way.'

'Yes, sir.'

Matthews replaced his phone, before placing his hands gently over his ribcage to soothe the pain. It seemed every time he spoke, the pain grew worse.

'Jasmine. Let's go back and sit in the jeep. We might have to wait a while.'

After a silent few seconds, he looked over his shoulder towards the bank of the empty canal, where Robson's daughter had been standing only a few moments earlier when he had sat down to make the call. Matthews sprung up and looked beyond the empty space across the lowered section beyond the steel perimeter. The girl was nowhere to be seen. He flinched at the sudden mechanical sound and watched in horror as the lowered section of steel began to rise. He knew he had a decision to make. *Shit! Which way did she go?!*

'Jasmine!'

Matthews felt compelled to act on instinct and ran the few yards between him and the ascending metal, leaping across the moving barrier before it became too high for him to scale. He limped across the canal bridge, continually scanning the barren area. This was going to be like looking for a needle in a haystack. *And the needle might not even be in the fucking haystack!* He began to shout as he prowled forward.

'Jasmine!'

Upon seeing freshly flattened vegetation, he attempted to follow its trail along the incline, towards the high fence in the distance and gathering storm clouds beyond.

*

Sarah groaned as Robson held a filthy, cold rag to her right cheek. The swelling continued to grow, and the surrounding area grew blacker by the moment. Miller had clearly enjoyed declining their pleas for a first aid kit and an ice pack before locking them into a small room without provisions. Ten minutes later, one of the other gunmen arrived with a small first aid kit, throwing the small bundle into their makeshift cell so it lay alongside the semi-conscious patient on the cold, hard floor.

Wilson paced the room, trying to evaluate their options. Robson looked up from his patient and interrupted her thoughts.

'So, it looks like Hart and Miller have powerful friends.'

Wilson's dark expression conveyed the gravity of the situation, but she seemed to be elsewhere. She finally responded to Robson's confused stare.

'Clearly ...'

'Connor?'

As Wilson nodded vacantly, Sarah groaned as Robson gently removed his arm from behind her head and stood.

'But what are the chances of swapping a prisoner without anyone knowing? They must have access to a fairly influential support network.'

'I know. Hart was only category C, but she was being monitored closely, as I understood it. Especially during visits.'

'I can assure you that I didn't see any evidence of that, Emma. Her lookalike substitute certainly wasn't under any kind of scrutiny, whoever she might have been. At least now I know why she looked so young – presumably, she was—'

They looked up at the sound of the door being unlocked. It opened abruptly to reveal the new, lean Jacob Miller standing in the opening. He held his gun in a casual grip and, as he entered, two of his gunmen followed and stood just inside the room. Miller's cold eyes were fixed on Wilson, as though she were the only person in the room. She began to feel weak at the knees as Miller approached her. Judging by the twisted excitement in his expression, something unpleasant was imminent.

'Officer Wilson, I'd like you to accompany me, please. I need to talk to you alone.'

Without waiting for an answer, he took up position behind her and shoved aggressively at her back. Robson considered reacting. He knew Miller was waiting, willing him to retaliate. The escaped convict sniggered as Robson knelt and began tending to Sarah.

'Oh, Jack, we shall tango together soon, I just know it!'

Robson looked at him in disgust as the two gunmen, having noticed him bristle, trained their firearms purposefully in his direction.

*

Jasmine's torn sleeve hung from her right arm as she retracted it from the ground, her top having been shredded on the security fence earlier as she squeezed through a small gap beneath the barrier. She double-checked her makeshift marker in the dirt. Satisfied that it should last long enough for her to find the same spot again, she rose from her secluded position and, with her heart thumping inside her chest, began to creep out of the low cover of vegetation.

Out in the open again, she suddenly felt vulnerable. She stopped and, remaining on her knees, removed a filthy hand from the ground to wipe away the rainwater that had dropped from the foliage on to her face when she had disturbed the leaf-laden branches of her cover. Her eyes were pale slits in her blackened, filthy face, as she adjusted her focus to concentrate on the small group of people in the distance. She quickly scrambled to the last remaining area of cover between her current position and her target, and began to breathe deeply as she contemplated her next move. She had a further ten yards to cover.

Jasmine ignored her growing feeling of helplessness and decided to look for an alternative entrance to the premises. The eastern flank of the building didn't seem to be guarded. However, there did not appear to be any obvious signs of access on that side. Only the front portal that sat a few yards from her appeared to provide a way in, but she already knew from the activity she had recently witnessed that she would not go unnoticed if she entered that particular door. She rested her backside on a tuft of long grass to ensure she remained fully covered by the small group of bushes that surrounded it, and squinted as she peered through the thin leafy branches to study the terrain outside. On noticing the spectacle to her right, she became momentarily distracted.

She had caught a glimpse of the giant antennae earlier, but her new vantage point gave her a better perspective to appreciate the sheer vastness of the installation. She had never been great at estimating measurements, but she knew that the huge pylons must have occupied several acres of barren terrain. There were hundreds, perhaps thousands of them, and they seemed to take on a sinister appearance as dense, black storm clouds began to gather and cover the tops of the towering metallic spires.

A recent physics lesson sprang to mind and, while she had no way of concluding what their purpose was, she had a hunch she was gazing upon more than just a communications hub. The air felt close and damp and, despite the mild temperature, she had begun to shiver. It almost seemed as though some dark energy was being emitted from the pylons and was now passing through her body.

With a surge of courage, she left her cover and darted forwards. Despite instructing herself that she had to remain brave, a rising sense of fear threatened to consume her. As she sprinted along the eastern perimeter of the building, she passed a window protected by vertical, metallic bars on the outside. The noise within made her freeze in dread.

She stopped and listened to a group of men shouting aggressively inside. The sound that followed made the hairs on the girl's arm stand on end. Blood pumped in her ears as she listened in terror to the sound coming from the other side of the barred, thick, frosted window, more than six feet up the building's wall.

Jasmine was certain that the source of the scream was female, and she began to shake with a deep sense of foreboding danger.

CHAPTER 127

Wilson suppressed a nervous shiver and did her best to appear confident as she maintained eye contact with Miller. Everything about his demeanour appeared calm and in control, apart from his eyes, which revealed an inner fire that seemed ready to explode. He looked dangerous. Crazy.

She had to admit to herself that the reports had been correct and not exaggerated – the ex-harbour master really had reinvented himself, certainly physically. Miller had removed his jacket to reveal a T-shirt which fitted snugly on his muscular physique.

The incongruity of the peace symbol tattooed on the side of his neck did not disguise the bulging veins beneath as he observed her intensely. It seemed to Wilson that he was reading her thoughts. A couple of metres behind Miller, the two gunmen were emotionless and stood perfectly still inside the small room. Miller's voice echoed inside the unfurnished box.

'So, Officer Wilson. Let's get down to business. Where is it?'

She swallowed, suddenly aware of the equipment to her right. She hadn't noticed it when she had initially been thrown into the room, but, out of the corner of her eye, she now noted a couple of thick chains dangling from the ceiling. She swallowed again, trying to generate some moisture in her dry mouth while resisting the urge to turn and look at the heavy-duty fastenings.

Miller seemed to read her mind, his eyes sparkling with intent. He could see that she had begun to read the situation. Wilson responded to break the tense silence.

'Where is what?'

She held his stare, but Miller seemed to be enjoying himself. He chuckled and leant forward with his elbows on the table, so that his chin rested on his hands, now only inches from Wilson.

'Don't mess me about, Officer Wilson. I really do wish we had longer to play, but we don't. So, I'll tell you what I'm going to do, shall I? I'm going to ask you one more time and, if you fail to give me a satisfactory answer again, then I'll be forced to use a little persuasion. Do you understand what I mean?'

He nodded to the chains so that she was forced to acknowledge the equipment.

'Jacob, I'm sorry, but I have no idea what you're talking about.'

Without warning, Miller delivered a brutal left jab, causing her head to fly backwards. He had ensured the thump possessed just enough venom so that she remained conscious … and seated.

He leant forward and grabbed her by the chin, raising her limp head to face him. Her bottom lip had already become twice its original size and blood ran down her chin and neck and began to soak her top.

'Sorry, Officer Wilson, but needs must. Do you know what those chains are for?'

Wilson shook her head. Her vision remained blurred, and blood sprayed from her mouth as she spat out an enraged response through gritted teeth.

'You're going to regret that, Miller.'

'Really?!'

He unleashed another blow, this time with less restraint, catching her between the eyebrows. The chair screeched against the floor as it skidded to one side.

Wilson lay motionless on the cold linoleum and, for a moment, everything was dark. Intermittently, she was aware of a ceiling light through her closed eyelids, before surrendering to the darkness.

*

As Wilson began to come around, she had no idea how long she had been out cold. Panic began to rise inside her and she felt her abdomen tighten. She looked towards the ceiling again, feeling increasingly disorientated. Her vision fluctuated in and out of focus for several moments, until she was finally able to make out the cause of the oppressive pain on her ribcage. Miller looked down wickedly from his seated position on her torso.

'Welcome back to the land of the living ... for now.'

She tried to suck in more air, but her attempt at expanding her lungs was met with immovable resistance and the pain in her ribs intensified.

'Please,' she gasped, 'I don't know what this is about. Tell me what you think I have!'

Miller sneered and rolled back on her ribs slightly, causing her to shriek in pain. For a moment, she hoped he was about to remove himself, but instead, he leant forward and tore her blouse open. He seemed to take great pleasure from the panic-stricken look in her eyes as she watched him withdraw a flick knife and bring it towards her. With a flick of his tattooed wrist, he sliced through the middle of her brassiere, nicking a section of skin in the process. Red liquid oozed from the wound in her cleavage as he pulled the two halves of the severed undergarment aside and, to add to her humiliation, leant forward and began to caress an exposed bosom. His two armed colleagues seemed to look on with perverse interest.

With huge hands now cupping both of her breasts, Miller began to address her calmly, as though they were merely communicating over dinner.

'Okay. Let's play dumb. Just briefly.'

Miller leant forward to increase the pressure applied to her breast.

'I want the electronic key fob you seized from Mark Connor. The MFA device that allows us to communicate remotely with our main server. Are we clear now?'

He removed his left hand and forced it into the top of her trousers, holding the top fly button between his forefinger and thumb. His right hand shifted and squeezed her left breast as he bent over to kiss it. As his left hand deftly undid the top button in her trousers, Wilson's voice trembled as she began to respond.

'W-what? I honestly don't kn— '

She felt relief as her ribs were finally relieved of his weight, thinking he had perhaps finally begun to believe her. Suddenly, Miller ripped the top of her linen trousers open and ran his knife down the front of both legs.

'Hoist the lying bitch up, lads.'

'No! No!'

Wilson screamed, beginning to hyperventilate as the two men dragged her by an arm each towards the thick chains. Her torn clothes fell to the floor as they dragged her, leaving her bloodied body exposed but for a pair of briefs.

Miller stood inches from her face as both of his armed colleagues secured the hanging cuffs around her wrists. Wilson's breathing was rapid. She felt the sharp, cold point of a knife press against her hip, before being whipped upwards.

She opened her mouth to scream in pain, but the sound refused to escape her constrained gullet. Feeling her briefs drop down one leg and land against her foot, she shut her eyes and forced her mind to meditate, engaging a skill which had resulted from the toughest part of her training – a skill she had hoped never to require, but somehow knew that one day would have to be invoked.

Survival mode.

They knew they had just about taken her steel and, as the three men surrounded her, seemingly examining every inch of her body in silence, Wilson reopened her eyes. As she absorbed the situation through blurred vision, she had never felt more vulnerable in her life.

'So.' Miller's voice was even and calm. 'How tall is this stunning little beauty do you think, lads? Five foot seven, or eight? This contraption is really based on a six-footer, to be honest, so the detainee can just about stand on the balls of his … or her, feet. Not that we've had to use it much, of course …'

Miller winked mid-sentence.

'I think you'll be on tiptoes though, Emma, so this really is going to be quite painful from the outset.'

Wilson had begun to shiver. The three men marched away without another word, leaving her naked and hanging from her wrists.

CHAPTER 128

The son and heir to the inimitable Sir Geoffrey Charlesworth watched the onscreen message calmly. It confirmed that the system was ready to be initiated. Months of planning had nearly come to fruition. The only thing out of his control now was who had possession of the key. The final piece of the jigsaw.

Once again, he ignored his vibrating phone, already assuming the caller's number would not be registered and therefore signalling another feeble attempt by the security services to contact him. This is what it had come to. He had been followed around the best part of northern Europe and, as he knew well, they had had their chances to catch him. But they hadn't taken their opportunities and now all they had left was to phone him.

He no longer needed to consider the risk of being located by the mobile signal. Every secret service in the world probably knew by now that the rogue British agent was holed up at the top of the iconic mountain, three thousand metres up in Iceland's atmosphere. But they still would not know what he was doing.

Arkwright was tempted to turn the phone off again, just as the vibrating finally stopped. He returned his attention to the control desk, not noticing that the caller ID had in fact been displayed on this occasion.

One missed call.

Jacob Miller.

CHAPTER 129

Jasmine Robson blinked to recalibrate her tired, bleary vision. She might have been young, but she knew there was something preternatural powering her body – some sort of reserve fuel supply.

Adrenaline, they called it, didn't they?

She had managed to find an alternative entrance and, from her hidden position inside the peculiar facility, had watched the three men depart the room from where the shouting had emanated earlier. There was no doubt, one of them was the man who had tried to get her thrown from a cliff – 'General Miller'. Seeing him again sent a tremor of fear through her juvenile body.

A dead-end corridor would not normally have provided the opportunity for a discreet surveillance position, so Jasmine was thankful for the array of boxes and apparently redundant furniture which had been discarded at the far end. She had buried herself deep within the debris. To the young girl, it felt like being inside an unlit bonfire, and she had to try hard to dispel the unhelpful thought, summoning another dose of courage.

Stay with me mum, I need you.

She caught her breath on hearing the lowered baritone voices at the other end of the corridor. Suddenly, the three men appeared again – General Miller, along with his two gun-wielding friends.

The new voice surprised her. There was a fourth member in the little party. She wasn't sure at first why it seemed so significant. It had been clear since arriving that the population of the complex was greater than three. Perhaps it was the fact that the fourth voice was female that seemed so unexpected to the girl. Or it could have been that, despite that the group was now walking along the corridor back towards her, the owner of the fourth voice could not be seen.

Jasmine felt panic well inside herself again as the three men passed the door to the room they had been in moments earlier and headed seemingly toward the pile of junk at the end of the corridor which concealed her. She tried to silence her breathing and regulate her pulse, but all she could hear was her own heart thumping. It seemed unusually amplified and she thought the others must have heard it thumping against her ribcage. The group were only a few yards from her when they suddenly stopped and unbolted another door, before disappearing inside.

Seconds later, Jasmine listened intently to the conversation inside the second room. She imagined herself as a naughty schoolchild, hiding from the teachers in the corridor. She was close enough to the room to be able to make out the faintest sound of voices. Did she imagine that she heard someone utter the words 'DCI Robson'? She desperately wanted to believe that, after weeks apart, her father was now within touching distance. However, she knew by now not to set herself up for disappointment. Jasmine Robson possessed a level of wisdom robustly built on a solid foundation of heartache.

She jumped as the door was flung open just a couple of yards in front of her. The leader of the men, Miller, walked with purpose into the corridor, followed by one of the gunmen, who quickly closed the door behind, apparently leaving their other, armed colleague inside.

Miller and his cohort burst back into the adjacent room where the noise had come from earlier. Within moments, there was a new sound. Jasmine tried to place the sound. She thought it was coming from a machine of some sort, perhaps the kind they used to dig roads. But the whooshing, gushing noise, did not quite align with the thought. After a couple of minutes, the noise stopped, but was replaced by further shouting. Only this time, she could hear the raised male voice clearly.

'For the very last time, Officer Wilson – where the fuck is the key?! And before you answer, you ought to realise that your next shower will be a great deal more thorough!'

The sight of water running from beneath the door made Jasmine's mind up for her. She leapt from her hiding place, sending boxes and a couple of wooden chairs crashing to the floor. She was already a couple of yards inside the water-drenched room when a lone gunman emerged from the adjacent door to investigate the source of the crashing sound.

Jasmine froze just inside the doorway, having instantly recognised the bruised face of the drenched figure hanging from the ceiling. The sound from the industrial-sized air conditioning unit as it started had covered up the sound of the door opening. She hadn't attracted the attention of the men inside yet.

The young girl watched 'General Miller' approach her father's ex-girlfriend. The veins in his neck bulged as he looked up aggressively, straining to bring his face as close to Wilson's as possible.

'That air con unit will remain on until you tell me what you've done with it.'

From where she stood, Jasmine could see Wilson's lips were turning blue, in contrast with the paleness of her face. Her naked, bloodied body shook violently. In fact, to Jasmine, she seemed to be as close to death as anything she'd ever seen, yet, remarkably, she managed a hoarse response.

'I-I don't kn-kn—'

'Bullshit! Fuck off!' Miller stood on tiptoes to spit out a final promise. 'You will die here, Miss Wilson, do not doubt that.'

He moved back casually before looking sideways at his colleague, who held a thick, firefighter-style hose. The man approached Wilson with the metallic nozzle. Jasmine gasped in horror as she watched him aim the hose at Wilson from only a couple of metres away. Miller's voice sounded evil.

'One final power wash it is then. Not a pleasant way to go, but you've had your chance, you stupid fucking cow. Farewe—'

'No! Stop it!'

The two men looked around, confused. Wilson didn't have the strength to raise her eyes, but somehow managed to tilt her head to reveal a blurry image of someone she recognised.

'What are you doing here, princess?'

Miller smiled as he addressed the girl.

'Sh-she doesn't know where the device is.'

Miller moved closer, inquisitive eyes peering into hers.

'Oh? And how would you know that, young lady?'

'Because I have it …'

Miller folded his arms to complete his condescending look.

'Show me.'

'Not until you let her go!'

He looked to his colleague.

'Search her.'

A female voice suddenly entered the room. Jasmine recognised it as the voice she had heard in the corridor minutes earlier. She looked across at the intercom on the wall as they all listened.

'She doesn't have it, Jacob.'

Miller remained silent, casting a puzzled look towards the speaker.

'But she knows where it is, don't you, Jasmine?' the new voice continued.

Jasmine nodded.

'And she also knows that if she were found to be lying to us, there would be consequences for all the people she cares about. Isn't that right, Jasmine?'

The silence was momentarily interrupted as Wilson coughed. A blood-speckled stream of bile escaped her mouth and splattered into the pool of water at her tiptoes.

'Will you show us where it is, Jasmine? If we let Emma out of those nasty chains?'

Jasmine suppressed a shiver at Miller's mock charm and nodded once more. She realised the source of the voice couldn't see her nodding, so she opened her mouth to voice her confirmation. The intercom sounded again, as though the owner of the voice also had eyes in the room.

'Good girl, Jasmine. Release Officer Wilson, Jacob.'

CHAPTER 130

Matthews ignored the corpse on the ground and continued probing the group of personnel they had found at the vast transmitter site. His armed back-up had arrived faster than expected. They had people searching inside the perimeter fence, but his instinct told him that Jasmine would not have been hiding. She was a girl with a destination in mind.

Matthews' voice had taken on a slight shriek every time he spoke, revealing a hint of his desperation at letting DCI Robson's daughter run off.

'How many are inside the main building over there?'

The tall African man shrugged.

'Don't know, man ... about forty, maybe?'

'What is the purpose of these aerials?'

'Like I keep telling you, man – communications.'

'And like I keep telling you, sir, stop lying to me. It won't help you in court.'

'I ain't done nothin' wrong, man.'

Matthews pointed towards the assemblance of recovered rifles on the ground.

'This really is going to be easy, Emanuel. I don't suspect that you, or any of your friends, possess licences to carry firearms. You really could do yourself a favour by starting to assist our enquiries.'

'Ah don't know nothin' else.'

'Who are you protecting, Emanuel? Is this loyalty? If so, it really is rather misplaced, I assure you. Don't you think that loyalty works both ways?'

Matthews continued, noting that the large man was becoming agitated.

'Do you think your seniors give two hoots about your dead pals over there? I'll answer for you – of course they fucking well don't. Just like they don't care a damn whether you live or die, Emanuel.'

'Fuck off, man!'

'Where are your bosses now, Emanuel? Inside the building over there?'

The big African's eyes now sparkled with aggression. Matthews became distracted by the sound on his belt. He withdrew the radio and replied to the voice.

'Matthews receiving. Go ahead.'

'DI Matthews. It's Sergeant Harris here, firearms team leader. Sir, team Bravo has breached the wall at the northern perimeter.'

'Okay, good. Move in … with caution.'

'Yes, DI Matthews … sorry … one moment, sir. It appears we have a further development. We've currently got eyes on suspect activity at the front of the building.'

'What sort of activity?'

'Sir, two men, both armed, and a girl. The girl appears to be digging something.'

'Shit! Is it Robson's daughter?'

'No positive IDs yet, sir.'

'Okay, hold your positions.'

'Sir, the girl – it looks very much like it is Jasmine Robson – she appears to be carrying out excavation work …'

'Excavation work?! Keep up your observations and do not move in until further notice.'

'Affirmative, DI Matthews.'

*

Sarah had regained a degree of alertness. Unfortunately, the pain from her injury grew proportionately with her consciousness. She looked at Robson, realising that the shouting from next door seemed to have subsided.

The slight, Asian, armed guard seemed slightly nervous. He hadn't taken his eyes off Robson since being left by his two colleagues. Sarah knew that Robson had recognised Jasmine's voice immediately, just as she had. Yet DCI Robson sat impassively gazing at the door, seemingly oblivious to the knowing stare that she had fixed on him for the last couple of minutes. *Poor Jack.*

The radio fixed to the guard's jacket crackled as a female voice echoed into the small room.

'Bingwen Liu, it looks like we have what we need. You can leave the other two locked inside and come and join us now.'

One hand continued to grip the firearm pointed in Robson's direction, while his other operated the button on the side of the radio.

'Understood. On my way.'

Liu walked silently to the door, keeping the gun aimed at the two guests. Sarah gave him a cynical look as she spoke.

'Oh no, are you leaving us already, sweetie? I was really starting to enjoy your company too!'

Distaste glinted in the small guard's keen eyes momentarily, but he seemed wary of Robson's emotionless stare as he backed out of the room pulling the door behind him. Sarah was instantly confused by Robson's hissed command.

'Get under the table!'

In a split second, Robson was at the door himself, his toppled chair still wobbling. He leapt up and landed with both hands on the door handle to apply the maximum possible downward force. As the handle moved, Robson sprang up off the floor as though he had been sitting on the most powerful spring. Pulling the door open into the room again, the guard appeared stunned, still holding the key in position despite the door being pulled away from him. Beneath the table, Sarah panicked at the sound of the firearm, quickly followed by a grunt.

'Get out from there, Sarah! Come on!' Robson shouted.

Sarah felt both relief and confusion in equal measures at the sight of Robson. Blood trickled down the centre of his face from a spot in the middle of his forehead. Outside the room, they stepped over the guard's body. Seeing the guard's smashed nose told her all she needed to know about what had occurred. She realised Robson's headbutt must have been delivered with great force as he had disarmed the man, mid-shot.

Sarah stopped as she reached the doorway and looked into Robson's eyes, already knowing what he was going to ask.

'Sarah, what on earth are you doing here?'

'I found the details in his garage, Jack. I had to confront him myself. I have to hear what …'

'Okay, forget it for now. Follow me and stay close.'

For a moment, the shocked tension eased from her body a little and she felt a small pang of confidence, assisted in no small part by the sight of Robson running with the firearm in his hand. As they fled the corridor together, she found herself hoping that they weren't too late for Jasmine and Emma, and she wondered if Robson had been thinking the same.

Seconds later, they got their answer.

CHAPTER 131

Jasmine found the hum of electronic devices hypnotising. The white noise seemed to amplify the surrealness of the situation. Having spent not much more than a minute in the company of Wilson, the young girl was now alone again and without an ally, just as she had been for the past couple of weeks. It seemed that nobody in her new world was sane any longer. She had no idea what they had done with Wilson. The gunman was still present, but he had been joined by a new armed man, both guards flanking her as she stood behind Miller, who was bent over the computer terminal inside the control room.

A few yards away, there stood an odd figure. Evidently, Jasmine assumed the elegant woman she now watched was the owner of the voice they had heard on the intercom moments earlier – the same, previously invisible woman whose voice she had heard from her hiding place in the corridor earlier. She appeared almost regal to Jasmine as she studied her, hypnotised.

The others referred to the woman as 'Naamah' and, as if to add to her mystique, she seemed to carry a kind of blurred complexion, as though she were being viewed through a camera filter. Jasmine couldn't put her finger on it, but the whole thing almost seemed like a dream. However, forcing herself to accept the reality, she trembled as she watched Miller enter the code from the device that she had just provided him with. Seconds later, he turned with a sneer.

'Oh dear, guess what?' he said in a mockingly parental voice, 'it didn't work, Jasmine. What shall we do now?'

The others watched unemotionally as Miller leant forward so that his nose touched the girl's.

'I-I don't know,' Jasmine responded. 'That's the key the Frenchman gave to me. He said it was from Mark Connor and I had to give it to my dad.'

'Aw, diddums! Well, what a fine mess!'

Jasmine felt faint with fear. The man who had already tried to kill her once seemed to be, if anything, even crazier now. He appeared to be on the brink. When he snapped, it was not unexpected, but through the numbness, Jasmine felt warm urine run down her legs.

'Nice fucking try, little girl. Now, either you or your friend, Miss Wilson, is going to tell me where the correct key is! I'm a tolerant man, but I have very little patience left now. In fact, you have no idea how close you are to—'

'Jacob!'

Naamah's tone was stern, yet she hadn't really raised her voice. It was clear that she held ultimate power over everyone in the room.

'Let's not be hasty. Perhaps Jasmine just needs a little persuasion.'

Jasmine watched the lady in horror as she recognised that the woman – Naamah – was crazy too.

'You're right,' Miller said. 'We mustn't be too hasty, must we?'

His eyes pierced Jasmine's once more.

'The fact that you have gone to such an elaborate diversion as to source a dummy key is all the confirmation I need that you are very much aware of what we are asking to be returned. So, I'll give you one more chance. Let's have it, please. I won't ask again. But, while you're thinking about it, I think we'll prepare you for the chains now, to save wasting time later.'

'No!'

As Jasmine screamed, the armed guards took an arm each and firmly lifted her from her feet. As they turned, the door to the control room burst open to reveal a woman with a badly bruised face, accompanied by yet another armed man.

'Put her the fuck down, right now!' shouted DCI Robson.

Unlike his armed support, Miller did not flinch, and began to emit a false chuckle.

'Hello again, Jack!'

'It's over, Miller. Release the girl, or I will fire!'

'Jack. I'm going to count down from five. If you haven't dropped your weapon by the time I get to zero, guess what?' He nodded towards the guards. 'Each of these boys will put a bullet into little Jasmine's skull from either side. And if you fire on either of them at any point, whoever remains standing will do the job before you get a chance to take them out too. Do you understand the odds, Jack?'

Miller smiled.

After a second's deliberation, Robson tossed his gun to the floor. Miller flicked his gun to usher Robson and Sarah into the room while the new visitors noticed Louise for the first time, their view having been obscured previously.

'Hello, Jack.'

Louise Hart – Naamah – spoke, as Miller and the two guards dragged a sobbing Jasmine from the room.

Sarah began to scream.

'No!'

Robson felt helpless as he watched his daughter being dragged from the room as the remaining guards trained their firearms on him and Sarah.

*

Outside the control room, Miller and the girl were greeted by DI Matthews and a team of firearms officers. Miller knew what the red dot on his shoulder indicated. It had occurred before. But he had been quick to react – too quick for the marksmen.

Certainly, it had helped that he had the girl as a shield. But while his comrades fell the instant the bullets lodged inside their skulls, he had been quick to withdraw his own firearm, which he now pressed against Jasmine's ear. He tried to disguise a wince as he wrapped his other, bandaged arm tightly around the girl's delicate neck. Jasmine's eyes bulged as Miller's huge fingers pressed deep into a pressure point in her neck, totally incapacitating her, so she could neither move nor speak. In fact, it was a struggle for her to breathe.

The senior firearms officer seemed to pay no attention to Matthews' pleading eyes as he shouted his command to his team.

'Hold your fire!'

As Miller inched forward, with the girl as his shield, the red dots of the laser sights remained trained on his body.

It was at that moment that Jasmine noticed Wilson for the first time. She looked terrible, her swollen face almost unrecognisable. But she was evidently being looked after and she was fully clothed again. And despite her haggard appearance, she still seemed alert to Jasmine. Somehow, her eyes still sparkled with understanding. Wilson turned away from the officer that had been giving her medical attention and ignored pleas for her to lay back down. Instead, Wilson held Jasmine's gaze.

A second later, Jasmine whimpered as Miller tugged at her ferociously, forcing her to turn. He dragged her, her legs bumping over one of the dead bodies. Jasmine knew that she had to take her only chance to dispose of the lump secreted in her crotch. Her trousers were just sufficiently loose to allow her to do so in a single swift movement and her aim was true. The small device's fall was cushioned by the body, preventing contact with the hard floor. She risked one final glance at Wilson to ensure the drop off had been witnessed, but the look that Wilson gave in return revealed nothing apart from the fact that she was not in good condition.

Instinctively, Jasmine returned her trembling hand to the immovable claw wrapped around her throat and, in desperation, she screwed up her eyes and tried to visualise an alternative, more pleasant scene. When she opened them again, both she and Miller were alone in a short corridor. After bolting the door behind them, Miller threw her against it with unnecessary force.

'Stay there, girl, and make yourself useful. You can be my shield.'

Leaving her shaking against the entrance, her knees began to buckle. Miller turned his attention to a keypad to the side of a second door and began entering a code on its small buttons.

Naamah seemed unmoved by the sight of the rifle that was pointed at her. Even as Robson moved closer, she seemed calmness personified. She even appeared impressed by the way Robson had so swiftly disarmed and then incapacitated the two guards.

'Still got it then, I see, Jack?'

'Not quite up to your talents though, Louise, such as your ability to fake death ...'

Louise Hart chuckled.

'You don't really think that was me do you, Jack? Come on.'

Robson felt his arm tense and tried to relax his trigger finger as he allowed Hart to continue.

'I got out of that dump a couple of years ago. There just wasn't much to do. Fortunately, my drug dependent little sister required little persuasion to take my place. But it was very clever the way we made the switch, you would have been impressed, I think.'

'And now she has died for your cause.'

'Oh, she was ready, Jack. Her poor little body couldn't have withstood much more chemical abuse anyway, so I think we did her a favour really.'

Robson scoffed.

'I hear she took quite a liking to you, is that right, Jack?'

The door to the control room flew open before Robson was able to answer. He turned and watched Matthews burst in, followed by an armed response team. Matthews stood at the doorway for a second to process the sight.

'James!' Robson hissed. 'You've just missed Miller. He's taken Jasmine into one of the other rooms off that corridor. Get after them!'

Matthews shook his head.

'We saw them, sir. We took two, but Miller is still loose. He has Jasmine.'

Robson cast an aggressive gaze towards Hart, who was now standing only a couple of metres away. Matthews had never seen his DCI shake before, but Robson's gun hand trembled now as he used it to direct the rifle towards her forehead.

'Where are they going?'

'How should I know, Jack?'

She smiled. For the first time, Matthews noticed how Louise Hart seemed to have taken on a deified image of herself. As though she were a ghost. Robson's words were laced with venom.

'Trust me, Louise. I'm quite happy to bend the rules if I have to ... perhaps you'd like to experience the chains for yourself?'

Robson, Matthews, and the marksmen all flinched at the sound of the strange alarm that suddenly echoed inside the room.

Naamah smiled at Robson after briefly glancing at something in her palm.

'Oh look, Jack, you're not going to believe this! It's your friend – Mark Connor. Shall we answer him?'

An electrical clicking sound echoed in the room before she continued.

'Harry!' Hart's voice was now emanating from speakers located in the corner of the room. 'Long time no speak! How are you?'

'Naamah ...' the speakers crackled slightly, due to the high-volume setting, but there was no disguising the cynicism in the caller's voice. In his peripheral vision, Robson was aware of Sarah, who had drifted in unnoticed. A scowl developed across her face. 'I thought I'd call rather than text. It's so much more personal, don't you think?'

'Absolutely, Harry, or should I call you *Mark*? Now, how can I help you, my dear?'

'Well, actually, Naamah, it's more what I can do for you, would you believe.'

'Really? Go on.'

'I have reason to believe that a key, very similar to the one used to access the HAARP mainframe, is currently in your possession.'

'What would make you think that, Harry?'

'I have my means. Anyway, you've probably realised by now, that it is not the key you thought it to be and is in fact a duplicate.'

'You are naughty, Harry.'

'Well, I'm afraid so. You see, that decoy key wasn't just a dud. It has actually activated a secret system installed on the Snowdon facility.'

'Secret system, you say?'

'I suggest that you and your friends vacate the installation as a matter of priority. You see, when that keycode was entered into the login database, while it might have appeared to have no effect, it has in fact set a timer in motion. Beneath your feet, enough explosive has been installed to blow the top of the mountain off, pretty much, and it will be detonated an hour after entering the code. That gives you and your pals about forty-five minutes to evacuate.'

Silence filled the control room before Arkwright continued.

'Now, I know what you're thinking – that hardly gives you enough time to get out safely, certainly not via the mountain surface. So, I guess you're going to have to make priority decisions as to who uses the secret stairwell and lift shafts.'

'Oh Mark, how very clever of you! But, before you go, I have a little surprise of my own. I'm here with a couple of your close friends, including none other than your stunning lady wife. Although, I must say, she doesn't seem very impressed.'

While Hart's mischievous smile grew, Sarah's eyes were vacant.

'Would you like to say anything to your husband, my dear?'

Sarah trembled, seemingly frozen to the spot.

'Agent Arkwright, it's DCI Jack Robson. She's not kidding. How do we stop the countdown?'

The calm voice on the phone disappeared, immediately replaced by one laden with anxiety.

'Oh no. No, no, no, NO! Jack – what the fuck are you doing there?! Where's Sarah?!'

'Right here with us. We're going to need your help to stop the explosion.'

They all heard a bang, before the phone line went silent, as though Arkwright had suddenly vanished. Robson noted Hart's delight and chose to ignore it. It was as though her own mortality did not concern her. *Always the most dangerous of terrorists.*

The speakers crackled again, while distant cursing could be heard. Then the voice became louder again.

'Jack. It cannot be stopped. Nobody has that power, not even me. Get the hell out of there, now! There is a secret elevator and stairwell that takes you directly to the bottom.'

'It can't be stopped?! Really, Mark?'

'No Jack, it's impossible. It wasn't meant to be this way! I didn't—'

Hart began to laugh loudly.

'I think you'd better show us the way out, Louise,' Robson spat. 'Is that where Miller has taken Jasmine?'

The speaker crackled again.

'Wh-what? Jasmine's there?! Why?!'

As though waking from a nightmare, Sarah screamed out.

'What the fucking hell do you care?! You lying bastard! You've used her!'

'No … she's not supposed to be involved! Where's Marchand? Sarah … I'm so sorry …' Connor suddenly sounded emotional. 'Jack, get them out! The lift. Head out of the control room and ta—'

A clicking sound signalled the end of the call. Hart removed her finger from the device in her palm and looked smugly into the room.

Robson gave Matthews the briefest of meaningful glances, then spoke softly.

'Protocol goes out of the window, James. Get everyone out of here. This is a code zero – alert control.'

'Yes, sir.'

As Matthews and the others exited the control room, Robson prowled with intent towards Louise Hart. The self-proclaimed *Naamah*.

After arriving within a foot of her, he leapt forward, arms outstretched. Confused at having grasped thin air, Robson reached out again, perplexed by the woman's speed of reflex. After another couple of attempts, Robson stopped flapping at thin air and stood upright to appraise his target again. He took a deep breath before sweeping a hand completely through her midriff. Naamah began to laugh.

'I wonder if we'll ever meet in the flesh again, sexy?'

She blew a kiss at Robson, then vanished.

CHAPTER 132

Robson was still locked in a pensive state when DI Matthews returned, slamming the door to the control room behind him. Unable to see the woman who had been in the room seconds earlier, Matthews wondered whether his DCI had finally cracked under the personal stress and assaulted their suspect. But as he edged closer to Robson, there was no evidence of an injured or felled woman. Robson seemed to snap into life in response to Matthew's increasing puzzlement.

'Where is she, Jack?'

'Gone.'

'Where?!'

'I don't know, Jim. Come on, let's move.'

Robson's eyes instinctively locked on to Sarah's as they were reunited in the corridor. Matthews spoke up behind them.

'Jack. Sir. I suggest we divide into smaller teams and concentrate on finding Miller and Jasmine.'

Robson looked into Sarah's glistening blue eyes. It was several seconds before he noticed a dishevelled Wilson, sitting on a chair a few yards away, watching in silence. Robson turned back to Matthews.

'No.'

'I beg your pardon, sir?'

'You heard what Arkwright said. Our only chance is either the elevator or the stairwell.'

'Sir, we don't know where th—'

'I think Sarah does, don't you, Sarah?'

Every person in the corridor watched Sarah nod her head absently.

*

Having already failed in his attempt to contact Jack Robson, Arkwright dropped his phone in frustration as his new wife's personal voicemail played again. He stared helplessly at his wristwatch, which had begun to time the moment he'd received notification that the device on the Welsh mountain had been activated.

Everything up until that point had been going according to plan. It was going to be a neat and tidy operation, and nobody would ever see him again. He had gone to great lengths to avoid inordinate collateral damage, but in the last few minutes it had become apparent that that key principle was no longer assured. And it wasn't going to be just any collateral.

Arkwright resigned himself to proceeding with the only task that remained within his control – the completion of his own operation in Iceland. A task that would undoubtedly result in collateral damage. But it would be for a greater cause, of that he remained certain.

He knew that, by now, those on the other side of the sealed doors would have made good progress in breaching the entrance, but they would be a little while longer yet and he was going to be using a different exit entirely.

He took one final glance at the control room before he left, one of the places in which he had carried out his greatest deception. He heard the machinery on the other side of the reinforced steel doors as soon as he shut himself outside the hum of the control room. Ignoring the sound, he walked, briskly now, to a doorway marked 'No Unauthorised Access', and swiftly inserted one of the keys attached to his keyring.

As he locked the door again from inside the small, cold room, the sound of the machines increased, signalling that the security forces had begun to penetrate the seal.

Not so far off after all. Ten minutes, tops. Plenty of time.

Standing at a second, heavy-set door immediately opposite the entrance to the room, Arkwright entered the very last code he would need and waited for the sound of the lock disengaging. The sound from the little keypad made him double take at the display.

INCORRECT CODE

He felt like kicking himself. Most people entered codes wrong routinely, but it was not the sort of mistake Agent Arkwright made. He had to acknowledge that he hadn't really slept since being in Paris with his newlywed, although not because of reasons typically associated with a honeymoon.

He re-entered the code which had been stored in his trusted memory for so long, this time taking even greater care to operate the correct buttons to accurately replicate the eight digit alphanumeric code in his mind.

INCORRECT CODE

Arkwright did not make mistakes.

The ringing inside his pocket interrupted his remarkably calm train of thought. But the name on the display caused even the ice-cool double agent's heartbeat to increase. He answered immediately.

'Sarah?'

The giggling female voice at the other end was familiar but had a sinister twang to it.

'Hello, Harry. Going somewhere, my darling?'

CHAPTER 133

At the bottom of the lift shaft, Jasmine watched the small but powerful man. If they were now truly at the bottom of the mountain, the speed at which the elevator had travelled through the heart of the mountain had been incalculable.

Her fear had begun to be superseded by disgust. Anger. After their short reunion, it now seemed even less likely than before that she would be reunited with either her father, Sarah, or Emma, nor any of their associates for that matter. There was no way anyone was going to reach her in time. Miller had secured the security door at the bottom and, according to his recent phone conversation, the elevator was now disabled, and the access codes changed.

Despite the odds, she felt a strange calmness. Not because she had faith that everything was going to turn out all right, more that she felt ready to accept whatever fate would throw in her path. She did not know where it came from, but she had already begun to observe that she had a different, less hysterical outlook on life compared to her young peers.

Her father and Sarah had both reminded her on several occasions that it was her mother's legacy. She couldn't remember enough to either agree or disagree, but for some reason, she always felt that her mother was by her side. Although, undoubtedly, if she had known that the facility almost a kilometre above her head was about to be blown to smithereens, her disposition might have been different.

Miller grabbed her roughly by the shoulder and shoved her forwards. Jasmine felt hope build inside her, expecting to be confronted by a significant police force as soon as they took their first breath of fresh mountain air. The vista before her made no sense. Miller read her thoughts immediately, letting out a wicked chuckle.

'Oh, expecting to see someone, were we?'

Jasmine refused to adjust her gaze, choosing to avoid looking at the vulgar man's contorted face. Instead, her eyes scanned the empty landscape before them. They had clearly alighted from the mountain in a region that was nowhere near any of the six, trodden paths that constituted the official routes. Miller shoved her hard enough to make her stumble. She was about to curse, but felt a strong hand on her collar, dragging her backwards.

A second later, she lay sprawled inside the cover of the secret mountain egress point again, looking up at the back of Miller's head. She finally discerned the sound, masked by the wind, which had previously escaped her. Her captor might have been a dickhead, she thought, but he certainly had acute hearing.

Miller turned to face her.

'Make yourself comfortable, girl. I think we'll sit tight for a little while longer.'

Jasmine looked away, unable to bear looking at his face for any length of time. Her eyes rested on the second locked security door – the entrance to the stairwell – making Miller comment once again, as though her thoughts were audible.

'Don't worry, there's no rush. Nobody will be coming out of either of those any time soon.'

CHAPTER 134

Arkwright fought hard to remain calm. He had waited years for this moment of sweet retribution – to destroy the maniacs that had seduced and killed his father, Sir Geoffrey Charlesworth. This was supposed to be his moment. But they had exploited his one weakness. Despite his ruthlessness – a product of both his specialist training and his extraordinary past – he was not devoid of emotion. The woman on the phone clearly knew that and was taking much pleasure from exploiting it.

'So, how long have your wife and her friends got, Harry?'

'I wouldn't sound so smug if I were you, Louise. You are only a matter of minutes away from losing both of your facilities and, along with that, any access to HAARP.'

'Hey ho, Harry, it is what it is. What interests me is how you are feeling about killing your own wife and several other innocent people?'

'Let them leave, Louise. They have nothing to do with this. Give me the new access codes.'

A chill ran down his spine as Louise Hart chuckled at the other end.

'Sure thing, Harry. Just like that, eh? I tell you what, young Master Charlesworth, let's do an exchange, shall we? A code for a code. Quid pro quo. Tell me how to override your naughty little device, and I'll give you the access codes, both for Snowdon and *Herdubreid. How does that sound?*'

'There is no code. The countdown cannot be stopped.'

'Come now, Harry!'

'I'm serious. The destruction of Snowdon is unstoppable. And you're about to lose *Herdubreid to the secret services. I've led them directly here. It's over, Louise, so why not let the innocent people go?'*

Hart laughed again. To Arkwright's disgust, her amusement sounded genuine.

'*Harry, do you know what? I couldn't really give a fuck about Snowdon. It isn't like it's our only facility, is it?'*

'*But without Iceland? As soon as you surrender this facility at Herdubreid, you will lose control of everything, and you know it!'*

'*Oh, don't you be concerned about that, Harry. I think you'll find the security services are after you, not us or our venture. And you might not be surprised to learn that there will be one or two among your imminent guests who will ensure damage limitation, and also that our table mountain HQ remains our secret.'*

Arkwright listened to her laugh again.

'We have clearly exhausted our negotiations, Harry. It's a pity. You are, in so many ways, so much like your father, just with a slightly different perspective. Nonetheless, it's been nice sparring with you. Such a pity you didn't feel you could work *with* us though – it would have made your father so proud. Goodbye, Harry.'

Arkwright let the phone drop from his hand and stared at the door's keypad. At his booted feet, his phone began to vibrate against the hard floor. The display lit up with Robson's caller ID. He did not want to answer it, but he had to. He knew he had to.

'Very clever, Louise. So, you've cloned everyone's phones. I'm impressed.'

'Agent Arkwright?'

Arkwright paused to validate the possibility that it really could be Robson before responding, still half-expecting Naamah to ridicule him.

'Jack?!'

'Are we still on first name terms then, Mark?'

Before Arkwright could respond, a new voice joined the conversation. A female voice laced with emotion.

'You fucking bastard!'

'Sarah? I'm so sorry. This wasn't how I'd planned it. I don't expect you to understand, but I couldn't let them get away with it. I couldn't tell anyone, not even you. They have allies everywhere. I had to go it alone, and I didn't want to drag in anyone that I cared for!'

All he could hear was sobbing, but he could tell from the slight change in tone that the irony of his last statement had registered.

'I'm so sorry. They destroyed my family. Sarah, deceiving you … and your family … that has been the hardest part in all this. I genuinely care about you, Sarah …'

Inside the small room, Robson eased the phone from Sarah's shaking hand, as she buried her head into Wilson's shoulder.

'How would you like to have a go at doing a good deed, Mark? We need some help.'

'Jack, I can't help you from here. It's too late for me, you just need to make sure you get well clear of the mountain.'

'Yes, that's what we need your help with.'

'What? You're not still on the mountain, are you?!'

'The codes aren't working. Something's wrong. We can't get into the stairwell.'

'Oh fuck! She's changed them all! I didn't know. I thought you'd—'

'Mark, is there any way we could hack into the server and override the security?'

'No. Naamah – Hart – has overall admin privileges. For anyone else to alter security preferences, both control stations must make the changes simultaneously. A cooperative reset. But I cannot believe she is going to prevent you from escaping at the cost of her own life …'

'Hart isn't here.'

'She's not? How ca—'

'Mark – going back to this cooperative reset – is that something you can assist with?'

'Not without you having your own synchronised pass key.'

Wilson gently released Sarah from their embrace and stepped forward, holding up a small device with a single display screen.

'This pass key?'

Robson, along with Sarah and the others, watched in amazement. Connor's voice crackled through the earpiece.

'Do I take it you have the key, Jack?'

'It would appear that is a possibility, yes.'

'Jack, go back to the control room. Stay on the line to ensure we don't get disconnected. Stand by – I'll just be a few seconds.'

Arkwright ignored the flying sparks from the steel doors, which had begun to fold inwards at the top corners. Several bullets sprayed through the small gap, hitting the doorframe of the entrance to the control room as Connor bolted inside.

Looking down at the monitor, he shouted towards his phone which he had laid on the desk.

'Okay, give me the passcode.'

Almost immediately, Wilson's voice responded with a six-digit numerical sequence. Arkwright jerked slightly at the deafening bang behind him but continued to work on the keyboard. There was no doubting what the sound of crashing steel indicated – the huge doors had finally given way. He estimated that he had seconds. Sure enough, a commanding voice boomed into the control room.

'Slowly put your hands on your head and move away from the terminal!'

Arkwright continued to operate the keys, as a familiar female voice crackled from his phone.

'Oh my God! Mark! Are you—'

'Now, Agent Arkwright! Or we will fire!'

Connor looked down at his still fingers, before slowly raising his hands. He felt the dampness of his sweat-laden scalp as he made two backward steps, aware of the sound of boots on the hard floor. He noted that some of the marksmen carried FN-P90 submachine guns, which transported him to the early days of his planning and training.

The Americans have come to join the party.

One of the men arrived at the desk and began to study the monitor, while another began roughly patting Connor down his sides. The female voice sounded from the mobile phone again.

'Mark! Are you okay?!'

The man at the desk lifted the phone to examine the display. Arkwright spoke evenly.

'Take care, Sarah.'

'I love you, Mark. When can I see you again?!'

Arkwright did not respond and focussed a steely stare at the nearest operative who had grabbed the phone. As he ended the call, another of the agents arrived behind him and gave a sharp tug on the back of his jacket.

'Silence!'

As handcuffs were secured at his rear, another man held the phone inquisitively at arm's length.

'Who was that?'

Arkwright casually shook his head.

'I'm afraid I can't tell you that …'

The man's expression blackened. As he opened his mouth to bark a command, Arkwright deftly operated the small device in his palm.

*

The explosion could be heard for miles around the Icelandic Highlands, and the gigantic plume of smoke that emanated from the former flattened mountain peak could be seen from an even greater distance. At the flick of a switch, the iconic beauty of the famous tuya had been reduced to a ball of smoke and debris. Most would simply believe that the former volcano had not been dormant after all.

*

The door's access pad beeped, and the two women looked up from their embrace. They watched in amazed relief as Robson pulled open the door.

Seconds later, a group of armed officers pelted down the spiral stairwell, while the remainder of the team nervously braced themselves, knowing that the lift they were entering would only exist for a short while longer.

CHAPTER 135

Miller's grip was relentless. It felt to Jasmine like an iron bar was wrapped around her throat. Each time she wriggled to try and ease the pressure on her tiny neck, the grip was tightened effortlessly and almost absent-mindedly by her captor. Miller remained focussed on the growing sound from their position of cover just inside the entrance to the lift shaft and stairwell.

The noise of the chopper above had only just subsided again. Miller knew that he had a little over five minutes before it would complete another circuit of the mountain.

*

'Hold it!' cried the firearms team leader.

Robson's hand remained gripped to the inner door handle while he turned in response to the sergeant's outburst.

'I'd suggest we set up some cover before you open that door, considering that this is also the only way out for the suspect. Please step away from the door, sir.'

As Robson stepped aside, the team leader nodded to two of his colleagues, both of whom immediately lowered themselves either side of the door, placing their eyes against their rifle viewfinders. Robson felt Sarah squeeze his hand tightly, as though sensing his thoughts.

Wilson, too, seemed to be tuned in to the anxiety that filled the small space between the lift entrance and the outside, despite her own recent trauma. She watched Robson out of the corner of her eye, noticing his unusually acquiescent demeanour. It seemed that he had finally surrendered to the overwhelming fear that his daughter remained in the hands of a killer, in an unknown location. They didn't even know for sure whether Miller and Jasmine had made it clear of the mountain, which was, if Connor was to be believed, only some fifteen minutes from being destroyed.

A crackling radio interrupted the silence.

'Delta-Five-One, Control. Please update.'

'Affirmative, Control. We are at the ground exit and about to move. Requesting radio silence.'

'Okay, Delta-Five-One. We are T-minus fifteen minutes, all operatives are positioned outside the anticipated detonation zone. Please prioritise personnel safety. Control out.'

The firearms sergeant faced the exit and barked his command at the remaining members of his team.

'Go!'

The lift began to charge back up inside the mountain, now empty and ready to collect another load. At the bottom of the lift shaft, the two marksmen tensed a notch as the door swung outwards, both intensely focussed on the dim hollow immediately ahead. The remaining surface water outside reflected the sun, creating a brightly lit backdrop of contrasting green, brown and dark patches on the slopes of the massif beyond.

The lead firearms officer chief inched forward with his rifle cocked and scanned the area outside as he breached the threshold. Two more marksmen followed, remaining a yard behind and providing continuous cover for their senior officer. Seconds later, Robson, Wilson, and Matthews were in tow, leaving only Sarah and one other firearms specialist behind, in accordance with his team leader's instructions.

The entire team reacted to the sudden sound. The wind had eclipsed the sound of the helicopter's rotors, but it wasn't enough to overpower the amplified voice that now boomed from the aircraft.

'Jacob Miller – listen carefully. Stay right where you are, we have you completely covered. Let the girl go.'

A gunshot immediately followed, but there was no further announcement. Robson's anxiety level threatened to consume him. Wilson, again reading his thoughts, placed a hand on his arm in a gesture of restraint.

'This is your final warning, Miller. That was a silly move. Release the girl. You have five seconds, or we will fire. Please be advised that we have lethal fire authorisation.'

Listening to the latest announcement, Robson imagined his young daughter somewhere outside with a gun to her head. As it happened, the image he pictured was an accurate representation of reality.

Following a second gun blast, the firearms sergeant looked knowingly at his marksmen, before drawing them forward with a slight jerk of his rifle. Robson shook himself free of Wilson's tender hold but was faced with the sergeant's upright palm.

'We'll cover this, sir. Please remain where you are.'

Everyone recoiled as another gunshot reverberated outside in the valley. On hearing the desperate mechanical sound that followed, they all instinctively gazed towards its source. Towards the sky.

The four specialists looked on helplessly at the helicopter, as it whirled uncontrollably while plummeting towards the ground. Seconds later, the serene landscape was overwhelmed by a giant ball of fire. The firearms chief immediately instructed his men to take up new positions, not noticing Robson and Wilson behind.

Robson froze as he watched the fierce flames, unable to escape the horrifying memories evoked by the sight of the present disaster.

*

Robson was abruptly snapped from his gruesome recollection by another, even more enormous rumble overhead, which seemed to shake the mountain itself.

Arkwright had been true to his word.

Wilson had regained some of her physical prowess. She knew that she and Robson were thinking the same thing now and followed hot on his heels as he flew out into the open. *Who was still up there?*

The emotion Robson felt was strange. The sight of his daughter being held hostage by a hostile gunman should have been horrifying. It *was* horrifying. But there was no denying the distinct emotion of relief he felt at knowing she was still alive.

The noise from above was deafening and all-consuming. Robson imagined the noise must have been similar to a large earthquake. A relentless, low-pitched rumble grew until it became something close to an almighty crash of thunder – a never-ending thunder.

If the thunder was the predominant note, the sound of the earth being ripped apart hundreds of metres above them was the percussion, as thousands of tonnes of earth and rock began to land again, having been catapulted into the Welsh atmosphere. The dramatic cacophony made it difficult for any of them to concentrate.

Contrary to the firearms officer's instruction, Robson had moved into the open and stood just behind the marksmen. He watched Jacob Miller, fifty yards away. He had an arm wrapped aggressively around Jasmine's neck and was allowing himself a fleeting glance above at the smoky consequence of the destruction.

Miller seemed to feel Robson's eyes and returned his gaze with an unreadable expression, while he continued to drag Jasmine towards a waiting vehicle, only metres away. He shouted towards the four men with their rifles trained on his forehead.

'If you're going to shoot, you'd better make it count. I have nothing to lose now! If you fuckers let off so much as a single shot, then I won't be held responsible for the reflex it might cause in my trigger finger … and the same applies if you shoot after we get into the jeep.'

The armed men remained fixed in position as their commanding officer barked in response.

'We just want the girl, Miller. Leave her and we'll leave you.'

Miller jeered at them.

'Of course you will! The girl remains my security for now. I will leave her somewhere safe when I know I'm clear.'

Robson and Jasmine made eye contact across the fifty yards that separated them, together sharing the same thought. *Miller was lying.* Robson knew he had to stop Miller getting away with his daughter. He turned and blurted at the firearms team-leader.

'Sergeant – you need to stop them getting into the jeep!'

The man looked across in disappointment that his orders had been disobeyed.

'We cannot risk a shot, DCI Robson. He could feasibly release a shot even if we hit him first time.'

'Even if?'

Robson knew the conversation was over. By now, Miller and Jasmine had moved to the far side of the vehicle, which now provided a barrier between them and the marksmen.

Jasmine screwed her nose in disgust at the scent of Miller's body odour as he momentarily adjusted his hold on her, trapping her in a looser headlock with his bandaged arm and allowing him to pull open the car door with his good hand. Miller followed the girl in through the driver's door, making sure that she remained sufficiently close to make it too risky for the marksmen to take a shot.

'Now, I don't need to hold this gun to your head do I, little lady?'

Miller grinned, visibly trying to control the sense of pain from his broken wrist, having forced himself to hold a firearm with it for the past half an hour.

'Because, as you will have realised by now, if you try anything silly, Mister Miller is going to blow your brains out, understood?'

Jasmine shuddered, feeling a combination of hatred and fear, before stubbornly looking away from him. She sat in silence, fixing her view out of the windscreen.

The front wheels span in the sodden, soft heathland as the car lurched forward. Miller knew he had to drive closer to the marksmen to access the road, so he made a clear show of holding the firearm against Jasmine's head. He pressed the cold barrel of his firearm unnecessarily hard into her soft temple, inwardly fighting the pain that seared through his shattered wrist as he tried to control the jerking steering wheel by stretching his arm through it and gripping it between forearm and bicep.

Jasmine decided to use the force of the gun pressed against her to her advantage and moved it in the direction of the door handle she had been surreptitiously inspecting out of the corner of her left eye. Miller seemed to realise he had let the intensity of the situation get to him and withdrew his arm a few inches as he concentrated on guiding the four-by-four on to level ground.

Twenty-five yards away, four trained marksmen watched him through the sights of their deadly weapons. Robson and Jasmine stared at one another for a second, before Robson nodded, opening his eyes wide to emphasise the gesture.

The passenger door had swung back against its stop by the time Miller registered the sudden sound beside him. As the girl rolled away from the car, Miller instinctively fired two quick shots in succession. The second embedded itself deep into the shoulder of one of the marksmen, who let out a scream as he dropped his weapon in reaction.

A volley of ammunition shortly followed, tearing through the metal exterior of the jeep, while some of the deadly ammunition flew in through the open door and ripped apart the interior. The door swung shut as Miller pressed the accelerator to the floor.

As Wilson helped Jasmine to her feet, Robson flew past the marksman who was administering emergency treatment to his colleague, ignoring the shouts from the others.

'Stay back, DCI Robson!'

Further shots were fired. Robson couldn't be sure which direction they'd come from and threw himself to the ground instinctively. He spat out a blade of grass and noticed another of the marksmen lying on the ground. The man trembled as he lay on his back with two hands pressed to his stomach. He moaned in agony while the grass around his body changed quickly from green to red. Meanwhile, the rear of the jeep disappeared in a swirl of exhaust fumes and dust.

Somewhere above, Robson heard the faint sound of helicopter rotors, but the sky had quickly become a dense blanket of fog as the smoke continued to billow from the ex-mountain peak. He looked behind and stared back at Wilson, who was now attending to one of the injured marksmen. Close by, Jasmine was on her feet, her head buried deep in Sarah's embrace.

Robson suddenly felt distinctly isolated, as though the world continued to spin its random tapestry, while somehow he had managed to get off and now, as an outsider, could only observe the chaos of it all.

*

A few hours later, water poured from the jeep as it began to emerge from the vast lake. As the huge winch pulled it on to the shore, water gushed from every orifice of the vehicle.

Matthews watched two members of the diving team wrench the doors open. Water poured out around their feet, before they climbed inside. Five minutes later, the two divers re-emerged from the vehicle. One of them looked at Matthews and shook his head, signifying that he hadn't found anything to recover. Moments later, the second diver approached him, his arm outstretched. Matthews placed a glove on his right hand before accepting the garment.

He held the prisoner's uniform aloft, already knowing whose it had been without the need for DNA analysis. A shout from one of the other divers interrupted his thoughts. He looked towards its source to see a diver's head bobbing on the surface of the lake. With one arm she held a rifle aloft for them all to see. Matthews nodded nonchalantly, while one of the diving team leaders signalled to the woman to come in. Matthews nodded to the waiting team of forensics officers.

'All yours.'

'Thank you, sir,' said a woman in white overalls.

DI Matthews threw her the prison uniform and left them to begin their futile analysis. He hopped into his car and departed the scene.

CHAPTER 136

Robson felt two pairs of mischievous eyes scrutinising him as he sat in an armchair and watched the beautiful woman enter the room. Instinctively, he rose, maintaining a plain, understated smile, so that no one could confuse his chivalry with anything less platonic.

He'd been promising to take her out for the past two weeks, ever since the events in Snowdonia had concluded. With more than a little encouragement from both his mother and daughter, he had finally booked a table at their favourite restaurant. They watched him now with overzealous eagerness and self-satisfaction, like Eros and Cupid combined.

'You look fabulous,' he said as he took her hand.

The sound of the mobile phone brought disappointed tuts from the sofa-based observers, while his date merely smiled and rolled her eyes.

'Sorry, just give me a minute,' he said, raising the phone to his ear.

'Hello, how are things going?'

The three females watched in silence as Robson listened to another woman on his phone.

'Yeah okay, thank you. What about you?'

There was a pause on the line before Wilson continued.

'Yeah, you know. Listen, Jack, I'm sorry to disturb you on a Friday evening, I'm sure you're busy.'

'No, don't be silly. How can I help?'

'Well, I just thought you might like to know, the analysis has come back on the vehicle found in the lake.'

Robson remained silent. He didn't require the confirmation that he knew was imminent.

'You were right – the car was the very same vehicle that Miller had used to transport Jasmine in.'

Robson sensed she was using the subject as pretext for another discussion. He wasn't used to such procrastination from Emma Wilson.

'Uh-huh. I know, I spoke to Matthews earlier.'

Robson spoke again to fill the silence.

'Was that it?'

Robson smiled, picturing Wilson's pretty frown at the other end of the line.

'We haven't been able to find a body, Jack.'

'Of course not.'

'What does that mean?'

'You won't find a body, because there isn't one. I told you – it's something to do with that second helicopter.'

Another pause.

'It was good to see you again, Jack. Perhaps we could meet some time? There are things I'd like to discuss.'

'Oh? Sounds ominous?'

Further silence.

'I'll call you. Bye, Jack.'

Robson couldn't read the glint in Sarah's eye. It was either emotion, or something else ... something he couldn't quite place. He walked across to her and, as he placed a kiss on her soft cheek, a car horn sounded outside.

'Your carriage awaits – shall we?'

Jasmine held her grandmother's hand as they turned to each other, exchanging impish grins. The elderly lady chuckled and squeezed her granddaughter's hand tighter.

'Come on, let's sort out our own dinner, shall we?

CHAPTER 137

Intelligence Officer Wilson observed the late-night crowds with detached interest. The scenes were a million miles from Friday nights in her former abode and she missed its peace and quiet terribly. The great city of London was supposedly a draw for the young, which could only mean one thing as far as she was concerned. She was no longer young. In fact, she couldn't remember *ever* feeling particularly young.

Her recent involvement with Robson had reminded her of the values she held dear. She had fought hard not to allow long-suppressed feelings to surface, out of respect for them both, and out of loyalty to her new relationship. If one could call it that. She had barely seen her current partner – her fiancé, no less – in the last few weeks, and even now, she didn't know whether or not an empty flat awaited her.

She pushed her way unceremoniously through the Covent Garden hordes like a true Londoner. After negotiating another bottleneck caused by a bemused crowd battling to get selfies taken with a levitating 'Yoda', Wilson darted off down an alley and off the beaten track.

As she rounded the corner to Floral Court, the light that could be seen shining from inside one of the first-floor apartments made her feel strangely nervous. She had barely seen Thomas over the past couple of months but decided to grab the bull by the horns. Lord knows, it was difficult to even contact him by phone these days. He hadn't acknowledged her last message.

Oh God, does he realise I'm home this evening?! I hope he isn't already entertaining.

She swallowed whatever was making her feel uneasy and called the lift. Minutes later, inside the cool flat, she was greeted by silence. She allowed the heavy-set wooden door to slowly close, before hearing the deadlock mechanism engage with a clunk. One thing was sure – there did not appear to be any welcome drinks on offer. The flat was in darkness.

'Michael?'

She removed her shoes and felt the cold laminate beneath her stockinged feet. She tutted at the fact that he hadn't even turned on the underfloor heating for her.

Definitely hasn't received my message ...

She approached the closed kitchen door first and threw it open, feeling frustrated now. The door slammed against the fridge. There were no signs of food preparation and, alas, no culinary smells.

'Mike? Anybody home?'

She heard the boiler fire up as she turned up the heating thermostat in the hall, and ventured into the modern living and dining room. The large room was faintly illuminated by the remaining dusk, along with the streetlights that had begun to flicker on in the busy streets outside, shining in through the large floor-to-ceiling windows. Turning to her left, she realised where the light she had noticed from the street had been coming from. She glanced towards the faint glow emitting from the direction of the study.

She detected the faint smell of Michael's aftershave as she approached the slightly ajar door. A grin began to form at the corner of her mouth. Perhaps he had something in mind after all. The study was a peculiar choice, but it had been a while. *A very long while.*

She pushed the door fully open and allowed her hopeful gaze to rest on the man in the comfortable leather swivel chair.

'Hello, Emma,' said the man.

Wilson's heart began to beat like a drum, but she answered evenly.

'Hello ... what brings you here?' Her instincts stopped her from entering any further into the modestly sized study. 'This is an unexpected visit. I trust Michael let you in?'

The leather chair creaked slightly as he crossed his legs and leant back, flashing the briefest of smiles.

'We were hoping for a chat.'

Wilson realised she wasn't going to get an answer to her first question. She took a mental note of the umbrella in the corner of the study, which represented the only feasible weapon in the room.

'What is it you want from me?'

'Well, we wanted to pick up where we left off – you know – back in Snowdonia when we were so inconveniently interrupted.'

'Who sent you?'

Wilson casually edged herself towards the umbrella, her eyes fixed on the unexpected guest as he elevated his tall frame.

'I think you already know the answer to that, don't you? So, let's not play games, Miss Wilson.'

The man's eyes displayed the same ruthlessness she had seen when he and his large colleague had assaulted her in her Welsh hotel room several weeks previously. There was an impatient edge to his voice when he spoke again.

'Oh, I'm sorry, how rude of me. Officer Wilson, this is Gary. You might remember him from our brief encounter with you in Wales. Gary is going to be our chauffeur. He's going to take us somewhere a little more secure. I hope that will be okay with you, Emma?'

In a single, lightning-quick movement, Wilson lifted the umbrella and swung at the head of the large man in the doorway. He lurched his upper body to the side in a seemingly effortless, yet lightning-fast, evasive movement. The metal tip of the umbrella rang as it connected with the floor.

Wilson began to fall towards the strewn umbrella after feeling a huge fist slam down on to the back of her neck.

CHAPTER 138

Naamah stood on top of the submarine and watched the sleek, jet-black helicopter deftly lower its passenger.

The man jumped away from the rope ladder in yet another impressive display of his newfound athletic prowess, his boots rattling on the metallic surface as he landed. Naamah opened her arms wide to greet Miller as he approached. Out of the corner of her eye, she was aware of the ladder being drawn up as the helicopter slowly gained altitude.

They both exchanged regretful, knowing looks, before embracing on the surface of the submarine. Miller pulled away gently, taking Naamah by the hand to lead her towards the open hatch but felt resistance in her arm. He turned to see what had gained her interest.

The sound of the ocean had prevented them from noticing that the noise of helicopter rotors had increased again. Peculiarly, the chopper hovered some twenty feet above with its nose turned down to face them. Instinctively, Naamah shouted as she became aware of the situation.

'No!'

She was the first to react to the sight of the machine gun protruding from the nose. The automatic weapon fired into action before either of them could evade the volley.

Moments later, their blood-stained corpses slid from the steel ship towards the ocean, the horror of each of the deceased's final moments recorded on their faces as they made their final voyage. On top of the submarine, the hatch was pulled shut from the inside.

The helicopter personnel watched the submarine disappear into the sea, then the chopper spiralled away. After several minutes, the once disturbed surface of the ocean became still.

CHAPTER 139

Robson studied his phone as Sarah continued her debate with the cabbie. The scruffy driver was not prepared to back down on his verdict. Having lived in the area all his life, he felt better placed than anyone to assess the finest kebab producer in Somerset. Still, Sarah, culinary critic that she was, continued to make a case for her own, personal preference.

The overgrown hedgerows scraped against his window as the taxi pulled in to allow an enthusiastic van driver to bounce past them in the opposite direction. As they resumed their journey along the undulating country lane towards their destination, Robson reread the cryptic message. The text from Wilson must have arrived almost immediately after their peculiar phone conversation had ended, twenty minutes ago.

Jack. You might have noticed – I've been trying to tell you something! Can we meet soon please? In case we don't, please store this info – Snowdon etc was a false flag. So was Arcam. This is confidential. Connor knew, that's why he went solo. The man in the woods has the answers (Hudson). He was assisting Connor. Delete this text. Much love, Em xxxxx

Robson realised the kebab debate had ended and looked sideways to meet Sarah's interrogating stare. He gave her a coy smile.

'Sorry, just catching up.'

She smiled sympathetically and placed her hand on his.

'Why don't you talk to her, Jack? Properly, I mean.'

'I'll call her tomorrow.'

The taxi suddenly stopped. Robson looked up and noted the driver eying them in the rear-view mirror, before looking out at the picturesque pub restaurant.

'Here we are then. Call it twenty.'

Robson handed over the cash and stepped out to join Sarah, leaning into the driver's window briefly.

'Enjoy your kebab.'

He winked and tapped the roof before they began to wander towards the pub.

For once, it was a beautiful summer's evening and, peering through the huge, drooping willows, the rural inn formed a postcard image. The smell of hops and cooking invited them inside. They linked arms as they walked past a small group of ducks at the side of a trickling stream, only just aware of the sound of the taxi speeding back along the road behind them.

Inside the cab, the driver spoke into the hands-free system.

'Did you catch all that?'

'We heard everything.' An emotionless voice entered the cab. 'What was he doing while you were talking?'

'He had a text. I think it was from her.'

'So do I. Okay, we're done.'

The line went dead in the cab before the driver could respond. A few hundred miles away, the caller leant back behind his desk and spoke to the large, suited man.

'How's our guest doing, Gary?'

'She's sleeping, sir.'

'We'll start work on her tomorrow.'

'Understood, sir. What about Robson?'

'I think his time is coming, Gary. Just continue monitoring him for now, while we await further instructions.'

CHAPTER 140

Martin Hudson had lost more than a week of his life since being brutally attacked by the colossus in the woods. The more he regained consciousness, the more he wished he hadn't.

It wasn't that he disliked being alone – that was not the issue. Nor was it the fact that his colleague, Bradley Morris, who had also been assaulted by the brute hadn't made it.

Hudson had lost all direction and sense of purpose. The doctors and nurses kept telling him that he was lucky to be alive, perhaps attempting to soften the effect of informing him that his friend has died at the scene. His memory of the incident on the Quantocks was sporadic and he had no idea what had happened to the young Robson girl that they had been pursuing. But even that wasn't what currently troubled him. There was only one question on Hudson's mind - what was he supposed to do next?

His employer, Arkwright, had made no contact at all and he had no way of finding out what had happened to them. He knew his ward was under close police observation and that it would only be a matter of time before the enquiries started. At least he would have someone to look after him when he went to prison. Perhaps that was his best option.

Hudson began to rub his head, confused by the sound. Seconds later, he remembered his phone.

They let me keep it?

He reached inside the bedside cupboard and, after several seconds of rummaging, withdrew the device which had, for some reason, been stuffed behind towels and spare pyjamas. Holding the phone aloft, it wasn't at all how he remembered it. He was sure he'd had a motorbike as his screen saver. *Or had that been a dream?*

He touched the screen to open the unread message. There was no name, and the sender's number had been withheld. But the message itself was even more obscure. He read it again before throwing the device back into the cupboard in frustration. Nothing made sense to him anymore.

Feeling suddenly exhausted, Hudson laid back and shut his eyes. In his mind, he saw the message again:

'*Seek out DCI Jack Robson. Trust no one else. Arkwright was correct about the conspiracy.*'

Hudson's jaw dropped open as he fell into a deep, morphine-induced sleep.

THE END

TO THE READER

Dear reader,

I do hope that you have enjoyed *DILUVIAN*.

If you have, I'd be very grateful if you could leave a review of the book on Amazon. As a new writer, such reviews are incredibly important, both creatively and in terms of sales.

To do so, just visit the *DILUVIAN* book page on Amazon, scroll down to the Customer Reviews section and hit the '*Write a customer review*' button.

I very much look forward to your feedback!

Best wishes,

Jason Minick

ABOUT THE AUTHOR

Jason Minick lives in the south-west of England. He has a passion for writing, and is a fan of reading many genres.

His debut novel, ARCAM, combines police procedural with conspiracy thriller. It is set in his favourite part of the UK: the south-west of England.

DILUVIAN is the second book in the DCI Robson series

Jason lives with his wife, Emma, and his three children, Lucy, William and Sophie. The family share their home with two very small dogs, Digby and Tizzie.

To learn more about Jason, please visit:

www.jasonminick.com

You can also connect with Jason on social media:

Twitter.com/JMinick_Author
Facebook.com/JMinickFictionAuthor
Instagram.com/jminickauthor

ACKNOWLEDGEMENTS

I would like to express my gratitude to the people who supported me in the production of this book.

As ever, thank you to Jon Turner, my proofreader. Your input is invaluable and I hope that my writing continues to improve under your guidance.

To Mark Thomas (coverness.com), my designer, who continues to produce epic material for me which always links perfectly to the story.

I would also like to give special mention to Carole and Michael for their expert analysis of the story and 'inside knowledge'. I feel very fortunate to have had access to some of your experience.

I thank my wife, Emma, for her frank assessment of my work and for her encouragement and support.

To you, the reader - thank you for reading this book. I hope that it has brought you enjoyment and even a degree of excitement!

Printed in Great Britain
by Amazon

65767667R00275